# CONSUMING
# FIRE

## THE STORY OF JOSIAH, KING OF JUDAH

ROBYN LANGDON

 FriesenPress

Suite 300 - 990 Fort St
Victoria, BC, V8V 3K2
Canada

www.friesenpress.com

ISBN
978-1-5255-4513-9 (Hardcover)
978-1-5255-4514-6 (Paperback)
978-1-5255-4515-3 (eBook)

*1. Fiction, Christian, Biblical*

Distributed to the trade by The Ingram Book Company

# CONSUMING FIRE

## THE STORY OF JOSIAH, KING OF JUDAH

# BOOK ONE

# PROLOGUE

*609 BC*

A fresh wave of pain washed over me from the front of my chest, through my back, and down my arm. I tried to grip the base of the arrows where they were embedded in my upper torso, thinking I needed to somehow keep a portion of my blood inside my body. The cry leaping from my throat was garbled by warm blood pooling in the back of my mouth. Two feathered arrows wiggled in my vision below my chin as Jared held me up with one arm and cracked the reins with the other.

"Please, my lord," he pleaded. "Don't die now!"

"No," I sputtered, spraying red from my mouth, "not until I've seen her … one last time."

I could feel the end coming now as a cold sensation began at my feet and spread up through my legs like a rising river. Jared, my chariot driver, looked down at me with a horrified expression—one I had never seen on his usually stoic face. Of all my commanding officers and bodyguards, he was the most calm and collected; he was quick on his toes and ready for anything the enemy could fire. The worry in his eyes frightened even me. I knew I'd be dead within hours—maybe even minutes.

This wasn't my expectation when we rode out to meet Pharaoh Neco yesterday. After all, who would expect a sphinx-worshipping, slave-driving pagan to actually hear from the LORD of Heaven's Armies? Certainly not I. And yet he had. His message was fraught with truth. The message I had regarded as blasphemy came from his filthy mouth. True nonetheless—I had indeed found defeat. But somehow this timing fit.

And now, as I realized how near my end was, I welcomed it, aside from one thing. I welcomed Sheol, whatever that held for me. I welcomed the pain I had longed to suffer if it could mean less suffering for my subjects. I even welcomed the warm saltiness of my own blood. But the one thing I could not welcome was the sight of her face when she realized this end. I was not ready to say goodbye to her. I would not embrace the pain I knew she'd feel after I was gone.

"Stop, Jared!" I cried.

Without moving the reins, he shook his head. "No, Your Majesty. We can't stop here. We're nearly there. Please, sire—just a little longer and we'll be at the palace."

"She should have ... a warning. Send a chariot ahead of us. The sight of my blood will frighten her. Let her hear of it ... before she sees it, Jared. I at least ... owe her ... that," I choked, barely able to get out the last words.

"My lord, I've already sent him. Prince Eliakim should be reaching the palace now," he said. Jared had thought to prepare her before I had.

I sighed—then regretted it. Attempting to breathe was more difficult than not doing so. The pain gripped me again and held me frozen. She would hear. She would know. I could hear her wails in my mind already.

My legs no longer had feeling. I buckled, but Jared held me tighter, his arm around my ribs, just below the arrows. He was right. We were almost to the palace. I could see Jerusalem in the distance. We had been on this jolting ride for hours as we sped back from the northern Plains of Megiddo, each gallop bringing more blood and more teeth-grinding pain. The horses seemed to glide across the ground ahead of us, but my ever-nodding head told the truth of our rough journey.

I allowed my eyes to glance back down at the blood seeping through the tunic I had chosen this morning. Not my tunic. Not the attire of a king. Not even the clothes of a distinguished soldier. Just a common wool garment any ordinary soldier might wear into battle. Once tan, it was now covered in my crimson leakage. This life was spilling faster than I thought possible.

I would meet my Creator soon enough. And I was ready. My subjects might mourn me, or perhaps they would celebrate my demise and the newfound opportunity to revel in the debauchery of their sins.

But this would be farewell to her. My queen. My angel. I watched her running toward the chariot with her skirts drawn high in her arms for greater speed. Already her tears streaked the beautiful, glowing face I had adored since my youth—the face that would cry for months and maybe years to come. And I could do nothing to stop her tears now. Nothing to comfort her broken heart.

There was only One who could do that.

# I. JOSIAH

*Twenty-three years earlier*

I had been disguising myself as a commoner and stealing away from the palace for a couple days at a time. I needed to get away. Away from my advisors, who constantly gave conflicting guidance and confusing recommendations. Away from the pressure of continued Assyrian encroachments on our northern borders. Away from my crying son and the memory of his mother who had died giving birth to him. Away from my palace priest, who seemed even more spiritually confused than I was. Just away.

So I removed all traces of my royal identity—crown, robe, and tunic—and I paid one of my errand servants for his clothes.

"Yes, my lord," he had answered automatically, but I knew my request confused him, evident from the way his eyebrows came down over his sideways glance. I didn't care what he thought, as long as he wouldn't tell anyone.

"And here is another silver piece to keep quiet. Understood?" I said with a glare.

"Of course. Your servant's lips are locked, as surely as the gods live."

I ordered him to find some extra clothes from the laundry but not to let anyone see him enter or exit. He nodded, embarrassed now by his own bare skin, and then bowed before exiting my quarters quickly. We both knew the laundry maids would be returning to their work soon and he had only minutes to find something to wear.

The moment I slipped his tunic over my head and tied his cloak around me, I felt the rush of a new identity cover my turmoil as completely as the fibers covered my flesh. It was both exhilarating and refreshing. I had been king since I was eight, one of the youngest in Judah's history. I didn't know why the politicians thought they needed to put me on the throne at such a young age, but such was my life.

I still felt so small. I did not *feel* like a man, but the looking glass told me otherwise. Although I was all of fifteen, my height and rough stubble of a beard made me look older. Inside, I still felt like that eight-year-old little boy, frozen in the confusion of my father's assassination and my new burden to rule the nation of Judah.

"Why me?" I had asked Hilkiah the priest.

"Why, you are the royal heir, of course," he replied frankly.

It no more answered my question than a cloud answers a bird in flight. And that brought me to my need for a disguise. I had to have some way to explore my kingdom and the state of its people on my own—without my advisors, without people watching my every move, and without my priest. I needed a way to find out who the gods were and of what they were capable. I had to know if there was one god who was stronger than the rest. Maybe I could seek *his* wisdom for my kingdom and its people. Perhaps he could help me find myself. Perhaps he could answer my questions. I had to look for him ... or her. I did not trust my advisors or the priests, who were always telling me different ideas.

"Well, no one can be sure, but this is what *we* believe ..." said Hilkiah, who had taught me as much as he knew about his god, Jehovah. Even he did not hold to his spiritual beliefs with any clear conviction. I was tired of their mindless theories. I needed to know for sure. With the rising sun behind me, I stole out of the palace courtyard, robed in my borrowed clothes and equally borrowed identity. I was determined to find some answers.

I began merely wandering the streets of Jerusalem for a few days at a time until I got too hungry or tired to stand. It was hypnotizing to watch men and women in their normal, non-royal lives rushing about town and purchasing goods from merchants along the way. I witnessed the men bartering their crops and flocks. I gazed at women working on their porches, beating rugs or hanging tunics out to dry. I stared as small children were playing in the streets or running off to their daily lessons and recitations.

At the end of my second secret excursion, I found a clue as to what I had been searching for in the city. It was a small, stand-alone building, not extremely ornate, but distinctly different from the brown mud walls of the homes and stores I had seen. The outer layer of mud had been dyed a reddish-purple, and a tasseled sign hung above the entry that read: *"Temple of Baal—Enter in Peace."*

I took a deep breath and ducked into the doorway, hoping no one would be there so I could have a look around. But my hopes were in vain, for there were many people inside—around fifty or sixty just in the room I entered, not to mention several stairwells and doorways leading to more rooms with more people.

What I had failed to notice before I walked in, however, was the *noise*. When I entered, I thought my ears would burst from the commotion. Pipes, flutes, and tambourines blared in one corner, playing as fervently and obnoxiously as they could muster (or at least so it seemed). People shouted at the top of their lungs in strange tongues I had never heard. Several women danced in seductive rhythm with the pipes and were dressed in sheer, brightly colored silk. As I turned to look at the center of the room, I saw other people chanting and dancing wildly around a silver statue the size of a small child, standing atop a table-like altar.

My senses could take no more. I felt my stomach lurch, and I had the uncontrollable urge to vomit. As I stepped back out onto the street and heaved, nothing came out. *Strange*, I thought, *I haven't eaten anything since yesterday, and I've certainly had no shellfish.* I had been allergic to shrimp, crustaceans, and the like since my youth, and each time I tried to consume the sweet-smelling meat, I would immediately throw it all up. "Just as well," Hilkiah had said one day after such an episode. "One of my grandfathers once mentioned that this kind of meat isn't clean for our people."

But I had eaten nothing to make me sick on this day. I resolved to go back into the temple of Baal but made it no farther the second time. The instant my eyes caught sight of that *thing* in the middle of the large room, I immediately felt sick again and barely stumbled back onto the dirt street before heaving once more. Sweaty and dizzy, I clambered back toward the palace.

That night, I dreamed of the scene I saw in Baal's temple—a nightmare worse than any I'd ever had. In my dream, I was trapped in the circle of chanting dancers, unable to escape their frantic ring. When I turned around, the growing silver statue loomed over me and threatened to topple. I awoke with my arms over my face in a muffled shout just before it fell. It took several minutes to catch my breath as I rushed to my basin, pleading with the poisonous cramps in my stomach to exit me. But once more, my retching was in vain. I determined never to return to that place again.

I did visit the temples and altars of other gods with similar, though not quite so sickening, results. Each time, I would muster the courage to enter, followed by the uncontrollable urge to leave almost immediately. What I observed of these gods disgusted me rather than impressed me. I never saw any wisdom or power emanating from the statues or Asherah poles; nor did I ever experience any peace or find answers to my questions as I consulted the prophets of these gods. I found nothing I had been searching for.

Nothing, that is, until I found the unmarked Temple of Jehovah.

# 2. HAMUTAL

On the day before Sabbath, my family traveled to Jerusalem for our weekly rituals. The weather was brisk but not unbearably cold. I loved the smell of the winter air—so clean and inviting, and different from the stuffy air that blew in from the desert during the spring and fall. On that crisp Friday afternoon, I wanted to bring as much of the cool air into my lungs as possible, taking deep gulps. My younger sister, Hannah, looked at me like I was crazy.

"What in the world are you doing?" she demanded.

"Doesn't it smell marvelous?" I asked, not really expecting her to answer.

"I smell nothing. It's freezing! How can you *like* this?" she said.

"Well, I don't like the cold, but the scent of this air is amazing! I wish it would always smell this way."

She eyed me again. "You're strange, you know?"

"Yes, I know," I laughed. And I did know. I was unlike my sisters and friends. While they had been swooning over young men, weaving their wedding gowns, and preparing for that glorious day when they would be married, I had been dreaming of something else.

My dreams were in the mountains. I had heard the LORD there as my family journeyed to visit relatives. It had been over two years since that day, but I could hear it in my mind as distinctly as the first time. We had cleared the peak where a few stray patches of snow stood their ground in rebellion; I stopped in my tracks, awestruck. I had never been so high above the world, and it seemed as if I could look out over it all.

The valleys around me sung of the LORD's beauty, with bright green trees and cool blue peaks in the distance. Though the ground was a hazy brown beneath me on the path, it seemed to shimmer in the distance as the bright sun bounced off at stray angles. The Voice was as clear as the rain and as deep as the ocean. He spoke one word: my name.

*"Hamutal ..."*

I had spun around to look for the owner of the voice but found no one and saw nothing but the clouds.

"Who are you?" I had asked.

Two words: *"I AM."*

That was all. He had said no more, but there was no need. I was sold out to answering His call, whatever that meant—wherever it would lead me; whenever He willed.

I would have worked a thousand hours and walked a hundred days just for the privilege of Sabbath, but my sisters and brother did not appreciate any of it. Had we been farmers, we would not have been able to do it week-in and week-out, but we were nomads, living in tents just as our ancestors had for hundreds of years. Our tribe was called the Recabites, and we were different from other Hebrews: we all lived in handmade tents, we refused to bow down to idols, and we abstained from wine. My tribe had not even tasted a sip from the vine to my knowledge.

The strange thing was, my family was the only one who made the trek from Libnah to Jerusalem each week. My father led the seven of us there every Friday and brought us safely home each Sunday. I could not remember a Sabbath that we did not go to the Temple for worship and prayer, but the other families in our village stayed home in their tents.

Though meant to be a holy place of pure and undefiled reverence, the Temple was in shambles. Rubble and debris lay everywhere, and only the altar and several lampstands remained intact, placed haphazardly around the courtyard. The Temple building itself, crumbling in so many places, looked more like a brick of hard cheese from my mother's shelf than the house of the Almighty. None of us ever went inside the Temple building. That place, along with a legendary curtained-off room inside, was only for Jehovah's priests and Levites. According to tradition, there should have been a lampstand, a table for the bread, a table for the incense, and most importantly, the Ark of the Presence. This was the place of His dwelling—the place between the wings of the cherubim where He had promised to stay.

I had asked my father about it one day when I was much younger.

"How do you *know* It's there, Abba?"

"I just trust that It is, Love," he replied.

"Yes, but has anyone ever *seen* It?" I asked.

"Well, I hope the priest has seen It. He's supposed to offer incense once a year, remember?"

"Have you ever asked him?"

"Well—" he hesitated. "No ... I think I'll leave that between him and the LORD."

"I'd like to ask him," I said.

"But you won't," he commanded.

I knew the tone. It was an unsaid, "*Watch your manners, young lady.*"

And I had said no more. I knew my father hoped the priest was interceding for us, but he would rather not know for sure. He preferred assuming the best over knowing the worst. At the time, I had dropped the conversation, but in my heart I wanted to know. Was the priest truly making the sacrifices that were required for me and all of Israel? Were the animals we took each week enough to make up for our mistakes against Him? To atone for the sins I knew of and even for those I did not? Did the Owner of the rich, mountain Voice accept me because of the lamb I brought? Would He ever allow me to hear His call again? Would I ever see the Face that matched the deep, musical Voice?

They were questions I would ask as long as I lived.

I was pondering these once again as we headed to Jerusalem on that Friday before my fifteenth birthday—the Friday before I first saw *him*.

He was easy to notice because even fewer people than usual had come to the Temple that Sabbath day. On most Saturdays, we saw at least twenty or thirty people bringing their offerings to burn and their songs to sing. But that day, there were only sixteen. I know because I counted.

*How can there be only sixteen today?* I wondered. *Are there truly only sixteen people in the whole land who follow the LORD? Only*

7

*sixteen who know their sins, and care to offer sacrifices to atone for them? How can there be only sixteen?*

My heart was mourning as I searched for an answer, and I was on the verge of tears when he stepped in and became the seventeenth. I could tell he had wanted to be inconspicuous by the way he walked quietly through the East Gate with his head bowed and hands clasped behind his back, but he stood out nonetheless. I wasn't the only one who noticed him either. Everyone else in the courtyard saw him come in and watched him walk to the back of our small crowd.

His appearance was not what made him obvious, for he was dressed normally enough in a long, cream tunic and a dark brown cloak—the kind my father or brother would wear, made of nice enough linen, but nothing ornate. His face, however, was not like that of anyone I had ever seen. His expression seemed full of both wonder and angst. But it was not his deep eyes or his stubbled, handsome jaw that made this young man awkwardly noticeable to the crowd that day. It was the fact that he was the only one of us who had come empty-handed.

He had brought no lamb, no ram, no bull—not even a pigeon! *Did he forget? Did he not know? What would he do?*

My wondering was quickly answered when the priest approached him with an extra ram he had brought for such an occasion as this. It had been tied to the post behind the altar with his own goat, although I had not known that before. He whispered quietly to the stranger and then returned to the front near the altar as we finished singing one of my favorite songs of King David.

> *Therefore my heart is glad and my tongue rejoices;*
> *My body also will rest secure,*
> *Because You will not abandon me to the grave,*
> *Nor will You let your Holy One see decay.*
> *You have made known to me the path of life;*
> *You will fill me with joy in Your Presence,*
> *With eternal pleasures at Your right hand.*

After the psalm, we approached one by one, bringing our sacrifices to the priest for the slaughter. I made sure to hand my lamb to my brother, who went with my father to take all of our animals forward to the altar. This lamb was harder to give up than others had been. I remember looking at him—so innocent and sweet—calling for me as my brother led him away. He had been so tiny when he was born a few months before, the smallest of three his mother had delivered one afternoon, which was unheard of among our flock. But I had helped him every day to reach her belly to nurse, and he grew stronger and sturdier each week. He was attached to me from the beginning, following my heels more often than he followed his mother's, which was not in his best interest. I made sure he got enough milk, though, and on some nights he even slept in my arms.

Even then, as he had but minutes to live, I loved him. Yet I knew what had to happen next, and I welcomed it. His blood would pay for mine, for it was I who deserved to die.

It was I who had sinned. I who had cursed at my baby sister, calling her a fool for throwing my best earrings down the well. I who had forgotten to clean the cushions in our tent after my menstruation had ended (though there had been no stains to clean). I who still held bitterness in my heart over my impending marriage to Matthias—that one I could never quite turn from, no matter how hard I tried. Yes, it was I who deserved to be led to my death, and I was thankful that the LORD would accept this little lamb that I loved on my behalf.

After the slaughter came the fire, and as the stranger returned to his place behind us, I stole a glance at him again. In the light of the blaze atop the altar, I could see pain in his gaze, and more wonder. His hair was brown, as were his eyes, which seemed to me like liquid pools of angst. I tried to look away, but his face continued to hold my attention. Oh, was he beautiful! He was lost in his thoughts and oblivious to the rest of us as he stared into the flames.

I couldn't help but wonder what he was thinking. Did he understand the meaning of the blood and the fire? Did he know the God I knew? Where was he from? Who were his people? If his facial expression could have answered my questions, I would have stared at him all day, but I was left with only more curiosity.

My mind snapped back to the Sabbath, and I refocused my thoughts on the last song we would sing. I chose to block my growing desire to know everything about him, and carefully thought about the Voice as I sang my best for *Him*. I also heard my father's and Hannah's voices above the rest. Father's was strong and clear—he never missed a note or faltered in his words—and he sang with even more conviction than the priest.

As I sang the final tunes in harmony beside Hannah's clear melody, I imagined a face behind the Voice from the mountain. I pictured Him smiling at our song just as Father did and hoped I was correct in my pondering. I earnestly wanted Him to be pleased with our offering of praise.

After the reading, the songs, and our prayers were finished, the strange young man rushed out of the Temple. I caught a glance of his face and thought I saw the glistening of a tear on his cheek. I watched him leave and felt as if my heart jumped out of my chest to chase after him. I wanted to know him and longed for him to stay so that I could read his face and figure out the answers to my questions. It took all of my willpower to keep my feet from rushing after him and to hold my stance beside my sister. And then he was gone.

The next morning, as we left in the stillness of the dawn, I saw a shadow entering the gates of the Temple. The silhouette was already familiar, for I had dreamed of him all night.

# 3. JOSIAH

By my fourth excursion out of the palace, I began worrying that someone would recognize me. It was a long shot because my subjects only saw me from afar, and always in my crown and robe (which were the only visible traits that made me stand out from any other man). Without those distinguishing markers, I doubted anyone would know my face. Still, I worried.

I walked with my head down to the place I had memorized from an old map Hilkiah showed me. As I walked up the hill from the exclusive rear exit of the palace, I could see the lonely temple sitting on the highest point in the city. I was astonished that it only a few minutes away on foot. *Why I hadn't been there before?* I wondered. Now that I was approaching it, the significant placement in the city and near my home was like an eyesore. I continued trudging up the hill until I reached the porch and then the gate.

But what I found there hardly looked like a temple fit for the God of all Israel. The rotting wood in the gate was splintered beyond repair, and only a few stones remained intact in the entrance. Two marble horses reared over my head at the opening of the gate, and I contemplated their significance. They reminded me of a similar pair of smaller horses I had seen in the palace.

A large, crumbled altar sat across from the courtyard gate, and a small group of people was singing a peaceful song as they stood in front of it. Not far from the altar sat a large, bronze bath-like structure filled with water. It seemed to be missing something at the base of it, as if someone had removed what was once meant to hold it above the ground. I saw other small incense altars and one large brass altar off to one side, but no one seemed to pay much attention to those.

I noticed a man of medium height and build, dressed in priestly garb similar to what I had seen Hilkiah wear from time to time. It was a darkly colored, tasseled robe underneath the top-covering of a vest of sorts, which looked like it held stones in the breastplate, although my own treasury held much larger and more beautifully colored stones. Two cracked and chipped pillars rose at the entrance of the large, dilapidated structure. However, no one attempted to enter—everyone seemed content to remain outside before the altar.

As I walked quickly to the back of the group, I noticed their confused, leery glances. It was then, just as I settled in behind them, that I realized why they stared. The bleating of a lamb pierced my thoughts, and it suddenly dawned on me that they all had brought animals with them. Despite my efforts to blend into this ceremony, I stood out like a black wolf among a flock of white sheep.

I had come unprepared.

A young woman who was around my age picked up the loudly protesting lamb to comfort it with soft caresses and whispers in his ear. This was my first real look at her, but I must admit my attention was more cued into the lamb than to her.

Just as I decided to leave because I had not brought a proper sacrifice, the priest laid his hand on my arm and I jumped, startled by his touch. In the palace, of course, everyone asked before even approaching, and never laid a casual hand on me.

He leaned in and stood up on his toes to speak into my ear with a hushed whisper as he placed the rope into my hand. "Here you are, my son," he said. "You'll need this. I had him on hand, in case of a traveler today. You can pay me later, if you wish."

"Thank you," I whispered back, chiding myself for not bringing any money. I had been in such a rush to leave that morning that filling my satchel had been the last thing on my mind. I decided at that point to return to this temple—at least to pay the priest, if nothing more.

I gripped the rope tightly as the ram pulled against it, but to my relief, he made no noise. I was already the recipient of too many unwelcome glances and critical eyes in that moment. I heard the girl's lamb cry once more and watched her soothe it. I could just barely see her profile behind her head covering. She had a thin nose and a delicately pointed chin. I watched her full lips kiss the soft, cream wool on top of the lamb's head, and my eyes widened. *Why, she loves that animal!*

Critically, I glanced down at my new ram. There was no way I'd have put my lips anywhere near that thing. The scent of its muddy wool and dung assaulted my nose, and my face wrinkled at the thought. Did she not know what I had only assumed? Was she prepared to let her beloved pet be killed?

She offered a sad but knowing smile as she set the lamb down, and then handed its rope-leash to a younger boy who led it and three similar sheep to the front beside the altar. I felt my jaw snap open at her willing gesture. She closed her eyes and raised her chin. As her head covering fell back slightly, I noticed for the first time her long, dark hair. It reminded me of the midnight clouds I had seen covering the moon the previous night, and I had a strong urge to run my fingers through it to see if it felt as soft as it looked.

My urge was interrupted by the realization that I should be leading my own ram to the front with the other men. I began to pull him along, to which he protested with low bleats. I tried my best to be gentle but firm with him. Shepherding had not been included in my palace lessons.

Just then, all of my focus pointed to the altar, as the priest lit the wood under the first bloody ram on fire and the scent of scorched flesh and fleece burned my nose. I waited, staring into the fire that held my attention. Deep colors of amber and blue flashed and danced at the base of the fire while sparks of bright white shot into the air in protest.

The priest cleared his throat at me, and I shook my head to clear it. I then quickly pulled my ram over to where he could raise his knife. He carefully spilled the blood in the moat that surrounded the basin and then hoisted the ram atop the flames. The cries of the animals echoed in my ears even after their bodies had caught fire.

Suddenly, silence surrounded me. I could not even make out the singing of the voices behind me and glanced around to confirm their lips were still moving. I looked back at the flames, and then my ears were blasted with a voice that echoed out of the silence.

*"Josiah, My fire ..."*

I jumped and turned my head from left to right to see who had spoken my name in this place. Who had known I was here? Was my identity revealed to these people? Did anyone else hear that voice? I noted that no one had moved from the reverent posture of worship and prayer.

The voice sounded as if it had come from inside the fire, so I looked again in that direction. It spoke to me once more.

*"I am here."*

As if caught in a trance, I continued to stare into the flames, painfully aware that I was the only one remaining before the altar. I was waiting for more of the deep, echoing words that emanated from the blaze. There would be no more—not that day. Keeping my eyes locked on the burning altar, I walked backward to my place behind the others.

I knew that in those last three words, my heart had heard even more than my ears. It was Him. God was here—THE God. A God who was alive and powerful! A God who saw me and knew my name. A God who spoke to me. It made sense now.

Of course it was Him. The God of my ancestors. King David's God. The God of Abraham and Isaac and Jacob. The others must have been frauds. My nightmare of the silver statue of Baal now seemed ridiculous. God was here. And He had revealed Himself to me.

An overwhelming sense of unworthiness washed over me, and I felt a lump building in my throat that rose up into my eyes and spilled onto my cheeks. I had found my answers—answers to questions I'd been asking for years. And I'd found them here, in this broken, tattered, ruined temple. This temple that no one had cared to repair or maintain. I found Him here—finally!

When the ceremony was over, I rushed out ahead of everyone else so no one would see my emotion or speculate my identity. I ran home to my palace, ducking into the secret entrance behind my private quarters.

But I would be back the next day—and the day after that, longing to hear His rich, mesmerizing voice again.

# 4. HAMUTAL

The following Thursday was my fifteenth birthday. As was our tradition, it was the only celebrated day in my life, other than my birth and my wedding. That was the way of my tribe, anyway. The inevitability of my life hung in the air around me as thick as the fog of that morning. I wanted to be cheerful for my family, but it was the sight of their faces that brought tears to my eyes. I ran out of the tent to hide them, but my mother followed and caught my wrist before I could get away.

"What is it, my dear?" she said.

"I'm sorry … Mother; I know you've worked so hard to make this day special for me … and I'll get through this. I just need a minute," I stammered, trying to fight back the swelling of my throat.

"Get through what, Love? Please, tell me."

I couldn't speak as I looked into her genuine, green eyes—eyes just like mine. My voice faltered uncontrollably, and I could contain my sobs no longer. She drew me closer into her arms and stroked my hair from the top of my head to the small of my back. I felt release and safety as she held me, but it was several moments before my tears slowed enough to speak coherently.

"It's this, Mother. It's you, and Father, and Hannah, and the children," I said quietly, while looking down at my feet. "This is my last year with you, and I don't want to leave. I'm not ready. I don't want to marry Matthias. I barely know him." The tearful explanation came fast. "What I want is to stay here with you, but from this day on—from now on—I'll just be counting down the days until I have to leave you."

She looked at me with surprise and knowing all at once—the way only a mother can. "Oh, Hamutal. I knew you were having a hard time, but I didn't know you were this upset!" She drew me close again and spoke into my ear. "It's normal to feel this way, Love. I had the same feelings for my family that you're having now. But it will all work out; you'll see. You accepted Matthias's proposal, and you signed the marriage contract by your own choice, remember? Your wedding will be beautiful, and Matthias is a fine young man, who is preparing his dowry for you, you know. Think of that and—"

"I *do* think of him, Mother, and who knows if he will even like me!" It was the first time I had let my insecurities be spoken aloud. "And besides, what does he know of the LORD? Will he take me to Sabbath every week in Jerusalem as Father does? Will he agree to that?"

"You know I can't answer that, dear." She continued in a soothing voice, "That will have to be his decision. But you may ask him, you know, once you're married. Just take it one step at a time. It will all be fine in the end, trust me. And if not me, trust Father. He was the one who thought Matthias was such a wonderful match for you, remember? You know he wants the best for you, too."

And I could not argue with that. It *had* been Father who had spoken to the young shepherd and his father, interviewing on my behalf. Surely Father knew what he was doing. He loved me more than anyone did, and I did trust him—completely.

*Yes, Mother is right; Father is right; I will be fine.* But even as I thought this, I didn't believe it.

At least my tears were drying now, and after my honesty with Mother, the emotions could be kept at bay while it was still my birthday. I could pretend for today, and tomorrow would worry about itself. I didn't have to see each day as a beginning of the end. I could make the most of each sunrise and every sunset. That is what God would want for me. At least, I would try.

As I walked back into our tent to finish my morning chores, Hannah surprised me by announcing that she had finished all of them for me. "Happy birthday!" she exclaimed for the third time in less than an hour, hugging me and spinning me around.

She then pulled away and, noting my swollen, red eyes, shot me a look that meant, "*We will talk later.*" I tried to reassure her with a feigned smile, but she would not relinquish her curiosity. My sister was always concerned when she saw me cry, mostly because I rarely did. She and I talked about everything, from chores and cooking, to the LORD and His ways, and even young men and marriage. She would be expecting to hear about my anguish later, and I knew I'd have to tell her.

Although it was a special day for me, we still had work to do with the flock and the rug-making and cleaning the tent. We all went our separate ways, and I was thankful for the gentle bleating of the sheep as I led them to the stream. It gave me time to think and to pray. I found my mind wandering to thoughts of the striking young man from the Temple, just as they had every day since last Saturday. I wondered if he would be there again this week and felt my interest spring back to life as I pictured his concerned, questioning eyes.

LORD, *who was that man? Does he know You? Please point him in the right direction, God. I can tell he was searching for something or someone. I pray that You would help him, today.*

I used my rod to prod the sheep back toward our tent as the sun began to dip lower in the sky. My family would be planning more surprises, and I practiced twisting my long face into an excited smile. I talked myself into doing the right thing, which was to choose to be thankful. I would thank the LORD of creation for all He had done for me and for each day I had left with my family. I would even thank Him for the young shepherd who was working so hard to earn enough money for my bride price. I would think on these things, rather than the one thing I could not have—more time.

After returning the flock to the pen, I readied myself for what was to come. My mother had made my favorite meal—boiled quail and potato bread, with fresh greens and yogurt dressing. It was a meal more extravagant than usual and I knew she'd spent all day preparing it. I made it a point to thank her after almost every bite.

After supper everyone smiled expectantly as Father went to fetch my gifts. They were extravagant, but I needed to use the smile I had practiced by the stream when I saw what they were. From my parents, I opened the package that held my wedding veil. They must have bought it at one of the markets in the city, for the sewing and beading were beyond even what my mother was capable of crafting. And from my sisters and brother, I opened the beautiful wedding slippers I would wear to cover my feet on that fateful day.

I held the gifts to my chest and gushed as many thanks as I could feign. Everyone cheered. My baby sister Sarah clapped her hands and shouted my name, and Hannah eyed me carefully for any clues to my previous tears. I made sure not to show the dread that was concealed beneath my forged excitement, at least not yet.

She would demand it from me later that night, though: "Why *don't* you want to marry him, Hamutal? Do you even have a reason?"

"Yes, Hannah, if you must know, I have several reasons," I countered. "For one, I've only met him twice. How in the LORD's green earth am I supposed to spend the rest of my life with a person I don't even know?"

Hannah shrugged next to me under our blankets, "Girls do it all the time. You act like this is a new concept, Hamutal. Mother was arranged to marry Father, after all, and she barely knew *him*."

"Maybe ... but I'm not like Mother, and I highly doubt there exists a man like Father in all of creation." I smelled my hair before I pulled it back away from my face and over the top of my pillow. It was clean and soft, and the rose and frankincense oils mother had brushed into it made me sleepy.

"You're so picky. It's hardly fair to compare anyone to Father. I, for one, think Matthias is quite handsome. And you can't ask for a harder-working man. Why, just the other day, he sheared half his flock in one afternoon. No other shepherd in the tribe is that fast—or efficient," she insisted. I wondered how she knew this bit of gossip and why she had paid such close attention to my betrothed.

"If I didn't know any better, I'd say *you* were interested in him," I chided.

"Of course not!" she snapped, though her crimson cheeks gave away more than she wanted to admit.

I blew out the lamp and lay back down next to her. I pressed her no further, but that blush and the truth behind it stayed in my thoughts. She dropped the conversation as well, allowing my earlier emotions to go otherwise unexplained in order to protect the secret she wanted to keep.

The truth was, my sister was far more interested in my fiancé than I was.

\* \* \*

The next day we left earlier than normal for Jerusalem. We had finished our chores early and were eager to arrive into town and get settled. We wanted to have enough time for a special Sabbath dinner that evening and to prepare our sheep for sacrifice the next day. Father had taught us a new song that he'd recently drudged from his deep memory of the psalms, and we were all excited to sing it together the next day in the temple.

Mother sent me back out to the cistern after we checked into the inn. It would still be daylight for a couple of hours and we had plenty of time to purify ourselves with the washing ritual before supper. However, we had not brought enough water in our skins and needed more from one of the deep cisterns in Jerusalem. I greeted the innkeeper as I left, smiling at him and his wife as I held up my empty carrying jar.

The innkeeper was familiar and kind. At first, he and his family had loved us simply because we brought in weekly income for them. But after a few years, we had come to know them well, and our friendship ran as deep as the Jordan. They saved a large room for us every Friday and Saturday night, also ensuring we had all that we needed for our Sabbath preparations. Though they rarely came with us to the Temple, we suspected that they feared the LORD, at least as much as they knew how.

The innkeeper's wife waved back at me and playfully called, "Don't spill, Love."

"I won't," I grinned.

It took less than a quarter-hour to reach the manmade reservoir. The townspeople were going about their business, chattering and bickering over the prices of merchandise, calling to children in the streets, hanging their clothes on lines to dry. Every once in a while, I would see a friendly face and smile. The walk was as pleasant as always, and quite a few people were out and about.

As I neared the water, however, I saw several rough men standing around and shouting at one another with slurred, angry words. I stopped in my tracks and hid beside a merchant's cart, waiting for them to leave.

"The master said to bring back three, and we only have one!" a large man said to the others. He had a long black beard and wild hair atop his head to match it. His cloak was made of heavy brown wool and he pushed it behind him and lunged forward as he spoke. "What have you been doing all day, you fools?"

The other three men sheepishly looked at their dirty sandals and shrugged. "You have only four hours until the deadline. Barak, you come with me. You two—go and look that way," he ordered as he pointed to the west. "We'll look down here. Meet back here in one hour and don't come empty-handed, or it will be your blood," he shouted and then swayed from his drunkenness.

The other two men ran unsteadily in the direction he'd pointed, and the black-haired man and Barak walked quietly away from the cistern, glancing around to see if anyone had witnessed their interaction.

I could not make out what they murmured to each other as they ducked into an alley. Creeping forward, I watched carefully for any signs of their return. I did not want to be anywhere near the frightening and loud strangers and hoped they were long gone.

But my hopes were in vain.

As I heaved up the drawing bucket, I heard their voices coming quickly behind me. Startled, I nearly lost the rope, but my left hand caught it just before it slipped back down. As fear ripped the breath out of my lungs, I poured the bucket of water into my own carrying jar, spilling much more than I should have.

I heard their voices drawing closer and felt their eyes on my back as the black-haired man said, "Well, what have we here?"

Gasping, and feeling more visibly frightened than I wanted to reveal, I spun around to meet their hungry stares. Cautiously, I picked up my jar, wanting to put anything I could between us. I backed around to the other side of the cistern, but said nothing of the warnings racing through my mind.

*Don't touch me! My father will have you stoned if you lay a single hand on me!*

"What do you think, Barak?" the black-haired man said slyly as he stroked his scraggly beard. "Will the master approve?"

The other man eyed me up and down and smiled. "Oh yes, he will like this one," Barak slurred, still just as drunk as before.

My eyes darted around, looking for anyone else who might be coming to fetch water at the usually busy cistern, but as irony would have it, not a person came near. *Please, LORD, save me from this danger. Rescue me, Jehovah. I know You see me.* I continued praying as they circled around and backed me into another alley.

I felt my head spinning as they each grabbed one of my arms and pinned me against the wall. My jar was slipping out of my hands and I fought to adjust the weight of it. The black-haired man was examining me, looking at me from head to toe as if he were inspecting an animal for purchase. He shoved my shawl off my head to reveal my hair and drew in a sharp breath through his teeth.

"My, my now, that *is* nice," he hissed, roughly stroking my hair down to my shoulder.

I pulled my head away from his touch, but was only rewarded with their tightened grips on my arms. I could feel my heart racing as the jar slid farther out of my hands. *What do they want with me? Where will they take me?*

I drew in a deep breath and prepared to scream, but Barak anticipated this and covered my mouth before I could let it out, knocking the back of my head against the brick wall.

"Let's go. We'll come back later for the others," the black-haired man whispered to his partner. "She's too feisty to hold until then."

My head felt as if it would split open.

With that, Barak grabbed my water jar and threw it down with a crash. He took both of my wrists in one of his large hands without removing his other hand from my mouth. I gasped through my nose in pain and stiffened, letting out a muffled groan as my wrists burned under his vice. He pulled me farther into the alley, and I struggled, torn between the ripping pain in my arms and the growing fear that admonished me not to proceed. My feet tried to brace against his force, but he was so much larger and stronger that I felt like a newborn lamb in the jaws of an enormous bear. It was no contest. I had no chance. No hope.

Until I heard the strong voice behind us: "Halt!"

The three of us stopped and turned to see who had spoken.

"Unhand the girl, at once!" the man ordered.

The alley was dark and I could not make out his face in the shadows, but his silhouette was the same form I had seen on the first day of the week, stepping into the Temple gates. He was even taller than my two assailants, and wore the same cloak I had seen him in last Sabbath. My stranger.

"This is no business of yours, son. We're just taking her back to where she belongs," the black-haired man lied. He stood behind me and Barak, and as he spoke, Barak pushed me behind himself so that I was trapped between the two of them.

I shook my head desperately, silently denying his lie.

Striding forward toward us with long steps, and seeing he would get nowhere with words, my stranger pulled his fist back and then slammed it into Barak's nose with a loud crack, sending him reeling toward me. I jumped out of the way so he would not land on me, and looked down to see him out cold and bleeding profusely from his nose.

When I looked back up at my stranger, the fiery rage in his eyes was terrifying as he came at us, while glaring at the black-haired man behind me. Although I was overwhelmingly grateful that he had arrived when he did, I now had an amazed fear of him that matched my wonder and curiosity.

My other perpetrator immediately seized me by the shoulders and pulled me back to his chest, pinning me with his forearm, and pulled a knife out from under his cloak. Bracing the knife against my throat, he took three steps back, dragging me with him.

"Stand back! Now—or she'll bleed the street red!" he ordered.

Though he was trying to stand his ground and act menacing, I heard his voice crack in fear, and felt his heart pounding against my back.

Seeing what the stranger had done to his partner had clearly frightened him. My fiery-eyed defender took advantage of his hesitation.

With one smooth motion, he clutched the man's knifed hand and pulled it away from my throat, twisting it behind his back. The black-haired man cried out in agony and released his grip on me to swing at my stranger. I tripped over my own skirts and fell on my knees beside Barak.

Slipping the knife from the now-screaming man's hand, my rescuer shoved the man's back against the wall with great force, his forearm choking him as he held both the man's knife and hand at bay.

"Where were you taking her?"

"None of your business," the man hissed back.

"Tell me now, or you die," my defender growled, now putting the knife to the man's throat.

Clearly terrified of the rage in the man's eyes and believing that he could and would kill him, the black-haired man said between choked gasps, "To ... to my master—a priest at the temple of Baal. She ... was going to be our newest temple prostitute, and bring in a handsome price, at that!" he spat with his last shred of defiance.

"Oh!" I breathed. It was even worse than I had thought.

Without hesitation, my defender drew the knife to the side and all that came next was the curtain of dark blood spilling onto his tunic before he collapsed against the wall.

I muffled a scream with my hand. I don't know what surprised me more—the fact that the large evil brute lay dying on the ground, or the knowledge that my stranger had so quickly and thoroughly ended the threat to my own life. He had moved smoothly, not like the young man he appeared, but rather like an older, experienced soldier, trained in the fine art of battle and warfare.

He stood frozen for a minute, breathing heavily now, staring out at nothing. I was also unable to move and sat on the ground gaping at him. I noted a trace of fury left in his eyes, and then he dropped the knife and looked down at me, sighing in relief.

Rather than simply extending his hand to help me up, he knelt, putting his arm around my waist, and lifted me to my feet. As I surrendered to his help and felt his touch through my thickly layered frock, it seemed as if I would melt in his arms. The terror still pulsing through my body and the simultaneous relief suddenly made me dizzy, as I looked up into those deep, brown eyes I had dreamed of all week.

"Thank you," I managed, my voice shaking violently.

"Are you hurt?" he asked, stepping back slightly to examine me.

His scrutinizing gaze combed over me and then returned to meet my face. Those beautiful, questioning eyes made my heart flutter, and it took a minute to regain my voice. *What did he ask me?* I tried to recall.

"Um ... I think my wrists are bruised, and, uh ... I hit my knee when I tripped."

He held up my arms and analyzed my reddened hands and wrists. They were both raw and almost bleeding, sure to be black and blue by tomorrow. The warmth of his hands on my forearms sent another surge through my body.

"You may need to bandage those. Let me see your knee," he asked, kneeling.

"I'm sorry, but I'd rather you didn't." I was imagining what my father might say. "It's probably just a scrape." He had already seen too much of me for a man who was not my husband or relation. This was certainly improper, and I didn't want to push it any further.

Suddenly, I remembered that my head was still uncovered. I searched the alley to find where the men had thrown my shawl. He noticed me gathering my hair, and he stood, turning to look for it on the ground around us. Finding it a few feet away, he picked it up, shook it off, and handed it to me. I quickly covered my head and thanked him once again, smoothing my dirtied shawl and frock.

Glancing back at the bleeding men in the alley, I wondered if he was apprehensive of anyone discovering the bodies. The king's soldiers and officials would surely find them eventually. Had anyone witnessed what had happened? Would my rescuer be accused of murder? As I glanced back up at him, I saw no trace of worry in his still-angry eyes.

Stepping out of the darkness of the alley, I noted the remains of my jar lying pathetically on the road. After all that had just happened, my errand to the cistern seemed trivial. Still, I did not want to return to the inn without our cleansing water. *What am I going to do?*

As if he had read my thoughts, my rescuer said, "I saw a merchant down there who sells water jars. I'll buy one for you." It was more of a command than a suggestion.

I hesitated. "Sir, how can I ask you to do that, when you've done so much for me already? You saved my life ... and I don't even ... know your name."

He shifted from one foot to the other, and it was obvious that he did not want to tell me. "You didn't ask me for help; I offered. You need water, do you not?"

"Yes," I agreed as I looked at my sandals. I couldn't hold his piercing gaze.

"This way, then," he said solemnly and extended his hand in the direction of the marketplace.

I conceded and stepped out in front of him toward the crowd. As we walked among the people along the dusty road, his hand protectively found the small of my back and I shivered at his gentle touch.

*Strange,* I thought, *I've lived fifteen years without any man other than my father ever touching me, and today I've felt everything from frighteningly violent to tender and compassionate. What more will this day bring?*

After he had paid for the water jar—a beautiful, hand-painted vessel that was about the same size as my broken one—we walked back through the crowd to the well. His hand never left its protective place, just barely touching my lower back, as he continued to scan the crowd for any other threats to my safety. When we reached the cistern again, he drew the water for me and poured it into the jar carefully. Picking it up, he turned back to me.

"Well, where to, now?" he said.

"I am able to carry the water," I offered, reaching for the jar. It was not customary for men to carry water, and I did not want him to break cultural norms for my benefit.

"I don't mind," he replied with a slight smile, palming the neck of it with his large, strong hand. Had I been carrying it, I would have needed at least one full arm, and most likely my other hand underneath the weight of it. "I wouldn't want it to hurt your wrists. I can walk you to your home, if you'll permit me?" His crooked smile compelled my cooperation, and I nodded.

"My family and I are staying at the inn down the road," I said, starting back along the familiar street.

I didn't want my time with him to end, and though I was not frightened to walk back alone among the crowd, I welcomed his presence, if only for a few more minutes. The sun was setting now, and I knew I would have to bid him farewell momentarily. The thought did not set well with me.

"We come here every week for Sabbath and stay on Friday and Saturday nights in order to be near Jehovah's Temple."

As I said the last words, he froze in his tracks. Curious, I stopped walking as well and watched his face for a clue. Aware of my gaze, he revealed nothing, and just started on the road again.

He was quiet for a while, and then asked me, "How long have you worshipped this god?"

"All my life," I answered. "Do you know Him?"

"I'd like to ..." he said, seeming to let his mind wander as he stared down the road. We walked in silence for a few moments longer and then arrived at the inn. I needed to hurry inside if my family was to have enough time for the cleansing ritual, but I was not yet ready to leave my rescuer.

"Won't you come in and meet my father?" I asked. "I know he'll want to thank the man who saved the life of his oldest daughter."

"I'll take my leave for now, but perhaps I'll see you in the Temple tomorrow for Sabbath sacrifice." I knew by his tone that there would be no convincing him to stay. "Please care for your wounds ... and get some rest. You've had quite a scare, young maiden."

"Thank you so much—for everything. I don't know how to thank you enough. Truly, my life is indebted to you. Is there anything I can do to repay you ... Anything at all?"

"No, nothing. You are not indebted to me in any way. It was my privilege to give those wicked snakes what they deserved," he said, scowling. I could see the anger building in his eyes, but then he immediately softened and looked back down at me. "As for what I've done for you ... I believe the pleasure of your company has been more than enough to repay me," he said with a sly smile.

I raised my eyebrows at his last statement, smiling in return, without really understanding the humor he intended.

"Until tomorrow, then?" he said.

"Yes," I replied. "Tomorrow."

# 5. JOSIAH

As soon as I walked away from the inn that night, I allowed my anger to come back to me. I had pushed it down so as not to scare the girl as we walked; I saw the fear in her eyes as I'd helped her to stand in the alley. Her assailants were not the only ones who terrified her. She was also frightened of me. With reason—I did not fault her for that.

Nearly running back to the palace, I let the rage rise up out of my chest and wash over me. *Is this the state of the nation of Judah? Is this what life is like for my subjects? I may be spiritually confused, but even I know this is wrong! Completely vile and beyond evil. How could anyone even conjure such a notion? To take an innocent girl and kidnap her, forcing her to become a religious prostitute in the temple of that … that … thing!*

As I continued replaying the events in my mind, I began to feel sick to my stomach again. And what of my own actions—murder? Of course he deserved it, but it was rash—even for me. My hands clenched open and shut, and I felt the need to hit something. As I ducked under the secret entrance into my quarters, I slammed my knuckles into the first thing I found—my bedpost.

I paced around my quarters, desperate for some retaliation. More retaliation. Death seemed an appropriate punishment. *Perhaps with a trial this time. Yes … I'll kill that priest! How many other girls has he stolen from that well? I'll kill all the priests of Baal. I'll burn that disgusting place to the ground.*

The thought of a fire that would send hot blazes high into the sky permitted me to take a deep breath and let some fury escape. I lit the kindling in my hearth instead of calling a servant to do it. After hiding my costume behind my bed and changing back into my own tunic, I stared into the flames, which had already begun to consume the smallest pieces of wood.

I was able to think more clearly as I gazed into the burning wood and sparks, and I pondered my actions of the day. *How long would I go on like this—sneaking out? What was my goal, now? Hadn't I found God?* Yes, but I knew I still needed more. I needed to consult Him somehow, and ask Him my questions. Finding Him was only the beginning. Now I needed to know what to *do* with my nation and monarchy.

Yes, I still needed my disguise. I had grown more comfortable with my new identity over the previous weeks. With my common clothes, I felt so sure of myself, so decisive, and completely unlike the boy king. I glanced out the balcony and noticed the last stripes of orange and pink in the sky as the sun set beyond the horizon. Gray clouds stretched as far as I could see in every direction, and a crisp half-moon shone down at me from behind them.

The beginning of Sabbath. I wanted to honor the beginning of LORD's day, but realized that I didn't know how. I didn't know where Hilkiah was, and I didn't have the energy to go looking for him. *What meal should I eat? Who should eat with me? What prayers do I say? What songs would honor Him? Should I light a candle, burn some incense?* I sighed. I had no idea ... but *she* did.

The fresh memory of her brought a smile to my face. As I replayed the scene of raising her to her feet, my arm remembered how it felt to touch her. She had seemed so frail kneeling on that dusty road. I pictured her looking up at me with wonder and fear. Her dazzling eyes had seen right through me. *Did she suspect?* I recalled skimming the softness of her hair as I lifted her and longed to be able to run my fingers through it. I was disappointed when she covered it back up, hiding it from view. Sitting there on my bed, I treasured the memory of being able to touch her. Her skin was silky-soft when I held up her arms to look at those reddened wrists.

But that thought snapped me back into my rage and I hurled my goblet into the fire, sending a scorching puff into the air from the wine. *How could he have hurt her? What kind of a person does that? Is that the kind of people who inhabit my kingdom? Does anyone care about justice and morality? Have they lost every shred of conscience?*

And so it went for me all that night—drifting in and out of my rage, staring into the fire, the thoughts of her my only peace. I don't remember when I fell asleep, but I do remember her face being the last thing on my mind before I did.

\* \* \*

The next morning at dawn, I awoke to the distant cries of a baby: my son Eliakim. It had been nearly a week since I visited him in his wing of the palace. I had been so busy on my excursions lately that he was the last thing on my mind. Feeling guilty for my neglect, I walked cautiously to his quarters in my nighttime garments. I found him still screaming, while his nurse cooed into his ear and rocked him from side to side.

The light hair on his head was almost white, and his soft, delicate skin was nearly translucent. He had all of his mother's features, including her gray-blue eyes, which momentarily were red with tears, pleading for help. Seeing me, he began afresh with his screaming and reached out with tiny hands.

Hesitating, I took him from her, trying my best to soothe him. "Hello there, little prince," I said, holding him out in front of me, hoping he wouldn't squirm from my grasp. "What's the matter?"

Hearing my voice, he calmed slightly, gasping in broken, staccato breaths. He looked at me curiously through tears, as if to predict my next move. My insecure gaze matched his skeptical one for a few seconds more before he wailed again. His hands balled into fists, and I realized this little creature possessed a tiny rage of his own.

Giving up, I handed him back to his nurse and shrugged. "Do you know what's wrong?" I asked.

"No, I haven't been able to quiet him all morning. I'm sorry for the disturbance, Your Majesty," she said.

"It's fine, Carah. I obviously can't do any better, and I'm his father. What more can I ask of you? I know you're doing your best. Just keep trying."

"Yes, my lord."

I watched him there in her arms, still whimpering. I could not get over the resemblance to his mother. Just as they always did when I visited my son, memories of Zebidah hit me like a sword, and I had to steady myself against the wall. My problem was not that she had died, nor that she had left me as the only parent of Eliakim. It was not even that I missed her. The problem was my guilt. Guilt for not caring about her more.

Unfortunately, she had become my queen before I had been ready for one. At only thirteen, my advisors and officials had decided that it was time for me to produce an heir for the throne, so they had chosen a young girl for me. Before I knew what was happening or how to protest, the wedding was already over and I was united to the blonde maiden from Rumah. Physically, I knew enough of what to do, but I never held any emotional ties to her. She had almost lost her life the first time she gave birth to a son, whom we named Johanan, even though he had only lived for two days. Her maids and mistresses had come to comfort her, convincing her she would conceive again. She wanted another baby so badly that it was not even three months later, after her body had healed, that she crept back into my quarters one night. When she found that she was with child again, her bright smile returned. The day she died was the same day Eliakim had lived, and I was left with nothing but regret, remorse, and an heir to the throne.

I sighed heavily, walking slowly back to my own room. I resolved to see my little son more often, regardless of how it twisted my emotions. His mother was gone, and he needed me, after all. None of it was any fault of his own.

I was no better at being a father at fifteen than I was at being a husband at thirteen … no better than being a king at eight. *No pressure, Josiah*, I said to myself cynically. I needed help—divine help.

Fortunately, I now knew where to find that help, and as I stepped into the Temple on Sabbath morning, I found a new comfort in its walls and surrendered to its peace. I had not come empty-handed: I brought the largest bull I could find in my barn. Hilkiah had once told me how he had watched his father offer an enormous bull at Jehovah's altar, so I suspected this would be an acceptable animal. Fortunately for me, a few other men had brought bulls as well, instead of mere sheep and goats.

As I stepped into my place behind the rest of the Sabbath-keepers, I looked around carefully for the beautiful young woman—the one who had not left my thoughts since the previous evening. I finally found her gaze and couldn't help but chuckle when she blushed and looked away. Shyly, she looked back at me and offered a crooked smile. She was careful not to look at me throughout the rest of the morning, but I was free to observe her from behind, every now and then. Free to notice how her long, black locks drifted out from under her shawl just below her waist. Free to watch how she bowed her head to pray and lifted it to sing. Completely free to watch as she genuinely worshipped her God—and my God now, too.

As the time drew near to bring our sacrifices, I spoke quietly under my breath as I led my bull to the front: LORD, *if You find favor with me, would You please speak to me again? I need to hear Your voice. I need Your help. I'm listening to whatever You want to say to me.*

The slaughter was messy, and the priest called for his assistant to pile pieces of the bull atop the altar. I stood back to watch the enchanting flames and to listen intently. I reasoned that if He would speak to me again, it would most likely be here: in this place, on this day, as I presented an offering before Him.

He did not disappoint.

A gust of invisible wind silenced all sounds around me. In my ears and my heart, I heard the same Voice as before, and I drew my breath in fear and amazement.

**"I AM your rock. I will be your strength and your help. I will use you because you have sought Me ..."**

Although I had not wanted to be conspicuous, I could not help but fall to my knees in awe. It was as if standing before Him was audacious. Before this moment, I had not completely understood the custom when my subjects would bow before me. However, here and now before the

Creator of all things, I knew. He reigned over me. And I would stay in this position until He bid me to go.

My ears were then reopened to my surroundings, and behind me I heard the prayers of the people once again. A few of them were singing in beautiful unison and harmony:

> *It is good to give thanks to the* LORD, *to sing praises to the*
> *Most High.*
> *It is good to proclaim Your unfailing love in the morning,*
> *Your faithfulness in the evening, accompanied by the ten-*
> *stringed harp and the melody of the lyre.*
> *My eyes have seen the downfall of my enemies; my ears have*
> *heard the defeat of my wicked opponents.*
> *But the godly will flourish like palm trees and grow strong*
> *like the cedars of Lebanon. For they are transplanted to*
> *the* LORD's *own house.*
> *They flourish in the courts of our God. Even in old age they*
> *will still produce fruit; they will remain vital and green.*
> *They will declare 'The* LORD *is just! He is my Rock! There is*
> *no evil in Him!'*

That divine moment has never left me. I knew His words were only for my ears. They were exactly what I needed to hear after my recent torment and desperation. And then, to be coupled by the praises of others, singing *their* song, which spoke directly to *my* life? I had no words to express my awe and adoration of this amazingly powerful God.

His promises to be my strength and my rock were so uplifting that I felt no trace of the rage that had been my constant companion for the previous six months. The joy of praising Him was so sweet that it replaced the turmoil I had held onto for years. *Yes—this is it! I will be planted in the* LORD's *house and I will flourish. I can be a king worthy of David's line. Jehovah will be my God, and He will help me.*

Yet, another aspect penetrated my thinking—an image not only of myself, but also of my subjects. *How many others know this God? Why are there so few people today in this Temple?* I wondered if they had met Jehovah as I did or if they were merely unaware of His power and peace. It was obvious to me that this God was the only one worthy of any worship or attention. It was clear that the lifeless statues I had seen before were merely that—graven and empty designs by human hands. A desire began to rise in my gut. It would expand like a hungry forest fire, consuming every part of my heart and will. I longed for all of the people in my nation to know and love this God just as I did.

And on that day, I resolved to do everything I could to bring this nation that I inherited—and now ... *loved*—into the same knowledge and peace that I had found.

# 6. HAMUTAL

As we left the Temple gates, each family going separate ways to head back and eat the sacred Sabbath meals, we all kept a quiet, reverent mood. I had explained to my father the night before that my rescuer was the same young man who had come into the Temple last Sabbath, so he insisted on calling to him before he could disappear into the throng.

"Young man," he called softly, not wanting to break Sabbath by speaking too loudly.

At first, he had not stopped. I don't think he meant to be rude; he simply did not understand my father was addressing him. "Jaazaniah— run quietly and ask him to wait a moment," my father ordered my brother in a whisper. Concealed beneath my manners, I secretly wished my father had asked me to run after him, because that was what my heart had done already.

My brother caught up to my defender and lightly touched his arm. For some reason he jumped at the touch and pulled his arm away. *Now that's strange,* I thought. Jaazaniah motioned for him to come down closer to him and then whispered into his ear as he pointed toward my father and me.

Straightening, he looked toward us and sighed. He was hesitating, but why? Hadn't I told him my father would want to thank him? *He was so full of mysteries!* I willed my eyes to look away from him and glanced down at my frock, smoothing it. When I looked back up, he was striding toward my father, a small smile on his face as he glanced over at me.

"Thank you for stopping. I will not take much of your time—I can see you are in a hurry," Father said when he reached us, Jaazaniah following closely behind.

Nodding slightly without losing my father's eyes, my rescuer extended the customary greeting of a loose embrace around the shoulders, and then stepped back in continued silence, raising his eyebrows in expectation.

"My name is Jeremiah ... I am Hamutal's father," he said. He paused before adding, "And you are—"

"Jude," he replied calmly. His voice was like music to my ears, and knowing his name gave me a small satisfaction. At least one of my questions about him was answered.

"I want to extend my high gratitude to you for rescuing my daughter, of course," my father said. "She told us last night, and said that without your intervention, those men would have taken her, and who knows what else? She said you fought them off and helped her escape."

Jude looked past my father at me curiously. Biting my lip and glancing down for a second, I shook my head slightly and returned my gaze back to him. So I had left out a few details for my father's sanity; I hadn't really lied—not technically.

"I find myself greatly indebted to you," Father continued, using almost the exact words I had used the night before. "What, if anything, can I repay you for your bravery and strength, my son?" At his last words, my stranger raised his one eyebrow, as if my father had challenged him, which he obviously had not. This confused me even more. *I wished I knew what he was thinking!* He kept looking past my father's shoulder at me.

Disregarding his offer, Jude changed the subject. "How are her wounds? Is she better today?" Though his words were addressed to Father, his eyes didn't leave mine.

"She'll be fine. Her scrapes and bruises are likely to heal quickly," Father replied. "However, you have failed to answer my question of repayment. It is extremely uncomfortable for me to owe you so much. I have many sheep and cattle at my home, as well as my trade of rug-making. I can pay you in silver—but even if I gave you all that I owned, it would never equal the value of her life—" He let the last words trail off into the air, as if this realization had just come to him.

"I don't desire anything," Jude said. "My actions were for justice, not recompense. I could not have let them hurt such a beautiful maiden," he replied to my father and then returned his gaze to me.

I blushed at his hidden compliment and looked down at my bandaged wrists and hands, which I found wringing around a piece of my hair in front of me.

"Well, then, won't you come and share our Sabbath meal today? It's the least you can do, so I can show *some* form of gratitude," Father said, almost begging him.

My heart leapt at my father's suggestion. Could it be that he would spend an afternoon with us? In the same room? I couldn't think of anything I wanted more at that moment and silently pleaded for him to accept.

Jude hesitated, as if calculating the ramifications or mentally checking his schedule for the day. Pursing his full lips and then drawing them in to form a line, he held his chin in one hand.

As if answering my silent plea, he replied, "I suppose that would be fine." He glanced back at me again. "Are you going back to the inn now?"

"Yes, you can walk with us. I'm very glad you will be joining us," said Father.

He and I both.

\* \* \*

The afternoon passed so quickly I could hardly bear it. Soon, the shadows were lengthening and the sun streamed in through the open windows as it set on the horizon. We ate our Sabbath meal together, said our memorized prayers, and sang all of the usual songs, but none of it felt the same with him. We sat on the floor around the table, reclining on the many pillows, after Hannah, my mother, and I had set the table with the food we had prepared yesterday. Jude had eaten everything politely, even though I assumed by his occasional hesitation that some of the food was strange to him.

After the meal, my younger sister Johanah took baby Sarah and laid her down in the corner for a nap. I was thankful when Jude and Father had turned the topic of discussion from my attack to the Sabbath traditions. My father answered Jude's many questions as best he could, both from what his parents taught him as a child, and from what the temple priest told us.

Most of Jude's inquiries were about the prayers of recitation and about why my father thought the LORD would ask His people to honor these rituals. About the prayers, he knew almost all of the answers, but about the reasons, my father was occasionally baffled.

"Hmm ... I'm not sure. I think the prohibition of work has to do with the Creator and His own rest day. Although, why certain actions, such as lighting of fire are not permitted—I can't say."

"And what of the animals sacrificed?" Jude continued, apparently not bothered by the unknowns. "There are certain animals that are not proper to offer, correct?"

"Yes, that's true," my father said, "but I don't remember all of the wrong ones, so I've always kept to sheep, goats, and bulls, though we don't really raise goats anymore."

"I see," Jude said, momentarily satisfied.

When he finally ran out of questions, he glanced at me across the table and smiled slightly. Looking out the window at the sun, he stood and stretched. We in turn rose from the pillows as well.

"Thank you so much for the meal and for permitting my inquiries. You've been very patient, Jeremiah."

My father blanched at the informality he used in addressing him, an older man, by his common name, but said nothing of it. Instead he asked, "Would you permit me one inquiry, son?"

Jude wavered for a moment, as if weighing the possible questions my father could ask. "I'll attempt an answer, yes," he said after a pause.

We all sensed there were things he was hiding about himself. "How old are you?" my father asked.

Chuckling a little, Jude replied quickly, "That's not too hard. I'm fifteen."

I gasped under my breath and felt my eyes widen. *Fifteen! Why he's my age! He looks so much older ... and acts more mature than any other young man of my age—not that I know many,* I mused.

Father said what I had only thought: "My, only fifteen! Why, that's Hamutal's age. I must admit, son, you had me fooled—that's for sure."

"I get that a lot," he said with a crooked smile.

"Well, then, we'll be leaving at dawn to travel back to Libnah, but perhaps we will see you at the Temple next Sabbath?" my father said.

"I plan to attend the Temple every Sabbath from now on," Jude said. "I *must* learn as much as I can of Jehovah, so that I can serve Him and do as He wills. The Temple and your room, here, have been the best places to learn."

My father's broad smile was his only response, and they hugged again in farewell. "I hope you'll be feeling much better by next week, Hamutal," he said as he turned to face me with concern in his eyes, and then, a wide smile on his face.

I'm not sure if it was the sight of his teeth in the light of the setting sun, or if it was the sound of my name on his lips that made my heart race in my chest. Nonetheless, it took a moment to catch my breath before I could reply, "Really, I'm fine. I can barely feel anything now."

And the last part was very true. His presence had left me numb.

\* \* \*

The days of that week passed slowly as I looked forward to the next Sabbath. My mind was tormented with thoughts of him and thoughts of guilt, each fighting the other in banter I couldn't control.

*He must care something for me. I could see it in his eyes when he smiled and turned to leave.*

*So what if he does, you fool—you're betrothed, or have you forgotten so soon?*

*I don't care! How could I marry someone else when* he's *all I can think about?*

*You have no chance with him! Don't be ridiculous. A shepherd girl like you and a gallant man like him—preposterous!*

*But it* could *happen. He wouldn't have bothered saving me if he didn't care!*

*No matter! Father will make you keep your promise and his to Matthias. That's your future! A shepherd's wife! He is working very hard for you, saving every shekel.*

I shook my head to free my mind of the hopelessness. I finished weaving the final strand in the rug, and headed out to call the sheep. They were only answering to me in those weeks, whereas just a few months before Father had been able to call them home too. I didn't mind, though, and as I set out to climb the hill behind our tent, I welcomed the stillness of the unseasonably warm afternoon.

I had almost reached the flock, and seeing them in the clearing ahead, I sat on a rock to breathe in the sweet breeze. My eyes swept around me to take in the grayish-brown grass, swaying in an almost musical rhythm. A few small acacia trees grew on the banks of the quiet stream, but they seemed lonely to me—as if they needed a few more friends. The sky was a vivid blue, and the clouds bright and fluffy—not gray and menacing like they had been the day before. I turned to check the sheep again, and they all seemed quiet. I would give them a few more minutes to drink. I had time. Time to think. Time to pray.

*O LORD, I feel so torn. You know I want to obey You, don't You? I deeply desire to honor my father and his choice for me, but I can't picture myself as Matthias's wife. Is that truly what You have planned for me? My dreams seem somehow bigger than that. I would stay here in this countryside if that is Your will for me, but am I crazy to think there might be something more?*

"Good afternoon, kind maiden."

The voice startled me out of my thoughts so severely that I dropped my staff, jumped to my feet, and twirled around to find its owner. *Jude!* How had he known where to find us? When had he come? What was he doing here?

I stepped back and looked past him for anyone else he may have brought along, but as I did, I tripped into a foxhole and fell backward.

"Oh!" I cried, landing on my backside.

Laughing at my clumsiness, Jude jogged over to me and lifted me once again by my waist. "Are you alright?" he asked. "What am I going to do with you?" he smiled, not waiting for my answer.

*I don't know, my lord. What* are *you going to do?* I pondered, looking up into those mesmerizing eyes.

*Stop that!* my mind scolded. His arm had not left my waist and his other hand held mine to steady me.

"I—I'm fine, my lord," I stammered, looking down in embarrassment. "You just startled me. How did you get here? I mean ... how did you find us?"

I was still reluctant to pull away from him, even as his touch sent heat through my palm and back. My left hand found the hard muscle of his shoulder and I held his fingers lightly with my other. I was close enough to smell his deep masculine scent, mixed with a hint of rich myrrh and something I didn't recognize as anything I had ever smelled before.

"I rode my horse. Libnah is not that far, or large, for that matter," he said, not retreating either. He looked down at me, smiling, and I felt extremely uncomfortable under his gaze.

With all of my will, I pulled my arms into my chest and forced my legs to take a step back, freeing myself from his half-embrace. He stepped back as well, dropping his hands to his sides and clearing his throat in embarrassment. I immediately regretted it, longing to be in his arms again. *If only my parents hadn't trained me so well in modesty*, I chided myself.

"You have a horse, then?" I asked. I didn't know what else to say.

"Yes," he replied, sharing no more information about his life than necessary.

"Well, I was just about to call in the sheep. Will you be joining us for supper?" I asked, turning my back to him and facing the flock.

"I don't think so. Not tonight," he answered, speaking to my back.

"Why not?" But I left too much regret in my voice.

Pausing for a moment, he replied, "Because I did not come to be with your family this time."

My eyes widened and my jaw dropped as I gasped. How relieved I was that he could not see my expression. He had ridden hours to see *me?* Carefully, I composed my mouth and turned around again to face him. In his eyes I saw a sparkle as he tempted me to take his bait.

"I'm not sure what you're implying, my lord." I feigned innocence, forcing him to say the words I wanted—no, *needed*—to hear.

He paused, grinning at me, his arms crossed playfully across his broad chest. "Fine. You win. I came to see you, Hamutal," he said with a sly smile.

I melted again at the sound of my name on his lips and had to turn away from his piercing eyes. I looked back up for a moment to see if he had noticed my blush. His knowing smile told me he had.

The voices in my head argued loudly again.

"I—I can't ... begin ... to tell you how ... how inappropriate this is ... on so many levels," I said, forcing my mouth to form each syllable and reaching out toward him. Even as the words left my lips, I wished I could take them back. As much as I wanted to be right here, right now, alone on this beautiful hillside with him, my propriety would not allow it.

The pain of rejection rose to his eyes. He took in a deep sigh and let it out in front of him. The draft blew over me and I involuntarily stepped closer to inhale his warm breath.

"It's not that I don't *want* to be here with you, Jude," I said. "There's almost nothing I can think of that I want more. It's ... It's—just that, that if my parents knew we were alone—well, they would certainly not approve." I bowed my head in defeat. "I can't dishonor them."

*Nice,* my mind scolded me again.

"But, we're *not* alone," he said coyly, pointing at my flock.

I burst out laughing, throwing my head back. "They are hardly acceptable chaperones, my lord," I said, still blushing.

His gaze never left my face as he chuckled along. After pursing his lips and thinking for a moment, he spoke again. "Alright then," he said with a slight bow, "I'll take my leave of you. Before I go, here's a question to ponder for when I return tomorrow to you and your *acceptable chaperone*. Fair enough?"

A nod of my head was all I could muster. My heart was racing, climbing still higher into my throat. *He was coming back? Oh, sweet bliss!*

"How does one find Jehovah's will for his life?" he asked without a trace of the warm smile left on his beautiful face.

Even as his question settled into my mind, my gut sank, for I knew I wouldn't have an answer for him. Not now, not tomorrow, maybe not ever. It was the same question I asked God every day, with seemingly no response. I felt my brow wrinkle in concentration and worry. If I honestly told him I couldn't answer, would he still come back tomorrow?

"Your question is not a simple one, my lord," I said.

"I know. But for some reason that I don't understand, I see a hint of what I seek in your eyes, and I trust that you can give me at least a clue. Think about it. I'll meet you back here tomorrow at about this time, if that is quite *appropriate* enough for you?" he asked, grinning again.

"Y—Yes, my lord."

"Good evening, then" he said, bowing his head.

# 7. JOSIAH

I had an excuse to go to Libnah other than to see Hamutal, but I hadn't needed one. I would have ridden all day to catch another glimpse of her slender frame and rosy cheeks. Two hours seemed like a moment.

After finding out from a villager where her family camped, I had spent a few moments with her on the hillside. Although I hated to walk away from her, I felt more at ease after seeing and touching her briefly.

I think she fell on purpose just to get me to pick her back up again, but that was fine with me. I knew that she felt torn between her propriety and her attraction to me, and maybe it was unfair to take advantage of that.

I couldn't help it—I was a moth to her flame. When she had laughed at my suggestion that the sheep be our witnesses, it sounded like a harp—musical and light. And her wide smile had so lit up her face that it took my breath away. But I realized even then that it wasn't all about physical attraction with her. What drew me to her with such power was her sincere devotion to Jehovah. I found that irresistible.

I hadn't guessed she would send me away so quickly, before she could even answer my question about God. She was stronger than I gave her credit for, and conceding to play by her rules, I tore myself away for a few hours to explore the village and its people.

What I found sobered me. After a few inquiries, I discovered half a dozen Asherah poles around the outskirts of town, under the tallest trees in the valley. Each was a looming, wooden statue of a nude woman who wore a prevalent three-pronged crown, the middle prong grotesquely phallic. Among the merchants, I found three vendors selling wooden, silver, gold, and bronze idols, while claiming that they had powers to perform a variety of miracles, from changing the weather to granting fertility. I came across a shrine to Baal, as well as several incense altars to various other gods—all in the town square. By the time the sun had set, I was too disgusted to eat, choosing instead to sit near the stream outside of town and rest my eyes.

The more I learned of Jehovah from the history scrolls of my fathers and grandfathers, as well as from the enchanting psalms of King David, the more I realized how disobedient my subjects had become against the God who once established our nation in the first place. It was as if they had taken all of His power and miracles and buried them in the ground. My people completely disregarded their heritage and the deep promises God made to bless us.

In one section of the History of the Kings of Judah scrolls, I had found one named Jehoshaphat, who actually acknowledged the LORD and served Him faithfully, leading the people of Jerusalem and all of Judah to do the same. Although the portion of the scroll that depicted the account of his reign was short, I had read it about fifty times, needing to discover, even memorize, his formula for leading the people to follow God—the One True God. One piece stood out to me, almost jumping off of the parchment as I read it over and over. It was something the king had commanded his judges and magistrates to do when ruling on a case among Judeans. As I lay on the bank of the stream, I recalled the words that held a mysterious secret that eluded me.

*"Whenever a case comes to you from fellow citizens in an outlying town, whether a murder case or some other violation of God's laws, commands, decrees, or regulations, you must warn them not to sin against the LORD, so that he will not be angry with you and them. Do this and you will not be guilty."*

I planned to do the same with my own judges in each of Judah's cities, but how? I had never seen these laws, commands, decrees, or regulations—and, as far as I knew, neither had anyone else. How was I supposed to keep myself, and ultimately my entire nation, from being guilty if I had no idea what the guilt was? I knew He must be angry with us, but how were we to please Him when mayhem, selfishness, and idol worship had all but erased God's mandates? I'd commanded my scribe, Asaiah, and the historian to scour the scrolls in the palace as well as in the Temple for what I was searching for, but they came up empty.

Exasperated, I could do nothing but ask God for help. As I prayed beside the stream, I felt a slight comfort for my anxiety. Though I did not hear His voice, I felt His peace, and I understood that I was not supposed to give up my search.

\* \* \*

When I returned to her tent, the moon was already high in the sky and she was sleeping soundly. I know—I looked. Of course I shouldn't have, and I did not really expect to see her through the thick layers of her family's shelter, but I was pleasantly surprised. As I peered through the openings among the tent cloths, I could descry her long, black-brown hair, splayed smoothly across her pillows.

Kneeling and peering a little closer, I managed to angle my eyes just right to see her face as she rolled over toward me. I drew in a sharp breath, due to my fear that she would awake and see me, and also in awe of her beauty. She looked like an angel, sleeping there peacefully, and it took all of the resistance I could muster not to reach in through the layers and touch her cheek to see if she felt just as soft as she looked.

But my shame caught up with me, as I knelt there outside her family's tent in the middle of the night. I sat back on my heels and dropped my head into my hands. *What am I doing? The king of Judah sneaking around at night, peeking into a tent at her!* What was I thinking? She would be the end of me. I was sure to be recognized sooner or later, and what did I plan to do then? I had to figure a way out of this web I was weaving.

I could ask her to be my queen. No, that wouldn't work—she didn't even know me as the king. She'd know I'd been holding the truth from her, and she'd be angry with me for that. But maybe she would forgive me … after all, I *was* from the tribe of Judah, so Jude hadn't really been a lie. She might. But how could I know if she would choose me? I scratched my head and ran my fingers through my hair in frustration. *Any other clever ideas, Josiah?*

I could stop following her and let her live her own life, which she seemed to be enjoying just fine without me. She had her family, her sheep, her Sabbath, and the LORD. What did she need me for anyway? I would only corrupt her innocence, her goodness—her righteousness. She would be better off out here in the country without me and my turmoil. But the thought of my life without her in it made me almost as sick as the idolatry I had witnessed that day.

I kicked at the long grass in frustration and walked back to town to retrieve my horse from the stable in Libnah. The moon was enough light to see by as I led him back to the stream. That is where I lay down to sleep that night, staring up at the stars and searching for God's answers to the mess I had made with my lies.

\* \* \*

I returned to Hamutal's hillside the next afternoon, reluctant to tie my heart to her, only to have to rip out the knots later. But I couldn't bear the thought of her disappointment, and I could not bring myself to leave her yet. I hoped that she would give me some answers about God's will, but I lacked the confidence in myself to follow through, even if she had shown me a golden path to the heavens.

I brought my horse this time, and not seeing her yet, tied him to a tree in the shade. *Another unusually warm winter day*, I thought to myself. *I wonder what she'll be wearing.*

My question was answered as she proceeded up the hill toward me, trailing behind her sister, Hannah. So this was her appropriate chaperone! I smiled at our sheep joke again. Inside, I was still brooding over my foolishness of the previous night, but I vowed not to ruin what little time I had with her today.

For now, my angel was walking toward me as I lay on my side under a tree, propping myself up on my elbow. She wore a deep red frock, in the same style as all of the others she always wore, with a matching white-and-red shawl that hid her beautiful locks from view. Her skin seemed to glow, and on her cheeks she wore a healthy blush, either from gaining sight of me or from the sweet, summer-like breeze. I could not yet tell.

Her sister, Hannah bowed her head slightly and kept walking about twenty more steps up the hill from us. Hamutal had clearly given her specific instructions beforehand. I was amused at this chaperone concept. I'm sure my smug smile showed it, too.

"Taking a nap, my lord?" Hamutal asked playfully as she walked toward me carefully. She was being deliberate not to fall again. "Have you no important business to attend to this day?" she said with a wry smile.

She had no idea. I had postponed an answer to my officials about whether we should attack the Philistine rebels who encroached on our western border. There was also the matter of Assyrian demands for a tribute in return for their retreat into Israel and away from our northern cities. I had not cared enough about either. Perhaps I should have stayed in Jerusalem yesterday, but I could always answer them tomorrow. One more day would not make or break the kingdom.

"Yes, kind maiden," I answered with my most dashing smile. "My important business is here with you."

*Ahh, that's the blush I was looking for.*

"Won't you sit here with me on this soft earth?" I said, patting the ground in front of me.

Eyeing me, she sat carefully, making certain her frock was appropriately concealing as she crossed her legs beside her. The spot she chose, however, was farther away than the place I patted. I smiled again at her genuine discretion. Checking for Hannah's watching presence, she turned back to me and raised her eyebrows in expectation.

"What is this business, my lord?" she asked.

"Why, my dear, a trade of course," I replied.

"And what trade would you propose? It's a fair one, I assume?"

"Yes, yes—quite fair," I said. "Quite fair, indeed. Here is my offer for you," I said, pulling her gift from my cloak pocket: two silver hairpins with small butterflies atop each one. I had seen several in my treasury that were far more ornate, with sparkling jewels and diamonds, and I had wanted to give her a set of those. They would have reflected her beauty and my feelings for her more accurately, but I thought better of it. Best not to draw too many questions.

She gasped at the sight of them. Maybe I had not toned them down enough. "They're beautiful. But—but I can't possibly have anything to give you that compares to the worth of these," she said. "How can I even think of offering a fair trade?" She merely looked at them in my hand, not even daring to touch the tiny trinkets.

I smiled. "So you approve? Here take them," I said. "Put them in for me."

Glancing at Hannah and then back at me, Hamutal scolded me with her eyes. We both knew it wasn't going to happen, and I shrugged to let her know I was playing.

She did reach to take them from me, though, and as she did, I saw something on her forefinger that I hadn't noticed before. It was a simple golden band. Instead of allowing her to take the hairpins, I held onto her hand gently and rubbed my thumb against the ring, my eyebrows descending in curiosity.

"What is this, Hamutal?" I asked.

I shouldn't have. I would regret it.

She pulled her hand from mine abruptly, leaving the hairpins. Standing quickly, she covered the ring with her other hand. She was breathing fast and on the brink of tears as I stood up also, very confused.

"What is it? What did I say?"

She did not answer me but turned around to hide her face in her hands.

"I'm sorry," I said, walking around her to catch her face.

When she finally looked up at me a moment later, I saw tears on her red and blotchy cheeks.

"Don't be sorry—you didn't do anything," she said, looking up at me.

Our playful tone retreated and tension filled the air in its place.

"The apology is mine," she said, choking on the words while looking away from me. She gazed over the hills and sniffled.

"I still don't understand ... Why these tears?" I asked, lifting her chin and brushing them away. Wasn't it this same cheek I had longed to touch last night? Yes, it *was* very soft.

"There's no use hiding it from you any longer," she said.

I was baffled. *She* was hiding something from *me*? This was a turn.

"I'm engaged. My parents have arranged for me to get married in less than a year. His name is Matthias and I've only met him ..."

But I heard no more. Her words hit me like a hundred arrows in the chest and I backed away from her, sputtering.

Of course—I had been right. She didn't need me. This was her life and I was a lost intruder. I had no right to do this to her and her family. Why had I come? Who did I think I was? This was her plan—her father, Jeremiah's plan—and, I assumed, God's plan.

"Jude ..." she whispered with more tears, reaching for me.

Recovering slightly, I grabbed her hand and shoved the pins into her palm, too roughly. "Here, you've made good on the bargain. You've shown me the LORD's will for my life." I stepped back and looked at her once more. "Or, at least, you've shown me what it's *not!*"

I spun around and untied my horse. I could hear her sobs as I mounted and rode off toward Jerusalem as fast as I could coax him. And I could still hear her cries echoing in my ears as I ran into my palace and flung myself onto my bed.

\* \* \*

For the next month, I walked around as if I was alive, but inside it felt like I died. I did everything I should. I addressed the needs and issues of my kingdom with my advisors and officials and even tried to seek the LORD in some of my decisions. I wasn't very good at it yet, but He had promised to help me if I would seek Him, so I did. I went to the Temple every Saturday and was very careful to avoid Hamutal and her family in the process. I even visited Eliakim more often. I stopped sneaking out in disguise, except for Sabbath. I followed the traditions of the LORD that I had learned, and I read as many psalms from King David and wise sayings from Solomon as I could, at night before falling into bed exhausted.

I still felt empty.

After I spent that first week forbidding my mind to think of her, I felt only slightly better. I was able to concentrate and focus a little more. I was even able to hear from God when I went to the Temple. He usually only said a few words, but they were continually the ones I needed to hear in that moment, and my heart almost always understood more than my ears could hear. One day, He even spoke to me about her.

*"I am her shield and her comforter ... "*

That had reassured and saddened me at the same time. She didn't need me for that. God would protect her. He would speak to her. He would brush her tears away. So why had I longed to be the one to do those things? Why had I not been content to let her go and be the wife of the man who deserved and cared for her? A man who would not lie to her and keep secrets from her. What *was* it that continued to tie my heart to her? She seemed perfectly fine without me. Why couldn't I force myself to be alright without her?

One thing I noticed that did not get any better with time, however, was my rage. It was back now—stronger than ever. I was angry with almost everyone and everything, especially anything related to idols. At night, I rushed into my room to light a fire in my hearth, just to catch my breath against my temper. Staring into the flames seemed to be the only thing that helped—and only marginally. Punching walls certainly didn't do any good. My knuckles turned purple before I could make myself stop. There seemed to be no dew to cool the burning fury that pulsed through every part of me.

\* \* \*

Five Sabbaths had passed since that awful day on the hillside, and I became accustomed to my inner torment. I pictured the rest of my life like this and tried to imagine myself as an old man, still fuming over the injustice in my kingdom, still longing for her. Although it was a dismal future, I could not picture anything else. It became all I knew.

That Friday, I was to appear before my people for the Annual Presentation of the King. It was a strange tradition that started long before me, but I agreed to do it again, against my better judgment. I was to ride through the streets of Jerusalem on my chariot in a parade, greeting the people and waving to them. I added my own twist, however, and planned to have a six-horse wagon behind me with bread and raisin cakes to be thrown to my subjects as we passed. I thought this an especially good idea for the children I saw begging on the roadside. When I had still been sneaking out during the week, I bought extra food from the roadside merchants to give to them as I traveled, enjoying their broken smiles as I shared my meals.

The parade was planned, and the entire city was made aware by royal proclamation. Messengers were also sent to many of the neighboring towns to bring in a crowd to "greet the king" and celebrate. I would ride in my chariot while my armor-bearer, Jared, held the reins, so that my hands would be free to wave. *Ridiculous*, I thought.

That morning, Jared assisted with my royal tunic and robes, along with my crown and rings. I felt like a peacock, too awkwardly adorned to function as I should. I stepped gingerly into my chariot, taking care not to snag my robe, and listened to the throng outside. When the gates opened, I saw hundreds of faces that belonged to the frenzied voices and forced a smile onto my face.

Taking a deep breath, I said to Jared, "I'm ready."

We rode along as planned through the crowded streets. I had not seen so many people in Jerusalem in my entire life. More people turned up for this greeting than ever before, and the noise was almost deafening. Though I was smiling and waving on the outside, my anger bit into me with new ferocity. *Where were all of these people last Sabbath? How can they come so far and so obediently for me, yet not even make an effort to honor the* Lord *in His house? Am I a god to be worshipped?*

I tried to see individual faces but recognized no one. Jared drove the two horses at a pace that was safe for me. No assassin could easily jump out at the chariot and attack me from behind in the open cart. I had not experienced any threats to my life yet, but ever since my father's cruel murder, no one took chances. Many of my officials and palace guards still remembered avenging him by revolting against *his* officials, who had strangled him in his own bed. They had been mere commoners then, but they protected me, and I promoted them to my own royal staff.

But it had been years since I had feared for my life. I knew most of the people liked me as the king. They knew I was fated to be next in line, and they welcomed my youth, even as I despised it. Regardless, Jared took no chances that day, urging the horses past the people who were cheering on the sides of the road.

Nearly half an hour passed as the sun rose high in the sky, and I began to sweat in my robe, despite the cool wind. It had finally turned cold for good, after that last warm day on the hillside *with her*. Chills racked my body for an instant, due either to the wind on my clammy skin, or because of my painful memory of that day. Probably the latter.

I turned to the side and looked behind me at the wagon. My servants were throwing the bread and raisin cakes to the crowd, just as I had ordered. People were shouting, cheering, clapping, and enjoying the food, music, and laughter. Nodding my head in approval of their happiness, and then shaking it in wonder, I turned back to face the front and continued waving. *Ridiculous!* I thought once again.

We were nearing the end of our circular route through the city, approaching the palace as I continued to scan the crowd.

Suddenly, my eyes inadvertently met hers among all of the other faces. My jaw dropped open in amazement and dread. Quickly, I snapped it shut, but I could not turn away.

It was her—my angel. Those beautiful green eyes trapped my own and I could not take my gaze from her, try that I may. I knew the longer I stared at her, the greater the chance she would recognize my face, but my head would *simply not turn*. She stood in the front row, smiling sweetly at the celebration and mirth. Dressed in a light green frock and a brown shawl, she was waving at the procession, looking directly at me. She did not show any sign of recognition, to my relief, and I did not see any of her family in the immediate vicinity. Her gaze then turned to the wagon behind us.

Just as my chariot passed, someone behind her tripped and fell into her back, knocking her into the stone street. Turning, I watched helplessly from my chariot as she twisted and fell, knocking the back of her head against the unforgiving cobblestone. She was the only one who had broken the invisible barrier that kept the people out of our path, and I realized the coming inevitability even before I glanced up at the wagon behind me.

Twenty-four menacing hooves pounded toward the young woman who still held my heart in knots—

That instant seemed to last much longer than it should have as I considered my choice. I could hold my royal posture, hoping someone else would save her from imminent death, or I could risk her finding out who I really was by picking her up from the street myself. A glimpse of her head being crushed by the speeding hooves of the very horses *I had ordered* flashed before my mind, and it did not take me long to decide.

I swung my feet out of the chariot and rushed over to her, as deftly as if I had not been wearing my heavy robe, while she struggled to stand. Tangled in her long, layered frock, she was getting nowhere fast.

I lifted her from her hips and quickly spun her out of the road, just as the horses pulled to an abrupt halt beside us. I glared up at the driver, who sat just a cubit away, looking down at me apologetically. The crowd had gasped and then hushed when I had leapt from my place in the chariot, and now everyone stood speechless, watching us as I steadied her.

She reached an arm back to clutch her head and looked up at me in awe. Then she squinted and drew in a sharp breath of recognition. "Jude?" she asked. It was more than she could take. Clutching my shoulders, her eyes rolled back into her head and her knees buckled. Before she could hit the street again, I swept her up into my arms and ran back to my chariot, nearly tripping on our garments as I stepped up into the back.

"Jared—the palace! Now!"

He snapped the reins and placed his arm firmly behind me as the horses jolted. I was relieved that he thought to do so, for we both would have spilled out of the chariot if he hadn't. I held my treasure tightly, drinking in her sweet floral scent, as she lay unconscious in my arms. I knew everyone was staring at me, but I could not have cared any less.

# 8. HAMUTAL

When I awoke, I was lying across a large, tall bed with dozens of pillows piled around me. My sense of feeling came back to me before I opened my eyes, as I realized that someone was stroking my hair. My eyes fluttered open to see Jude gazing affectionately at me from behind his long, dark lashes. He smiled carefully, not wanting to frighten me, and held me down by my shoulder. He was sitting next to me on the bed while one of his hands pressed lightly on my collarbone, and he leaned on the other hand, as his arm crossed over me beside my waist.

"Please don't sit up, my angel," he said, "you'll only faint again."

Silently I obeyed. I could not pull my eyes from his magnificent face, no matter how hard I tried.

"I see you didn't throw my gift into the stream."

He touched the butterfly clips in my hair. I hadn't dreamed of such a thing. They were all I had left of him after he had raced away from me.

"You must not hate me *too much* to wear them, then," he said quietly with a pleased smile. My brow creased in confusion. I shook my head slightly.

"I thought it was you who hated *me*," I said. After all, it was he who had shoved them at me as he spat his cruel, yet very true words. We couldn't ever be together, and it was time we both faced it. How could he not hate me?

He shook his head. "Never ..."

I carefully looked around now, trying not to turn my head too much. I did feel dizzy. Why was I so dizzy? Was I dreaming again? If I was, I prayed not to wake up. Closing my eyes again to fight off the spinning in my head, I surrendered to his touch. He lightly stroked my hair as it rested on the pillow beside my head. I had no strength or sense to resist him now. Nor did I want to. His fingers played down my jawline and brushed against my neck, drawing a shiver down my back.

I opened my eyes again and peered at the small table beside the very high bed. On it sat an ornate crown, ordained with jewels that sparkled in the sunlight, which was spreading into the room from the open balcony. The crown looked familiar—I had seen it earlier today on the king's head as he waved to the crowd during the parade.

It all rushed back to me, as I blinked at the reflecting crown, and then gasped deeply as I snapped my eyes back to him.

"You're the king!" I frantically whispered, sitting up to get out from under the bridge of his arms over me.

"Please, Hamutal ..." he said. "Allow me to explain ..."

And I couldn't resist his pleading eyes. I nodded, leaning back against the pillows carefully.

"It's true, and it turns out I was holding an even bigger secret from you than you were from me. I *am* King Josiah," he said. "And, although my name is not technically Jude, I *am* of the tribe of Judah." He sighed apologetically. "The reason I used a false identity is because I needed to seek God as a commoner, not as the king. I had to find Him in private, without any pretense or fanfare—and, as you know, I did," he continued with a smile, holding my hand as he spoke.

I believed every word, for he never looked away and his voice was clear and deep. I was held in his gaze, unable to resist his power over me.

"For reasons that are still beyond me, I also found you in the process. And no matter how hard I try now, I can't let you go. You seem to just keep falling into my life." And at this, he smiled crookedly.

I couldn't help but smirk in return. I suppose I did have my own clumsiness to thank for that. And, of course, his courage and strength.

"Will you forgive me, Hamutal?"

My eyes grew wider and I placed my hand to my chest. *The king, asking me for forgiveness!* I nodded. "Of course, my lord," I said quietly. "But I'm not sure you've done anything that merits *my* forgiveness."

"I've deceived you, and that was wrong. I lied to you about my name and led you to believe I was someone else. That wasn't fair to you."

But I had not felt offended. His reasoning seemed valid enough—I had needed to find God for myself once, too. Those eyes implored me, and I still could not believe I was sitting this close to such a strong man—one who was at the same time genuine and tender. And now to have this new knowledge of his royalty astounded me even more.

"But—you're the king!" I repeated. "What could you want with me, and you actually rode to Libnah—for me?" I asked.

Despite the pounding at the back of my head, I concentrated to recall each of our previous encounters. *At the Temple ... in the alley and walking through Jerusalem ... in my family's room at the inn ... on my hillside ... I had been with the king on each of those occasions? With him—the king! And me, the shepherdess!*

"The king!" I repeated, closing my eyes and shaking my head to clear it.

Some things made more sense—his informality with my father, his evasiveness at my questions. But there was one thing in all of his explanation that still did not make any sense—me. The room spun again and my head felt like it would burst from the inside. I tried to lie back down, and he helped, resuming his position over me again.

"Are you in very much pain? Your head looked like it bounced on the street. I'm sorry that I could not catch you before that happened," he said.

*The king! Apologizing to me! Again!*

"My head does hurt, Your Majesty," I said, trying to address him correctly. "But I think I'll be fine if I just lie still and keep my eyes closed for a moment. Please forgive me for not taking my knee."

"Stop that!" he answered. "It's me. The same me."

I heard him walk away for a brief moment, and then he returned with a cup of cool water.

"I have one question of you, and then you can ask anything of me. I promise to tell you everything about me, and it will be only the truth. Is that acceptable?" The need was dripping from his clear, deep voice.

"Yes, of course, Your Highness," I said, sitting up to drink with my eyes closed so that I would not get dizzy again. To be honest, there was almost nothing he could ask of me that I wouldn't have done, king or not. He had held my heart since the first day I had seen him in the Temple, and the knowledge of his royalty had not changed that. I only hoped he wouldn't ask me to predict the future again. I had no idea what Jehovah was doing now.

"Is your mind decisively set on marrying this other man?"

I opened my eyes and saw his penetrating gaze meet my eyes. I looked as deeply into his heart as I could and saw nothing but genuine desire and truth. This was his one question? About Matthias?

I knew I could tell him anything. "No, of course not, my lord. I've only met him twice. I hardly know him." I stared past his shoulder and pictured my future. "Marrying him has been the cloud hanging over me for two whole years, ever since the arrangement was made," I said, feeling guilty as the truth spilled out of my mouth. "I don't want to live as a shepherdess the rest of my life. I've always wanted more, and for a while, I thought the LORD had given me a vision of more—of what my life could be. But I don't know anymore … I guess I've just given myself into the predetermination of it, hoping God will show me what to do when the time comes to be his wife."

I looked back into his eyes as he breathed deeply and put his fingers into my hair at my temple, holding my head. I closed my eyes and gave into the warmth of his touch, leaning into his hand.

"That's all I needed to know," he replied.

I didn't know why he seemed so satisfied with my answer; it changed nothing for me.

"I think that helped," I said, handing the empty goblet back to him.

"Would you like to see the palace, now?" he said.

I shrugged and nodded. "Of course," I said, feeling insignificant. He put his hands under my arms to help me up off of the bed, leaning very close to my face.

"Wait," I said, barely able to breathe from his proximity.

"What is it?" he asked, not lifting me yet.

*Consuming Fire*

I put my arms around his neck and looked at him, so close to me—so striking. "Nothing. Do you know where my shawl went?" I asked.

"No, but I had a few brought in," he said as he lifted me to my feet and then waved his hand across the room at a table where several beautiful cloths lay folded neatly. "When you were asleep, I had my servants find a few for you to choose from, knowing you would want one. I was going to put one on you, but … well …" he trailed off. I recalled how he had been stroking my hair when I opened my eyes.

I walked over to the table and ran my fingers across the fabrics, all much finer and softer than anything I owned. I saw blues and reds, neutrals and greens, all very beautiful.

"These are wonderful," I said. My head was still pounding, and my heart was still racing.

"Take them all, if you like," he said.

"I think one will do for now, Your Majesty." I smiled. "Which one do *you* prefer?" I asked, curious as to what he might like to see me in. Of course, I realized a second later, he preferred me not to wear any of them. I smiled again, to myself this time.

He walked over to me and drew a light green one off of the table. "I think this will go well with what you are wearing, and also with your emerald eyes," he replied. "It's the one I was considering as you slept."

"Very good taste, my lord," I said with a satisfied smile as I reached for it and secured the corners of it around my locks. It was longer than my others and actually covered the bottom of my hair in the back. I smoothed it behind my shoulders as I looked back up at him.

He smiled at me and then turned to the window. "You are quite lovely, you know." It was not a question. After a moment, he sighed and turned back to me. "So, may I show you around, now?"

"I should probably get back to my parents soon," I forced myself to say. There was no part of me that wanted to leave him now. I knew my family would be worried, though, as I looked out the window to see where the sun was in the sky. It was dipping lower, turning into late afternoon.

"I took the liberty to send a messenger to the inn," he said. "They will know you are here and being cared for. I told them I would either

63

bring you back or summon them to come and get you when you are feeling better, but not to worry. I do not recall seeing them in the crowd with you."

"No," I answered, "they weren't. Baby Sarah wasn't well today. I asked Father to let me come to the parade," I said. "Actually *begged* is more like it. He hasn't been permitting me to go out alone much lately," I said, looking at him sideways.

"And with good reason, I'm sure."

I scowled at him.

"I am thankful he let you out, though." He smiled back.

"And I'm thankful you were there, too," I said, sobering at the memory. "I remember the horses now. I felt so trapped ... and helpless. I honestly thought my life was over. How did you do that?"

"Like I said, you just keep falling into my life," he said and shrugged. "Well, these are my quarters ..." he began, sweeping his arm around the room.

I let my eyes wander from his face now, as I took in my surroundings for the first time. The bed seemed very high to me, almost as high as my waist, and was surrounded in sheer fabric that stretched from the top of the bedpost near the high ceiling to the floor. It was almost completely covered in pillows of all different sizes, colors, and shapes, sewn with luxuriant fabrics and textures. The bedclothes were made of deep–crimson–woven wool, with gold trim and tassels around the edge. As I admired it, I still could not believe I had been lying in *the king's* bed. In *his* bed.

Next, my eyes found the enormous bear hide, complete with head, lying on the floor in front of the large hearth in the center of the room. I stepped around the bear and admired the hearth, which was a hollow square structure made of beautiful, unfamiliar stone. The walls of it came up to my thighs, and I could have lain down inside of it, it was so big. Someone had lit a small fire in it and I warmed my hands over the flames.

"This is a very large hearth," I said, almost as a question.

"Um ... yes. I—well, I like fire," he said. "It calms me."

"Oh," I said, nodding. *Good to know.* "I've seen you lingering in front of the altar sometimes on Sabbath."

He nodded. I raised my eyebrows, wanting him to share more. He sighed, knowing his short answers were not going to be enough for me anymore. "Uh, the LORD, well—Jehovah ... speaks to me from the fire on the altar," he said, hesitating.

My eyes widened. "You've heard His Voice?" I said. I hadn't known anyone else who had heard Him speak like He had spoken to me on the mountain.

"Yes. I believe so. Usually it's only a few words, but it is as if there's so much more meaning in them," he said. "I feel like He's talking to my heart, not just my ears, you know?"

I nodded, still amazed. It had been the same for me.

"Have you ... have you heard His voice, too?" he asked.

"Only once. But I can still hear it in my mind when I recall the moment. I was walking high in the mountains and He called my name. Then I heard 'I AM ...' and that was all ..." I stared into the small flames in the hearth.

When I looked back up at him, he was gaping at me. I guess we were both surprised at each other and our new, shared experience with God. With a slight smirk, I walked over to him and closed his jaw with my fingertips under his chin.

He smiled and shook his head in disbelief. We both leaned our elbows on the broad balcony window and stared off into the setting sun. After a few moments, he said in reflection, "You know, that's the way many of His messages to me begin, too—'I AM ... I am your Rock, I am your comfort and peace, I am your guide, I am your strength ...'"

And then, reflecting on his words and delighting in the LORD's greatness, I could not keep the song from my mouth. Thinking of His Voice and how amazing it was that He had spoken to us mere humans was humbling and encouraging all at once. It was as if my spirit itself began to sing from within me in worship and thanksgiving—a song my mother had taught me years ago:

*"Praise be to the LORD,*
  *for He has heard my cry for mercy.*
*The LORD is my strength and my shield;*
  *I trust Him with all my heart.*
*He helps me and my heart is filled with joy.*
  *I burst out in songs of thanksgiving.*
*The LORD gives His people strength,*
  *He is a safe fortress for His anointed king.*
*Save Your people!*
  *Bless Israel, Your special possession.*
*Lead them like a Shepherd,*
  *and carry them in Your arms forever."*

When I turned back to him, his eyes were closed and I couldn't tell whether or not he was breathing. A moment later, when he opened his eyes, I saw wonder and appreciation in his strong face. "You have not only the face of an angel, but the voice of one, too," he said.

I shrugged. "You should hear my sister."

I looked back out the window and saw the sun disappearing behind the hills. Long streaks of orange clouds draped across the graying sky, and I could see only half of the bright red sun behind them. It was then that I suddenly remembered what day it was.

Drawing in a short gasp, I turned to him and whispered in desperation, "The Sabbath!"

He looked at me wide-eyed and shrugged with his hands out in front of him.

*Oh! He doesn't know what to do!* I realized.

"We need water, hurry!" I cried, looking around his room. Glancing over to the basin in the corner, I saw a water jar beside it. I rushed over to see if it was full. *Good!*

"Do you have any food?" I asked, though not because I was hungry. We should have First Meal as the sun set. I was desperately trying to remember everything my mother and father had shown me. I had not ever missed a First Meal in my life and did not want to ruin the beauty of that moment by dishonoring the LORD.

"I can order anything you want; my cooks will prepare whatever I ask," Josiah offered.

"No, my King, it's too late! We can't force them to work—we will be making *them* break the Sabbath! What do you have already prepared?" I asked, looking around.

He seemed just as desperate as I was to figure a way to keep the laws of the Holy Day, as he quickly walked into an adjoining room, beckoning me to follow. This room was smaller than his bedroom, but still very grand, in and of itself. There was a sizeable table on the floor with a few large pillows on one side of it. There was also another, smaller table beside it that held a bowl of fruit, a plate of bread, and a few pieces of dried meat. Also beside the fruit bowl were two pitchers. He held my hand and led me to the small table and asked as we knelt together, "Will any of this do?"

I looked at the food on the table. I took the plate and placed some of the bread and the fruit atop it, avoiding the meat, which I could not tell from looking at it what it was or how it was prepared. I smelled the two pitchers, backing up from the second as the sharp fermentation of wine burned my nostrils. I handed the first pitcher to him along with two goblets and carried the plate to the large table.

"Do you have candles?" I said, glancing at the light disappearing faster and faster outside the window of his room.

"Yes, how many?"

I thought for a moment and looked around—one for each of us, plus the extra. "Only three," I answered. I knew there had to be several other people in the palace, but at this late hour, I had no hope of including them, though I desperately wanted to do so.

He rushed to his room and returned promptly with the candles in holders and a freshly lit wick.

"Did you get that flame from the hearth?" I asked.

"Yes, is that right?" he asked.

I nodded. "But you cannot make any more fire once that one burns out. Not until sunset tomorrow, yes?"

"Yes, fine."

I took the candles from him and placed them on the table. "Bring the wick back in here, please," I said, walking quickly back to the basin in his room. "I need to wash before I light."

He poured the water over my hands as I rubbed them together over the basin and then dried them on the soft linen beside it. I then carefully took the wick and poured for him as he followed my lead. I glanced out the balcony again at the sunset.

We were rushing, and I knew it. Once the candles were lit, we could slow down and pray, but my heart was racing. I did not know if I was going to be able to do it all in time.

He was nervous and unsure as well, so I forced a reassuring smile at him. After he dried his hands in haste and tossed the towel back onto the basin table, I took his hand and we ran back into the table room. Kneeling beside him, I took a deep breath to compose my voice. As I lit the candles and started the prayer, my words were steadier than my hand as I said, "Repeat after me …

"We keep the Sabbath day, for it is a holy day for us …"

Josiah repeated it and continued to do so as I went on:

"Anyone who desecrates it must be put to death; anyone who works on that day will be cut off from the community … We have six days each week for ordinary work, but the seventh day must be a Sabbath day of complete rest, a holy day dedicated to the LORD … Anyone who works on the Sabbath must be put to death. The people of Israel must keep the Sabbath day by observing it from generation to generation … This is a covenant obligation for all time … It is a permanent sign of the LORD's covenant with the people of Israel … For in six days the LORD made heaven and earth, but on the seventh day He stopped working and was refreshed …"

As he finished the last line, he turned his gaze from the candles to my face expectantly, as if asking what came next. I smiled into his eyes as they reflected the candlelight and sighed as I felt the blood rise to my cheeks. I pushed the meager plate of food toward him and said, "Please, begin to eat."

My father was always the first to take a bite at all of our meals, and I did not feel it proper for me to do so. He took a few grapes and offered them to me. I shook my head. I had always wanted to taste the delicious-smelling fruit, but Recabites were not permitted.

"My clan does not eat or drink of the vine, but it is fine for you, my lord," I said. Instead, I reached for a pear and a piece of the bread. I chuckled. "I'm sure you're used to eating much finer meals, aren't you?"

He shrugged. "Sometimes," he replied.

We had both been able to slow our breathing now that the sun had set and we were able to stop running back and forth. I couldn't contain my laughter.

"What is it?" he asked.

"Nothing," I said, shaking my head. "Just us and our little First Meal. And me here in your palace. I never would have dreamed of this in a thousand years."

"I, on the other hand, have been dreaming of it for weeks. Ever since the first day I met you in the alley. I knew you would know what to do. I knew you could show me how to honor the Lord," he said.

His boldness was still so shocking—so different from my own timidity.

"You really do want to learn His ways, don't you?" I asked, feeling the sincerity emanating from his every fiber.

"I need to … There's nothing I want more. And I want to know them well enough to show the people of Judah how to honor Him, too. I'm supposed to be leading them—supposed to show them who He really is. Before I can do that, I need to know for myself. I cannot waver—there can be no doubt in me." He stared into the small flames of the candles, as if he saw a vision there of what could be.

I tried to picture it, too: Judah obeying the Lord. People turning from their idols and false prophets and sorcery. Men and women and children coming to the Temple every day to confess their sins and sing to my God. And this king, the one to lead them there. Yes, I could see it, too …

We both knew his role in all of it, but where would I fit in? I longed for answers to my lifelong questions from Jehovah. Could I, a woman, a shepherdess, be used to bring Him great honor? Though I still had no idea what my future held, I was relieved to be able to trust him—my king. As I knelt there on the pillows next to him, I was humbled in his presence. This young man, who had been so mysteriously forbidden to me for weeks, had now opened his life to me—revealing a secret desire that I sensed he had shared with no one else. He wanted to be a king worthy of the LORD's calling. Whether or not I had anything to do with that plan, I felt a new peace. The peace of surrender.

# 9. JOSIAH

"I care not, Hilkiah!" I shouted. "That is what I'm commanding you—either do as I ask, or consider yourself dismissed. I can find another high priest!" I concluded, waving my hand in emphasis.

I was sitting on my throne while all of the so-called priests and officials were on their knees before me in the throne room. The sun was setting and I was quickly tiring of Hilkiah's insolent arguing.

"But consider your people, Your Highness," he said, trying to reason with me again. "They need a high priest who is well-versed in *all* of the gods they serve, even if the king himself only serves one."

"I *am* doing all of this for the people of Judah!" I snapped. "They need direction and clarity! How can they find it when there's a medium on every corner and a different household god in every home and tent from here to Samaria?" I didn't wait for him to answer. "You *will* serve Jehovah, and you will speak to me and to everyone in this palace about Him alone—no other gods! Not Baal, not Asherah, nor any celestial body! You will serve as Jehovah's priest if you want to be the royal high priest!"

My voice was loud and angry now; I lost the calculation and control I had when I started. Hilkiah and the others looked at me apprehensively, wondering where all this had come from, no doubt. I knew they were speculating how far I would take this and if I was really serious.

Hilkiah had been my father's and grandfather's high priest, and he had seen firsthand how the two of them had taken idolatry to its present state. They had silenced his talk of Jehovah and commanded him to do just the opposite of what I was asking of him now. My grandfather, Manasseh, had been especially diverse in his practices, believing that people should follow the "god of their mind's choosing," and that he had had no right as the king to choose for the people who their god should be. He had also been influenced by the Assyrians, who had threatened for years to overtake our land and make us into slaves. He had been afraid *not* to worship Baal and the other Assyrian gods; and so he made all options viable, and had delighted in the fact that Judah had become so varied, so closely resembling the nations surrounding us—the nations he coveted.

This was Hilkiah's past, so in part I should not have blamed him for balking at my new command, which went against his every grain. Nonetheless my rage flared at him, and my compassion for his upbringing was dissipated by my irritation. If he had dared argue with me one more time … I felt my muscles tensing to strike him onto the floor and have him carried off to be dumped in the wilderness.

I took another deep breath to calm my voice before I addressed them again. "The present state of this nation demonstrates the futility of worshipping false gods. There is murder … chaos … threatening invasion every other month from neighboring nations—no one ever agrees on anything in this administration. To me, it is perfectly clear that God is fed up with our wayward disobedience. We, the people who were once called His portion, the apple of His eye—now reduced to *this*!" I waved my arm around me as I lectured. "Starting with my reign, we will turn back to the only God who can help us, and we will do *everything* we can to prove to Him our faithfulness."

"As you wish, Your Majesty," Hilkiah replied. There was a slight defiance in his eyes, as if underneath this acquiesce he was also saying, *We'll see if this works, but I doubt it.*

I sat on my throne looking down at him with scrutiny in my thoughts, but I allowed his underlying attitude to slide for the moment. I knew of other Levites who could serve as my priest. I would give him *one chance* to follow this command, but I already had a few men picked out as his replacement, should he prove himself a vacillator.

I glanced around at the rest of my council and sighed. Obviously, it would take them a few weeks to get used to my new leadership style. No longer was I about to let them tell me what needed to be done or debated. They had led me for long enough—it was my turn to be king.

My recent weeks with the LORD had empowered me. He had spoken to me, proving that His was the only voice with enough credibility and decisiveness to hold authority. I resolved to surround myself with those who were willing to listen to Jehovah for counsel about this kingdom, or at least those willing to listen to me. Everyone else would have to go. History or no history, regardless of rank or age.

This was the one test I would have for my officials, my advisors, even my servants: Were they willing to serve Jehovah alone, or did they keep other gods? Hilkiah had been the first, but I looked around at all of their expectant faces, knowing that there would come a time for each of them to declare as well. Not that day, but soon.

*I have to give them time*, I thought, softening. *It has taken me months of questioning and seeking to turn to the LORD—they might need time.*

"That is all," I said with conviction, dismissing further banter. "I will be riding out to Libnah on personal business tomorrow. I will take two guards and no more, and I will be back on Friday to resume our talks about border security and trade embargoes. You are dismissed," I pronounced, the finality firm in my voice.

I saw a few of them furrow their brows in confusion. My decisiveness was new to them and they wanted to protest. Instead, they rose from their positions quietly and did not begin their murmuring until they were almost to the exit of the throne room.

I let out a heavy sigh. This was going to be every bit as difficult as I had anticipated. I had served as their vassal since I was eight. Becoming their true leader years later would not be a simple transition of authority. I knew I would have to prove myself in some ways—to earn their trust. And I didn't know if I had enough time for that.

\* \* \*

The next morning as I set out for Libnah to meet with Jeremiah, I shook with uneasiness as my royal carriage rattled along the dusty path. I knew what I would say, but his unknown response unnerved me. When meeting with him as the king, not as Jude, I did not want my authority to coerce his decision. But my pretenses would have to be put aside if he was to trust me.

I stuck my head out of the carriage and shouted, "Faster!" to Jared. This ride had already seemed to last for days, and we were not even halfway to the small town. I had sent a messenger ahead of me the night prior to tell Hamutal's family that I would be paying a visit to their tent to discuss some "matters of business." Thinking of my wording to my messenger, I smiled. I wondered if she would recall our "fair business" on the hillside when she heard the message.

When I had taken her back to the inn that Friday evening, I gave her permission to reveal my identity to her family but asked her not to spread my secret beyond that. After all, I could not allow all of my subjects to assume their king a complete lunatic. Jeremiah and I had seemed to share a good friendship on the day he invited me to join in a Sabbath meal with him and his family. I was hoping he would remember that, and perhaps conveniently forget the fact that I had misled him about who I was. *Hardly!* I thought to myself cynically.

I said a silent prayer, asking God to give me favor even beyond what I could earn. LORD, *I need Your mercy today. I don't think I can do what You've called me to without her. I know that no part of me deserves this, but I also know that You can do anything. I may be king, but You alone are God.*

I put my head in my hands and ran my fingers through my hair, reciting in my mind the speech I had practiced. I tried to anticipate his answer and considered the best possibility and the worst, preparing my response for either. I felt ready. So why were we still not there!

Another hour passed before we finally arrived in Libnah, while I sat alone with my tense thoughts in the rocking carriage. My guard and attendant Asaiah opened my door, and Jared handed me my crown as I stepped onto the street. I looked down and took it in my hands, thinking of how it would be perceived. I decided to carry it rather than put it on my head. Sighing, I resolved not to worry about the crown. It was part of who I was.

Although I told my guards to not draw any attention, the people on the streets naturally noticed me and began to shout in excitement, "The king—he's here!" Then they commenced dropping to their knees as I passed. I hurried by the few shops on that street and turned to take the narrow path that would lead to her family's tent, which was about a fifteen-minute walk into the hills from there. Jared walked in front of me with his sword bared beside him, and Asaiah followed behind, directing the people not to follow us.

As we neared Jeremiah's tent, Hamutal emerged and bowed to one knee, dropping her head in reverence. The rest of her family came out as well, Hannah holding the baby. They all followed Hamutal's gesture, making me feel like squirming out of my robe so that I could just be Jude again. I glanced over at Asaiah and noticed him eyeing Hamutal for an extra moment. Jealousy rose in my abdomen, but I breathed a sigh and pushed it down. I could not fault him—she was beautiful. Of course other men might see that, and I couldn't blame them for noticing, could I?

"Welcome, Your Highness," said Jeremiah when he stood.

The rest of them rose as well, and I caught Hamutal's glance with a smile. Her eyes were pleased and curious. She had no inkling of why I was here. And that was how I wanted it to stay—for now.

"Hamutal, would you mind if I have a few moments alone with your parents?" I asked, getting right down to it. I had waited all morning to be here, and my patience would not last through any more formalities. I could feel the practiced speech springing into my mouth. Determined to wait until she left, I swallowed them back.

My angel looked back at me with a quizzical glance and then bowed her head obediently and replied, "Of course, Your Majesty. As you wish." She whispered to her sisters and brother and then beckoned them all to follow her up the hill, I guessed to check on the sheep that were grazing there.

"Won't you come in out of the wind, my lord," offered Hamath, her mother.

"Thank you." I nodded and followed them into their dwelling. It was larger than it looked from the outside, and a few of the corners were closed off in drapes for sleeping areas. In the center of the tent was a large pole that supported much of the weight of the coverings and curtains. Close to it was a small fire pit, lined with large rocks, and over that a spit for roasting and a hook that held an aged kettle. Jeremiah motioned me to the one seat in the room while he knelt and sat on some pillows. Hamath poured me a cup of the hot liquid in the kettle and then sat beside her husband, looking back up at me in expectation. I held the cup but did not drink, fearing I would not like its contents and that I might offend her if I couldn't control the look on my face.

"I appreciate your time today, Jeremiah … Hamath," I said, nodding to each of them. "I should not need long."

"The pleasure is all ours, my lord," he replied courteously. "Hamutal has had quite a lot to say about you these past few days. You've given us quite the surprise, you know," he said with a slight smile. "And I have you to thank, once again, for saving my daughter's life. I'm wondering if you'll refuse to accept any payment from me this time," he said with a grin.

I was taken aback. I did not expect this, but why not? I wasn't thinking of the near-trampling when I had composed my speech to him in my mind on the way over. He was playing into my plan without even realizing it!

I cocked my head to the side thoughtfully and pursed my lips together. "Actually, sir, I can think of something to ask for this time, though please consider before you answer too quickly."

"Anything, Your Majesty; if I own it, it will be yours," he said in complete reverence.

I was impressed at his comfort with my new role to him. Almost immediately I had gone from being a naïve boy to his honored ruler, and he seemed not the least bit uncomfortable. This, then, was turning out to be easier than I had dreaded. I responded quickly in hope, yet not quite convinced he would keep this new promise.

"I desire Hamutal's hand in marriage. I want her for my queen—her and no other," I declared. This was not really what I had rehearsed, but it seemed fitting, nonetheless. I then leaned forward toward him and held my breath for his answer.

He balked, blinking once, and then opened his eyes wide. He hadn't seen this coming, after all. Standing, he sighed and thought for a moment, looking back at me. He began to pace back and forth across the tent, looking from me to her mother and back again. His silence was torturing me, and his delayed answer twisted my stomach into knots. Hamath was silent but seemed just as curious as I, and yet just as confused as he.

Finally Jeremiah stopped and faced me. I stood to meet his stare, anticipation winding my muscles tighter and tighter.

"You know, Your Highness, that our family is not of any nobility, don't you?" he asked.

"That is exactly why I am here this afternoon rather than my representatives or council members," I replied. I paused to collect my nerves. "This union is not about social standing or military strategy. I love your daughter, sir. And I've decided that I want my wife and the mother of my children to be someone who serves Jehovah and serves Him alone. Hamutal's lineage is irrelevant."

He furrowed his brow as he listened to me, turning to pace again, and kneading his forehead in concentration. Once again he squared to face me. "I apologize, Majesty, but I cannot give you what I've promised to another man—not in accordance with the law and my faith. She is betrothed to a man from our tribe named Matthias, and he would have to give her a legal divorce—the pact is binding. Much as I believe you would provide for her and lead her well, her hand is no longer mine to give," he said solemnly.

I sighed, expecting this possibility.

"I believe this is something you must take up with Matthias," Jeremiah said. "He is the one who has prepared his bride price for her. I've promised Hamutal to him."

"I'm willing to pay twice as much as he has prepared," I offered—I knew it would be a long shot.

"That is fine and well, Your Highness, but it changes nothing. Besides, my daughter is not an item to be auctioned to the highest bidder," he chided me gently.

"Of course not, sir. That's not what I meant. Only that I am prepared to offer the proper payment, once everyone is in agreement, that's all," I said.

He was right, and I didn't *want* to buy anyone off, though that would have been easier. What I really wanted was to know that Hamutal would choose me, if the choice were hers to make. I closed my eyes, desperate to figure out a way to make that an option.

I said the first thing that came to my mind: "I need to speak with Matthias, then. Do you know where I can find him?"

"Now?" he asked

"Now."

"I might guess he's out in the field with his own flock, but I wouldn't know exactly where," he replied with a shrug. Hamutal's words echoed in my mind from our last Sabbath together: *"I don't want to live as a shepherdess my whole life. I've always wanted more ..."* This Matthias was a shepherd, then. That was part of why she dreaded marrying him.

With new boldness, I asked, trying not to sound too demanding, "Would you please send your son with my guard Asaiah to bring Matthias back here? I'd like us all to speak together, with you ... and Hamutal as well." I turned to Hamath: "Would you mind?"

"As you wish, Highness," she replied with a slight nod.

I turned to Jeremiah for his answer.

"I can't stop you from asking him. As for my son, he does know the way, so I'll permit him to do this errand for you," he said. I could tell he was hesitant, but he suspected what I was planning.

A few moments later, Hamutal, Hannah, Johanah, Jaazaniah, and the baby all came back into the tent, rosy-cheeked from the cold. I suddenly felt guilty for sending them out of their shelter. After handing the baby over to Hamath, Hamutal smiled, bowed slightly to me, and walked past me to the corner to pick up a blanket.

"Allow me," I offered, unfolding the blanket and wrapping it around her shoulders. I let my hands and arms linger around her as I did. Blushing, she smiled up at me and glanced over at her parents to see if they had caught our little embrace. They had. As her mother turned her back to us to stoke the fire, I saw a knowing twinkle in her eye. *Good. They should see how she cared for me, too.*

Hamutal turned to pick up a few more blankets, brought them to the other children, and then sat by the fire to warm her hands.

Jeremiah took Jaazaniah outside, and I heard them speaking lowly to Asaiah, who peeked into the tent at me. I nodded, agreeing to what Jeremiah had told him, and he bowed to me in acknowledgement. Though I had not told her parents of my intention to keep our discussion from their daughter, I was thankful that they had picked up on it intuitively.

Hamath and her eldest daughters began preparing a meal for the evening, discussing the extra mouths at the table and the need for additional food. I sat back and watched quietly, keeping my attention on my angel as she washed, chopped, and stirred. She stole small, questioning glances at me as well, as if trying to ask me with her eyes what was going on and why I was here. I replied with a sly half-smile.

Jeremiah returned from some chores outside and began to talk to me about Jerusalem and what new structures were being built in the city. He expressed concern for security at the borders, to which I quickly reassured him that our troops had taken a heightened guard and were well prepared should the Philistines or the Assyrians threaten to attack. He seemed pleased and honored to speak with me about such matters, though I must have been obviously distracted by both Hamutal's presence and by the pending arrival of Matthias.

It was another half-hour before I heard men's voices coming from outside the tent, and I stood to greet the one man who stood between me and my future bride.

As he entered, I sized him up carefully, even as he saw me and took a knee in respect. He was dark-haired and tall, though not quite as tall as me, and had a full, squared-off beard, making my estimate of his age about eighteen or nineteen. Hamutal took one look at him and looked back at Hamath with panic on her face.

"M-Mother?" she said.

Matthias then rose and turned to her, taking her hand and bowing to lay a kiss on top of it. "It is lovely to see you again, my dear," he said in all innocence, gazing at her.

She stood there, frozen in speechless confusion and swallowed hard.

I clenched my fists so hard I thought I would draw blood under my nails. An envious rage welled up in me as my shoulders rose to my ears. Quickly I stared into the fire at the center of the tent and took a deep breath, working hard to control myself. This could go very wrong if I lost it here. *Easy, Josiah,* I thought. *He has more right to look at her that way than you do. Let's talk this through. Get back to business.*

"Thank you for coming, Matthias," I said.

"Your Highness," he acknowledged, nodding again to me. "I'm not sure what I, of all people, have done to draw your attention and require a guarded summons, but you definitely have my curiosity, that's for sure."

*I'll have more than your curiosity before the night is through—I'll have your bride.*

"I want to propose a compromise with you," I began, cutting through the formality. "I'd like to ask you to discharge your agreement with Jeremiah for his daughter's hand. You see, I am in love with her, and I suspect she might have feelings for me as well. Jeremiah has agreed to give her hand to me on matters of royal debt, but says he cannot do so until you have granted her a legal divorce, releasing her from your current engagement. Would you be willing to do this, if I were to pay you what you would have given Jeremiah in bride price for her?"

As I spoke, my eyes danced between Matthias and Hamutal. I needed to read the reaction in his face, but I also longed to know what her response would be to my proposal as well. She stood unsteadily, holding Hannah's hand with both of hers and gasping for air. I was going for surprise—I ended up with shock.

He paused for a confused moment before he spoke: "Well, I don't suppose I have a choice, do I, *Your Highnesssss?*" he asked, hissing the last word in sarcasm and raising his eyebrows slightly from their furrowed position.

"On the contrary. I'm asking you, not demanding that you agree to this. There is no force involved, just an agreement between two fellow

Judeans," I replied. And it was true; though I must admit I would have done anything for her, even throw my authority over someone. But I knew that was not what she wanted, and she deserved the greatest man, not just the powerful one. I had to hope that he would consent.

"But I will still be left without a wife," he replied matter-of-factly. He had a point.

"Would you prefer to marry a woman who is in love with someone else?" I asked. I had a point, too. His eyes snapped back to Hamutal, who turned a bright red and looked at her sandals, confirming my assertion quite conveniently for me.

I redirected: "There are plenty of other young women in my kingdom, and, with twice as much money now, you're sure to find one who suits you well."

He stood there thinking for what seemed like hours—but was probably only a few seconds—then took a deep breath and let it out slowly. "Very well, Your Majesty. I release Hamutal and Jeremiah of this marriage arrangement," he said, regret dripping from every word.

I let out a sigh of relief and looked over at my angel. She was clearly still dazed at what had just happened. Rising to my feet again, I walked over to Matthias and took the sandal from his hand in pledge. "If you meet me at the square in Libnah in one hour, I will have your payment and her papers ready for you," I said.

He nodded in agreement and then turned to Hamutal.

I watched their farewell closely. She slipped the gold band from her forefinger and placed it in his open hand. He walked out of the tent and out of her life—just as it should be.

# 10. HAMUTAL

I was still reeling.

Inside, my stomach was tied in knots and my heart felt like it had stopped beating. Did that really just happen? I thought about it again, replaying the conversation in my mind. *Yes ... I think the king asked Matthias to free me from my prison, and ... yes ... I think Matthias actually agreed to it.* I let it sink in and tried to breathe like normal. I felt my heart fluttering like a dove just released from its cage.

There was something more, something bigger, but I couldn't reach it yet. It loomed before me so huge it was like a boulder I could not wrap my arms around to take hold. What did he say again? I knew I was close, but my shock held it just out of reach. I strained to concentrate, aware that I had many eyes on me as I gawked into space—including Josiah's.

And then his words came flooding into my mind like water loosed from a dam.

*"You see, I am in love with her, and I suspect she might have feelings for me as well. Jeremiah has agreed to give her hand to me ..."*

He was in love with me? He had asked my father for my hand? And my father said yes? *Amazing, I go and check on the sheep for a few minutes and look how much I miss!* I thought. I broke my stare and looked up into his delighted eyes. He was absolutely triumphant. So this had been his purpose. I had been wondering why he had come and then so quickly asked me to leave him with my parents. Curiosity had nearly driven me insane up on the hill. He was here to negotiate me out of hopelessness.

"Would you mind if Hamutal and I step outside for a brief moment, sir?" he asked my father. My heart commenced to racing at the idea of being alone with him again—freezing wind or not.

"Yes, of course, Your Majesty. Please also ask your guards to come in and warm themselves by the fire, if you like," he said. And I knew Josiah would not turn him down.

"Thank you," he said. Then added, "For everything."

My father smiled and nodded in understanding. I threw my arms around him in thankful bliss, unable to contain my excitement. He patted the back of my head and held me close. "I would give all the silver in the world to keep that delight in your eyes, Love. May you be blessed in this union."

I brought my blanket with me this time and stepped under Josiah's arm as he held the tent flap open for me. He then gave my father's warm message to his guards. The two towering men bowed to him and stepped in, rubbing their hands together.

I stepped out into the chilly afternoon that loomed with gray clouds in every direction as a gust of icy wind took my breath away. I hugged my blanket tighter around me. Josiah placed his hand gently on my back and led me a few cubits beyond the tent.

"Before I ask you something, Hamutal," he began, "I have to tell you one more thing about me that you don't know yet, alright?"

He was preparing me for *another* revelation about himself? Would this man's mysteries ever end?

I nodded. His nervous eyes were making my insides swim.

"I was married before, and she died giving birth to my son," he said. My eyes widened, but I remained quiet. "I was so young, and it was very strange. Her death has haunted me, but not for any of the right reasons … What I'm trying to say … is … is that I've finally been able to put her behind me because you've taught me what it is to love someone—the way I believe the LORD intended."

He waited for me to respond, but I didn't know what to say. Since I first learned of his true identity, I had feared that he might have several wives, mistresses, and concubines. Before this moment, I had tried to dismiss this dread as insignificant, since I would not really allow myself to imagine that I would end up with him. And so, this new piece of information hurt me, but not necessarily because I was jealous. It hurt me, because it hurt him.

"Does that affect the way you feel about me?" he asked.

I pondered it a little more. I wanted to be completely honest with him, since I believed he had been truthful with me.

"No, my lord," I said, answering his gaze with my own. And it didn't. My heart was still in his hands. I still would do anything for him, had he merely asked. There was still no place I'd rather be than in his arms.

But I had more to think about now. He had been married before, and I never had. He knew everything that went along with having a wife, and for me to picture being with him, I couldn't help but picture being fully *with* him in every way—when he had been with someone else. Truth be told, it affected the way I felt about *myself*.

Even as he looked at me with nothing but fondness, I couldn't hold back my insecurity. "Was she beautiful?" I asked.

His brows descended over his eyes, and he realized what I was thinking. "Yes, she was," he confessed. He looked past me, staring into his memory. "She was lovely to look at, but I never knew her; never saw who she really was. And she never really knew me, either. We weren't married for very long, and she stayed in her own quarters most of the time. We were both so young and ... and then she was gone." He shivered as the wind blew a new, fierce gust over the hill.

I offered him my blanket, and he took it, and then surprised me by throwing it around his back, stepping behind me, and wrapping his arms and the blanket around me, standing very close to encompass us both in it. I felt my back against his solid stomach and chest, and relished his arms around the front of me. His hands wrapped around my shoulders, and it was suddenly very warm underneath our makeshift shelter.

He leaned over my shoulder and whispered into my ear with very slow and deliberate words: "I knew you better, and loved you more, the first day I met you."

His warm breath wafted down my spine and I shuddered involuntarily, in reflex leaning back into him. He drew his arms even tighter around me and buried his head in my neck, breathing in deeply through his nose. He held me that way for a few moments, and it felt like he was drinking me in. I could smell him, too, and inhaled the warm scent of rich myrrh that was so uniquely his.

Then he took a golden ring with a large emerald in the setting off of his smallest finger and opened one of my hands, laying it gently in my palm. After giving me a chance to see his gift, he asked into my ear, "Will you be my queen—the only one I'll ever marry again?"

And there was no way I could say no. Not my insecurities, not my fear, not his past, or his secrets—nothing could have kept me from surrendering to his love. I trusted him with my life, the very life he had rescued twice. I was confident that he would hear from God for our lives and His purpose. I wanted nothing more than to spend the rest of my days by his side.

As I turned around, I felt a comfortable smile spread across my face. Holding my hands up for him to see, I placed the ring on my forefinger. I was closer to him now than I had ever been, standing there under my blanket. His long arms wrapped around me and pulled me in, and he looked down at me with a beaming smile, which faded into longing when I slipped my arms around his waist and leaned into him.

Neither one of us knew what was happening next until his lips were already on mine. I closed my eyes and reached up to him, feeling the warmth of his mouth and responding with my own thirst.

When he pulled back slightly and placed his forehead against mine, he offered a gasping, "I'm sorry."

I looked into his eyes and replied my own breathless "I'm not."

"I won't be able to wait very much longer for you, Love," he whispered.

"You won't have to."

And true to my promise, I rode out with him the next day, headed for Jerusalem to make plans for the wedding. I filled a saddle basket with some frocks and shawls, along with a few other belongings but left the wedding dress I had sewn. I told my mother she could keep it for one of the other girls, or sell it in the market. While I was making it, I had put in many hours with my shoulders hunched over the painful stitches, picturing Matthias, and trying not to cry. There was no way I would marry Josiah clothed in another man's memories. I was still undecided about whether or not I would wear my birthday presents, so I left them too, knowing I would be back.

Though my parents seemed very willing to allow me to leave with him for a week, accompanied by only his guards, Josiah insisted that Hannah come along, too. My father was reluctant for her to leave, especially since Mother would already be left without my help, much less Hannah's as well. He had conceded in the end, however, giving in to my mother, who instinctively knew how much we would need each other.

My sister seemed even more excited than I was for the week in Jerusalem, her eyes beaming as she packed a few of her own belongings. "I can't wait to see the palace, Hamutal—tell me all about it!" she squealed.

"Honestly, I only saw the king's quarters," I replied. "I guess we can have the grand tour together." And then it hit me that I was about to see the splendor of what would become my home in a matter of weeks. My mind was constantly overflowing with thoughts of Josiah, of loving him, and of becoming his wife; I didn't have much room for thoughts about becoming the queen. When the idea of stepping into my role of royalty passed before my mind, it still felt surreal.

Leave it to Hannah to keep reminding me, though. She had asked endless questions the night before as we lay together on my sleeping mat. Most of them I hadn't even thought of, like "What will your crown look like?" and "What do queens eat?" and "What will you *do* all day in the palace?"

Shaking my head in the dark, I must have said, "I don't know" to almost everything she asked. *Why do people keep probing me to tell the future when I can't even fathom what tomorrow holds?*

I was glad when her questions had switched directions and turned to him: "What did he say to you outside, tonight?"

"He asked me to be his queen and promised I'd be the only one for the rest of his life," I said dreamily. I was so relieved when he added the last part of his proposal. I knew there would be no possibility of me sharing him. I could scarcely get over the idea of his former wife, much less any others. I wanted all of his embraces, each of his adoring gazes from his jeweled, brown eyes, and every last kiss to be mine and mine alone. And the memory of his lips on mine brought back a burst of fire to my mouth, and I suddenly drew in a sharp breath and tensed next to Hannah.

"What?" she demanded.

"Nothing," I lied.

"Tell me!" she whispered, and clutched my hand viciously.

"He kissed me," I confessed, excitement palpable in my breath.

Hannah gasped. "I knew Father shouldn't have let you go out alone! What was it like?"

"I thought I was going to disappear right there in his arms," I said, hugging myself. Every part of my skin remembered his touch, and I savored my body's sweet memory of him.

My sister sighed next to me, bringing me back from my bliss.

"What is it?" I asked.

"Nothing. I'm just trying not to be jealous. The LORD would not want me to covet what you have, but it's very hard not to," she confessed.

"Your husband will come too, dear. I just know it," I reassured. And I really was confident that God had a wonderful husband for her too. "Matthias is single now," I teased.

A quick punch to my arm in the dark was her only response.

"I'm glad you're coming, Hannah. I need you with me," I whispered. And I did.

"Yes, you need me to make sure that king of yours doesn't steal any more kisses before your wedding day!"

"Of course—you keep him honest." I nudged her. Though a very big part of me hoped he might steal a few more.

\* \* \*

The carriage ride was comfortable as the three of us sat on the purple cushions, Hannah between my king and me. The top section of the carriage was overlaid in gold and caught the sun in bright reflections as we traveled. Josiah's guards rode on the seat outside the carriage and we heard their muffled voices occasionally. I listened to the birds singing in the branches that draped over the road and wanted to sing along with them—I was so thrilled. We were back in Jerusalem in what seemed like moments—much shorter than the journey on foot.

Just before we reached the palace, Hannah turned to him and asked curiously, "Your Majesty, I'm honored by this privilege, but may I ask why you insisted that I come along?"

He smiled and hesitated, and then leaned forward to look at me while he spoke to her. "Well, you see, I don't trust myself. I'm like a very thirsty soldier who has been out all day in the throes of battle. I'm very hungry, too, and when I come in from the field, I find a banquet table before me." Here, he paused and gestured to me. "But it's not yet time for the festivities, so I need to sit at the table and wait. There's fresh, cold milk, sweet wine, and fluffy cakes of honey, but the problem is, I'm so famished that if I take just one taste, I'll end up gulping it all, devouring every last crumb. My biggest difficulty, however, is that last night I *was* somehow able to sample this delicious feast, and so now I *know* how truly wonderful it will be," he finished.

My cheeks had been burning the entire time as he spoke, and now I could no longer hold his gaze as I looked down at my trembling hands. Hannah squirmed next to me.

"So, you see dear sister, I need you here, to stay by her side this entire week so that this ravished soldier doesn't forget his table manners," he crooned with a crooked smile.

I closed my eyes, drew in a deep breath, and held onto the carriage door to steady myself. Hannah cleared her throat in embarrassment. "Yes, Your Majesty," she finally spoke after an awkward silence. "I'll do my best."

# II. JOSIAH

Once I showed Hamutal and Hannah to the guest quarters, I needed to get back to duties and meetings. My officials, commanders, and advisors were waiting for me, and our debates dragged into the evening. I was still trying to establish my credibility and authority with them, so I listened carefully to their concerns and advice, making decisions based on the wisdom they offered, along with my knowledge of God and His desires. Finding the balance was not easy.

Every time I decided against a motion they recommended, and instead honored what I believed the LORD would have wanted, I feared revolt or rebellion. I tried to acquiesce in a few things they requested when not in direct violation of my beliefs so as to give them some semblance of a voice, but it was like walking over a bed of coals as I attempted to honor God and keep my country's leadership intact.

The most pressing issue of the day was the argument over what to do in Israel, where Assyrian troops had been disappearing by the thousands. My magistrates stationed near the border brought reports of the once domineering and violent Assyrian empire, now weakening. Subsequently, they were sending their entire army south to Egypt in order to secure the rebellion there. This left the previously enslaved Israelites with their freedom, albeit an impoverished one.

My council members and army commanders agreed that we should take advantage of the situation and invade Israel, in order to assimilate those tribes back into Judah. I, on the other hand, with the surprising support of Hilkiah and a few other priests, favored a trade agreement with our brothers. I knew Israel was just as much Jehovah's wayward son as were we, and I wished to reach out to them in compassion. Because the wealth in our government storehouses had grown since I had taken the throne, we would be able to afford such an alliance, offering a more peaceful option for uniting. We didn't come to an agreement, but my heart was set. Rather than enforce my command, however, I chose to resume talks the next day, hoping my generals would come around.

By the end of these debates I was utterly spent and retreated to my quarters to gather my thoughts before having dinner with Hamutal and Hannah. Unfortunately, my room did not offer the solace I was seeking. On my bed lay a small, sealed message scroll. In curiosity I opened it and read the only sentence written on it:

*What abomination of the* Lord *has the king permitted in the Valley of Hinnom?*

I was dumbfounded. I did not remember ever visiting the valley just south of Jerusalem, much less giving permission or orders for any *abomination* to be there. I stepped back into the wide hallway outside of my quarters to catch a glimpse of the messenger. I didn't even see a guard, and I heard no clues in the silence, either. I walked back to my bed and sat down to reread the scroll.

As far as I was concerned, my kingdom was filled with abominations; I just hadn't quite figured how to remedy that yet. My permission, or lack thereof, was irrelevant. People seemed to be doing what they wanted when they wanted, with whomever they wanted. The only public religious stand I had ever taken was just two days before, when I had told Hilkiah that he was to be a high priest of Jehovah alone.

*What does this mean?* I thought. The confusion was nearly painful. My head was still pounding and I knew Hamutal was waiting for me in the dining hall. Dismissing the note for the moment, I tossed it back on my bed and walked out to meet her.

Before I got to the table, I saw one of the guards patrolling the halls and pulled him aside. "Do you remember seeing anyone in my quarters today?" I asked.

He thought for a moment and then said, "Yes, Your Highness; the priest was there with his son. He said you wanted him to remove all of the incense. Is there a problem?"

"No," I replied calmly. "Thank you. That will be all." I would talk to Hilkiah after dinner.

Hamutal and Hannah rose from the table and curtsied to me. "My lord," they echoed in unison.

I nodded at them and offered a polite smile. I was truly happy to see her after a long day, but I was preoccupied by my mystery messenger. They had been waiting on me for a while, evident by the already-set banquet before us. I sat down and invited them to begin, still feeling distracted.

"Thank you, my King," said Hamutal. Her voice had a ring to it that forced me look at her again. It sounded different from when my servants or officials addressed me as such, almost as if I were her king and hers alone. I liked it. I took a deep breath and refocused my attention on her again, silently repenting of my preoccupation. I took her hand in mine and kissed the top of it.

"And how was your day, Love? Tell me what you have been doing while I have been away so rudely," I said.

She left her hand in mine, her touch as thrilling as ever. "We were able to have a tour of the palace with Asaiah," she said. "It's so very grand! I'm lost already, and I haven't even seen it all."

"Yes, it is. I don't even think I've been into all of the rooms yet, either," I said.

"Oh my!" Hannah exclaimed. I nodded in reassurance of my declaration.

"Will you be able to show us more tomorrow?" Hamutal asked with pleading eyes.

I hated to refuse her anything she wanted, but I knew where I would be tomorrow, and it was not here in the palace.

"I'm afraid not. Something has come up—just before I came to dinner, actually—and I'll be traveling to the Hinnom Valley come morning," I replied, not wanting to worry her with my secret note. Then, reconsidering, I asked, "Do you know anything about it?"

"Only it's location," she said.

"Mmm, that's about all I know, as well," I said, the disappointment too thick.

"I'm sorry I can't be of more help."

"No, no—don't worry about it. I'll find out what I need to know tomorrow. It's not far, so perhaps I won't be gone very long. Maybe we will be able to spend the afternoon together. How does that sound to you?"

"Perfect," she said, gazing into my eyes.

I smiled, delighting in her adoration. "Besides," I said, "the tailor and his assistants will be coming to make arrangements for your gown in the morning. I spoke with him today, and you should have seen the excitement in his face when I gave him this newest assignment. Do you know what you want yet?"

"No, I'm not sure. I was hoping they might have some suggestions. I don't know what a future queen wears to her wedding," she said, biting her lower lip.

"I'm sure they will know." I was confident that Shallum would be working on sketches and fabrics late into the night in his anticipation.

"I only want to look my best for the groom," she teased. "Do you think *he'll* approve of the tailor's suggestions?"

"You would be gorgeous to me in rags. I will love looking at you no matter what you're wearing."

I took a few bites and allowed the sisters to do the same. Despite the wonderful company, my head was still pounding, and Hamutal caught me rubbing my temples.

"Please, Your Highness," she said, "you should retire and get some rest for your errand tomorrow. We'll be fine until you return."

"Thank you for understanding," I said as I rose to my feet. I hated to leave her, but my thoughts would not stay where they ought, and I desperately needed some time alone. My hearth beckoned me, and I nodded to her as I rose from the table.

"Sweet dreams," I said.

"They will be, if they are of you," she replied with a sly smile.

"When were you in here?" I demanded.

"Just this afternoon, Your Highness. I removed the incense as you commanded," Hilkiah answered, clearly confused at my anger.

"Did you leave me this message?" I asked sharply as I walked around the hearth and held up the scroll to him. I had lit a large fire and the flames and sparks were leaping into the air now.

"No. No, I've never seen that," he replied. "What does it say?"

I handed it to him to read. He glanced back up at me with a furrow on his brow. Shrugging and shaking his head, he handed it back to me. "What does *that* mean?"

"I was hoping you could tell me," I said.

"I'm sorry," he replied. "I don't know what could be in the valley that would be an abomination of the LORD. What are you going to do?"

"I'm going to check, of course. And you're coming with me. We'll go first thing tomorrow morning, so tell Jared and Asaiah as well. I'll need a few others, too, but not more than that, understood?"

"Yes, Your Highness. Will there be anything else?" he asked, bowing to leave.

I looked over at his son, who looked to be a few years older than me. He wore a priestly robe and kippot, which covered the crown of his head like his father's, but he lacked the vest of a priest. His hair was dark brown and very neat, and his beard a bit longer than my own stubble that I preferred to keep short. He met my gaze with a bit of scrutiny under his practiced reverence, as if trying to predict what I would do next.

"I'd like to speak privately with your son for a few moments. I'll not detain him long," I said.

Hilkiah's brow wrinkled yet again, but he did not protest. "Of course. I'll give the message to the guard, and I bid you good evening." He walked out, but I had a feeling he was eavesdropping in the hallway.

I walked over to Hilkiah's son and asked, "What is your name, young priest?"

"Jeremiah."

"Really? I know another Jeremiah. He's about to become my father-in-law," I said.

He raised his eyebrows and turned the corners of his mouth downward, nodding. "I like him already." Then he smiled.

"He's a good man who fears the LORD, as does his daughter, my future queen," I said, not realizing the pride in my voice until it was too late. I watched his response to the mention of God's name. I was trying to keep the conversation light while testing his convictions. His eyes narrowed, and then he nodded once in approval.

"And how would you *know* that they fear the LORD? For certain, I mean?" he asked, slightly tilting his head to the side. I sensed he was probing my faith, not Hamutal's or her father's.

"That is a difficult issue, knowing the beliefs of another person ... but you are the priest—I'd like to hear *your* opinions first," I said.

He narrowed his eyes and pursed his lips, knowing he should not refuse me, but acknowledging that this conversation may have sounded different had I not held authority over him. He wanted to test me just as much as I wanted to test him.

"Well, it is not always easy to see from outward appearance or behavior," he began.

I nodded in agreement, thinking of Hilkiah and others I knew. They had seemed to accept any god as equal to Jehovah. It appeared that the priest in front of me might not have aligned with his own father in his sundry theology. "There are many aberrations that people do in secret," Jeremiah said, lowering his voice and looking sideways, "even if they claim to worship the LORD, and few are even doing *that* in these days." He continued with a disgusted look on his face. "Only the LORD of Heaven's Armies can judge the heart of a man; only He can know everything that His people do and think in the darkness of their hearts," he declared, boldly now. As he spoke, his mistrust was capitulated and he continued unabated—almost as if he wanted to keep a secret for tactical maneuver but could not hold it from bursting out.

I was too amazed to speak for a moment. Never had I met a priest so devout. I knew then and there that he would be instrumental—not just for me and my aspirations, but truly used by the LORD.

"I agree with you wholeheartedly!" I blurted out, and then, suspecting Hilkiah may have been listening, I lowered my voice. "Come into the other room," I whispered, beckoning him with my hand. We quickly stepped into my private dining quarters where I had shared a First Meal with Hamutal. We spoke in hushed tones, aware that not many held our same stance or passion.

"How long have you been surrendered to the LORD alone?" he asked me.

"Only a little over a month," I answered with a smile. "I found Him in the Temple and He spoke to me from the altar," I recalled. "And you?"

Before answering, his eyes widened with amazement. He seemed impressed and excited at my testimony of new faith. "I chose to forsake all other gods about two years ago, and have been trying to read as much as I can of the scrolls of David and Solomon. But my father does not know that. No one does. They are, after all, located here, my King," he confessed, bowing his head.

*Hmmm*, I thought, *how ironic. Jeremiah was sneaking into the palace while I had been sneaking out—both to find God.*

"No, I'm glad you've read them, Jeremiah," I said. "Please, feel free to come any time—you have my permission. Only, don't take them out, understood?"

"Of course not," he said. "I wouldn't think of it!"

"So, tell me, my new friend," I began, putting my arm around his shoulders, "was it you who left me the note?"

"Yes." He was suddenly sobered, the previous smile drained from his face.

"Well," I said, "what is it? What's in the Hinnom Valley?"

"I'd rather you see it for yourself. I can't even say the words," he said, staring into the air. He was very serious now, and almost frightened. He shuddered and dropped to his knees. "I wouldn't have told you about it if I didn't think it would make a difference, but ... but, when you commanded my father to only speak of Jehovah and no other gods, I somehow ... I thought you *must* be devoted to the LORD's ways ... and that you might want to lead your kingdom accordingly. Was I correct?"

"Yes, yes—of course! That's exactly what I want—I just don't know how yet."

"I'd like to come with you, if you'll permit me, but I don't want to even speak of it if it's not true. I heard from a servant last week that something there had frightened him, but it's merely hearsay until I see it with my own eyes. My note was only to get you to investigate for yourself."

"Then we ride out together in the morning. I'll need some trusted eyes and ears." Jeremiah nodded in agreement, though he did not quite share my enthusiasm. Instead, he wore a foreboding look.

I embraced him in farewell and said, "Get some sleep, Brother."

He nodded and then bowed as he left.

\* \* \*

As we neared the valley, I couldn't stop my heart from racing, as fear of what we would find gripped me. I heard nothing but the pounding of hooves underneath me and behind me. Ten of us had ridden out, but I suddenly regretted not bringing more troops. What if it proved to be more than we could handle? I looked back at Jeremiah for a moment, and reassured myself that my new friend would have warned me if that were the case.

LORD, *please give me strength to do Your will. I'm afraid, God; and I don't even know what holds my fear! Show me, LORD. I beg You; show me what to do.*

We had ridden across the plain, descended the northern slope of the valley, and then made our way eastward. I had not seen anything out of the ordinary yet, but the gray clouds overhead sent an ominous message, as if revealing some impending doom.

After a few minutes, we reached the bottom of the valley and rode along the dry streambed, slowing only slightly. The horses were kicking up a thick cloud of dust behind us, and there was no telling how far we had come.

I returned my gaze forward and pulled my reins up hard at the sight of the billowing smoke cloud appearing around the bend ahead. My horse skidded to an abrupt halt and the others behind me did the same, some of them surpassing me, unable to stop fast enough. I narrowed my eyes and guided my horse forward slowly, trying to make out the source of the black cloud. My comrades murmured in quiet wonder behind me. Although I couldn't see them yet, I could tell by the size of the smoke cloud that the flames would be quite large. We were about a thousand cubits away, but I could make out a crowd of people gathered around the base of the billows.

I waved my cavalry forward now, curiosity piercing.

As we drew closer, I perceived a large statue, about the height of three men, in the center of the crowd. *This is going to be horrible.* I prepared myself. I glanced back at the faces behind me. Hilkiah seemed confused and concerned. Jeremiah looked amazed and sorrowful as he shook his head. My guards seemed to be apprehensive, yet still bold and resolute. *They seem ready. Am I?*

I picked up the pace slightly. We rode in closer and my stomach lurched as I saw what they were bowing before. At the base of the stone statue was a tunnel of bricks, from which poured mountainous flames, leaping high into the air. Above the tunnel sat the chest and arms of the statue, which resembled a man's torso and arms. The arms seemed to wave randomly in the air, and within the chest were several holes that revealed smaller flames. Atop the statue sat the large silver head of a bull with golden horns.

My tongue was thick and heavy in my throat, and I felt my heart drop. The group of about a hundred people rose from their knees in unison and chanted, rocking back and forth on their heels, unaware of our nearing presence.

"Molech, Molech, Molech!"

I shook my head in disgusted wonder. I was afraid of whatever god this was, and I wondered if it held any power against Jehovah. What they did repulsed me, but that did not compare to the fury I felt as I saw what the idol-worshippers did next.

They continued to shout their chants as one man brought a large bundle forward from the crowd. I looked back to the statue and saw that the flames at the base were dying down slightly as we rode closer.

When I looked more carefully at the man, I saw that he held a young boy of about three years old, just as I heard him cry. I felt my eyebrows tense and lower over my eyes. *What is he going to do with him?* I asked myself, feeling my body trembling now. I looked back at Jeremiah, whose terrified expression answered my silent question.

Suddenly I heard my own mouth cry out "NO!" as I leapt from my horse and rushed into the back of the circled crowd, but their bodies were too tight as I shoved them aside. People fell as I pushed, but I kept going. I was not going to make it. The guards behind me were shouting at people to step aside in the name of the king, but everyone was rocking back and forth in a slow, drunken daze.

I clamored ahead in horror as the man tossed the screaming boy into the blazing tunnel. His tears of terror turned to screams of agony as he caught ablaze right before my eyes.

I felt not the slightest hesitation as I ascended the steps to the coals and flames. I ran up, reached into the fire, and pulled him from the tunnel, unaware of my own pain as my robe caught on fire and my skin singed beneath it. I held his tiny body in my arms even as the smell of his scorched flesh burned my nose. I turned and rushed him to Asaiah, who wrapped us in his saddle blanket, extinguishing the flames on our clothes. I proceeded to hand the wrapped and still-screaming child to Jeremiah, as Asaiah tried to pull me by my shoulders back to our horses.

Realizing what he meant to do, I stopped and backed up the steps away from him. For the first time, I saw their crazed faces as I addressed them, my rage burning hotter than the flames that had charred my arm.

"What are you doing?" I shouted. "Get out of here! How could you do this? I will not have this in my kingdom! If you do not leave *this instant*, I will have every last one of you imprisoned!"

The people turned to leave, dazed and confused, but they were not moving fast enough. I pushed through them, knocking them over again to get back to Jeremiah and the screaming boy. When I reached them, he was staring down at him wide-eyed and shaking his head. I looked down at what he saw and winced, turning my head away.

Taking a breath to steady myself, I looked again. He was bleeding from his head to his feet, soaking the blackened clothes in red stains.

There were places on his arms and legs where I could see the flesh; his skin was entirely gone. His screams stopped abruptly, and I assumed he passed out, because I still saw his tiny chest rising and falling with breath.

*Oh, God, please save him!*

"Hurry—back to the city," I cried, taking him for a moment as Jeremiah mounted his horse. I looked down, feeling more sorrow for this child than I had ever felt in my life—more than I felt for myself. More than when my father was murdered. More than when my mother died. More, because of what I knew.

When I handed him back to Jeremiah and mounted my own horse, I felt the desperate need to get him help, mixed with the aching fear that no help would be enough. Though my arms were blistered and bleeding, we rode as quickly as possible, and I did not look back to see if the people had actually left. I didn't want to know if they hadn't. I had to merely *hope* that they would not stay; it was all the strength I had. I rested one arm and then the other, transferring the reins as we rode faster and faster, my hands and arms seizing with pain as we rode.

We could have made it to the city sooner, but Jeremiah had slowed us, saying it was too much for the child. Nonetheless, we were back to the gates in less time than it took to ride out, rushing him into a place Asaiah knew, with a physician ready. As I laid him down on the table, I finally allowed my tears to flow. Tears of horror. Tears of shame. Tears of rage.

## 12. HAMUTAL

My sheep bleated loudly as I led them down to the stream, breaking my silent thoughts and prayers. With our wedding only a week away, I should have been thrilled, but instead I was worried. Josiah had sent a gift and message today, written in his own hand, but instead of reassuring me, the note troubled me:

*My Dearest Bride,*

*My patience drains and I wish you were back in the palace with me. We could sit by my hearth, and I would hold you in my arms. I hope you are well. Only a few more days before I see your lovely face! Please give my greeting to your family.*

*Your King*

My first concern was that it was so brief—his other messages had been much longer, detailing his business in Jerusalem or travels around the kingdom. My second concern was seeing no mention of the little boy who had been burned in the valley. I didn't know if he had lived through the day yesterday. Before this note, he had written to tell me his progress every day, sending a messenger to Libnah to greet me in the afternoons. *What if he dies? What will Josiah do?*

Although he didn't admit it to me before I left, I knew that so much of my king's emotions rode on the survival of the child. He wasn't able

103

to concentrate on anything else other than his healing—not even me. Although he took me with him to see the boy at the infirmary once, he remained distracted for the rest of my stay.

Not that I didn't understand the significance this event had on his kingdom and his leadership—Josiah was so passionate about moving Judah *away* from idol worship. In his mind, this child's life was the one thing that kept the kingdom hovering above the dung pit of idols. I contemplated the boy's chances of survival and thought Josiah might be too discouraged to even try to bring reform to our people. And so, I had been considerate, even brushing off his apologies as we left at Sabbath's end to return early to Libnah with my family.

I realized then on an even greater level how much this was weighing on his shoulders for him to be so preoccupied the week before our wedding. *The child must survive. Not only for the good of the kingdom, but for the sanity of my fiancé.* I said a silent prayer again for the boy and for Josiah.

I opened the package wrapped in beautiful purple silk and found a new set of hair clips that were extravagantly ordained with garnets and rubies, shaped like delicate flowers. I turned them in the sunlight and watched the dazzling reflections dance against my clothes and arms. I also found wrapped in the silk another note that read, *These were the ones I wanted to give you before, but I thought they would give me away. I can't wait to see them in your midnight hair. I love you.*

I smiled and pictured him choosing them for me in his treasury room. In my mind, he looked peaceful and contemplative, smiling as he picked them up. I cherished the fantasy of his happiness and wondered when or if I would ever see that look on his face again.

\* \* \*

The next afternoon, the same messenger arrived at just the same time as the previous days and dismounted, handing me yet another letter and wedding gift. I opened the gift first, treasuring his words more, wanting to make them last. As I unraveled the soft cloth covering, my breath was caught in my throat as I saw the contents. I unrolled a stack of crisp parchment paper—the kind only bought from Egypt. Each page was the same, with no blemishes or snags like the other paper I had seen. A smaller sheet fluttered to the ground and I bent to pick it up, careful not to let the rolls touch the earth.

*Because I know you'll want to write your family often,* the smaller sheet read.

Tears flooded my eyes and spilled onto my cheeks. *Well, perhaps he wasn't so distracted.* This gift was well-planned, and he knew me better than he should have, given the short time since we had met. It flattered me that he paid attention so well and chose such a precious thing—not only for me, but also for those I loved. He knew I would need to see them, too, and had offered to send or bring me home for a visit whenever I asked. *He really does give me too much.*

After admiring the paper once again and painstakingly rolling it up exactly the way it had been packaged, I could wait no longer to read his message. I peeled back the seal slowly and noticed right away that this note was longer. But as I began, I could hardly contain my sobs.

*Lovely Hamutal,*

*These days are dragging slower and slower, it seems. I don't know how I did it before—only seeing you once a week for Sabbath. Although I know my royal duties will take me away from you at times, I'm looking forward to spending the rest of my life with you close to me. I know it doesn't make sense, but my world seems so much harder to control when you are away. Just to let you know, the child is no better, and, in fact, he is worse. The doctors are not able to stop his bleeding and there is a new fever again. I was visiting him every day to check on his progress, but can bear it no longer. The past three days I've sent a messenger to bring word of anything new.*

*Also, in case you were wondering, the physician said my arms are healing well, but I will still have to wear these bandages for a few more weeks. It seems they will be part of my wedding attire. Not that I mind. I would have gladly been burned more, if it meant he would have been burned less. I don't know if he'll make it, Love. Please keep praying.*

*Four days more. Every night I look up at the sky and remember our kiss on your hillside. I feel so spoiled to think that God has given you to me and that I'll have you always.*

*Until Sunday,*
*Josiah*

The next two days were a blur of packing my belongings, finishing wedding preparations, and traveling to Jerusalem for Sabbath. My heart had never felt two more opposite emotions at the same time—drowning sorrow and dizzying excitement. Each time I would allow myself to smile in anticipation of seeing his face, I would immediately feel guilty over my joy, when a boy was simultaneously suffering.

I stayed by myself at the inn on Saturday so that Josiah and I would not see one another before the wedding, missing my first Sabbath in the Temple since I was a little girl. Instead, I paced around our room, praying the prayers they would be praying and singing the songs they would be singing. I imagined my groom and felt the memory of his arms around my shoulders. I prayed for his heart and his healing and pleaded for the little boy to live. When my family returned, I hugged them all and then made Hannah tell me every detail from start to finish of the Sabbath ceremony, though it had been no different from the week before. What did make it different, however, was the message that came to the inn later that evening, after the sun had set.

The boy had died that day.

I wept into my father's shoulder and pleaded, "Why, why, why?" Though I had not known him, the memory of his tiny, bandaged body, and the knowledge that his own parents had been the ones to murder him for a sacrifice to Molech, ripped grief through my soul like my fifteen years had never known. My spirit wanted to demand justice from my God, demand that He exact the same penalty on the idol worshippers that they had inflicted on the boy who was barely more than a baby. I knew the statue in the valley Josiah had described to me was no real god and held no true power. He had died for nothing, for a vain imagination of someone's sick mind. *Why? Why? Why?*

My father's quiet humming would be my only solace as he rocked me in his lap. I wondered if my groom would be asking "Why?" even as I was sobbing it. It felt too much like defeat, as if the lifeless Molech had won. I knew Josiah had voiced similar words to me the last time I saw him. I didn't know how he would respond—his faith in the LORD was still only several weeks old. Would he think God had abandoned him? Would he lash out in anger at the people who had put their little son in the fire? Although I wished I could be with him that night, I knew the LORD's words were his only hope for comfort. My silent prayers for him were my last thoughts before I closed my eyes on the eve of my wedding day.

\* \* \*

Hannah shook me awake as she whispered, "Get up, Bride—we've got to get you dressed!"

I pulled my stinging eyelids apart and winced at the burning sensation behind them, and then winced again at the pounding in my head. For what was supposed to be the happiest day of my life, it was not starting well.

"Mmm," I groaned, "get me some water, please." I could tell already that I was not going to look my best for my groom. My puffy, red eyes did not impress my mother, either.

"Hamutal, wash your face with the cold water—it will help," she said. It didn't.

My father and my brother left to buy me some special date cakes as a treat since I had fasted all of the previous day, and Mother and Hannah took the opportunity to get me into my under-things and cover me with some blankets until after breakfast. My gown had been delivered on Friday, greeted with all of our amazement. Shallum had promised not to show it to the king so that it would be a surprise. It was a cream, beaded dress with miniature, gold threads woven into it, and delicate, gold tassels around the bottom of the skirt. It was more form-fitting than my normal frocks, with a neckline that dropped in a slight curve below my collarbone and wrist-length sleeves that opened from the top of my shoulders to my elbows. As I carefully slipped it over my head and smoothed it down my waist, my mother gasped, pulling her hand up to her face. She smiled and shook her head in awe. As she walked around me to admire the full view, tears rolled down her cheeks.

"I've never seen anything so elegant!"

Thankfully, the tailor and his assistants had made a blue wrap with gold embroidery for my shoulders, which my mother draped around me, securing it as best she could. I had never shown my shoulders in public before and it hardly seemed appropriate to start today. I chose to wear Josiah's ruby hairpins, even though they did not match the dress. Hannah disagreed with my choice, and I had to remind her that this was my wedding day, not hers.

After I ate and got dressed, I draped a plain shawl over my hair gingerly, so as not to pull any hairs out of the pins, and stepped into the slippers my siblings had given me for my birthday. Father had sent the veil he and Mother gave me to the palace on Friday when we arrived into town, since Josiah would be the one to pull it over me as the ceremony began.

My mother once told me about this custom, which began a long time ago after our ancestor Jacob had been deceived into marrying lazy-eyed Leah, instead of his beloved Rachel. Now grooms were the ones to veil their brides so that they could be assured of the woman's correct identity.

My father kissed me on the cheek and slid a golden band onto my wrist. "I know it pales in comparison to any jewelry the king has given you, but I hope you will still wear it occasionally and remember that I was the first man to love you." He wiped a tear from my cheek and then one from his own. "And I will always love you, no matter where you travel, or what nation you're queen of," he choked with a crooked smile.

"Abba," I cried, calling him by my childhood pet name, "my eyes are already too red," I chuckled and sniffed. "Thank you. And I *will* wear it, and I'll never forget how you've loved me and cared for me. I will always adore you. Will you remember that?"

"Yes, Love. Always."

When we arrived at the palace in two carriages to accommodate my large family, we were greeted by several attendants who led us to the inner courtyards where the banquet tables were already set with plates and rolls. I remembered Josiah's anecdote about the soldier's wine and honey cakes and suddenly felt a shudder. *Am I ready for this? Will he even come for me?*

This was the location where I was to wait with my family for my groom to come and veil me. The other wedding guests, which Josiah promised me would not be more than his closest and most trusted servants, attendants, officials, captains, and advisors were waiting for him in the west end of the outer courtyard, where the ceremony would take place.

I half-expected him not to show. He had been distraught by the boy's death. *I shouldn't expect him to concentrate on me today. Maybe we should wait,* I thought. *Maybe in a few weeks.* When he stormed in, looking around at the courtyard, followed by Hilkiah the priest and two guards, my logic began to agree with that fear. He had the same furious look on his face as the afternoon in the dark alley. It appeared that he would just as soon kill me as wed me. Then his eyes met mine and he immediately softened, sighing and then swallowing. He lowered his head with a more gentle resolution and stepped slowly toward me and my family, carrying my veil.

My mother carefully lifted off my plain shawl and laid it down next to the table where we stood. It was at that moment as he stopped to look at me from head to toe that a slow smile spread across his mouth and even reached up to cool the rage burning in his eyes. I observed him admiring what he saw until I felt my skin burning and I could no longer hold his gaze. I found myself looking down at my slippers, waiting for his next move, without allowing even a half-breath to escape my chest.

Instead of spreading the veil over me, he touched the pins that held all of my heavy hair on top of my head and then lifted my chin gently with his knuckle. Although he said nothing, his eyes told me that regardless of what had happened yesterday, he wanted nothing more than to make me his wife. I saw peace and composure in his face that had not existed when he had come in just a moment earlier.

He spread out the beaded veil and draped it delicately over my head, allowing my mother and father to wrap it properly around my face and hair. He narrowed his eyes and gave me a smoldering smile, before turning on his heel and walking back to the outer courtyard.

Only then did I allow myself to exhale, feeling my breath come back to my face as it reflected against my veil. As I peered out from the fabric, my parents each took one of my arms and led me into the same doorway through which my groom had just passed. I could hear my blood pounding in my ears as the rabbit in my chest commenced its racing.

Seeing the small crowd that was gathered for our wedding ceremony, I was pleased that he had kept his promise not to invite too many. Although we were outdoors and it would still be a couple of hours before dark, thousands of candles were lit atop hundreds of bronze lamp stands. I noticed the heavy scent of eucalyptus and lilies floating through the air, before I saw the green stalks and large white blooms in huge vases at the front of the standing group. The people were divided into two sections with a wide aisle between them. My family followed me and then stood with the rest of the group, except for my mother and father, who continued to walk me toward my groom.

As he stared at me, I looked back at him though the thin slit in my veil and wondered what could have happened that I of all people would be marrying the King of Judah. *Who would have thought it would be him?* I asked myself.

"*I knew,*" said the Voice of the LORD. I gasped and stopped in my tracks, frozen. I realized who had spoken, but I couldn't yet bring myself to believe it. I felt my parents urging me firmly by the elbows, but I didn't budge.

*I don't deserve him, LORD.* Doubt and anxiety filled my judgment, and I didn't think I could go any farther. Josiah's brow furrowed in confusion.

"*And yet, I have called you both. Together.*"

And, like before, it was exactly what I needed to hear.

*Help me, Jehovah. Show me how to be the wife and queen he needs.*

When He spoke no more, I resumed my slow steps, followed by the relieved sighs of more than just my parents. Josiah smiled once again and stepped forward slightly. As we began the seven circles around him, the crowd began to say a prayer of blessing over us. When we were finished, I stood to his right, and two of his attendants raised a wide cream-colored shawl over our heads as the priest spoke his part.

"Welcome! He who is the Almighty and Omnipotent, over all … He who is Blessed over all … He who is the Greatest of all … He who is Distinguished of all … Shall bless the groom and bride."

The rest of the ceremony was somewhat of a blur to me, though I do remember my father signing our marriage covenant, and also the way Josiah's eyes never left mine as he promised to provide everything a husband should. After that, they sent us alone into a small white tent for a few moments, where the king gathered me into his arms and whispered a secret into my ear.

"It's my birthday." He grinned.

"No, it's not!"

He nodded, raising his eyebrows for emphasis. "I'm sixteen today."

"But my lord, why didn't you tell me? I didn't get you a gift!"

"Yes, you did."

"What? Where?" I asked, confused. Had someone else sent him a gift in my name?

He leaned closer to me again. "It's right here in my arms," he breathed into my other ear, sending an uncontrollable arch down my back. I gullibly looked down at his bandaged arms around my waist and then glanced back up to him and smiled bashfully. I thought for a moment.

"Well, it is probably the only thing I could give you that you didn't already have," I said with a shrug.

"And you're all I've ever wanted."

His hands carefully unwrapped my veil, and then a satisfied look settled on his face when he could see me again. He looked like he might have bent down to kiss me, but suddenly his attendant swiped open the entrance to the tent and we were whisked away to the banquet for hours of feasting, dancing, singing, and laughter.

* * *

Later that evening when we were finally alone, he laid my veil across the balcony wall just outside of his room, and we stood closely together under the stars, holding hands. The night was cool, but warmer than it had been, with a careless breeze that fluttered through my gown every now and then. The sky was clear, and I delighted to see so many stars twinkling happily above us. They reflected my perfect mood exactly.

"You know," he told me, "I almost called it off today—or rather postponed it, I mean."

"Because of the boy?" I asked. But I knew his answer before he spoke it.

"Yes," he said, nodding. The sadness was still so close. Even for me. "I just didn't think I could make you my queen today when I couldn't even stand to be around myself," he whispered, hanging his head in shame. "I broke a few jars this morning ... and some other things, too—I can't even remember now. I was just so furious!"

"I knew you would be. I was thinking the wedding might be better at a different time, too. I almost thought ... maybe you wouldn't come."

"But I did, and when I looked at you, it was like it all melted away. Not the pain or the need to fix this somehow, but my anger dissipated." He paused to turn away from the stars and look down at me. "When I saw how beautiful you looked, and how you were so willing to put all of it aside for us, I decided I wanted to do the same—and I'm glad I did." He grinned.

My knees began to bend involuntarily and my breath caught in my throat, along with the pounding rabbit that knocked against the walls of my chest and back.

He drew me close and kissed me, and I found my hands wrapping around his neck and my fingers playing in his wavy hair. But this kiss didn't stop abruptly the way the first had, and I had to retract myself after a moment to catch my breath. He briefly let go of me to reach up to my head, and carefully pulled out my hairpins, watching as the layers tumbled to my waist. He held my hand and walked backward, guiding me inside, his eyes taking in the view of me within the frame of my hair.

He must have felt me shaking as he pulled me back into his chest, because he asked, "Are you alright? You're trembling." With one hand he ran his fingers over my shoulder that my gown left exposed.

I nodded and swallowed hard.

He stepped back, keeping my hands in his firm but loving grip, and concentrated on my expression. I tried to hold his gaze, but my eyes kept looking away, out of my control. I didn't want him to sense my fear. But he noticed despite my wanting.

"You're scared, aren't you?"

I shrugged. I couldn't lie to him, but I didn't want to tell him the truth, either.

He smiled then, realizing something. "Too much talk of hungry soldiers and banquet tables, I think," he said. "Sorry about that."

I bit my lip nervously, trying to force a smile.

He drew me back into his warm arms and traced the curve of my back under my hair. His other hand cupped my jaw tenderly. "Don't worry, my angel," the king whispered as his lips glided down my neck. "I've promised myself I would be very gentle with you tonight."

And he was …

# BOOK TWO

BOOK TWO

# 13. JOSIAH

Words were not getting me anywhere. Decrees were useless. Even my officials and task forces were not making any progress worth mentioning. My frustration with these people was growing, and, though I knew what I had to do, I would rather have found another way. The problem was—there were simply no other options.

One year before, when Hamutal and I had been married for three years, and on the day after our son, Jehoahaz had turned two, we were worshipping at the Temple, and He had spoken one word to me. It was the only option in His mind. The only choice that would work.

*"Burn ..."*

*Burn what, Jehovah?* I had prayed, with no answer.

It had taken me a full twelve months to figure out what He meant, and now, as I prepared my guard, the soldiers, and the priests for what was to come, no one was delighted at Jehovah's plan. They raised skeptical eyebrows at me and murmured amongst themselves. None of them directly challenged me, however. They had not done that for years. I had established the authority of my monarchy by then and was no longer the boyish vassal king in their eyes, or my own.

"How long do you expect all of this to take, Your Highness?" asked Acbor, one of my leading magistrates.

I looked across the table at his curly red hair and beard, which he stroked as he pondered the current prospects. He had shown significant loyalty and wisdom in recent months, and I had offered him a position as head magistrate, which he had not yet accepted. He said he needed to ponder the role and what it meant.

As with all of my surrounding leaders, I demanded absolute allegiance to the LORD of heaven and earth and complete denial of all other gods. He was not yet sure he could align with the dedication to one God, and unbeknownst to him, his time was running out in *this* circle of chiefs and leaders if he could not give me a clear answer. As he looked quizzically into my eyes, I could see the wheels in his mind turning all of this around.

"It may take years—I'm not sure," I responded calmly. "But think of the time we've already wasted in trying everything else. None of *that* worked, and nothing else will convince this nation of the LORD's fierce wrath over their idiotic, impotent gods. They have to see it ... and hear it ... and know it—personally. It's my only hope to persuade them."

"And how long will Your Majesty be with us? You come tomorrow, but how can we be assured of your support the next day, and the days after that?" Acbor asked. It was not so much a challenge as a need to be aware of the details before he committed wholeheartedly to my strategy. He was being wise, calculative.

"I've taken a vow in the LORD's name that I will personally supervise each cleansing," I said, addressing everyone in the room. "I'm not sending you out alone without my covering. I will be wherever you are. I need to know it, to see it with my own eyes. Jehovah has asked that of me—and it's the least I can do.

"We will move as one rather than spreading out and dividing forces. We will not return to our homes and our wives until everything is completed." They all seemed to take a deep breath of comfort as I spoke, which turned to sighs of understanding at my last statement.

I was hoping that these sighs meant their loyalties, but that was still to be determined. Their affections for me would not be enough, nor would their admiration of my crown. The only factor that held any levity was their unified stance for Jehovah—acknowledgement that He was LORD, King, Priest, and Ruler of this nation. What lay ahead of us was not for the lighthearted. I had no room for cowards, shifters, or idolaters. They either followed Him or they didn't. And if they didn't follow Him, they didn't belong in my ranks.

Unfortunately, I could not as easily hold the same ultimatum over the commoners in my kingdom. Granted, my subjects revered me and listened to me. And they actually liked me, or so it seemed. They had become more civilized, refraining from stealing each other's land and water, and murders had decreased in great numbers. My guards had cracked down on blatant prostitution on street corners, and more brothels were being closed than were opened each month. The only mandate they were not yet conforming to was this matter of handmade gods and their altars. I could not be everywhere, in every town, on every corner, and neither could my soldiers.

For the previous four years, I had tried everything I could think of to stop the evils of these people, but they kept returning to their detestable practices like a mangy dog returns to its vomit. I had set up guards around the Asherah poles on the outskirts of the city, commanding them to threaten anyone who came to offer incense or food to the sex goddess. I set a permanent blockade in the Valley of Hinnom around the shrine of Topheth so that no other parents could sacrifice their children to Molech.

I wrote royal decrees that were sent from one end of my kingdom to the other, forbidding the people to worship any god but Jehovah alone. I threatened to take all of their wood and incense away, denying them access to the materials they needed for their wayward, misguided offerings. I had even bribed the people, proposing to provide them with proper animal sacrifices if only they would come to Jerusalem and make offerings at the Temple of the LORD.

None of these tactics had worked. I should not have been surprised, though. Jeremiah, the son of my high priest, Hilkiah—now my most trusted, but unofficial, advisor and friend—had warned me of as much. Although I had asked him a dozen times to join my royal cabinet, he preferred to refrain from the "games," as he called it. I could not blame him. Though I had sought to surround myself with the wisest men of my kingdom, we still faced too many decisions for which no consensus could be found. I often made decisions that circumvented or blatantly contradicted their recommendations, and they had grown accustomed to that as well.

Jeremiah was the only one I could trust completely. I listened to his voice even more closely than my own, for he regularly heard directly from God and was discovering a remarkable gift of prophecy that I relied on more times than I could count. He and I discovered a few buried scrolls in the Temple signed by a royal priest named Isaiah. This man had been as devout a Levite as any I'd ever met or heard of, daring to speak out against my evil great-great grandfather, Ahaz, and ministering to his righteous son, Hezekiah. We would often sit up late at night together reading his words and trying to decipher their meaning.

I asked Jeremiah to come with me on this delegation of cleansing my nation, but he'd refused, declaring his intentions to fast and pray in the wilderness for a time. He heard Jehovah calling him there in preparation for something he could not yet see. I gave him my blessing, but I was inwardly reluctant. I wanted him close to me for selfish reasons. His presence gave me courage beyond my own.

When I had finally been able to tell him what the LORD had spoken to me, he confirmed it so clearly. He shuddered as if with a chill and then prophesied, *"Plow up the hard ground of your hearts! Do not waste your good seed among the thorns. O people of Judah and Jerusalem, surrender your pride and power. Change your hearts before the LORD, or my anger will burn like an unquenchable fire because of all your sins."* I could surely use his wisdom and reassurance on this trip. The only other person who had been able to encourage me like he had was my wife.

My Hamutal. She was still the smile on my lips, the strength in my muscles, and the cool water that eased my impatient rage. The thought of leaving her made the tension twist in my shoulders. Since our wedding, not a single morning had passed that I did not wake up to her loveliness. Even on the day she had given birth to our son, I had not allowed her to be taken away to the empty palace harem. The midwife had come and tried to shoo me out the door, but I would not budge from her side, holding her hand as she screamed and writhed in pain.

I was more afraid than she had been, though I didn't dare reveal as much. I could not push away my fears that childbirth would take her in the same way it had taken Zebidah. With each set of cramps that twisted Hamutal's face, I silently pleaded with God to allow them both to survive. I pressed a cold towel to her forehead and whispered into her ear how much I adored her. When she and the baby survived the terrifying ordeal, I was nearly alarmed that God had answered my desperate prayers. Later that night, I repented for doubting His faithful loving-kindness.

But this would be my first mission that was longer than a day's trip from the palace. She would wake up without me morning after morning, and I would long for her night after night. I was not expecting this operation to be short, but I was determined to do as the LORD had asked of me and see it from start to finish. As much as I needed her, I ached to do God's bidding even more.

And I recognized this would be the breakthrough I sought. Not just because it was my command, or even because I enjoyed a healthy bonfire from time to time. Not because it was another desperate attempt—*No!* It would be a success because I had finally known what to do from *Him*. Because the Holy One's way was always sovereign, and always best.

"This is a volunteer mission," I continued to my brave audience, snapping back from my memories. "If you refuse to go with us, you will be part of the force that stays to guard the city or the borders," I said. "I realize that what I'm asking will be a sacrifice. I'd like at least fifty of you to come with me, and I believe everyone here in this throne room has proven himself in battle, in dedication to my crown, and most importantly, in devotion to the LORD." I tried to look each man in the eyes as I spoke, willing them to believe my sincerity.

"Hilkiah, would you please read what you found in the annals of King David?" I said. I didn't just want this edict to come from me—it had to be substantiated by our nation's historical figures of authority to convince some of them.

He began in an authoritative voice with cadence and grace, just as if it had been the great psalmist-king himself: "*Great is the LORD! He is most worthy of praise! He is to be feared above all gods. The gods of other nations are mere idols, but the* LORD *made the heavens! Honor and majesty surround Him; strength and joy fill His dwelling. O nations of the world, recognize the* LORD, *recognize that the* LORD *is glorious and strong. Give to the* LORD *the glory He deserves! Bring your offering and come into His presence. Worship the* LORD *in all His holy splendor."*

About a hundred men filled my throne room—men I had hand-picked as the most valiant in the kingdom. "If you are willing to serve your God and your king in this way, remain with me now. If you refuse my request, feel free to go back to your previous post, and you will not be held in contempt for doing so."

I waited a few moments for their unspoken response. I counted twenty men who left, walking away quietly and filing out the door, one at a time. Acbor was among those who stayed, keeping his eyes on me. After no one else appeared to be moving away, I spoke again.

"Very well. We will meet at the Golden Gate at dawn and set up camp in the Kidron Valley. We start with the Temple of the LORD, and then we'll move from south to north through all of Judah." Though my palace was located closer to the Temple than the valley was, I would keep my word, not returning to my opulent lifestyle while my men were suffering in their tents. This was *my* mission, and I refused to allow myself to be distracted. I hoped my example would inspire them as well.

"Say goodbye to your families tonight. Make love to your wives, and kiss your sons and daughters. I need all of your attention and all of your devotion. We fight not against seen enemies, but against the evil desires of our own countrymen."

\* \* \*

A few gray shapes appeared outside the window in the darkness of the morning. The dawn had come sooner than desired. My head rested on my elbow and I remained in my bed, treasuring the warmth of the soft blankets and the sound of her whispers into my back. We hadn't slept all night, talking about the mission and enjoying one another, holding each other until that very moment.

"Don't go," she pleaded as her arm tightened around me.

The fire in the hearth at the end of our bed shed some dancing light around my quarters. I rolled over to look into her languishing eyes.

"You know, this is not even dangerous. There is virtually no possibility of me getting hurt in any way," I said.

I was not afraid for my safety. There were plenty of guards to surround me and dozens of soldiers were recruited who would reinforce the leadership I had spoken with last night. Regardless of my own confidence, she remained apprehensive. She eyed me with an unbelieving glare, trying to find the lie in my voice. I did not doubt whether I would return, but the *when* was ominously unknown.

Her concern softened and turned into a mischievous grin. She traced a soft finger along my lips. "Can't you leave *tomorrow* morning? Stay with me one more day ... Please," she said. "I'll make it worth your time ..."

As her leg wrapped around mine and her hands brushed along my skin, I began to burn with fresh desire. The kisses she offered were more delicious than ripe grapes from the vine and I almost gave in to her idea. *They wouldn't leave without me ... and one more day couldn't hurt anyone ...*

I abruptly pulled away from her intoxicating caresses and swung my legs over the bed, sitting up with my back to her. She left her hands on me, but stayed under the blankets.

"That's not fair and you know it," I said. "If I stayed today, you'd say the same thing tomorrow morning, and the morning after that. And you know I can't resist you."

"Then don't." She smiled.

"Do you *want* me to disobey the LORD, woman?" I asked much too abrasively.

I turned my neck and looked at her critically. She said nothing, sheepishly shaking her head. Her eyes closed and she sighed deeply. When she opened them again, they were soft and understanding.

"I know you have to go—and I want you to get it over with. I want the people to understand that their gods are not gods at all. I want you to burn every last one of them, so that the only God left will be the Real

One." Her voice was strong and convincing. Maybe she should have given the pep talk to my troops last night.

"Then get dressed and stop tempting me," I said. "You know I hate this just as much as you do."

"Why don't you take me with you, then?" she asked playfully. "No possibility of getting hurt, remember?" But she knew I'd never agree to it. She just said it to remind me that she'd do anything, endure any discomfort, and risk any danger for me. I didn't need the reminder, though.

"Hilarious."

She tied her robe and knelt on the bed in front of me as I pulled my short tunic over my head. Straightening my sleeves for me under my royal armor, she pulled me closer and kissed me again. It was amazing how in only four years I'd learned to understand her thoughts by the way her lips met mine. The subtle difference in this kiss was that it was less about her desire for me, and more about her unease, as if she knew this could be her last piece of me for a very long time. I embraced her and wound my hands in her long, silky hair, treasuring our last moments for myself as well.

"Now I'm running late! Please go and get the boys," I said, tearing myself from her. "I'd like to see them before I leave."

"Yes, my King," she said with a slight bow.

\* \* \*

As we marched in procession from the palace to the Golden Gate to meet the rest of the infantry and the priests, I prayed to Jehovah to help me.

*LORD, I know what I have to do, but I need Your direction in all of this. I know some of the people will be distraught. Although theirs is a misguided love, they do love these statue gods, nonetheless. Will they hate me when I destroy them? Will they move to other nations where they can fill the lust in their hearts? God, show me what to say to them. Help all of my men to be courageous and obedient to You. May their hearts not falter—may their love of Your Holiness grow during this mission as they see who You truly are.*

Jeremiah had helped me seek the LORD about the priests and Levites who could be trusted to know about the Temple and its regulations. I wanted this done right and did not trust myself to know everything. God had long ago called the tribe of Levi to care for His house, and I wanted to be sure to include them, at least those who had remained true to the Almighty without prostituting themselves to other gods for the purpose of wealth or fame.

Jeremiah had also given me a series of interview questions for the priests and Temple officials, and I meticulously combed through all who were in Jerusalem, promoting those who met my qualifications and dismissing those who did not. He told me that during the reigns of my father and grandfather, many Levites had betrayed the God of Heaven's Armies, and several of those who had been faithful to God's laws had left the area since the Temple had been so disgraced and defamed by the addition of idols, statues, and foreign altars.

And this led us to our present task. With the help of those I'd chosen, I was going to make God's House clean. I trusted Jeremiah's prophecies to be accurate. As I recalled his words in the Temple only a few months ago on Sabbath, I clung to the trace of hope God offered.

"*O Israel, My faithless people, come home to Me again, for I am merciful. I will not be angry with you forever. Only acknowledge your guilt. Admit that you rebelled against the LORD your God and committed adultery against Him by worshipping idols under every green tree. Confess that you refused to listen to My voice. I, the LORD, have spoken! Return home, you wayward children, for I am your Master. I will bring you back to Zion—one from this town and two from that family—from wherever you are scattered. And I will give you shepherds after My own heart, who will guide you with knowledge and understanding.*"

I allowed my mind to wander and imagine what it would be like to witness such repentance in my subjects. What if they would give up on their idols that had forsaken them all these years? What serenity could come to our nation if they could only hear His call of love, as I once had? Would Jehovah really be merciful and welcome us back to His bosom if these stubborn-hearted shrine-lovers acknowledged their guilt before Him? I could only hope and trust His promise.

Shaking my head clear of the daydream, I continued marching up the hill and the steep steps to the Temple gate. I halted about thirty cubits away and scanned the group of priests before me.

When we arrived, I called for Hilkiah, Zechariah, and Jehiel, as well as the rest of the Levites who had demonstrated faithfulness to Jehovah. I was anxious to see Hilkiah and beckoned him immediately. He wore his most ornate robe, complete with the ephod-vest, which held twelve gemstones, representing the original tribes of Israel, although many of those entire tribes had abandoned God's ways to follow other leaders and foreign gods. Though the high priest held his head up as he walked toward me, I saw a hint of apprehension as he knelt to bow at my side.

"Have you taken the inventory, then?" I asked.

"Yes, Your Highness. And there is much to do," he answered carefully. "Are you certain this is what needs to be done? For everyone, I mean."

"Absolutely."

"There are other worshippers in the Temple as we speak, my lord. This will not be pleasant—" His near-black eyes narrowed as he fidgeted with his vest. He was even more nervous than I, which did not set my thoughts at ease. Was there no other man in my ranks who held this ground with me? For the second time that day I wished Jeremiah was at my side.

I took a deep breath and motioned for Hilkiah to fall in beside me. Unsheathing my sword, I raised it up high in the air for my forces to see. I felt a surge of strength through my arm, as if a power other than my own joined with each fiber in my body and my hand came back down with my blade pointed straight ahead of me in the direction of the Temple. We marched forward as one, our steps in unison on the gravel beneath our feet.

# 14. HAMUTAL

I clutched Jehoahaz close to me as we both waved to Josiah. His tiny hand fluttered in the air long after the king had marched away with his guard. I tried to hold back my burning tears so that the boys would not be afraid, but I couldn't. They spilled from the corners of my eyes and ran down my cheeks faster than I could swipe them away. My heart chased after him just as it did every time he left, but my mind was still there to lecture me back to logic.

*Stop crying. He will come back. You are a grown woman who has children more important than your tears.*

*But this could take months! There are so many idols in this nation, and he intends to torch every last one of them. He may never come home!*

*Don't be ridiculous! God will protect him. Would Jehovah send him to do this work just to allow him to be killed?*

*But people can be fanatical about their "gods." Remember the woman who sliced open her breasts before an Asherah pole because she thought the sex goddess could give her a child? Who knows what these mad people will do?*

*He wasn't concerned, and neither should you be.*

*Well, he was either deceiving himself or just appeasing me. I know there will be hundreds who will want him assassinated for this. You don't just defile someone's religion and then expect that he will swear allegiance to you for doing so.*

*There's nothing you can do about it now, so get on with caring for the boys.*

I looked down at Eliakim, who stared blankly after the procession. This beautiful, fair boy, who was my son in every sense but birth, remained so difficult for me to read. His look was a confusing combination of fear, sorrow, and apathy. He glanced up at me just as I brushed the last bit of moisture from my cheeks. I gave him a reassuring smile and reached for his hand.

"Come along, boys; let's get some breakfast," I said cheerily, as if today was no different from any other. "Abba will be back before you know it." I only wished I could believe my own words. Eliakim took my hand without returning my smile and walked with solemn steps beside me toward the stairs that led down from the palace roof. Just as I was about to take the first step, however, I glanced to my right and noticed something. Perhaps the rising sun now shone more light on the two incense altars, but as I looked more carefully, there was no mistaking them.

"Just a minute, Eli," I said, backing up the steps and pulling him with me gently. I readjusted Jeho in my arms and walked carefully toward the two foreign altars.

"What is it, Mama?" Eliakim asked.

"Hmm," I said quietly as I squinted my eyes and shaded them from the bright morning sun with my hand. "I think the king will have to come back sooner than we thought." I had no idea which of Josiah's grandfathers had built the blasphemous shrines on the roof, but they were clearly altars to other gods—probably Baal or Chemosh. Though the sight of these small structures built to summon the nonexistent powers of lifeless figurines infuriated me, I was also inwardly rejoicing that Josiah would have to come back here to destroy them as part of his quest. I made a mental note to write him as soon as I got the boys started with their lessons.

We walked together back down the steps and into the courtyard where our breakfast was set and ready for us. I thanked our private cook and servants. They bowed slightly and walked back indoors to their duties. I offered the fresh, hot eggs to Eliakim, since they were his favorite, and scooped some cold fruit onto Jehoahaz's small plate. They began picking up small pieces of food and shoving them into their little mouths, getting messy already. I couldn't help but chuckle to myself at how adorable they were.

The sweet joy of that simple moment made me think of my own mother. She had always been so patient and tender with all of us, faithfully teaching us about the LORD and His commands, and showing His love just as much in her actions as she did in her words. I longed for her generous example in my life once again, as I struggled each day to be the mother God desired for these two precious boys.

I wondered how my family was doing and thought to invite them to the palace for a few weeks. Maybe they would be a good distraction while my husband was away. Although my parents and siblings still came to Jerusalem almost every week, it had been so long since we enjoyed an extended visit. Most of our time was spent in hushed reverence for the Sabbath. We barely laughed or played together the way we used to do so. They refused to stay at the palace instead of the inn, because my father thought Sabbath should be about sacrifice, not luxury. And I could not argue with that. But if they would come for a longer stay, we could enjoy one another once again. I could sing and dance in the firelight with my little sisters and brother.

Perhaps even Hannah would come to cheer me up. She and Matthias had been married just over a year ago. I went to her wedding alone because Josiah was called away that week for negotiations with Israel's trade emissaries. He might not have even been aware of the wedding, except that I mentioned it to him later. He'd barely looked up from the scroll of Isaiah when I did.

It seemed like forever since I had seen my sister, and I had to stretch my mind to remember when it had been. "Oh my!" I exclaimed to myself. Eliakim and Jehoahaz looked up at me with curiosity.

"What, Mama?" Eliakim asked, his words muffled by the eggs that filled his mouth.

"Such manners for a prince!" I said. "You must learn to eat smaller bites, dear," I added with a smile. "And don't speak when your mouth is full. Your magistrates will never be able to understand your orders!"

"Sorry," he muttered once he had swallowed.

"I was just thinking how terrible it is that I haven't seen Aunt Hannah since her wedding day. Do you even remember her, Eli?"

His brow wrinkled as he tried to recall. After just a moment, he shrugged lightly.

"Oh," I groaned. "This is inexcusable! It's settled, then. I'll send carriages for everyone tomorrow. It has been far too long."

The boys looked at me as if there were a snake crawling out of my hair. They had no idea why I was acting so strangely, talking to myself and carrying on. I ruffled Jehoahaz's dark, curly locks and rose from the table.

"We'll be together after all!"

\* \* \*

Two days later, my family arrived in one of the royal carriages, and I rushed to greet them in the courtyard. My mother stepped down carefully while holding her chestnut frock, and her olive skin glowed in the afternoon sun as she grinned at us. I rushed into her outstretched arms and danced her around the horses. I was a bird frolicking in the rain with the thought of her staying for days and weeks. Jaazaniah, Johanah, and little Sarah stepped down as well, and I stared into the carriage for my Father's appearance next. But he didn't come.

"Where's Father?" I demanded from my mother, looking from her to the driver and back again. I had specifically asked him to bring my *whole* family, and had sent two servants to care for the sheep and the tent. The driver helplessly looked to my mother for a rescue.

"He couldn't get away, Love," she said, tucking a strand of hair behind my ear. "I'll tell you more later." She whispered so softly that I had to read her lips.

I gave her my most pathetic pout.

She scolded me with her eyes and then turned to my siblings. "Come, children, let's get our things," she said. *Always so gentle*, I thought.

"Don't worry, Mother," I called, just as the servants arrived and took the bags and trunks from the back of the carriage.

Mother and Johanah thanked them and smiled graciously, even offering to help. I realized in that moment that I did not know the servants' names, though I had seen their faces every day for the last month, at least. I suddenly felt like a spoiled princess.

*What kind of person have I become? Didn't I vow not to become the haughty queen I had despised in my imagination? Just how many steps away am I from evil Jezebel, the wife of the most vile and idolatrous king of Judah? Hadn't she become so greedy that she stole someone else's land for her own political agenda? And surely that attitude started with taking the lives of others for granted.*

Leave it to the beautiful grace of my mother to bring me back to myself. She had not been here more than a few moments, and already I was grateful for her presence.

"And what of Hannah and Matthias, Mother?" I asked. "Will they be joining our little family reunion?"

"Yes, Love," she replied with a sly smile, "and wait until you see her!"

"When?" I demanded with exhilaration.

"Tomorrow. Matthias said he had to tie up a few loose ends first with his new land, and then he could get away for a week."

"Oh! A whole week!" I said. "My dear sister for a whole week!"

My servants eyed me warily. Jehoahaz clapped his hands and shrieked just because he saw me doing the same, but Eliakim stood there with another strange, blank look on his pale face. Mother smiled at me and looped her arm through mine as we made our way through the corridors to the guest chambers. It was a moment later before the rest of my mother's words registered.

"Land? Why has Matthias bought land? Recabites don't own land," I said. "Is he drinking wine now, too?" I chuckled sarcastically.

"I'll let you ask your sister that one," she murmured.

I stopped in my tracks and stared. I couldn't understand what would bring Matthias to break the ancient code of our ancestors. Concluding that there would be time to discuss it later, I dropped the conversation, too thrilled to let anything spoil the day.

When we walked into the guest chambers, my little sister Johanah gasped in surprise at the luxury. She meandered around the room, fingering the delicate fabrics on the bed and the rich tapestries on the walls. I smiled, but said nothing, remembering my own awe when Hannah and I had taken a tour of the palace before my wedding.

Sarah and Eliakim, who were the same age, eyed one another shyly and stayed far enough away that they would have no chance of accidentally bumping into each other. My mother took Jehoahaz from my arms and bore her nose into his neck, sending loud giggles from my son around the entire palace.

"Oh how I've missed this sweet grandbaby of mine! Why have you not brought him to the Temple yet, Love?" she asked.

"Josiah said it's to be purified before his sons will go. He doesn't want them to see it with the other altars, because he wants them always to remember it as it should be. He is very careful to show them the LORD's way and shield them from exposure to other gods." I spoke proudly of my husband to my mother, knowing she would approve of his strict stance. "But it won't be long now. He is excited to show them Jehovah's house and teach them what it means to bring a proper sacrifice."

"Good," she replied with satisfaction. "These princes are sure to be brave leaders, just like their father."

Just then, the tutor came to the open doorway and bowed, summoning my sons to their lessons. They were learning Hebrew already, per Josiah's orders, as well as training to spar with little wooden swords and shields. It was so delightful to watch that I would often peer out of my window at them in the courtyard. Only after several of these days of observing them did I recall how skilled Josiah had been at combat when I met him at such a young age.

I invited my brother and sisters to go with Eliakim and Jehoahaz, and they leapt at the opportunity. I knew Mother and Father taught them many skills and lessons at home, so they would enjoy the instruction together, and my mother and I would have an opportunity to talk in private. Once they had all disappeared down the corridor and I could hear their distant voices in the courtyard, I turned once again to face her.

"And now you can tell me why Father did not come," I said.

"Come, Hamutal, sit down with me," she said, patting the bed beside her. She was stalling, waiting as long as I would allow before opening the package of news I already realized would not be pleasant. "Let me braid your hair like I used to when you were a little girl."

I sat down next to her and bent my head toward her obediently as she unwound my shawl and combed through my hair gently. I savored her knowing touch and relaxed my head into her lap. She was preparing me for her news, and though my body melted in her gentle hands, my heart raced in anticipation and dread.

"Your father has not been feeling well, Love. He wanted to come but was ashamed for you to see him in his condition," she said, pressing her hand soothingly around my shoulder. Though she meant for me to stay there in her lap, I sat up in shock and bore a look into her eyes to find any hint of a lie.

"What do you mean 'condition'?" I said, my voice rising. "Is he sick? Was he hurt? I saw him last Sabbath and embraced him. He seemed fine. Why would he not want me to see him?" The last question was bathed in pain and offense. My questions had come so fast and I wanted answers to all of them immediately.

My mother just ran her fingers through my hair and shook her head. "Don't fret. We're not sure what is wrong with him. He has just been ... very ... well, very tired lately. He doesn't have any energy to do the things he used to, and he is spent after almost every task, even the simplest ones. Sometimes his chest hurts, too, or his head. I wouldn't worry if I were you, Love. He will feel better soon."

The words she had meant for comfort had the opposite effect. "Why did he not come here and rest? I sent plenty of help to care for the sheep and your home, and if he needed more, I could have sent as many servants as he wanted," I said. "This is absurd!"

I was infuriated now, and downright angry at the thought of my precious father suffering under the burden of his labor while I was living in such prosperity. I longed to rush to him that instant and help with the weaving or the shearing, or whatever he wanted done. "I wanted him here, Mother. I wanted us together. Even if it meant he would be reclining here on this couch the entire time, eating from the king's table."

"Your father is a proud man," she said. I knew there must have been something more, though; something she was keeping from me. "It's hard for him to let you and his grandsons see him so weak and weary. You know it would be no blessing to him if he were confined to a couch and waited on hand and foot. Your servants will help him while we're here, and perhaps his strength will return by the time I go back."

"I'll be praying that it will," I said with resolve, rising from the bed to pace.

In my memory were many stories of how God had healed our family and our nation. Our oral tradition spoke of His power to restore health. I would seek His sovereign power for my father. If anyone could restore his body's vitality, it would be the One who had created that very same body and had known it since he was born. Surely God could give my father many more years to live.

I wished I could go to the Temple to offer a sacrifice on the LORD's altar, but Josiah still hadn't finished purifying it yet. I hadn't expected him to take this long in God's house and was discouraged at what that could mean for his mission around the rest of the nation. He had spent several days on just the one structure—what remained were many journeys through the land, hundreds more blasphemous places of worship to destroy, and thousands more idols to burn before the nation would be cleansed to his satisfaction. And I still didn't know if even all of that would be enough for God's satisfaction.

At the thought of how many more months it could be until my husband was home for good, I wanted to let my tears loose from behind my anxious heart and stinging eyes. Instead I faced my mother and asked, "Do you long for Abba much when you are apart? Are you missing him now?"

"Of course. Every hour seems to last longer than it should. Even after we've been married for so long, I miss being near him. Your father is such a gift from the LORD to me." Her nostalgic smile faded into a blank, worried stare.

"Mother?"

"Sorry, Love," she said quickly, snapping her glance back to me. "I just miss him. And how you must pine after your own groom! You two are still practically newlyweds." I knew she had changed the subject back to Josiah to distract me, and I wasn't going to let her get away with it.

"Mother, you tell me right this instant what exactly is going on with Abba!" I said, my voice growing low and deliberate as I sat back down on my bed and held her shoulders.

She met my stare for a moment and then glanced down in defeat. She wrung her hands, turning them over and over, grasping one aged and calloused palm, and then the other. She looked back up at me through wet eyes.

"Oh, Hamutal, I'm so afraid to lose him. I don't even remember what life felt like before I knew him. I was so young when we were married …" Her vulnerability was surprising. Never before had she shown this much pain and worry. It frightened me to be the one comforting her. "We've taken him to a priest and a physician, but he won't go back. He says if Jehovah wants to heal him, He will. If not, he said he is ready to face his end."

"Oh, Mama," I said, pulling her into *my* arms now, "I'm so sorry. Shhhh, now—I know."

But I didn't. I didn't know what to say or how to make her anxiety and pain go away. I had no idea how to stop her tears. If anything happened to my father, I would just as soon go with him. And I knew my mother felt the same. We held each other and cried. And then we prayed.

\* \* \*

"Hannah, you're as big as a tent!" I shouted as she emerged from the carriage, with her expecting bulge preceding her by two full handbreadths. I recalled how I had felt at that stage of pregnancy—awkwardly uncomfortable. Or perhaps uncomfortably awkward. Probably both. No wonder Mother had said, "*Wait until you see her.*" I bent over her belly to hug her as best I could then reached down to rub her abdomen and coo to the baby inside.

"And just who are you, Little One? Why don't you come out and meet your Aunt Hamutal and your cousins?" I was so excited for my sister that for a moment I forgot my tears from the previous afternoon. I laughed as I danced around her and then hugged my mother.

"I told you, didn't I?" she said to me with a sly smile.

"Yes, Mother, you're quite the secret-keeper lately," I said. Sobering, yet not wanting to steal Hannah's joy, I asked, "How many more weeks do you have, little sister?"

"I think still four! Although I have no idea how I'm supposed to get any bigger. This child is already bursting my seams, if I have any," she said, laughing and massaging her sides.

"But where is Matthias?" I asked.

"He sends his warm regards and gratitude for the help but decided at the last minute that he could not be away. He's expecting some important guests this week and needs to be there when they arrive," she replied. "He was reluctant to let me leave with the baby so close, but I reassured him that I would be back before his birth."

"His?" Mother and I said together.

"Well, we're hoping, anyway," she said with an embarrassed smile, caressing her stomach with both hands now.

Jehoahaz reached up as high as he could to pat Hannah's tummy, too, but Eliakim kept his distance. Like always, my shy one was ever-hesitant, ever-brooding, and always observing. Though he didn't always relate well to people, he usually watched them with intent and curiosity, and something else I couldn't quite put my finger on. Suspicion, maybe?

Dismissing an urge to analyze his behavior, I hurried everyone to the king's table for a feast with my family. Although the king wasn't with us, why we couldn't indulge as if he were? As we entered the dining hall, the heavy scent of spices, roasted meat, and freshly baked yeast bread filled our noses, and I smiled proudly as my family salivated over the lavish meal. We sat on the pillows and mats that surrounded the table and found ourselves at an awkward pause. We were without a man to lead our mealtime prayer.

"Jaazaniah, would you like to say the prayer?" I asked.

As if the king himself had awarded him a medal for valiant heroics, my brother smiled proudly and bowed his head. "Jehovah, we ask Your holy blessing over this delicious meal ..." he began. The food was cooling by the time he finished.

"Hannah, tell me about your new land," I began once my brother had finished his prayer, asking the question that had been burning in my mouth since she had arrived.

"Well, my meddlesome sister, if you must know, my husband has purchased a section of rich soil near Libnah from an Assyrian who claims it was his by inheritance." As she spoke, I felt my jaw drop almost to the table. "Matthias thought it was better for a Recabite to break our outdated tradition than for a foreigner to lay claim to Judean land. Ironically, they've become good friends over the deal," she said with a pleased smile I didn't comprehend.

"Your husband is friends with an Assyrian?" I said. I could not stop the disgust dripping from my words and face. "But they're our worst enemies!"

"Hamutal, would you stop living in the past? Assyria is retreating from Judah's lands. We don't *have* to be so prejudiced against them, you know." As she spoke, she shook her head and held her palm out in front of her, as if I were ignorant and needed an education in foreign policy.

In the many months since I had seen my sister, she had changed so much. Not only was she a woman now instead of a girl, but she had obviously also traded some of our family's values for new ones. As I stared at her in disbelief, not even recognizing the sister I had grown up with, I could not help but blame Matthias for the unflattering transformation. And I suddenly realized I could have just as easily lived her life instead of my own. Matthias had almost become my husband. I mentally placed myself in my sister's sandals. *What if I had married him? Would I be willing to sacrifice my family's regulations and customs? To befriend Israel's hated enemy? To give up worshipping at the Temple?* The thought made me shudder.

Later that evening, I went to the guest quarters to bid my family goodnight, but overheard my mother and sister in a heated argument before I stepped over the threshold. In curious guilt, I stood in the corridor, too paralyzed to walk back to my chamber.

"It's the opportunity of a lifetime for him. Surely you can understand that," Hannah said.

"No, I can't understand," Mother said.

137

"Oh, you and Hamutal are both refusing to see what the future holds. You'll all be blindsided, and you can't even listen to anyone around you for the warning!" My sister was nearly shouting now.

"But, Hannah, Bethel is so far away. My grandchild ..." my mother pleaded.

I shook my head in confusion. Bethel? The northernmost part of our country? What in the world could be in Bethel that would be of any interest to my sister or her husband?

"Don't be ridiculous, Mother. *We* won't be going to Bethel. Matthias will go for a year to be trained, and then he will return, and we can live on the land. He doesn't leave until after the baby is born, and he'll be back next year."

That disrespectful tone gave me cause to stomp into the room and slap some sense into her. My feet resisted the urge, and I held my frozen stance, afraid even my breathing was too loud.

"I don't see you disputing Hamutal about her husband's religious travels away from his family! What—just because he's the king, your self-righteous judgment doesn't apply to him?"

I could contain myself no longer. I stormed through the doorway confused, insulted, and outraged.

"How dare you, Hannah? What do you know about the king's mission?" I said.

"Hamutal!" Hannah said. "How long have you been here?"

"Long enough to hear your ignorant ranting!" I said.

She stared at me in speechless disbelief, her mouth hanging open like a cistern; her eyes narrowed in retaliation.

"Tell me right now what Matthias is doing in Bethel, and why exactly Mother doesn't want either of you to go," I said.

"Fine, Your *Majesty*," she replied. "My dear husband travels to Bethel to be trained as a priest. He aspires to give his life to the ministry. And I stand behind him in complete devotion." As she stated her case, she folded her arms in front of her and raised her chin in defiance.

It made no sense. Priests were only allowed to be descendants of Levi, and if they were trained anywhere, it would be here in Jerusalem, close to the Temple.

And then my heart stopped and my breath froze in my chest. "A priest ... of ... what ... god?" I whispered.

My sister knew she was in hot water with me already, but she placed her hands on her widened hips, took a deep breath, and replied without a break in her voice: "The very same god that blessed me with this child, who gave us a prosperous plot of land, and who continues to shower wealth on our growing family. The god of prosperity and goodness—Baal."

The breath that I had been holding escaped in a scream. I looked over to my mother, who lowered her eyes, too afraid or ashamed to face me.

"No, Hannah! You don't understand!" I cried.

"I think it's *you* who don't understand, sister," she said.

"Hannah, he mustn't! The king ... he'll ... you can't let him!" I said. I had fallen to my knees at her declaration of idolatry, tearing my nightgown with my hands to bare my chest before them.

When Josiah had spoken of the pain he felt over the nation's waywardness, I had never understood why it hurt him so badly, sometimes even causing him actual physical symptoms of sickness. But now that it was my own sister, I felt it, too. I recalled the many times our entire family had stood together in the LORD's Sabbath service, singing and praying beside one another. Had she forgotten all those years? Was she so willing to trade the Living God for a dead one? Her words continued to stab my ears like knives. I covered them and began to cry.

The set of her jaw and the look of insubordination in her eyes told me that any amount of pleading would make no difference.

# 15. JOSIAH

Each day of cleansing the Temple brought with it a different set of challenges. The first day had been revolting, to say the least. Since I had found the Temple as a youth, I had only been attending services at the Temple on the seventh day of the week for Sabbath, which I now learned had been reserved for Yahwists and our traditions. However, on the other days of the week, unbeknownst to me, the sacred house of the Living God was being disgraced by other religious ceremonies. The day we began the cleansing was the first day of the week, and, as Hilkiah had warned me before we entered, there were other worshippers—devotees of Asherah, the sex and fertility goddess.

The tallest statue I had ever seen of her, carved of wood and plated with gold, stood in the entry of the Court of the Israelites while several women and a few men bowed on their knees before it. They were chanting in stentorian voices something I could not understand, and several drums accompanied them in a steady rhythm. Just as I was about to interrupt their "service," a beautiful young girl with striking red hair was brought out from one of the rooms of the Temple, shoved in front of them, and then stripped naked for them to gawk.

Two of the men in the crowd each raised a fistful of gold coins, and the officiator shoved her toward the one who seemed to hold more. This procedure was repeated with a male prostitute, only the second prize was bid upon by both men and women alike. They didn't seem to notice our intrusion yet, so I stepped a few paces closer to them and cleared my throat, just as the prostitutes were returning to the rooms from whence they emerged, along with their highest bidders.

"Your Majesty!" I heard a few of them gasp as they bowed before me.

"'Behold, Israel, the LORD, the LORD your God is ONE'," I quoted. "This is Jehovah's Temple. It will be used for the worship of Him alone, from this day forward. I hereby declare it a national offense to worship any other god, including Asherah, to be punishable by death. This is your official warning. All of you must leave at once, and you are not to return to this place until you're ready to declare allegiance to the Most High God."

My subjects began milling around in confusion, but none of them made a motion to leave as I had ordered.

"Acbor," I ordered, "the statue."

He immediately left my side and motioned to several of his fellow troops to help him as they lifted the disgusting shrine off of her stand and carried it out to Solomon's Porch. Checking their aim so as not to hit any of my soldiers below, they tossed it down into the Kidron Valley where the other half of my officers and troops waited to destroy it with fire and our enormous crushing stones.

I followed Acbor and his assistants a few steps, but suddenly a shriek rang out behind me. "No! No! What have you done to our goddess?" I turned to see several women screaming and beginning to wail in desperation. They rushed to the wall of the Temple pinnacle to see where the statue had landed.

The priest of the lewd statue-goddess rushed at me with his fists balled over his head. Asaiah and Jared intercepted his futile attack before he could get close enough to even spit at me, but he began shouting, "You can't just do this! Who are you to—"

"I'm the king!" I shouted back. "And this Temple was built by my ancestor, Solomon, for the sole purpose of honoring One God, and One God only." I raised a finger in the air at him as I shouted. "I most assuredly have the authority to destroy your precious non-god and to remove you and all of your followers from the premises. You can either choose to walk out, or I can have them throw you down to meet the same fate as your dear Asherah!"

Asaiah gave him a last shove, commanding him, "Get out!"

The priest stumbled out of the gate, shaking his head in disbelief.

"That goes for all of you!" I barked. They slowly began to file out, one at a time, down the porch steps, mumbling to one another as they went. I stepped back into the place where I had seen Asherah's prostitutes disappear and found a group of people huddling in each of the two rooms. Hanging on the walls were brilliant-colored tapestries, sewn with as fine of craftsmanship as I had ever seen. The stitching and embroidery rivaled even the hangings in my palace.

"What are these?" I demanded, pointing to the walls of the room.

"Coverings for our goddess, Your Majesty," one woman said.

"Who made them?" The female prostitute raised her hand hesitantly. "Burn them!" I ordered.

She stifled sobs in her hands as my men tore them off of the walls and placed them on the carts we would take down to the valley that night.

"Get dressed—now." We had only just begun, and my patience was already spent. "Where do you live?" I asked the prostitute. If she was some homeless slave, I readied myself with enough compassion to find a temporary living situation for her and the others.

She said nothing but motioned to the bed on which she was cowering as she covered herself with a few meager garments. I was too shocked to breathe.

"And you?" I asked, turning to the male prostitute.

He pointed to the room my guards had pulled him from just moments before.

I clenched my fists and brought them slowly to my forehead. I turned to Hilkiah, who was a few cubits behind me, among the rest of my guard and the other priests. Looking into his eyes, I asked as calmly as I could, "Why have I never known that the Temple of Jehovah is the very living quarters for Asherah's prostitutes?"

He stammered for a moment. "Be ... cause ... you ... never asked?" he stammered.

I struggled to control myself. Jeremiah had once told me that regardless of my preference, his father would remain the high priest, delegated by his peers. And contrary to my previous belief, I actually had no control over that fact, according to the law of the Levites. Though I wanted to curse at him and strike his jaw to send him sprawling across the courtyard for allowing such sacrilege in this of all places, I suppressed my rage and mentally handed him over to God to exact His own justice.

I turned back to the prostitutes and pointed toward the gate. "Out." What little compassion I had mustered was dissipated, and I couldn't have cared less if they slept on the streets.

Looking for Jehiel, the Temple administrator, I found him standing among the Levites, watching for my next move.

"Jehiel," I called, and motioned for him to come closer. I had appointed him only recently to study what he could find in the palace and Temple scrolls of God's standards for His dwelling place. When he stood before me with Hilkiah, I said, "Tear these two rooms down and rebuild them—"

"But, Your Highness," Hilkiah interrupted, "these are part of the original structure from King Solomon. He constructed these outer housing quarters for the priests and Levites." I looked into the two rooms once more. The stench of their activity filled my nostrils and made the contents of my stomach turn violently.

"Very well, then. They are your new quarters, Hilkiah," I said, bowing my head and sweeping my arm toward them.

He balked in disgust. "My lord ... you can't expect the High Priest of Jehovah to ..."

"Exactly. Tear them down," I repeated, turning to face Jehiel. "Today. Rebuild them with new stones and cedar. Understood?"

He sighed and replied, "Yes, Your Highness," and then began choosing a crew from among the men we had brought into the Temple. I sent the rest of my men to find anything else that might have been associated with Asherah and pile it onto the carts to be burned that afternoon.

"Hilkiah," I said once we were alone, trying to be as patient as I could. "Are there any *other* idolatrous prostitutes living in the outer rooms of the Temple about whom you might like to inform me?" I asked, pronouncing each word carefully. "Now that I'm *asking*," I added with a tilt of my head.

"No. Not that I know of. I took the liberty of making a list of the occupants as a part of the inventory you requested. No other prostitutes," he answered.

"And," I breathed deeply to control myself, "are we clear about why it is unacceptable for this Holy Place to house the dung of all humanity or contribute to their profits?" I asked.

I saw surrender in his eyes. He nodded slightly.

"I can't even ask if you ever received a portion of that lust money, High Priest. I don't know what I would do if you told me you had. Hopefully, it is apparent that *none of this* is to happen *anywhere* in my kingdom, and least of all here."

He averted his eyes. "I understand."

"You'll read me that list tonight. God *will* come and dwell in this place again if we purify it for Him."

Before I left the Temple for the afternoon, I went to the altar and knelt. I was not accustomed to seeing it cold and empty. I prayed quietly under my breath: LORD *Almighty, please forgive Your people. Come back into this land, into this place, and into our hearts. Show us Your power over all other gods, and send Your word to us once again. This day was the first of many, LORD—and I need more fortitude. I don't really want them to die, LORD, though they deserve to be executed for their detestable actions. I want them to know You, as I do. Help me to control my anger, Almighty. Give me Your compassion, even as I must look upon their filth. May Your command be done. So let it be.*

\* \* \*

That afternoon in the valley, as my men were preparing the fire, two soldiers approached me, one with a message scroll and the other with a question from Asaiah. The first handed me the scroll as he bowed, and said, "From the queen, my lord."

I laughed heartily and realized it was the first happy moment since I had left. "It hasn't even been an entire day yet, and she's sending me love letters already?" I held it without reading it, thanked the messenger, and then turned to the second man.

"Yes?"

"Your Highness, Master Asaiah would like to know what you want to do with the gold once it is melted away from the idol."

"Catch it as best you can and then have it melted into bars," I replied. "We will be using it for collateral during the international trade agreements this fall."

Although the Temple desperately needed several talents of gold for its repairs, I was reluctant to use what we would confiscate for that. Even destroyed and melted down, the precious metal still seemed defiled to me. I would instead buy spices, food, and perhaps weapons with our melted "gods," and planned to fund the refurbishing of the Temple from the gold and silver in my own treasury.

"Tell Asaiah that I need a few moments alone in my tent but that I'll be out shortly. Don't start the fire without me."

While we had been up at the Temple, the rest of the crew had been making camp, setting up dozens of tents and preparing meals for everyone. It felt as if we were in a far-off land, preparing for battle with our enemies. I could have walked home in less than a quarter of an hour, but I was receiving messages from Hamutal as if she were days away.

I smiled, shaking my head at the irony of my self-inflicted predicament, and stepped into the privacy of my quarters. Although I had asked the workers not to make my tent superior to any other, they hadn't quite followed my instructions. Instead of a simple straw pallet, a thick mattress sat atop a wooden frame on one wall, along with a small desk and seat on the other side. Several floor pillows were piled in the corner, and there was a basin, a plate of date-bread and grapes, and a skin of water atop another small table beside them.

I took a drink of the water, which was refreshing to my raspy throat, and fell onto the pillows to read the note from my angel.

*Hello, dear husband.*

*I know you'll laugh, but I miss you already! I pray your day has been productive and that everyone is following orders as they should.*

*It is with deep regret that I draw your attention to a matter that will require you to return to the palace immediately. I have found two altars atop the roof, above the upper room of Ahaz. It appears as if they were once used to burn incense or offer food to the gods of your wayward grandfathers. As this is within the specifications of your present mission, I expect your arrival shortly.*

*I'll also expect you to make a brief diversion into our chambers, as my arms will crave your embrace. As this matter is of utmost importance, I should not anticipate any delay in your arrival.*

*All my love and affection,*
*Hamutal*

I shook my head and laughed again. Although the matter of the altars was serious, and the fact that my own home needed to be cleansed of impurity left me irritated, it honestly paled in comparison to what I had witnessed that day. Her wit and playful tone increased my longing for the cooling comfort of her smile. *Deep regret, indeed,* I mused. I took some parchment and ink from the desk and began a reply to her.

*Very well, my Love. As you have decreed, I shall return to the palace as soon as I am finished here with the Temple, although I should warn you, it could be several days. I apologize, my lady, that immediacy is not possible. I pray you'll not have my head for the delay. I, too, long to see you, and to touch your lovely skin. I wish you could be here with me now, but I am also very thankful that you are not. I love you—especially when you make me laugh. It was good to do at the end of this deplorable day.*

*Longing for you already,*
*Josiah*

As I stepped out of my tent and called for the messenger, I noticed that my men had finished the preparations for the fire and were beginning to position the two square crushing stones beside the fire pit. One was stabilized on the ground in a carefully measured groove, and the other sat atop it, rigged with several ropes that my strongest soldiers would raise, using a pulley that hung over a large branch of an olive tree. It was the largest tree in this portion of the valley, and fittingly, we knew it as another location of Asherah ceremonies. This was where they held the infamous orgies, and they believed the magnificent tree itself had powers of fertility and ecstasy. Avoiding the work area of the grunting stone-bearers, I walked over to evaluate the tree and placed my hands on its massive trunk.

I neither felt power emanating from the bark, nor heard any voices of the tree speaking to me. I had once asked an Asherah worshipper what it was about the trees that held such awe for them, to which she had claimed the trees talked to her and revealed her fortune. To me it was nothing but bark and leaves. Beautiful? Naturally. Powerful? Hardly. After its function in our pulley system, I would have it cut down and brought with us for wood at our next cleansing site.

I turned back to the massive stones and nodded to the muscle. Originally, I had observed this as part of Assyrian execution tactics in my war strategy course with my tutors, but I had chosen to modify it with larger stones in order to crush any rock, metal, or wooden object. I was eager to see how it would work on the statue.

Asaiah handed me the torch, and I carefully touched the flame to the fresh kindling in the pit. The tinder lit immediately, warming the sticks and small branches above. One by one, they caught and added height and heat to the flames. Soldiers placed larger branches and logs until the fire filled the enormous hollow and raised the blazes high into the air, sending billows of gray smoke into the bright blue sky. I stepped back a few paces when sweat began beading on my forehead, and I signaled for them to stop bringing wood.

At another signal from my hand, twenty men pulled on the ropes to lift the top crushing stone, straining against its load. At first, their feet just slipped against the loose gravel beneath their feet, but within just a few minutes, the stone was high in the air, dangling as if weightless. Three other soldiers carried the idol past the fire and began to place it between the two stones.

"Stand back!" Asaiah ordered his men, and everyone around the fire and the crushing stones obeyed without hesitation. They had all seen what the contraption could do to a simple rock and did not want any shard of gold or wood to catch a wrong angle and become a projectile weapon.

Once we had all moved a safe distance away from the stones, I gave the signal for the men to release their ropes. With an ear-splitting crack, the goddess was smashed into pieces, a few of which bounced out from between the crushing stones and landed near the fire pit.

It was not until that moment, when I had just begun to feel the coolness of satisfaction and progress, that I heard the wails behind my soldiers. A crowd of the previous worshippers had followed us down and was observing the death of their religion. I carefully stepped back and peered around my men to get a glimpse of them. The men had ripped out patches of their beards and the women had covered their faces and hair with the dust from the valley. I sighed and felt my jaw clenching in an angry rhythm at the pitiful sight.

*If only they would show such remorse at the tragedy of abandoning Jehovah,* I thought. *How can they be so blind to His power and faithfulness? Was it Asherah who brought us out of Egypt? Did she give us this land, handing it over to us from its previous inhabitants? Do they not remember who fed their ancestors in the desert with manna and quail, and instant springs from rocks? Have they so easily forgotten how God was the one to rescue us from our enemies for generations? How can they be so distraught over a powerless statue, and yet so oblivious to the power of the* LORD*?*

I sighed and waved to Asaiah, who then commanded the troops to pick up the pieces of the idol and drop them into the refinery bowl. This was a large iron basin designed to withstand the heat of the hottest fire. It sat to the side of the blazes among the coals that were pulled aside for this purpose. As the fire attendants placed the shattered pieces of the statue into the bowl, the gold began to melt almost immediately and pool in the bottom of the basin. The expert refiner whom Asaiah had handpicked for this mission began to fetch out the scraps of wood with long tongs, tossing them, aflame, into the fire once the gold had dripped off completely. I marveled at his skill and coordination, nodding in appreciation of his proficiency. Whether the impotent statues we destroyed on this mission were gold, silver, or bronze, I knew his knowledge and agility with the fire would be priceless for this campaign. I made a mental note to ask Asaiah to reward him generously.

I stepped around my troops to address the group of idolaters. "Look at your beloved Asherah now!" I called, sweeping my hand toward the flames. "Would you still bow to this, or might you choose to serve the God of heaven and earth, a God who cannot be destroyed by stones, fire, or men?"

While the fire burned hotter, I motioned to my scribe, Shaphan, asking him to bring the scroll he would read at each of these fires to anyone who would listen. He hurried into position at my side in front of the crying and wailing crowd and unrolled his parchment. It was a passage Jeremiah and I had found in the many scrolls of Isaiah, and I had the scribe copy it carefully so we could bring it with us on the mission without endangering the original.

He began in a loud, clear voice, "This is what the LORD says—Israel's King and Redeemer, the LORD of Heaven's Armies:

*"I am the First and the Last; there is no other God. Who is like Me? Let him step forward and prove to you his power. Let him do as I have done since ancient times when I established a people and explained its future. Do not tremble; do not be afraid. Did I not proclaim My purposes for you long ago? You are My witnesses—is there any other God? No! There is no other Rock—not one!*

*"How foolish are those who manufacture idols. These prized objects are really worthless. The people who worship idols don't know this, so they are all put to shame. Who but a fool would make his own god—an idol that cannot help him one bit? All who worship idols will be disgraced along with all these craftsmen—mere humans—who claim they can make a god. They may all stand together, but they will stand in terror and shame.*

"*The blacksmith stands at his forge to make a sharp tool, pounding and shaping it with all his might. His work makes him hungry and weak. It makes him thirsty and faint. Then the wood-carver measures a block of wood and draws a pattern on it. He works with chisel and plane and carves it into a human figure. He gives it human beauty and puts it in a little shrine. He cuts down cedars; he selects the cypress and the oak; he plants the pine in the forest to be nourished by the rain. Then he uses part of the wood to make a fire. With it he warms himself and bakes his bread. Then—yes, it's true—he takes the rest of it and makes himself a god to worship! He makes an idol and bows down in front of it! He burns part of the tree to roast his meat and to keep himself warm. He says, 'Ah, that fire feels good.' Then he takes what's left and makes his god: a carved idol! He falls down in front of it, worshiping and praying to it. 'Rescue me!' he says. 'You are my god!'*

"*Such stupidity and ignorance! Their eyes are closed, and they cannot see. Their minds are shut, and they cannot think. The person who made the idol never stops to reflect, 'Why, it's just a block of wood! I burned half of it for heat and used it to bake my bread and roast my meat. How can the rest of it be a god? Should I bow down to worship a piece of wood?' The poor, deluded fool feeds on ashes. He trusts something that can't help him at all. Yet he cannot bring himself to ask, 'Is this idol that I'm holding in my hand a lie?'*

"*Pay attention, O Jacob, for you are My servant, O Israel. I, the* LORD, *made you, and I will not forget you.*"

And then I began my rehearsed speech as well: "Nation of Judah, the greatest of all tribes of Jacob: God has not forgotten us, but we have forgotten Him. I, Josiah, King of Judah, son of Ammon and descendant of David, forbid you to make false gods and bow down to them any longer. Choose instead to worship the Creator of gold, wood, stone, mountains, livestock, and the stars and the seas. He will not be created or made, for He alone is the Maker of all things. Jehovah is His name and He longs to bring you back to Himself, if you will only choose to obey Him. Your dead god is destroyed; you are now free to choose instead the God who is alive!"

After several minutes of grumbling and futile attempts to argue their rights, most of them began to dissipate, and soon all I could hear was the loud crackling of the fire. The blazes died down and became pulsating coals of intense heat, and I watched in near hypnosis as the air above them wavered gently. I waited to hear some affirmation from the LORD, but He was not in this fire. His presence seemed unreachable and cold, and I wondered if He had even noticed what we had just done. In the logic of my faith, I realized He could see all things and reassured myself once again that this was His plan, not mine.

After about an hour, the refiner was ready to scrape the dross off of the top of the gold in the basin. He carefully pulled his long iron tool across the edge of the molten gold, scooping the impurities into another bowl, which he held carefully with tongs. He brought me the dross and asked what I wanted to do with it. I thought for a moment of an appropriate demonstration for the people.

"Have it cooled and then demolished again. Mix the remnants with the ashes from the fire. We'll bring it with us for now."

\* \* \*

Every day of that week was worse than the first. I found more to destroy than I had expected in the Temple, and it took much longer than I had anticipated. Regardless of the magnitude, I was determined to be thorough. By the second day, word had spread of what we were doing and people of all different religions and walks of life came to protest. I put the rowdiest ones under house arrest or threw them into the palace dungeon.

On the third day, as we were pulling out two incense altars carved with star-and moon-shaped images and throwing them down into the valley, I was surprised to turn around and find my friend Jeremiah in the courtyard. I went to greet him with an embrace, but he held up his hand in a warning not to approach him. His severe countenance told me that he was not here for a sociable visit. I eyed him carefully. He looked nervous, the way a man looks when he is about to ask a father for his daughter's hand in marriage. His whole body was shaking, his knees knocking together as he stood. But in addition to fear, I saw determination, as if there was nothing that could stop him from saying what he had come to proclaim.

He squarely faced the crowd of protesters and the soldiers who surrounded them. Though his back was now facing me, I heard every deliberate word as it bounced off of the Temple walls in acoustic glory, as if he were slowly plucking the strings of a lyre one at a time. His body continued to shake, but his voice was nothing but sharp, and echoed all around us.

"This is what the LORD says:

"*I remember how eager you were to please Me as a young bride long ago, how you loved me and followed me, even through the barren wilderness. In those days Israel was holy to the LORD, the first of His children. All who harmed His people were declared guilty, and disaster fell on them. I, the LORD, have spoken!*

"Listen to the word of the LORD, people of Jacob—all you families of Israel! This is what the LORD says:

"*What did your ancestors find wrong with Me that led them to stray so far from Me? They worshiped worthless idols, only to become worthless themselves. They did not ask, "Where is the LORD who brought us safely out of Egypt and led us through the barren wilderness—a land of deserts and pits, a land of drought and death, where no one lives or even travels?*

"*And when I brought you into a fruitful land to enjoy its bounty and goodness, you defiled My land and corrupted the possession I had promised you. The priests did not ask, "Where is the LORD?" Those who taught My word ignored me, the rulers turned against Me, and the prophets spoke in the name of Baal, wasting their time on worthless idols. Therefore, I will bring my case against you," says the LORD. "I will even bring charges against your children's children in the years to come.*

"*Go west and look in the land of Cyprus; go east and search through the land of Kedar. Has anyone ever heard of anything as strange as this? Has any nation ever traded its gods for new ones, even though they are not gods at all? Yet my people have exchanged their glorious God for worthless idols! The heavens are shocked at such a thing and shrink* back in horror and dismay," says the LORD. "For my people have done two evil things: they have abandoned me—the fountain of living water. And they have dug for themselves cracked cisterns that can hold no water at all!"

As Jeremiah spoke of God's faithfulness, answered only by His children's betrayal, he had begun to weep, and it was as if I were watching God Himself bemoan the actions that had separated us from Him. The crowd was struck silent, as was I, recalling all of the seemingly impossible miracles our forefathers had testified to, which my generation and those immediately before me had either forgotten or disregarded. The anguish in Jeremiah's voice pulled me so hard I found myself on my knees with a large, uncontrollable lump in my own throat.

I had never before considered so deeply the full gamut of God's *feelings* for us. Rage, I was familiar with. Anger, I knew. But this new picture Jeremiah had so distinctly painted was different. It was not only God as the justifiably wrathful Father, whose sons and daughters had disgraced His orders, but it was the LORD as a jealous husband, gawking in confused horror at finding his beloved enjoying herself in the bed of another man. The image wrecked me.

I tried to put myself in Jehovah's position. What if Hamutal had forgotten how I had loved her—how I had rescued her from death at the risk of my own life? What if she had chosen not to pour out her affection to me any longer? How would I feel if I returned from a trip such as this one, and she had decided to give her heart and her body to another man, as God's people had given their precious worship to foreign gods? How would I remind her of our love? How would I win her back? Would I even want to try?

Jeremiah walked away, leaving the Temple quickly and abandoning me on my knees before my soldiers and subjects, tears streaming down my face. The gaping silence hung in the air like a thick fog as I stared into their contemplative eyes. A thousand lifetimes could not make me forget the anguish and despair I heard from Jehovah's heart through the prophet's voice.

# 16. HAMUTAL

The day Josiah came home, I could see the change immediately, even in the way he walked up the palace mount; he held a different posture than the man who had left me just nine days before. It was as if he now carried a large sack of sand across his shoulders. His steps were more careful, more deliberate, and he stared ahead of him in deep thought, not even seeing the boys running at him until they nearly knocked him over in the courtyard of the palace. Whatever had happened during that week of cleansing the Temple had transformed him, peeling away the man I knew and leaving a stranger in his place.

All of my intentions to rush into his arms were halted, and I stood in the entrance to the royal garden wringing my hands for lack of anything better to do with them. He greeted the boys with no more than a simple pat on each of their heads and continued moving forward with the same deep stare, now pointed in my direction. When he reached me, I suddenly wondered if I had done something to upset him. His eyes bore into mine like daggers, and then suddenly he wrapped me in his arms and squeezed me so tightly, I thought he might break me in half.

"Oh, my angel," he whispered.

"Josiah! What—"

He shook his head next to mine, unable to express whatever pain had struck him.

"Is everyone alright?" I asked, pulling away enough to look into his watery eyes. They still bore into me so sharply that it nearly hurt.

"Yes, my men are fine." He sighed heavily before continuing, "You'd never run away from me, would you?"

"What—where is this coming from? You know I could never even imagine life without you!"

"And you'd never abandon God, either—no matter what?" He had taken my face in his hands and he kept looking at my eyes, moving his gaze back and forth under his furrowed brow.

"Josiah, you're frightening me—you know me better than that," I said.

"Yes … yes I do." He pulled me back into his crushing embrace. I placed my hands on his shoulders and pushed him away from me as firmly as I could to demand an explanation of his strange behavior, but as I did, he winced and pulled his left shoulder from my grasp, clutching it with his right hand.

"What happened?" I gasped.

"It's nothing, Love. Just a little nick."

It was my turn to bore holes into him with my eyes.

"Fine—you were right. I have a lot of people angry with me right now. My soldiers accidentally let a hidden dagger slip by. One of the priests of Chemosh threw it at me yesterday, and it grazed my shoulder. Security has been doubled, and we're going to start frisking the crowds before we begin. Trust me, I'll be fine."

"Oh, Josiah," I cried as I pulled his face down to me to kiss him. It felt like it had been years since our lips had met, and I felt no condolence in being right about the danger. He kissed me back fully, demonstrating the desire for me that I only assumed had been building every day we were apart. Before I wanted him to, he pulled away and sighed.

"Can't you just tell them what to do? Why must you be there? It's too risky—you're too important!" I exclaimed.

"We've been over this, Hamutal." He paused to look over my shoulder, the desert dunes visible in his mind's eye. "I must be sure. God asked me to burn them all. How can I stand before Him and declare this nation pure if I don't see it with my own eyes? And how will people know that I'm in earnest if I send a mere messenger?" He looked back down into my eyes. "Don't you see the necessity of the crown being present for all of it?"

I couldn't answer him. A part of me still did not see. But I knew better than to argue. It would only waste our precious time together and rouse his anger toward me when it should be saved for the idolaters. Nothing I could say would ever change his mind, and if this was truly God's plan, who was I to interfere? Somehow I had to trust Him to protect Josiah, even when his guards could not. I gently caressed his shoulder and tucked my head under his chin, drinking in the wonderful scent of his skin and clothes.

"Listen, I have a favor to ask you." He pulled away suddenly, his previous brooding tossed aside by fresh excitement.

"Anything."

"Well, I found a young girl who has been living in the Temple," he said. "At first, I was so disgusted by her that I turned her out into the street to fend for herself, or else die, but then I remembered something. The first day we met, *you* were almost kidnapped and forced into temple prostitution. I had my men look for her on the streets, and they found her, thank God. It turns out that she didn't choose her life of selling religious sexual favors. Her father sold her into slavery, and she was coerced to work for Asherah's priests." Here he stopped and shook his head, cringing at his thoughts. After a moment, he continued, "Hamutal, could you help her? I'd like her to stay here in one of the guest chambers, or even in the harem, though you must make sure no one gets the wrong idea. She has no family to return to and nowhere to go. What do you say?"

I shrugged. "I'm not sure I can help her, but I'll try—for you."

"She's quite frightened, but I think she could learn to worship God. Will you show her His ways—like you showed me?"

"I'll do my best."

"Wonderful! I'll introduce you—"

"Wait … my lord …" I wanted to tell him about my family. I didn't know how long he would be able to stay before rushing off again.

"Don't worry—I haven't forgotten about the altars upstairs. Asaiah is pulling them down as we speak."

"But—"

"I have to get a few things and then rejoin the troops. We're burning the temple of Baal today—the one I told you about, you know—the one that made me sick. I can't wait to see the flames when it goes up in smoke!"

"You mean, you're leaving already?"

"Not before I kiss you again." He drew me back into his arms and took my chin in his hand. I quickly tried to memorize the feeling of his lips and his arms as his body pressed against mine. "Now, I have to go, but remember—the sooner I leave, the sooner I'll be back. Was there something else you wanted to tell me?"

I thought about how my news could be nothing but a distraction to his focus and determination. What could he really do about any of it, anyway? I didn't see any sense in making my burdens his when the weight on his shoulders was already so heavy.

Swallowing, I answered, "No, my King."

*Just that my father is dying and my sister has become a Baal worshipper.*

"I'll go and get the girl, then. Stay right here," he said. I nodded, forcing a smile. When he came back with the stunning redhead in rags, I felt compassion mixed with a twinge of insecurity. She was so beautiful, despite the smudges of dirt on her face and the way she stood as if the slightest breeze could blow her over. Josiah led her into the courtyard by the arm, and though there was not an ounce of betrayal in his eyes, I fought the urge to rip his hands away from her.

"Hello," I said, carefully composing my voice before I spoke. "My name is Hamutal. And you are …"

"Tirzah," she whispered.

"Welcome to the king's palace, Tirzah," I said, taking Josiah's place at her arm. "My husband tells me you've had a painful past, but he wants you to know the beautiful hope Jehovah can offer you."

She nodded slightly.

"Would you like me to show you to your room?"

She shrugged her painfully thin shoulders and nodded again.

Josiah tenderly grasped my elbow and murmured, "I have to go, now. I love you."

"I love you, my King. Come back to me soon—in one piece!"

He kissed my cheek, and with a half-smile and a squeeze of my shoulders he was off, and my heart followed. I let go of the girl's arm and turned around to watch his back for as long as my eyes could see him.

"Would you like a hot bath, Tirzah?" I asked, turning back.

Her cold, brown eyes widened at the thought. I noticed that her skin was young and soft, but her eyes were somehow old. They were empty and frozen, dripping with hidden fear. Now that Josiah was gone, my jealousy vanished, and I felt such pity for her that tears stung the back of my eyes. I took her hand, which felt like a cool, limp olive leaf, and led her into the palace. As we walked down the empty corridor toward the lavish harem, I tried to imagine what her life must have been like: how horrible it would have been to be used for her beauty—sold again and again as if she were an object and not a treasured creation of the LORD.

I tried to picture her face as my own, because my life very well could have been hers. I could be the homeless one, the one without anyone to love her or hold her except those who did so for self-serving motives. I could be the girl with empty eyes and ancient, crystallized dirt all over her body. But I was the queen. I was the one who had been called by God and rescued by the king. Humility threatened to drown me and then left me with an overwhelming need to help Tirzah climb out of her pit of shame. A few minutes before, I had agreed to welcome her into the palace simply because Josiah had asked me, and because I would do anything to please him. But in that moment, I desired nothing more than the chance to help Tirzah find full recovery from the nightmare of her life.

When we reached the room I had in mind for her, I thought it best not to call any servants. I wanted her to trust the privacy, though the concept must have been foreign to her. I lit a fire myself and put on a pot of water to boil for hot tea and a bath. I looked in the wardrobe for some clean clothes and found a simple, ivory, linen robe that would be soft and warm on her skin.

"Would you like to sit on the sofa," I asked.

She only shook her head hopelessly from side to side.

"It's alright. This is your home for now. Please, rest a minute."

Tirzah said nothing and continued to stand as I prepared her bath in the laver, pouring her a cup of tea once the water was hot. She sipped it gingerly and held the cup with both hands to warm them. Though it was late spring, the afternoon was cool, and I felt a breeze coming in from the balcony that must have chilled her. I caught her looking at the bath as I poured in soap and the precious oils, and knew this would be just what she needed.

"Would you like me to leave you to bathe in privacy?"

Tirzah seemed torn. Though it was obvious that I was earning some rapport, she did not yet trust me. I handed her a towel and told her I would be back in about an hour with some food. However, as I walked out of her room and closed the door behind me, I had a sinking feeling that she might run if I left her for that long. When I returned to my chambers, I sent my own guards to her room with specific instructions not to let her leave and to come get me if she tried.

A bath sounded relaxing to me as well, and I began to draw water from the basin and heat it over the fire. I sent a messenger to the tutor and the nurse to keep the boys for the afternoon and that I would see them for dinner that evening. Once I had bathed and dressed, I looked into my mirror and brushed the knots from my hair as I prayed.

*God, please help me to reach this girl. Only You know what she's been through, and only You can help her. Would You soften her heart and demonstrate Your power to heal? Please show her the great depth of Your love for her—how You can forgive and restore everything that has been so cruelly ripped from her life.*

As I walked back into her room, I was shocked to see her still covered in rags and the same coating of filth, lying in the middle of the marble floor and rolling back and forth as she moaned. I stepped carefully toward her, wondering if she was having a nightmare. As I drew close enough to see that her eyes were open, the empty look of death in them frightened me.

I withdrew suddenly, taking a few steps back as I clutched my stomach. As I watched her suddenly flinch and then begin to writhe in agony, my thoughts and emotions were divided between disgust and sympathy. I shook my head in confusion and reached my hand up into the air in a frantic plea for Jehovah's help. *What's wrong with her, God?*

Finally, my compassion won out, and I knelt, reaching out to stabilize her shoulder. "Tirzah?"

She began to sob, moaning in incoherent pleas and frightened screams. Tears poured from her cheeks and wet the marble beneath her. Despite the fetor exuding from her skin, I picked up her shoulders and laid her across my lap, drawing her close to my bosom in attempt to hem in her fleeting heart.

"Tirzah, it's me—Hamutal," I said.

At the sound of my voice, she calmed slightly, but only momentarily. Within a few moments, she began to writhe again, and finally, I was able to decipher a few words: "Please ... no ... no ... not again ... not tonight ..." Instantly, her body went rigid into a line; she collapsed into my arms with continued moans and wails. At first, she pushed me away, but when I persisted in a firm, but gentle embrace, she surrendered and allowed her arms to fall into my lap.

LORD, *what do I do? What's wrong with her? What is it that she's so frightened of—that's tearing her mind apart? Help me, God. Help me reach her, please.*

*"Speak My Name,"* He said to my heart.

Confused, but willing to try anything He asked of me, I began to speak over her the names of Jehovah I had learned in the Temple and from my father: "Jehovah ... God Almighty ... the LORD your Provider ... the LORD your Healer ... the LORD who sees you ... the Most High God ... the LORD is Peace ... the LORD your Shepherd ... the LORD of Heaven's Armies ... God of Righteousness ... the Great I AM ..."

As I gently stroked her back and arms, I continued to repeat as many of His names as I could remember, over and over again. Miraculously, Tirzah began to grow quieter, her sobs becoming broken gasps as she calmed. Her eyes remained closed, as she lay curled around me, her head in my arms and her shoulders settling into my crossed legs.

Suddenly, a vision of her life hit me like a stone in the back. I tried to picture what she had been screaming to ward off, and each new vision was like another rock pummeling into my flesh. I winced at the images that I could only conclude were coming from God. I had certainly never seen anything so wicked. I closed my eyes and surrendered to the visions in my head, knowing I could not fight them now. I had asked Him to show me what was plaguing her, and He was not about to mask any of it.

A large fist threatened to slam into the vision of her face. Still holding her in my arms, I felt myself wince at her pain. Then visions of men's faces, one after another, loomed over her body. It was surreal; I had become Tirzah in the vision. The stones were pummeling me now, faster and faster.

I was suddenly inside a room that reeked of body odor and semen, staring out the door at what looked to be the Temple courtyard. Just as I was about to attempt an exit from this apparition, the door slammed shut, another stone slamming into my stomach. I could not reach the door to reopen it because a chain held me trapped to the wall. I was handed thread and a needle by another man, my intuition understanding him to be a priest or master of some sorts. With another stone to the side of my head, my fingers sewed tapestries during the day, until the time came for performing other services. A wave of helplessness drowned my mind just before I felt the LORD rescue me from the hallucination.

"Oh, God ..." I gasped. "How did she ever endure *that?*"

I shook my head as the vision cleared, but the memory of it clung to my mind the way the wool of a sheep clings to the briars of a bristle bush, forcing a shepherd to cut the fibers away from the thorns. Only I could not cut it away, no matter how much I fought.

I looked back down at her and stroked her fire-colored locks. I wished to take away her nightmares, her pain, her shame, her anguish. I didn't know where to begin. Josiah had asked me to introduce her to God, and with new determination in light of what I had seen—in light of the compassion He had given me for her—I resolved to show her what I knew of Him.

"Tirzah? Let's get you into the bath, alright?"

Coming out of her hallucination, she choked on her breath and looked up at me with an empty stare. I pulled her up to sitting and smoothed down her shoulders. She dropped her head at my gaze, but I lifted her chin gently.

"Maybe you don't feel worthy of a bath in the king's palace, but today is the beginning of a new life." I held her hands in mine, and for the first time, she did not look away from me as I spoke to her. "I'm going to show you a new kind of love—a kind you probably have never known. And before I show you anything, I want you to know that this love does not come from me. The love I offer you is from the God of heaven and earth—Jehovah. I have served Him all my life, and I want you to know Him, too. He is the only God worth serving. The only One who holds power. The only God who offers love."

Her eyes narrowed as she tried to take in my words, and then she sighed. I wasn't sure how long our conversations would continue to be one-sided, but I was determined to care for her, regardless of her response, or lack thereof. I rose from the floor to re-warm the bath water and get a new cup of tea for her. I poked my head out the door, asking one of the guards to send for some food, and then quickly returned to help Tirzah undress.

I pulled the rags over her head as she limply raised her arms in hesitant cooperation. I looked at her bare skin, which held pockets of yellowing bruises, as well as a few old scars atop each of her shoulders, as if someone had painted pink stripes across the crest of them. The only thing I could speculate was that they must have been a ceremonial branding. The idea of how much they had hurt sent a new hatred for the priests of Asherah through me, and I clenched my fists in and out as I had seen Josiah do so many times before.

Tirzah caught sight of this and cowered, hiding her face in her hands.

"No, dear, I'm not angry with you—please ..." I gently held her shoulders and caressed the scars. "I was only saddened by what they did to you—these must have been painful ..." I pulled her hands firmly away from her face and bent down so that her eyes were level with mine.

"I'll never harm you, Tirzah. I promise you—never. That's not why you're here."

A pained expression filled her face. She still did not trust me. *This is going to be laborious.*

Not wanting her to get chilled, I led her as gently as I could to the laver and helped her to step in, easing her down into the warm, perfumed water. I began to sponge it over her shoulders and hair, and she relaxed slightly, leaning back against the side of the copper basin. Handing the sponge to her, I got up to pick up her clothes from the floor.

*Well, I could have them washed, but what's the use?*

"Tirzah, look at your filthy rags," I said. She snapped her head up. "Just like your old life, we are going to get rid of this gown, and I'm going to give you new clothes—just like the LORD is going to give you a new life."

I tossed the gown into the fire and watched her while she gasped and met my gaze with shock, as if she felt betrayed.

"It's alright. That part of you is gone."

Just then, I recalled a passage of something Josiah had read to me once over dinner. He had brought a scroll with him that evening, as he did often. It was from Isaiah, the prophet to the great King Hezekiah. A part of what he read me that night applied directly to Tirzah's life at that very moment. I could almost recite it word for word because I had asked Josiah if I could write it down for my own prayers. Even as the words rolled off my tongue, it was almost as if God had spoken the words especially for her.

*"'The LORD will hold you in His hand for all to see—a splendid crown in the hand of God. Never again will you be called "The Forsaken City" or "The Desolate Land." Your new name will be "The City of God's Delight" and "The Bride of God," for the LORD delights in you and will claim you as His bride. Your children will commit themselves to you, O Jerusalem, just as a young man commits himself to his bride. Then God will rejoice over you as a bridegroom rejoices over his bride.'"*

"Tirzah, you don't have to be forsaken or desolate any longer. If you will turn to God and obey Him alone, He will delight in you like you're His bride. I know it's hard to imagine right now, but you'll see." She fidgeted in the water, uncomfortable under my direct stare, but I continued, "He rescued you for a reason, and He can restore what was stolen from you. Whenever you're ready to turn to Him, He will be more than ready to welcome you into His arms and call you His child."

But it was too much for her to absorb all at once. She looked back at me under a furrowed brow and then glanced back down at the water. Realizing her limits, I washed her hair with jasmine oil and soap, and I prayed that her pain would rinse off of her heart as easily as the suds flooded off of her hair when I poured the water from the pitcher down her back.

She stepped out tentatively when I held up her towel, and then I wrapped it securely around her shoulders. I had brought my favorite fragrant oils with me and began to rub some onto her back and then bent down to take her feet. But she drew her foot back from me before I could touch it.

"No." It was the only word she had spoken to me since she told me her name in the courtyard.

"I don't mind, Tirzah." I lifted her calf and spread the lotion down her ankle and over the rough soles of her feet. "I haven't always been a queen, you know. I used to rub oil into my sister's feet after we came in from taking care of our sheep. Don't think of me as anything special— I'm just as human as you are."

She relinquished her foot into my hands after a moment and closed her eyes as I massaged her instep. I worked the magnolia oil into her other foot and her legs, and then I proceeded to pour some into her hands to rub over her arms.

"Well, I must say," I teased as I stood, "you do *smell* like a new woman." I shot her a grin, as I turned to put away the soaps, oils, and lotions, noting her slight smile as well.

The guard brought her meal, and I managed to give her a few bites before she stifled a yawn behind her hand. Since she was visibly exhausted from traveling here and adjusting to her surroundings, I showed her to the bed and forced her to lie down in it. From the way she resisted, I had a feeling she would have slept on the marble floor if I had let her. She still did not feel worthy of the royal treatment, and I didn't blame her. I might have felt the same had I been in her place. I stroked her back and prayed that she would not have any nightmares.

I didn't return to my mother's room until after I heard Tirzah's slow, steady breathing and felt her body relax under my hands.

# 17. JOSIAH

If the first few weeks of cleansing the nation were exciting, thrilling, and promising, the months that followed were nothing short of exhausting. As spring turned into summer, our energy began to wane, and we were drained by the tedium of smashing idol after idol, destroying shrine after shrine, and burning altar after altar. In the evenings, my soldiers, priests, and servants fell into their beds on the verge of fainting from the heat, and I began to doubt whether my own resolutions would be enough to sustain them. As we moved from north to south and then back north once we hit Kadesh Barnea, the sweltering waves of heat reflected off of the desert sands while the skin-reddening sun provided a double attack. I found myself begging the LORD for the relief of a simple breeze but was not granted any comfort.

The two most rewarding demolitions had been that of the altar of Molech in the Hinnom Valley, and the temple of Baal in Jerusalem. I was more pleased to see those atrocities burn than any others. There was a deep satisfaction welling up from the pit of my gut, and a literal unwinding of the tense muscles in my neck as I gazed into the coals. It was as if something that had been twisting and grinding in my mind had finally been unraveled, and I could at last breathe deeply without the catch of anxiety in my lungs.

If this was not what I was made to do, I doubted there was any purpose at all for my life. If burning false gods and their detestable temples was my reason for drawing breath, I thanked God for it every day. On the hottest, most punishing days, I thanked Him even then.

Every idol I destroyed was one that could no longer rob Jehovah of praise. Every shrine and temple I burned was one less that could keep my subjects away from *Jehovah's* Temple.

But it became evident in the heat of those summer months that without my commands, cleansing the nation was the furthest thing from anyone's mind. Though a commander and a sentry were sent ahead of us to each town and village to prepare the people for our arrival, the false priests and idolaters were surprised almost every time we arrived with our crushing stones and flames. It was as though they had to watch me destroy them to believe that I would.

On our way from Beersheba to Gath, as we passed through the dry forests near the Philistine borders, I expected to meet an ambush party at any moment. Acbor ordered several scouts to move ahead of us in all directions, but the only suspicious activity they found was a caravan ambush just shy of the border. Our scouts ordered them with threats to retreat off of our land, and they were happy to heed the warnings.

We pressed on into the dry heat and brush, rounding the plateau ridge in the east. Though Judah's ever-changing terrain had been my heritage and home all of my life, I viewed the scenery with fresh awe and astonishment. My guard had stopped with me as I stared, but I waved them on ahead so I could take a moment to observe what God had fashioned in the distance. Several bluffs rose up violently from the plains in contrasting colors of grays and browns, only to end just as suddenly near the clouds in squared-off peaks, as if God had sawed off the tops of the mountains to make tables for Himself. I stood in wonder at the Maker and His amazing ability to create beauty in the midst of a bleak desert. *LORD, would You make something beautiful of Your people, just as You have of our land? Show them how You can be the God of their longing.*

In Gath, I saw the first evidence of my people beginning to understand our quest. A few who feared the LORD heard of our arrival by way of our sentry, and they made our intentions widely known in the town. As we set up the camp, the crushing stones, and the fire pit, men and women came bearing their idols to be destroyed.

We all looked at them askance, obviously unaccustomed to surrender when we previously had been confiscating all the idols and shrines by force. One man bowed before me, holding up his golden statue of Ashtoreth, the detestable goddess of the Sidonians from the north.

"What say you, man?" I asked.

He swallowed loudly and then confessed, "We swear allegiance to you, King Josiah, for it is you who sent seed-grain to our village when disease killed our crops these past three years." He shuffled closer to me to lay the statue at my feet. "If you want our gods, you may have them, as long as we retain your favor."

I combed my mind to recall what he was talking about, and suddenly remembered the brave youth from Gath who had come to my judgment court one afternoon last spring on behalf of his family, unbeknownst to anyone in the village. He had only asked for enough grain for his widowed mother and five siblings, explaining the strange death of all of the crops in the region, but I had seen it fit in Jerusalem's abundance to send enough to feed as many people of the village as possible, and with seed to plant as well.

Nodding in remembrance, I corrected the man before me: "It is not allegiance to me that I seek, but your allegiance to God Almighty. And keep my favor in return for your willingness to renounce your false religion, but I ask you now to seek the favor of Jehovah. Come to the fire this afternoon to hear the readings from His prophets, and bring as many people of the town as will come. God seeks your repentance, and I am grateful for your surrender." I picked up the statue and tossed it casually beside the stones that the workers had recently removed from their carts.

Turning to face the rest of them, I shouted, "If you are willing to surrender your shrines and statues, place them next to the large stones. If you are hiding any household gods, we will find them and destroy them, along with any Asherah poles or trees. The more cooperation we get from you, the less force will be necessary."

Our work in Gath was completed in one day, whereas other towns and cities had taken several days before I felt peace to move on. Many people came to hear Shaphan read from Isaiah's scroll and listen to me plead with them to seek the God of Abraham, Isaac, and Jacob. Although I still suspected that some kept hidden idols in their homes or fields, as I did in every place we cleansed, Gath was a pleasant stop simply because of their cooperation. On top of the thrill of melting the figurines and cutting down Asherah poles and groves, I had an added satisfaction of believing that my subjects might one day know and obey the LORD.

# 18. HAMUTAL

"You should see her, Mother; she's so scared."

"Where is she from? Is she a Judean? An Israelite? A foreigner?"

"I have no idea. She hasn't really been able to talk yet." I sighed helplessly and sank back next to her in the bed. There were so many things for me to worry about, and my mind was cluttered. It was as if I couldn't concentrate on any one problem for long enough to find the solutions. What should I do about my father? *Send the royal physician home with my mother next week?* And what of Hannah, who had rushed back to Libnah after our spat? *Should I go to her and Matthias and beg them to turn back to Jehovah, if only for their own safety?* And now there was Tirzah. *What could I do to reach her through the stone wall she had set up around her heart?*

"Would you like to pray, Love?"

"Oh, Mother, that's exactly what I need. Let's go to the Temple now. I'm sure it's not too late. We can pray and offer a sacrifice and see what Josiah has done." I sat up excitedly to get dressed and cleanse myself.

"Wait, Hamutal, that's not what I meant. Why don't we pray here? God can hear us, you know. His ears work all over His earth, not only in the Temple." She raised her eyebrows and knelt beside the bed. Though I desperately wanted to be near the Presence again, I could not argue with my mother's reasoning.

"You're right. We can always go tomorrow."

"Let's pray together—like we did when you were little. Do you remember how much you used to talk to Him? I would catch you in the meadow with the sheep, just having a little conversation with Him, like He was one of your playmates. I didn't know whether to scold you for being silly, or praise you for praying so much."

"Thank you for not scolding me, Mother. I've always loved talking to Him—both our memorized prayers and the ones that come from my heart. I wish I still talked to Him that much. It would no doubt help me to stop worrying the way I do. If I can't fix things, there is always One who can, right?" I knelt beside her on the floor the way my father had taught me, facing the window that was nearest the Temple.

"Absolutely," she said.

"God Almighty …" I began, and did not stop until all my fears and doubts were dissolved in my faith of His power and worth. I asked for Josiah's protection, Hannah and Matthias's repentance, my father's health to be restored, the nation's reforms, Tirzah's healing and surrender, my sons and their own devotion, and my admitted inability to hold all of it together—that was His work, not mine.

When I was finished, I looked back up at my mother, who wore a smile full of wisdom. I laughed softly at her innate ability to know what was needed. I could only hope to be as full of understanding someday.

"So, what did you do today?" I asked. "Did you see the king as he swept through in a whirlwind?"

She nodded, understanding my disappointment. "I caught a glimpse of the two of you in the courtyard from my window. He's still so besotted with you, Love. I think he spent just as many minutes kissing you as he did speaking with you."

I touched my lips in memory of him and sighed.

She winked and hugged my shoulders. "I was in your garden today with the children. I've never seen anything so spectacular in all my life."

"Yes, the bulbs must be blooming already, aren't they?"

"You mean to tell me you haven't seen them yet?" Her surprise bordered on insult, as if I had betrayed the blooms by not visiting them.

I shook my head in regret. "Not this spring. I've just been so busy, I've honestly forgotten them."

In years past, I could not be kept away from the extravagant terrace, spending every moment I could there, especially the long afternoons and evenings when Josiah was busy with delegations and council meetings. That year, I had all but forgotten its draw; but her reminder beckoned me to a memory of Josiah and I during our first fall together, planting the hyacinths, tulips, and daffodils among the already established lilies. He had them imported from the East when he noticed how I adored the other flowers. We were going to let the gardener plant them, but I insisted that Josiah get his hands dirty with me. Though he refused at first, he enjoyed himself in the end.

"When do you think they'll bloom?" he had asked, doubt in his voice over whether the strange brown and purple knots could produce anything as beautiful as I had promised. I knelt to face him on the earth.

"Not until the spring. You'll just have to be patient."

"I'm not very good at waiting, Angel," he said.

"Yes, I'm aware." I smirked and wiped a smudge of dirt off of his cheek. He took my hand and began to kiss my wrist and forearm, which brought a tickle from his beard, and a laugh escaped my throat.

"You're the most beautiful thing in this world," he said as his eyes moved from my arm to my face.

"You say that every day."

"I can't help it if I adore you," he said, acting quite offended. "Would you like me to stop saying it?"

I shook my head. He pulled me on top of his chest as he leaned back against a large olive tree. His hands drew circles on my back as my head found the familiar crook between his shoulder and his chest. We lay there for a long time until he had to leave me for a meeting with Jeremiah.

I fell asleep under the tree and didn't stir until that evening when I awoke to his laugh above me.

"My Queen, did you overexert yourself today? I shall have to tell the foreman to lighten your workload," he said, chuckling, and then resumed his place next to me as I yawned.

"What a pampered palace brat I've become! Napping until dark ..."

"You wanted to become more than a shepherdess, didn't you?"

"I don't think this is what I had in mind," I said, rolling my eyes.

"Well, I can't say I'm disappointed to find you where I left you." And his lips found mine in the darkness of the sunset ...

I treasured the memory of our love in our garden and hugged the impression of his body against mine. Perhaps that was one reason I hadn't gone yet this spring: it just wasn't as beautiful without my king to share it with me.

\* \* \*

As I said farewell to my mother and siblings a few days later, I put on a smile, though all I wanted to do was cry. They had to get back to my father, and I wanted to go with them. But I was dubious to leave Tirzah alone, and she was still too unstable to travel with me to Libnah. I was spending almost all hours of the day with her, neglecting my houseguests to tend to her.

"Don't fret," my mother said. "We've had a wonderful time. She won't let anyone else in, you know. And her life is so much more important than our entertainment—that's obvious. When she's doing better, you can bring her to Libnah and we can be together again. Your father wants to see you too, Love, so come as soon as you think she's ready. Alright?" She shook my shoulders gently and turned her chin down to eye me expectantly.

"Thank you for understanding. I'll be out as soon as I can, and I'll bring the boys, too." I clutched her to my chest and considered my dilemma. I had specifically asked God to use me in His plan, had I not? And now that He had given me a husband to encourage, two sons to mold into heirs to the throne, a palace and kingdom to influence, and now the life of a young woman who teetered on the edge of losing her mind, I wanted to take it all back. I wanted to crawl back to my mother's lap and retract my lofty request.

Heavy as the burden was, I couldn't bring myself to refuse His bidding. LORD, *I'm overwhelmed. I don't know how to do any of these things well. I'd rather not do them at all. But I love You too much to quit on anyone. I'll do my best, but I need Your help. I surrender—You're in control here, not me. I know you can take the evil around me and turn it into something good—just like you did for our ancestor Joseph when he was in Egypt. I am nothing without You, Jehovah. But with You, I believe all things are possible. There is no limit to Your power.*

"Give Abba my love," I choked, letting go of her quickly, and nearly pushing her away.

Everyone waved from the carriage, and I finally put my arm down when they were out of sight beyond the cloud of dust and the grove of trees in the distance. That was the first hot day of spring—the first taste of the heat that would grow more and more sweltering, until men would swipe the sweat from foreheads and beards, and women would take afternoon naps in the shade to escape the stifling winds.

That same heat would drive me nearly mad.

# 19. JOSIAH

Not every town showed the same allegiance as Gath, but a few of them came close. As we made our way through Beth-Ezel, and neared the town of Bozkath, the heat of the August sun became nearly unbearable under our loads of precious metal, wood, and tents. We lost several camels, oxen, and donkeys to the heat, and planned to purchase animals to replace them. As the stone dwellings of Bozkath appeared in the valley, we all breathed a collective sigh of relief.

An older man came out to greet us and offered his home for me to bathe and rest. Asaiah insisted that I take a reprieve and promised to find the public baths for the rest of the troops before beginning the cleansing the following morning. After refusing a guard or escort, I consented to his suggestion, and asked the man who hobbled before me his name as I followed him to his home.

"The name's Adaiah," he said, "Your Majesty's humble servant." His gait was broken and labored, and though I understood his difficulty, I couldn't help but wish he would lead me to his bath and bed a little quicker.

"I appreciate your generous offer. We've been on the road for several days without rest. I hope my men find hospitality in the city as well."

"We've all been expecting you, my lord." He looked back at me with a half-smile and a nod. "Especially your servant."

His sly tone caught my attention. "What did you say your name was, again?"

"Adaiah. Do you know it?"

"I do, but I can't say from where. Have we met?"

He turned around to stop and look at me in the face. There was something familiar about him. Something about his features, something in his deep brown eyes staring back at me with a lack of the subservient fear to which I was accustomed.

"No, Your Highness, we never have." His voice dripped with too much regret.

We arrived at his home within a few minutes, and he led me to a seat where a servant girl immediately appeared and knelt to wash my feet, removing the sandals nearly etched into my flesh. Her soothing touch eased my pain, and I forced my thoughts to Hamutal as best as I could. Six months on the road without her had suddenly taken its toll, and in that moment, I wished more than ever that I could finish this mission and be done once and for all with the traveling, burning, and lecturing. The girl's hands moved up to my calves, and I pulled away quickly.

"Thank you, that is fine."

Adaiah led a small woman to me. Her eyes were graying with age and her hand, which gripped his, was twisted from years of work. Nonetheless, her face was kind and warm, and a hospitable smile accentuated the excitement in her eyes.

"My King, permit me to introduce my wife, Danelle. When we heard you were coming to our city, the two of us agreed it would be of highest privilege to host your stay, however long that may be. There were rumors that you camp with your men, however—."

"I have been, yes."

"Would you reconsider your policy, at least for this evening? Danelle has prepared a lovely meal—surely better than camp food, but perhaps not as extravagant as the palace feasts."

Both of their faces pleaded with me to accept, and Danelle's hands were even clasped, as if in prayer.

"I'll consider it. The reason I've been dining and sleeping with my men rather than paying an innkeeper or requesting a host for myself is because their faithfulness to my mission does not go unseen or unrewarded. I have no desire to flaunt my authority and privilege in front of them when they are giving up so much to serve me—to serve the

Lord," I corrected myself. "I'm sure you can understand how that hardly seems appropriate."

I sighed as they nodded in understanding.

"Let me see what kind of accommodations Bozkath can offer the rest of them. Perhaps if they can find comfortable lodging and food, I can stay here in your home. I would appreciate that bath, however, regardless."

"Of course, Your Highness, of course. Right this way ..."

After enjoying the warm, floral water and indulging in the myrrh and frankincense oils for my hair and beard, I finally emerged from his bathhouse into the courtyard of their home. I thanked Danelle and Adaiah extensively and asked if they had a servant who could act as a messenger to Asaiah and my men.

"Your guard is at the gate now, requesting orders," Adaiah said.

I stepped outside of their doorway to a freshly bathed messenger and two clean-scented guards standing post. A pleased smile filled my face, and I said, "At ease, Dalit. I've found a place to stay here. Did you find enough accommodations for everyone in the city? We don't have to camp tonight if you have."

"I was hoping you would say as much, sire. We have found several inns. We've all had a bath and the offer of a decent meal. Asaiah sends word that we are ready to set up camp, though, if you command."

"Not at all. Everyone deserves a rest. A bed and a meal for every man! See to it that I pay for everyone, understood?"

"Yes, Your Majesty! Most generous, Your Highness! Is there anything else?" If the other men were as excited as this young runner, I would be the hero of the day. I did think of one limit to their indulgence, though.

"Yes, there is, Dalit—*no women*," I said clearly and slowly.

"I understand." His disappointment was not hidden, but neither did it appear he expected anything different. "I will relay the message to every man. Thank you, once again."

He ran off quickly, though I thought he was more skipping than running. I dismissed my guards as well, who trotted off after minimal reassuring that Danelle and Adaiah hardly seemed the assassin type.

I stepped back into their home and told them I would indeed be able to stay the night, thanking them once again for their hospitality.

"The honor is all ours," Adaiah said. "You grace us with your presence. Please, come and sit at the table—the meal is nearly ready."

I sank onto the pillows around the table and drank the smooth wine. I speculated that it must have been the best they owned, something they had saved for a special occasion.

"Now, tell me where I might know you from, Adaiah" I asked once he had filled my goblet again. "Have you ever been to Jerusalem?"

"Not for many years. The last time I was in the great city was when my daughter was married. Perhaps you may have known her ..." The twinkle in his eyes was unmistakable.

"Perhaps. What was her name?"

"Jedidah."

I inhaled sharply, catching the wine I had just swallowed and began to cough uncontrollably. I had not heard or spoken my mother's name since she had been murdered with my father. Could these people really be my grandparents?

After a few more moments of hacking, I was finally able to speak again. "Are you saying that your daughter married my father, Ammon?"

"That's the man I gave her to, though I can't say it was the best decision I ever made for her."

I wanted to ask why they had never come to Jerusalem to visit me, or at least lay claim to some riches for being royal in-laws. I also wanted to ask how their daughter, my mother, had won the heart of the king. Was theirs an arranged marriage? Was this couple who sat before me of nobility? So many questions swarmed in my mind, and I didn't know which one to ask first. Instead I sat there in bewilderment.

"I take it your mother never said anything about us to you, my King," Danelle said.

"She may have ... I can't remember for certain. But now come to think of it, she did talk about her home here in Bozkath. She wanted to bring me here once when I was about four or five years old, but King Manasseh would not allow it. Shortly after that, my father became king, and there were too many threats on our lives to even think of leaving the palace. I've always believed all my relatives were gone." At that point, I could not help but stand and embrace them both.

Danelle reached her hands up to my face and patted my cheeks gently. "My son."

Though I wanted to know so much more, I sat through almost the entire meal in silence, not knowing where to begin. The three of us just kept looking at one another in disbelief.

"The food is wonder—"

"How have your travels—"

I chuckled. "Go ahead."

"No, no—please, you first," Adaiah said.

"Thank you for the meal; it is delicious—especially compared to the dried beef and hard rolls I've been used to for the past months. I'd almost begun to forget what a proper meal should taste like."

Danelle beamed a proud smile at me as she scooped more potato cakes and stewed lamb onto my dish.

"Oh, that's plenty. I won't be able to get up from this cushion if I eat much more!"

"Tell me of your travels, unless that information is classified, of course." His robe had fallen open as he reclined back onto the pillows behind him. His obvious informality and friendliness cheered me, encouraging me to trust him.

"The heat of the summer sun on the loose and rocky hills of this region are unforgiving at best. I pine after my wife like I never expected I would. My company is weary and often disgruntled by our incessant stop-and-go pace. In almost every town and village, I come across someone who tries to assassinate me. I've become overwhelmed by how much more ground I have yet before me. And I've discovered there's nothing I enjoy more than watching idols burn in the flames of a fire I've lit. All in all, I'd say it's going quite well," I added with a slight shrug.

Both of them stifled a snigger and shook their heads in sympathy, as if they were connected by unseen strings that held them in unison.

"How far will you go?" Danelle asked.

"As far north as I can, to be honest. Bethel seems to be a natural stopping point, as it is our northernmost city. But I've been hearing more and more rumors of the Assyrians retreating from Israel. My ambassador to Samaria reports they are gathering their troops in preparation to fight the encroaching Babylonians, though it's merely speculation at this point. If I find unoccupied territory up there, though, I just might keep going. Israel is part of our Promised Land, you know—it always has been. God planned for His people to conquer all of this territory, not just the Southern Kingdom ..." I stopped, realizing I was giving a history lesson to people of a generation who should have been teaching me. They both looked at me expectantly, however, clearly not offended.

"But, Your Highness, if you are already weary of this mission, why push yourself? Wouldn't all of Judah be enough?"

"We'll see." I don't know why I expected them to share my zeal just because they were my mother's parents, but this clear lack of enthusiasm chafed me. Though I dreaded their answer, I had to inquire of their loyalties. "Do you serve the Most High?"

"Jehovah?" he asked. I nodded. "There was once a time I would go to the Temple for holidays, but I never worshipped him exclusively. King Manasseh was so open, you see. He encouraged his subjects to explore all faiths. Yahwism seemed so restrictive to me. So many rules to follow—eat this meat, prepared this way on this day, but not that day. Cut your beard, but not on the sides; wash your hands in this special water; clean your robes before you go to Temple; bring your best lamb, no spots. I couldn't keep up with it—too hard!"

"So you gave up on Him? Because of what He asked of you?" The disappointment in my voice was much more evident than I desired.

"I suppose that's why. I really don't bow down to any gods anymore. They never did anything that I asked of them anyway. I never had the sons I prayed for when I sacrificed to Asherah. My crops died shortly after I married off Jedidah, depleting my herds as well. Baal certainly did not answer my prayers for prosperity of the land. And all of the others seem to want money or sex or food offerings. They're statues—what could it matter to them?"

"What, indeed," I muttered. And I had no idea how to convince this dear, generous couple of their mistake to reject the Sovereign LORD along with the trash of idolatry. I somehow knew that no matter what I did or said, that rejection was final. And it hurt.

# 20. HAMUTAL

The hot wind whipped our skirts as I dragged Tirzah up the Temple Mount. Her feet slowed with each step, but my determination assured that her hand never left my grip. After months of coaxing her from her shell, she finally began to talk about her life, and she was able to put into words the brutality God had shown me in my visions. Each day, we would read from David's Psalms or from Isaiah's scrolls and drink in the sweet Word together. And each day, she would soften a little more, the light coming back into her eyes and the color returning to her cheeks.

"You're going to love it—it's so different from what you remember."

"But my memories are the same," she said.

"Tirzah—please … give Him a chance. The LORD desires to show Himself as good to all of His children."

She said no more but continued to drag her feet. I had waited on this day for weeks—the day when I thought she was finally ready to return to the Temple. As we drew nearer to His Presence, I could feel the anticipation rise onto my skin. The walls that I found so comforting and safe were the same that had held her in a prison of torture and shame. As I put my arm around her shoulders to offer reassurance, I felt her shudder. I watched her gaze race back and forth across the walls and gates of the Temple Mount and felt her heartbeat quicken beneath my fingers.

"Tirzah—remember your new identity. You are no longer that other woman. You are an honored guest of the queen. My friend. And one who seeks the God of Heaven's Armies." I spoke in steady calming tones and she began to breathe in rhythm again.

Our entourage went before us and followed behind as well. All eyes were on me as we approached the Porch of Solomon and passed through the gates into the courtyard. Tirzah kept her eyes downcast on the marble floors, refusing to look at the place where she had been sold time after time. I touched the arm of my guard, Ruben, asking him to tell the priests and temple scribes not to stare at me or Tirzah, and to allow us to bring our sacrifices without extra attention. Ruben nodded and left my side to speak with Hilkiah.

"The Presence of Jehovah rests within a secret room in the Temple," I said, pointing into the darkened building past the pillars.

"Will it come out here?"

"No, Tirzah. The Presence doesn't leave the Ark of the Covenant. If we were to see Him, we would die. But His Spirit is here, and He'll come close, though not in all of His splendor. He needs to protect us from all of Himself. That's just how powerful Jehovah is. He can only reveal Himself in part."

I reached inside to my deepest understanding of Him to try to explain the unexplainable.

"Try not to be scared, but keep a reverent fear, my dear. The racing in your heart as you draw closer to His glory should never wane. Here, feel mine." I placed her hand on my chest below my collarbone. Her face jumped up to mine in surprise.

"Yes, I'm fearfully excited as well. This is a Holy Place—the home of a Holy God. But I've learned to manage my fear so that it draws me closer to Him rather than frightening me away. He doesn't want to scare us—He wants us to honor Him for who He is, for how majestic and loving the LORD has always been and will be forever."

She shivered and we knelt together before the altar. The courtyard was now pleasantly emptied of everything but the necessities. Josiah had removed all extraneous altars, statues, and other fixtures. All that remained was the altar, the lamp stands, and the laver. To me, the emptiness felt so clean, so ready, so surrendered. My king had done a good work for his people. I felt privileged to be counted as one of his subjects and his queen.

Tirzah survived her first sacrifice, though only just barely. During the songs and prayers, I fought to focus on God rather than on her trembling beside me, but by the time our lambs were led to the altar, I was aware of nothing but His restoration over me. His healing peace flooded my conscious as it did each time I knelt there. I inhaled Him and prayed He would wash over Tirzah, too.

"There, now, that wasn't so painful, was it?" I asked as we stepped outside the gate.

"Painful—no. Frightening—yes." She tucked a strand of her flaming hair behind her ear and gripped the edge of the limestone wall as she stepped off the porch onto the gravel path.

I looped my arm in hers and felt like skipping down the hill in triumph. "But you saw how wonderful it is to praise Him, did you not? How thrilling it is just to be near His Spirit and sing our sweet psalms that I taught you at home in the palace? Tell me you didn't feel His love today."

"Well, I didn't feel unwanted ... or wanted for the wrong reasons."

"I guess that's a start," I said with some disappointment.

If only she knew how much He could offer. If only I could make her see His loving kindness. She would know Him only when she chose to seek Him. And nothing I did would force that. In fact, I had to be careful not to end up pushing her further away.

"So, you'll come back with me tomorrow?"

"How about next week?" she said.

"I suppose I'll take what I can get."

\* \* \*

As I was putting the boys to bed that night, Jehoahaz asked once again for Josiah.

"Abba comes tomorrow?"

"No, my Prince, not tomorrow," I replied with a pout.

"Next year?"

I laughed. "It better not be next year!" His little mind still held no comprehension of time. If not tomorrow, it might as well be forever. "Would you like me to read the letter to you again?" He nodded his head enthusiastically.

"May I read it, Mama?" Eliakim asked.

"Oh, of course, my little scribe. Go right ahead," I said, but I suspected that he would be reciting rather than actually reading. At five years old, he was so very intelligent, though, I couldn't be sure. He kept amazing his tutors by his rapid advancement. I handed him the scroll with the king's seal.

"'A message for the Princes of Judah,'" he began shyly.

"Go on, dear, that's right ..." I coaxed.

> "'Brave Sons—your kingdom is grand and vast. Once I have cleansed it, I will show it all to you. What a grand adventure we will have! Climbing the hills, crossing the dunes, exploring the valleys and streams—such thrills we'll see. I hope you are taking good care of your mother and being on your best behavior while I am away.
>
> "'I must tell you of a sand scorpion I saw today—the biggest I've ever seen. He crept out of the sand near the pit where we were burning the idols, and by chance caught his stinger on fire. I wish you could have seen him dance! He hopped back and forth across the pebbles, holding his flaming tail as high as it would reach, as if he was waving a banner. My men and I laughed until our bellies ached!
>
> "'Rest assured that I am safe and in good health. Aside from this blasted summer heat, I am enjoying myself as I watch the false gods of our kingdom burn in the blue and orange flames of our fires. I hope you are well and in good health, also. You are both sure to have grown a cubit by the time I see you this winter!
>
> "'If all goes as planned, I should be able to return in Shevat, but it could be longer if God desires to send me into Israel or Samaria. I will keep asking Him.
>
> "'Kiss your mother for me. I will ask her to do the same for you. And don't you worry, because I'll have plenty of gifts for all of you when I return.
>
> "'Peace and love, Abba.'"

"Wonderful reading, son."

"Again!" pleaded Jehoahaz.

"That's enough for tonight—it's late," I said.

"When is Shevat?" Eliakim asked for the tenth time.

"In about five more months. Not too much longer now."

"I wish Shevat was tomorrow," he replied quietly.

"So do I, son. So do I. Mama misses him too." *Strength, LORD … please.* "Do you remember why Abba is away? What he's doing?"

"Burning the gods!" Jehoahaz exclaimed with a fist in the air.

I couldn't suppress my laughter at this enthusiasm. "Yes, that's right! He's making your kingdom clean before Jehovah—getting it ready for your rule one day."

"There's lots of gods to burn, huh, Mama?" said Eliakim.

"Sadly, yes. Our people have rejected the God of our forefathers and have chosen instead to bow to the gods of the nations that surround us. Do you understand why this is wrong?" Eliakim shook his head, though I know I had explained it several times. "What did Mama say about the prophets?" Shrugs.

I exhaled my breath through puffed cheeks. "They tell us of Jehovah's jealous heart. He wants all of our worship and all of our devotion—not just some, or even most of it. We must follow His ways and His commands and realize that others are but empty statues made by wood carvers or metal workers. They make their gods, but Our God made us. So the king is destroying all of those statues, and soon the people of our kingdom will turn to Jehovah. Right?" Nods.

"Good night, my sweet boys. I'll see you tomorrow." I kissed each of them on the nose and moved to walk out, but Jehoahaz held my frock.

"Wait, Mama!"

"What now, Jeho?"

"Abba said to kiss you for him," he said and then puckered his soft pink mouth.

# 21. JOSIAH

A false sense of accomplishment plagued me as we neared Bethel on the twelfth of Shevat. My company was expressing eagerness to finish the mission here at our northern border, but my plan was to press on into Samaria if we could bear the cold months in our tents. When summer had finally surrendered to the crisp breezes of fall and winter, we had all found a fresh revitalization, and I prayed it would last until the LORD gave me our leave.

Though I longed for the comforts of the palace, and I dreamt of Hamutal each night, I refused to give up when we were so close to completion. I commenced to giving daily motivational speeches to the men and promising lucrative incentives for those who persevered without grousing.

But as we neared Bethel, I sensed a different atmosphere than what we had previously encountered. God stirred in my spirit a strange caution. The discontent was reminiscent of my early years as king before I had encountered Him.

I pleaded with the LORD for wisdom, and dismounting my chariot, I discovered the answer.

Several rows of limestone steps lined the hillside and led to the same point about two-thirds of the way up the mountain. From where I stood, I could see the towering altar, and as I ascended the stairs, a golden calf came into focus.

I stopped for a moment to catch my breath and noticed Jared, Asaiah, and Hilkiah looking around at the hillside with the same hesitation and apprehension. They guided the troops closer to the shrine and drew their swords in preparation.

Suddenly, out of one of the cave-like tombs strode a man dressed in highly ornamented robes, whom I assumed to be a priest. He walked out to meet me as I climbed the stairs. The foreboding in the moment was palpable, and I spoke a silent prayer under my breath to ask God what was different about this place.

**"Burn the rebellious nation,"** He spoke to my heart. It was the courage I needed.

I climbed higher still as I saw others join the priest from the cavern.

"Your Majesty, what brings you to Bethel?" the priest asked in feigned innocence.

"You know very well why I'm here." I looked to his armed priests who had drawn their swords halfway from their sheaths.

"Now, now, my King, we are harmless here. Why do you trouble our quiet lives with such raids?"

"You haven't seen trouble yet," I said through clenched teeth.

I calmed myself amidst my rage and carefully eyed the enemy. Among those who had emerged from the temple was a man I recognized but could not place. It was not until he spoke that I remembered him.

"You have no power over our gods, Your Highnessss," he hissed.

*Matthias!*

"Quiet!" the priest ordered. "My lord," he said, facing me once again. "Tell me exactly what you request, and I'll tell you what Baal requires. Perhaps there is some compromise we can come to—"

"I'm afraid not. Regardless of what you think that statue might want, the Living God alone is to be worshipped in Judah. I've outlawed idol worship in my nation. You may either hand over your statue and altar, or I'll be required to take them by force."

"But why the sudden change in the law?" asked the priest. "For years, your forefathers have allowed the people of Judah to choose their own gods. Since when does a king have the right to choose our god for us?"

"Since I took the throne," I said.

"And who gave you that authority, may I ask?"

"Jehovah."

"Well, I find it impossible to follow the commands of a god I can't even see or touch," he said. "How am I supposed to believe that some invisible voice told you to destroy my beloved Baal, the deity I've served for years—the authority that protects me and blesses my family?"

His blasphemy lit a fuse in my gut, and my voice came louder than I intended when I spoke. "I honestly don't care how you believe it; only that you do. 'Behold, Israel, the LORD your God is One,'" I quoted. "The God of our ancestors is the only true God—He is the Creator, the Beginning and the End. He is a jealous God, and your worship of that atrocity has enraged His anger against you," I said as I pointed at the calf.

"With all due respect, Your Majesty, I find that preposterous—" the priest said.

Matthias interjected, "How can that be true if we've been so prosperous in serving Baal? We're wealthier now than we've ever been as a people. We have more cattle and livestock in the nation than we've had in years, and our neighboring nations are vying for our trading caravans. There has been nothing but happiness since Baal has been honored in Bethel and the rest of Judah. Why should we give up his prosperity for you?"

"Think again, you fool!" I shouted. "If you have anything at all, it is from Jehovah, who owns the cattle on every hill. He's the maker of livestock and harvests. And if you don't credit Him, at least acknowledge that two years ago Bethel faced a crippling famine and these people only survived because I sent them food from the storehouses in the palace. You'd better get your facts straight, young man, if you're planning to contest me."

"The *fact* is that we don't care who you are—we'll defend our god to our deaths!" Matthias shouted back, fully drawing his sword now.

"Young apprentice," warned the priest again, but he was too late.

"Have it your way," I shouted back, enjoying too much that I was going to put his arrogance where it belonged.

I drew my sword just as the first arrows whizzed past me to strike down every man exposed on the hillside, including Matthias and the priest. As they toppled down the hill, a second set of men emerged from the caves in the hillside with swords in hand, shouting and chanting the name of their god.

I lunged at the man closest to me, blocking his swing with my shield and plunging my sword into his chest. Jared was on my heels, and Asaiah was right beside me, striking down with ease every zealot who dared face us. They were priests and farmers, not soldiers, and it showed.

I'd like to say that I felt some remorse or sorrow at the ease with which we killed those men, but when I searched my heart in that moment, all I found was the morbid satiation of my rage. It refreshed me to throw off all restraint and any attempt at patience. As I looked into the eyes of those dying men—the ones I was killing and those all around me on that hillside—I saw nothing but rebellion put in its place. Justice. Revenge. Defense of the Good Name of Jehovah. And it felt right.

For a moment.

I looked up the hillside after several minutes of fighting to see the remainder of the priests and prophets running for their lives.

"Should we let them go, my lord?" Asaiah asked.

"No. Bring them back. Let no man escape the destiny he has chosen."

"Your Highness?"

"I have an idea. Just bring them back."

Taking a deep breath in the silence that followed, I looked at the macabre massacre on the hillside of Bethel with disgust. Most of the priests and guards were still, but a few were still groaning in their last bloody moments. Though I held little in common with them, I was acutely aware of our brotherhood. It was not Assyrians we had put to death today. They were my subjects, my countrymen—my should-have-been brothers.

*It didn't have to turn out like this,* I thought. I stood atop the stone steps and reached up to where the golden calf stood on his perch behind the altar. It was somewhat smaller than my son Eliakim, but it took all of my strength to topple it.

"That one's solid," I cried down to the metal workers who were beginning to ascend the hill and ready the site for destruction. The gold from this Baal would fund my army for an entire year or more.

"Jared, Acbor, Ahikam," I said.

"Sire?" they answered in unison.

"Find out what is in those caverns and give me report."

"Of course, my lord," they answered, setting off to climb the hill in bounding strides.

"Asaiah, ready the fire."

"Yes, Highness."

When all of the men were on task, I took one of the iron hammers we had used to smash the smaller statues and began to demolish the altar. I merely shook the stones the first time but then concentrated my aim and put all of my strength into the next swing. After several blows, the rocks began to crumble one at a time and fall off the altar in bits. Blow after blow, my fury exuded as I deliberated over the lives of the men lying on the ground all around me. The muscles in my arms and back grew fatigued after only a few moments, but the pain was cathartic—an exit for my disappointment and anger.

Jedaiah, one of the stone bearers, eventually wandered over to me with a bewildered look on his dusty face. He stood several inches taller than I, and his arms were approximately the size of my thighs. He carried with him an iron mallet larger than the one I had been swinging.

"Can I be of assistance, my King?"

"Yes, please," I said, huffing for breath. "Gather the men. Smash it to pebbles."

Asaiah suddenly appeared beside me and asked, "Where would you like the fire, my lord?"

"Here." I pointed to the growing pile of rubble. "But not until we're finished." I turned back to Jedaiah. "Leave no stone intact."

Never again would any of my subjects lose their lives and souls for the sake of this. When we were finished, there would be nothing here to worship, much less take notice of or even remember. I swung around to punish the altar again. The rhythmic sound of our pummeling was exploding music to my ears.

When my shoulders refused to swing the heavy hammer any longer, I stopped for a moment, tossed the iron to the side, and collapsed in the dried grass. Jared approached with a skin of water. I guzzled it quickly and nodded for his report.

"Bones. In all of them."

*Strange.* "That's all?" For some reason, I thought there would be more in the caverns than just tombs. More shrines, perhaps, or other statues. I was imagining something like the lamp stands, tables, and altars, as were in the depths of my own Temple.

"Just one Asherah pole on top of the hill, my lord. But all we found in the caves were human remains." I looked to Acbor and Ahikam, and they nodded in agreement.

Graves around the shrine; they must have all been worshippers of Baal. There was only one thing to do, and I dreaded it just as much as I felt compelled to complete it. Before I could commit such an atrocity against their remains, though, I had to be sure.

"Find me a citizen of Bethel, Acbor," I said. "Some old man who has seen many years. Someone who can tell us about who these people were. Bring him to me."

"Right away, sir," he said, turning on his heel and loping down the hill to the village.

He returned with five men who dropped to one knee when they saw me. I shot him a confused look and demanded an answer with my eyes. "They all insisted on coming, Your Majesty," he said in apology. "May I present the noble lords of Bethel."

Rising to greet me, they carefully took in the scene on the hillside that Acbor must have explained on the way. Nodding, they turned to one another with knowing sighs, glancing askance.

"We've been expecting you, my lord," said the man before me. Of all of them, he had the grayest hair, and his eyes were light blue with blindness. He leaned heavily on a walking stick as he approached with broken steps and turned to me with his withered face.

"Good, then," I answered and gestured at the fallen image, "you know this abomination is about to be destroyed."

"Yes, we knew you would burn the idol ..." He paused and looked at the bodies that littered the ground. "... and the priests."

But I hadn't even revealed that piece to my own assistants. "What did you say?"

He nodded his silver head slowly. With a careful step up to the mound beside me, he sighed and took in the sight of each lifeless body strewn about the dead grass.

"Can you tell me about the graves here?" I asked.

"All the caverns are filled with the bones of those who bowed to this god. They wanted to be buried close to the altar so Baal could lead them into the next world in safety."

"And what about that one?" I pointed up to a sealed tomb—the only covered grave on the hillside.

"That, my King, is the grave of the holy man who came here to pronounce judgment against Jeroboam, the first king to put a Baal here in Bethel."

I nodded carefully. This I had read in the palace records. Jeroboam was the first king of separatist Israel. He placed a new worship site in this very place so that his subjects would not return to Jerusalem to worship, and so kept their allegiance away from the throne of David.

"This man, a prophet of God, told the people that one day you would come to bring the fire of the LORD—the fire that would burn not only the statue, but the bones of its worshippers."

Now it was my turn to drop my jaw agape. So this wasn't my idea—it had been His all along.

**"Burn the rebellion in My land."**

"Yes, LORD," I said aloud, dismissing the confused eyes of the elderly men.

By now, the altar was satisfactorily demolished, and the men were helping Asaiah to prepare the fire atop the pieces. They threw dark acacia logs down first, followed by smaller branches and twigs from the brush for kindling.

"More trees!" shouted Asaiah down the line of my loyalists, who worked as one, tossing massive pieces of firewood to one another uphill to where we stood. This would be our biggest blaze since Topheth, and they were prepared. Once the pile of fuel was prepared in such a way as to burn long and hot, Asaiah handed me the torch, as always.

In the few seconds that lingered between the torch and the blaze, I thought strangely of Hamutal. With a sharp longing that suddenly

*Robyn Langdon*

emanated from my gut, I wished she could be by my side to see this bittersweet victory for God. That she could witness this day that I had worked so hard to accomplish. Her words rang in my ears again, as they had each day on this outrageous mission:

*"… burn every last one of them, so that the only God left will be the Real One."*

*Yes, my Angel. Every last one.*

I touched the torch to the kindling and motioned for everyone to stand back. As Asaiah helped the elders move up the hillside for a safer vantage, we all stood back a few paces as the flames climbed higher and consumed the first branches in a flourish. In an instant, I became those flames, melting into the wavering orange air and crackling loudly in fury. I was one with the fire, and it felt sweet to devour the air, the breeze, the wood. Hotter and hotter we burned, the fire and I.

"My lord, the statue?" Jared interrupted, bringing me back to my flesh.

"Yes, when you are ready."

When the disgusting defilement of gold began to melt into the refiner's pit—all of that yellow metal swimming and dripping and swirling—relief took over me like an amazing weight lifted off of my chest. Though previously imperceptible to me before that very moment, I had been breathing too shallowly. All of the sudden, hot air rushed into my chest, and it was as if the LORD had suddenly freed me from an unseen oppressor. I drank deeply of the roasting waves as I inhaled again and again.

No longer would people who should be bowing before Jehovah in His Temple kneel to this beast. It would never rob Him of worship again—ever.

*I've burned it, LORD, just as You commanded.*

**"And the bodies—to desecrate the altar and this unholy place."**

I almost argued. Thoughts of the families of these men cascaded into my mind—families who would have no remains of their loved ones to visit or mourn. But if that was the price Jehovah demanded, I would not withhold it from Him.

"Bring the bodies and bones, Acbor," I ordered. In my head, it came out clearly. In my ears, my voice sounded broken and afraid.

"Which ones, my lord?" he asked.

I looked into his curious eyes and envied him. Oh, how I wished in that moment that I could trade places with my newest general, to be the one receiving this order, not the one giving it. What if I hadn't heard God right? What we were about to do was no stroll in the garden, no mere target practice amongst sparring-mates. These were lives, souls, memories.

But Jehovah was God, and I was not. I was the one following orders. Acbor raised his eyebrows, waiting for my answer as I pondered.

"All of them. Throw them on the fire. And then bring out the bones from the graves. As many as you can remove."

Not a single man moved. They simply stared at me as if I were an apparition.

"Do it, and do not think. Jehovah's anger will be fed with the flames of their flesh. It will be cooled with the ashes of their bones. Israel and Judah will learn the price of their disregard. This is the beginning of the end, my friends. Do it, and do not think!" I repeated.

# 22. HAMUTAL

I readied my servants for our trip to Libnah. Mother had sent word that Father's health was worse, and I knew I had to go—with or without Tirzah. At the last minute she backed out, claiming she felt too ill to travel. I insisted she stay at the palace while we were away, and she reassured me that she would most likely stay in her room the whole week.

The boys kept getting caught in my skirts as I was packing our things and ordering the servants about. To the measure that I was distressed, they were equally excited.

"Go and get some of your scrolls, Eli. We'll read and write on the way."

"Yes, Mama," he said.

"Oh!" I turned and stumbled over Jehoahaz for the third time. "Jeho!" I shouted angrily.

"Sorry, Mama."

"Oh, child!" I stopped to exhale and draw a slow breath. "Mama needs to be able to pack our things now. You can't be following me everywhere. Just sit here on the bed ... and try to help me remember everything, please?" I worked to calm my voice and recall how my mother would handle her own tension.

Once everything was packed in the caravan bags and onto the camels, the boys and I ascended the royal carriage steps. I sighed heavily, waving to Tirzah and my treasured palace servants, and turned to shout our readiness to the driver, but the sight of Jeremiah running up to us stopped me.

"My Queen, please ... a moment ..."

"Stay in here, boys," I said.

I climbed back down from my seat to greet him with a loose embrace.

"Where are you off to today?"

"I travel to Libnah. My father's health is failing. This could be my last visit with him. Is there something you need from me, Prophet?"

Jeremiah hesitated. His eyes diverted to the carriage where the boys peeked their heads out from the curtained openings.

"How are the princes, my lady?"

"They are well, though they miss their father. I'm afraid I'm not as enjoyable a playmate as he is. But they lack for nothing else. Why do you ask?"

Jeremiah took my elbow and pulled me farther away from listening ears, into the shade of a nearby fig tree. "As you know, my lady, I've been in the wilderness, seeking the LORD," he began. His eyes beamed straight into mine.

I sighed in frustration. "Please, Jeremiah, can this perhaps wait until I return—we must make Libnah in good time—"

"I'll only be a few moments. To get straight to the point, I need to warn you of what Jehovah has shown me—the vision of Judah."

Now he held my attention. "Yes?"

"It is quite bleak, Hamutal. We are all besieged and carried off ..."

He trailed off, though I willed him to finish.

"What! When? Should I not travel today? Should we summon the king home immediately—" I asked.

"No—not today. He returns when he finishes Jehovah's work. It is for your sons I am most concerned, for it is they who were wearing the crowns in my vision."

"What ... What does that mean? What are you saying? Are my children in danger?" I clutched his robe and demanded an answer—not from Jeremiah—but from God Himself.

The priest held my shoulders. Perhaps he thought I might swoon. "Queen Hamutal, please. I don't mean to alarm you. There's no need to call in the cavalry. This vision was far into the future—years down the path of our lives. But you know that the fate of our nation rides on the faithfulness of our king, do you not?"

What was he saying? That Josiah was not faithful to the LORD? I knew no other man who loved God more than my husband. That my sons would be unfaithful? I taught them every day what I knew of God.

"I don't understand. What am I to do? To whom are you referring?"

"My Queen, I beseech you—guide the princes in the way of their ancestor David, who never turned to the right or the left. With their father away, you are their instructor in the LORD's ways." His eyes searched my face for understanding, and his hands gripped my arms even tighter. "You know as well as I that not even the priests in the Temple can be trusted. I don't know whether they follow God or merely the king."

I stepped back and shook myself of his grasp. Confusion made me stagger and raised my defenses against his accusations. My hand found my head and I sighed. Not only was this nonsense and confusion at the time of my grief and loneliness, it was responsibility over matters that were beyond my control.

"Prophet, you of all people should know me and my family. You know I raise my sons in the ways of the LORD and that we have no other gods before us in the palace. I have no idea what your intentions are in this conversation, but I must ask you to leave this matter be and allow me to take my leave to Libnah to tend to my dying father. Thank you and good day!" I spun on my heel and walked quickly back to the carriage where my sons made room on the seat for me.

"Wait!" he cried after me. "I meant no ..."

I wrapped my arms around each of the boys tightly and shouted to the driver without even a glance back at Jeremiah. I could not imagine what he was describing. Eliakim and Jehoahaz both followed Jehovah as best as they knew in their childhood understanding. As much as they could comprehend of God, they followed. They were learning to sing the Psalms of David. They knew the prayers and traditions of Sabbath. What, if anything, could I do that I wasn't already doing? What did God want from me? What did Jeremiah want from me? A deep insecurity washed over me, and I felt a constricting in my chest as I saw Jeremiah's hopeless vision passing before my mind.

LORD, *I'm trying my best to follow You—to raise these children to know You. Are You trying to tell me I'm not doing an adequate job? Are You saying they might turn away from You? Oh God, please—anything but that! Help me, Father. I don't know what more to do …*

I was helpless in so many ways. Helpless to save my father, helpless to mold my sons, helpless to win over Tirzah. It was as if in challenging my motherhood, Jeremiah had questioned the very validity of my purpose. I gasped shallow breaths through my silent tears, brushing them away before the boys could see.

As we rode over the hills and through the forests on our long trek, I could do nothing with my grief and desperation but cry.

\* \* \*

Near Libnah, I found my parents in the same tent in which I had grown up, with my mother kneeling beside my father as he rested. I led the boys in quietly and settled them in the corner with some bread and goat cheese.

Eliakim said he would try to get Jehoahaz to sleep for his afternoon nap. I was relieved with his mere offer to help. He must have known how fragile I was. Even if he could do nothing in quieting his younger brother, I was glad he was willing to try—and I hadn't even asked him. There are times in a mother's life when all she can do is beam with pride at her eldest. I kissed him on the top of his head before I rushed to my father's bedside.

He looked like a pale apparition—a fragment of what he had been when last I had seen him. His eyes were closed under darkened folds around the sockets, and his cheeks held none of the joy I was accustomed to seeing. The skin hung off of his bones just as our animal skins hung off of the posts of our dwelling. As I looked him over, the lump in my throat threatened to choke me, and the uncontrollable sob that came from my chest was loud enough to wake him.

He blinked a few times before coughing and reached out for my mother's hand. "Hamath? Hamath!" he cried.

"I'm here. Here I am." She turned to whisper to me, "He's not seeing well."

"I forgot where I was," he said with a slight chuckle.

"You're home in the tent. Hamutal and the boys have come to see you."

"Hello, Abba," I managed. *Oh, if I could only hide the tears in my voice.* I took his hand from my mother and leaned closer to kiss him. He brought his other hand to my cheek.

"Hello there, Love."

I rested my head on his hand and tried to memorize every part of that moment: the fragrant sheepskin draped over him, making his lower half seem disproportionate to the rest of him; the lingering touch of his hand that still held the strength of my father, though there was little left; the salty taste of my tears that mixed with the aloe on his cheek; even the sound of the wind rustling the tent curtains and the soft words of Jehoahaz asking his brother for more milk from the corner. I etched it all into my mind and vowed never to forget it.

"It must be hard for you to see me like this," Father said.

"Not so hard that I'd stay away. Not so hard that you should be ashamed."

"You know me too well. I am very happy you are here—very happy …" His voice faded into a coughing spell that wracked his body and wretched him off the mat. When he finally settled, we offered him some dark, hyssop tea, which he sipped thankfully.

"Can I get you anything else?" I offered to both of them.

"No, Love. I'm alright now," he said.

My mother merely shook her head.

"Would you like me to bring the princes now?" I asked.

"Of course. And didn't you bring that king of yours?"

"No, Abba. He is still away on his mission."

"Still away? Do you mean to tell me that he is still burning idols and shrines?"

"He is. The last letter I received was from Amasa. He makes his way into Samaria and then intends to come home to Jerusalem soon after that."

My father thought for a moment, creasing his eyebrows together. "There must be much to destroy if his mission has lasted so long. Does it never cease to amaze you how rebellious our people can be, my dear? How they can see Jehovah at work and then walk away from Him?"

"No, Father. Their ability to ignore the Almighty and fall all over their statues never does. I can only hope that once Josiah has finished the cleansing, that people will turn back to Him. It's the first thing I ask for in the morning and the last thing I pray at night: that Judah would seek the one true God and Him only. Somehow I believe that if they would seek Him, they would find Him. And if they found Him, they would love Him. And if they loved Him, they would obey Him." I stopped to imagine the vision again, letting it sink deep into my desire and become a silent prayer in that moment.

Another coughing attack from my father brought me back. I held his cup to his lips and let him sip again. He leaned into me and I helped him to lie back again. My mother went to bring Eliakim and Jehoahaz to the foot of the mat.

Once he was settled back in, I spoke again, "Abba, Eli and Jeho have come with me. Haven't they grown?" I pulled them to his side and motioned for them to kneel so he could see them.

"My, what strapping sons you've raised, Hamutal! May they be blessed with many years of peaceful reign in Judah."

Eliakim stretched a little taller on his knees and Jehoahaz bounced into my arms. "Well," I said, "they do seem to be growing by the minute. I was hesitant to bring them, but now that I see you together, I'm glad I did."

"Thank you," he whispered through his tears.

# 23. JOSIAH

On Sabbath I knelt, facing south—toward Jerusalem—to pray for my family and my kingdom. Longing for my wife's arms around me, I worshipped Him in my heart, though my sorrow prevailed. I thanked Him for open borders into Samaria and Israel, as well as for the privilege of being His instrument of purification. I asked God for strength to endure to the end of this seemingly endless mission. After the cremation at Bethel, I had only wanted to turn around and go home to her. But He bid me onward and northward to continue burning idols beyond the border of Judah.

*Please, Father—let this be over soon. Release me, LORD.*

When I returned to camp that evening, a man was waiting for me with Jared and Asaiah. He was tall and thin—too thin. If one would poke him, he might very well fall over. His beard was full and long, and the darkest black I had ever seen. His hair matched in color, though it was very scarce atop his narrow head.

"Your Majesty, this man says he brings you a message from the LORD," Asaiah reported.

"And who might you be?" I asked.

"Let's just say we're cousins, my King."

"You are of noble blood? Of David's line?" I inquired.

"Yes, King Hezekiah was my great-great grandfather. I hold no ties to the throne, however. Please do not take my presence as a threat to your crown." He appeared benevolent enough. I saw no evidence of weapons

205

concealed in his belt, though I knew Asaiah and Jared better than to let anything slip their inspection.

"Then what do you want? What is this message?" I was growing impatient and hungry. "And tell me about the god for whom you speak." I knew better than to give audience to a divine message without first authenticating the true divinity of it, cousin or no cousin.

"From the God who is our Redeemer—the LORD of Heaven's Armies, from Jehovah," he answered.

"Go on, then," I said, shifting myself down into a makeshift throne. *A fellow relative who feared God. Imagine that!*

*"Gather together—yes, gather together, you shameless nation. Gather before judgment begins, before your time to repent is blown away like chaff."*

"When?" I demanded.

*"Act now, before the fierce fury of the LORD falls and the terrible day of His anger begins,"* he continued without missing a beat. *"Seek the LORD, all who are humble, and follow his commands. Seek to do what is right and to live humbly. Perhaps even yet the LORD will protect you—protect you from his anger on that day of destruction."*

And with that, he turned to leave.

"Hold on," I called after him when I was able to speak again. "I need answers. When is the day of destruction? Haven't I *been* following His commands?"

*Do what is right and live humbly* … Had I not been doing that? With a sinking sense that God was somehow displeased with my actions, even though I had done my best to complete everything He requested, including torching every idolatrous priest in Bethel, I ran after this prophet to demand answers from him—no … answers from God.

"Wait—you didn't even tell me your name!"

"Zephaniah," he called over his shoulder without stopping.

I gave up trying to chase him down and knelt to my knees in defeat. I put my face in my hands and sighed. Jared's footsteps came up quickly behind me.

"My lord?" It was a query of concern. And I knew a request for orders would follow closely.

"Gather the troops, Jared. I can't take this any longer. I've got to get back to Jerusalem." *Back to the Temple where I can worship. Back to my Angel.* "We will split into five companies tonight and break camp in the morning. If we've got to purify Israel, too, we'll do so as quickly and efficiently as possible. This travel and tent-dwelling is driving me mad!"

"What about the men with the stones? Do you want me to divide them up?"

"No, send them home. Confiscate all of the idols and bring them to Jerusalem where we'll reconvene. We'll have a public demonstration of what God thinks of these trinkets."

"A grand idea. The men will be delighted," he said. His voice urged reassurance, as if he knew I was about to become rash and wanted to stop me before I went too far. He knew me too well. I stood up, hurled the sand I had been strangling, and met his gaze with determination.

"If the day of destruction is coming, Jared, and we have a chance to repent ... then repent we will!"

He nodded. "I'll rally the men for you, sire."

# 24. HAMUTAL

It was four months later that I went back to Libnah to bury my father. I arrived to find my youngest siblings, Jaazaniah and Sarah, quietly weeping over his body. Johanah and Mother were preparing the anointing oils—myrrh, cinnamon, aloe, sandalwood, and frankincense—outside the tent. I had brought Hilkiah with me to perform the rituals and rights of death, and a thick silence hung in the air, pierced only occasionally by a sparrow's song.

I tried to comprehend the numbness I was feeling, but it was so far out of reach that I could do nothing more than stand in the middle of my childhood home in the haunting stillness. I didn't know where to go. I had no direction to mourn. It was as if I was a shell and all of myself had gone to Sheol with my father. There were no tears to cry, no sobs to moan, no words to speak.

I don't know how long I remained frozen there, but my mother and sister came in from their preparations and found me at some point.

"Oh, Hamutal, I didn't know you were here. I just came in from behind the tent and saw your carriage," mother said blankly. She stood behind me, waiting for me to acknowledge her. "Children, please leave your sister and me for a moment," she said to my siblings.

I still could not face her. If I looked into her red eyes I would lose control. I would have nothing to give. I would fall apart. She drew closer to my back, put her arms around my shoulders, and held me like that for a long time. She must have shared my numbness, because she did not cry, either. We were still—so still. The only movement in the tent was our slight breathing that was strangely synchronized. After several minutes, I realized she had begun to lean into my back—I was holding her up and she was holding me together.

The man who had done that for all of my life was now taken from us. We would have to learn to do it on our own. But we did not know how—not yet. I stared at his lifeless form on the mat where I'd left him. Though I wanted to close my eyes, I forced myself to look. The grayness of his skin. The lack of movement in his chest. The silent, frozen lock of his lips—those lips that had kissed me and taught me and comforted me. The void in his hands, those rough hands that I loved to hold and touch. His strong arms that would never hold me again, never tuck my hair behind my ear, never break bread and hand it to me at the table. I tortured myself in silence, knowing that if I didn't do so in that moment, missing him would haunt me forever.

I couldn't pray yet. I knew I would soon. But standing there on my fragile legs with my mother leaning hard on my back and my empty father within arm's reach, I had no strength to acknowledge the God who had allowed this—who hadn't healed him, though I'd pleaded every day.

My silence to Him was not in rebellion. In my mind, I knew He was still good, still sovereign, still loving. But my heart felt none of that. My heart was weak and broken. It was ignorant and blind.

I've lost the rest of my memories about the remainder of my time in Libnah spent honoring him. There are some vague images in my head about the funeral ceremony, and I do remember huddling in the tent with my sisters and brother after he was finally in the tomb. I don't know if I cried. I don't remember tears, though I must have shed some, for I do recall my shawl being damp as Hilkiah and I rode back to the palace.

Hannah came only for the ceremony. She was confined to bed by her mistress, who said that her birth pangs were coming too early and she must lie down all day, every day, until her second baby was closer to its time. It was probably for the best. I would have fought with her about her choices again, I'm sure. My father's memorial was no place for harsh words.

I felt as though I had lost her too, though. I could have used the chance to mourn with her. I might have allowed the tears to fall more, if only my dearest sister, who had shared almost all of my memories with Abba, would have cried with me.

But Hannah had walked out on him when she walked away from God. Abba would not acknowledge her husband when they visited. Matthias was the one blamed for her conversion to Baal. But how could she just turn her back on our father? How could she betray his love in that way? I did not understand her thoughts and motives, nor would I ever.

But she was still my sister. And I still loved her.

I remember the carriage ride back to the palace because of the awkward silence between Hilkiah and me, as well as the strained conversation that followed. The priest tried to console me in my loss, but when he recounted a psalm of David, he misquoted the verse, and I remember being so bold as to correct him. I don't know why I did it. Usually I tolerated his mistakes with the holy texts, but that day I had nothing else to give. No grace, no understanding, no allowances.

He then attempted to comfort me with a reminder that Josiah would be home in less than two months, but that seemed like a lifetime when all I wanted was his strong arms to hold me in that moment. In my mind, it was the only thing that could have brought me any relief. I imagined my head on his shoulder and closed my eyes to the daydream. I sighed deeply in the revelry of it, but immediately shook it off. The void of both him and my father was too exceedingly painful to face.

Josiah had not been able or willing to leave his mission and travel back to Libnah for the ceremony. When his messenger brought the news back to me the day before, I had cringed. All I wanted was for my husband to hold me, but those ridiculous foreign gods and their disgusting shrines had robbed me of him when I needed him most. I let out a frustrated groan at Hilkiah's mention of the king.

When I arrived back at the palace that evening, I found the boys eating dinner with their nurses. My stomach churned at the thought of food, so I kissed them on their heads lightly and withdrew quickly to my room. I dismissed my servants and didn't come out for over a week.

211

It was Tirzah who finally forced me to emerge from my quarters. She brought me to the royal baths behind the garden and washed my hair, like I had done for her not so long before. She said, "I'm sorry for your loss, my lady," and rubbed rose oil over my arms and shoulders. It was in that moment that I remembered how to feel again, and with the memory came my tears. I cried deep, heaving sobs, calling "Abba, Abba!" over and over again. Tirzah held me for hours and then brought me back to my bed where I slept and cried for a few more days. I lost count of the number of times the sun rose and set, but I finally did regain my appetite and gave in to my handmaidens begging that I eat something.

My memory illuminates soon after, when Jeremiah found me staring blankly at my sons as they sparred in the courtyard one day. They clanked their wooden swords together clumsily in the cool winter frost as I wrapped my cloak around my shoulders to block out the wind.

"My Queen," the prophet said with a bow.

"Jeremiah." I nodded.

"I was sorry to hear of your father's passing," he said. "I know from what the king said that he was a man who feared the LORD."

"He was ... a man ..." But I could not finish. My nose stung with the onset of tears and I could not hide my grief from him, try that I may. There was no use. I was in such desperate need for someone, anyone to lead me back to sanity. Or perhaps back to God. When Jeremiah reached to comfort me, I acquiesced gratefully into his arms.

"There, there, my lady. This too will pass," he said.

"When?" I said. "When will this pain ever pass?"

Eliakim and Jehoahaz heard my sobs and dropped their swords to come running.

"Mama?" they asked in unison.

"Run along, Princes—I'm fine." I lied to protect them once again, brushing away the tears and feigning a smile. "Go and fetch your slings now—you must work on your target practice." Reluctantly, they obeyed.

Jeremiah allowed me to cling to him. I expected him at any moment to push me away, but he didn't. I buried my head into his arm and tried to stifle my sobs. I knew it was somehow improper for me to need him so much in that moment. My conscience screamed at me from inside my head, but it felt safe to be held together, when for so long the pieces of me had been falling away.

"This would be much different for you if he were home, wouldn't it?" Jeremiah asked once I had quieted. I nodded into him. He pulled away slightly to look into my eyes. "You know he wanted to come back for you, don't you?"

"What do you mean? Did you receive word from him?"

"No, but I know him. I know how much he loves you. It was no easy thing to stay out there in the countryside. Were it up to him, he would have been home immediately," he said.

"Then the LORD bid him to stay?"

"That's my hunch. But, my lady, you must not be angry at the Almighty," he said. "God has reasons we will never fully comprehend. Have you been to the Temple to offer sacrifice since you came back from Libnah?"

I shook my head in embarrassment.

"Would you like me to accompany you this evening?"

I was not sure if I was ready to face Him yet. I had cried out to Jehovah in my pain, but I was still harboring so much resentment. I knew going to the Temple would require a surrender of my soul and my grief, and of that I was still terrified.

"Hamutal …?"

"Of course, Prophet. I know …I've been avoiding the One who holds my comfort in His hands."

# 25. JOSIAH

It was not until we finished raiding the capital city of Samaria of its idols and shrines that we reunited again in Bethel and began our lively march toward Jerusalem. I could almost feel her in my arms, and the mere idea of her skin made me spring off of my sluggish camel and walk ahead of the infantry.

"Thank you, sire," Asaiah said to my back.

"For?"

"For taking us home. Finally. And alive."

I slowed my pace to match his stride. "This was never meant to be a mission of fatalities," I said.

Jared, who had been one step behind me since we departed Samaria, chuckled softly. I turned back and shot him a grimace, to which he shrugged in feigned innocence.

Asaiah nodded reflectively, and I watched him from the corner of my eye as he sighed. "Nonetheless, it's good to be facing south again. Come tomorrow night, I'll be in my own bed next to my own hearth, full with a meal of my own grain and meat, kissing my own wife, drinking my own wine."

"What makes you think she'll let you kiss her with that dirty rug on your face?" Jared said.

Asaiah stroked his beard from his lips to his neck and examined his filthy hand before shooting us a nervous frown. The three of us burst out laughing, along with several others behind us who had been eavesdropping.

"Perhaps we should all stop at Solomon's Pool as we head into the city," I said. Asaiah offered me a thankful grin.

We picked up our pace even more and were jogging the rest of that afternoon, provoked with longing in our loins and dreams of clean beds not full of sand and our own stench.

\* \* \*

My first glimpse of her the next afternoon was from the street as she waved down at our parade into the city from atop the palace roof porch. Her light smile did not reach her sorrowful eyes, however, and she seemed to have aged five years in the previous one that I was away. Losing her father had left her frail. When I waved back to her, she folded her arm delicately across her chest and rested her hand on her smooth neck. Even from my distance, I could taste her in the back of my mouth.

But when I raced into our chambers, I didn't find her waiting for me. I spoke to the guard in the corridor to inquire of her whereabouts.

"The queen asked me to relay that she'll be in purification for you until this evening. She invites you to dinner with the Princes in the interim."

Strange. Perhaps she could have done that earlier ...

"Very well. Are they in the dining hall?"

"Yes, my lord, or they will be shortly, along with their nurses," he answered.

The boys greeted me with tackling hugs, to which I responded by tossing each of them above my head and ruffling their hair.

"And how are Judah's strongest princes today?"

"Abba," Jeho giggled, "we're the only princes there is."

"Really?" I teased, looking over their shoulders. "No more princes since I've been gone?"

Eliakim chided me silently and rolled his eyes. He seemed to me to be more like sixteen than six, so I tousled his hair again and drew him in for a crushing hug that he returned without complaint. They had both grown even more than I had anticipated, and Hamutal had let their curls grow long—though Eli's were almost white, and Jeho's were just as dark as mine.

216

"Where's Mama?" I asked. Perhaps these little spies could give me more information than the guard had.

"Taking a bath," Eli retorted, rolling his eyes yet again.

"She said she wants to be pretty for you, Abba," Jeho said.

"Well, she doesn't need to take a bath for that, now, does she?"

Jeho shrugged in exasperation. "Girls!"

There was no holding back our laughter. From the mouths of my babes ...

Jeremiah entered with a bow and rose to greet me with a warm embrace. His eyes looked tired, and I could tell he had been pouring over Isaiah's scrolls all night again.

"Ah, my friend—so good to see you again," I said.

"You took the words right out of my mouth," he replied with the same smile I had seen in Hamutal earlier—the smile that was glad in his mouth but guarded in his eyes. "How were your travels?"

"Let me see ... long, hot, windy, sandy, frustrating, rewarding, flaming ... Need I go on?"

"Only if you want to."

"Why don't I tell you over dinner? Will you join me and the princes?"

"As you wish. And the queen?"

"We were just discussing that, the boys and I. It seems she's passing on dinner to complete her beauty rituals. Have you seen her?"

"Not today."

"Then yesterday?"

"Last evening. She arrived from Libnah upon the news that you were on your way home."

"Really? How long had she been with her family?"

"A few weeks. Her sister has been quite troubled."

"Hannah or Johanah?"

"Hannah. Her husband was killed at Bethel, as I presume you know," he said.

But I was somehow ignorant. *Hannah's husband ... Who was Hannah's husband?* I strained to recall.

"Hannah was married?" I asked. "Why was I not told this?"

"I'm quite sure the queen told you, Highness. Hannah has been quite devastated," he whispered quietly with a sigh.

"Oh no—" I suddenly realized the connection.

He leaned even closer to me so that the boys would not hear. "She attempted to take her own life and that of her unborn child ... I think Hamutal said something about poison from a witch doctor. By the grace of God, she was not successful. The child was born too early, though, and needed a nurse. The queen said Hannah would not even look at him. Two days ago, she disappeared."

I sighed and dropped my face into my hands. "What a mess!" I looked up into Jeremiah's eyes. "And my wife?"

He paused to think before answering. "She's definitely shaken."

*So that's why she's avoiding me.* "Thank you."

* * *

Hamutal stole into our chambers as I was watching the familiar moon from our balcony. Peculiar how no matter where I was—desert, mountains, plains, north, south, even home—the moon always looked the same. If it was a crescent here in my palace, I could rest assured it was a crescent in Samaria and a crescent in Egypt. Aside from the moon, however, life held so few guarantees.

She cleared her throat lightly before she spoke: "Good evening, my King. Welcome home." It was forced and awkward, even coming from the lilt in her voice I had missed for so long.

I turned around and drank in the sight of her. "Did you have a nice bath?"

Offering a smirk, she shrugged and nodded.

"And?" I said.

"And what?"

"Well, for starters, this isn't the joy of you leaping into my arms I imagined my return to be."

She sighed again and looked askance. "My journey back from Libnah yesterday was—"

Meeting my eyes, she stopped herself short, perhaps realizing she was about to complain to *me* about a hard afternoon's carriage ride.

"Was what?"

"Nothing. Um … my sister is recovering from a self-inflicted poisoning, as well as premature childbirth, and … and, well, I suppose I'm just worried and preoccupied with her."

"Alright."

"And also, she's gone," she finally spilled, "absolutely and neglectfully gone." Her hands animated her words, flailing as she spoke. "We have no idea where she went, and her baby needs her. It's not easy to be here, knowing she's out there alone. I left a servant in Libnah as my messenger to come quickly and tell me of her rescue … but there is no word." Through all of this, we stood several paces apart, each not willing to risk the first step.

"Shall I send out a search party?"

She shrugged one shoulder. "If you think it would help."

"It might."

"It's just that—what if she doesn't want to be found? If we find her and bring her back, would she just run again?" Her voice sounded desperate.

"She might."

She pushed her fingertips to her forehead and sighed. "I just don't understand."

"What?"

"I don't understand why."

"Why, what? What is it?" I was losing my patience trying to pry everything from her.

"Why you had to kill them."

So it had come to this. I turned my back to her and stepped even farther away, feeling a familiar anger swell into my throat and hands. This was not what I needed nor longed to come home to—not even remotely close.

"Wasn't your plan just to take their statues and altars away? Why did you have to take their lives?" Her voice faltered with a cry but she continued. "I just don't see why that was necessary."

I fought to keep control by inhaling deeply, but fire surged through every fiber and muscle. For a few moments I just stood there raging, with my back to her.

"Hamutal," I said through clenched teeth, "you of all people should know—" But I could not finish. My temper was too hot, and I could not control my own voice. I spun quickly and reached for the table behind me to throw it into the fire.

Only instead of finding the table, my furious hands found her. By the time I realized what had happened, it was already too late—

She let out a sharp cry as her hip snapped against the corner of the hearth. Her hands reached into the flames to stop her momentum.

Frozen by my mistake, I panicked.

I strode forward to reach for her, but she pulled up with her hand in front to stop me.

My beloved angel looked at me as if I were a fearsome brute. With a few quick breaths, she gathered herself and limped away, clutching her side with one hand and raising the scalded wrist in the air.

"Wait—come back, I didn't mean to—"

But I was too disgusted with myself to move after her. In my mind, I berated my hands and my rage, grasping to understand how that could have just happened. She must have stepped closer to me while I was turned.

It was not until several minutes later that I was able to run down the corridors to find her. I looked first in the boys' room but then scolded myself for it. Turning on my heel and darting into the harem, I stopped short when I caught sight of her in Jeremiah's arms.

*No. Oh no.*

"What is this?" I yelled.

Hamutal was sobbing. When she heard my voice, she caught her breath in her throat and looked up at me. Jeremiah eased her onto the couch and held her burned hand gingerly.

"I think I should ask you, King Josiah. What is this you have done?"

"*This* is none of your business!" I shouted. "Take your hands off my wife!"

Just then, the palace physician entered and bowed before us. Rising quickly, he trotted over to Hamutal to examine her hand and wrist, asking her what had happened. She glanced up at me for a moment before turning to answer him.

"I fell into the hearth."

Jeremiah glared at me and motioned to the corridor so we could speak in private. I felt more like striking him than talking to him. Seeing one's wife in the arms of his best friend will do that to a man.

"Do you mind telling me why you pushed the queen into the fire?" he asked. He put one hand on my shoulder, which I quickly shrugged off.

"Do you mind telling *me* why your hands were groping the queen just now?"

"That's not true, and you know it, Josiah!"

"Then how does she find such ease in coming to your touch?"

"Don't be ridiculous. She's hurt—that is the matter here—not me. I found her limping down the hallway and brought her here by her own request. I sent for the physician, and you walked in." His eyes never left my own. "Now, what happened?"

"It was an accident. Beyond that, it's none of your business!"

His eyes widened in surprise and pain.

"I want you to leave the palace now," I said. "I'll send for you when you are needed again." Even as the words left my lips, I wanted to retract them. We both knew I needed his wisdom and friendship, especially now that I had made so many new enemies, both here in Jerusalem and around my nation.

"As you wish," he said after a moment. "I was actually on my way to tell you that God has called me to Samaria to deliver a message. I suppose this works out perfectly."

"Yes, indeed." But it was anything but perfect.

"Take care of her, my lord," he said.

"You don't have to tell me that!"

"Alright, alright," he said with his hands raised in front of him.

I returned to my wife, who looked back at me with the same fear I had seen in her eyes the day I killed her assailants in the alley. I didn't know how, and I had no idea how long it would take, but I had to remove that fear from her eyes.

# 26. HAMUTAL

I couldn't sit or kneel, so I was forced to stand behind the congregation at the evening sacrifice. The pain in my hip was excruciating—like knives digging into the bones of my pelvis hour after hour. The agony in my hand had dulled to a throbbing ache once the doctor wrapped the burns.

It was an accident; I knew it was. But my pain was real, and most of it had nothing to do with my injuries. Once again, Josiah's anger got the best of him, and this time, I was the one to pay. I winced again with a sharp breath between my teeth. How could he have been so oblivious ... so careless?

*Jehovah, I feel so neglected and useless. What am I doing here? What do You want me to do? Maybe I should just stop trying. I don't know what You want from me. I don't understand my purpose here ... God, protect my sister and bring her home. Heal her child. Bless my mother and give her strength to go on, even without Abba. Nothing is impossible for You. But it all feels impossible for me.*

Tirzah helped me to turn and walk out of the gate. As we descended the Temple stairs, she held tightly to my good hand and slipped her arm behind my back. The wind whipped up sand into my already dry eyes and threatened to drive me mad. As my other attendants held my skirts, Jeho and Eli skipped ahead through the swirling hot wind down to the palace.

"Mama—can we eat now?" asked Jeho.

I looked at Eli, whose eyes pleaded even more persuasively than Jehoahaz's whines.

"Fine, boys—see what you can get from the cooks," I said. "Come to the harem when you're finished."

Eliakim shot a disapproving glance at us. "Are you sleeping there again?"

"It's no concern of yours where I sleep, young man."

"I was just asking."

I glared at him for a long moment. "Run along, now. I'll see you after you've eaten."

"Yes, Mama," they said together.

\* \* \*

"I like this one best. Could you read it to me again," Tirzah asked, handing me a scroll. I opened it to see what she had chosen. Another of King David's songs.

"Read it or sing it?" I asked.

"Oh, sing it!"

It was one of my favorites, too. I sang the words to Tirzah and my mistresses, Adah and Oshri. The notes and words pushed away my pain:

"'*The earth is the* LORD'*s, and everything in it.*

*The world and all its people belong to him.*

*For he laid the earth's foundation on the seas and built it on the ocean depths ...*

*Who is the King of glory?*

*The* LORD*, strong and mighty; the* LORD*, invincible in battle.*

*Open up, ancient gates!*

*Open up, ancient doors, and let the King of glory enter.*

*Who is the King of glory?*

*The* LORD *of Heaven's Armies—he is the King of glory.*'"

Their eyes pleaded for more, and I laughed in embarrassment. "Why did you choose that one, Tirzah?" Oshri said.

"Oh, I love thinking of God, the Maker of all things, and our Maker, too. Remember how the high priest said at the sacrifice tonight how there is nothing He does on accident, no mistake in His doing?"

"Yes?" I said, not knowing where this was going.

"Well, doesn't that mean I'm not a mistake, either?" Tirzah looked back to me for the answer.

"Of course you're not a mistake. You're anything but that."

"And I love how it ends—the King of glory. It's like He's on His way to rescue me right now!"

Adah laughed aloud at her. "Rescue you from what, you fool? As if Jerusalem were under attack!"

"Adah!" I scolded.

"From myself," Tirzah said. "From my past. From anyone who would ever want to harm me again."

"Oh ... well, I suppose," Adah said.

"Yes, I love that part, too," I said. "And the part about opening up the gates. As if it were our choice whether or not we let Him in to save us."

"Is it? Our choice, I mean," Oshri asked.

"What would you say, Tirzah?"

"Oh yes, my lady. God loves us and comes to save us, but we have to choose to be saved. At first, I didn't want Jehovah for my God. I thought He would be cruel and demanding like the statues. But He's not. Like the song says, if we purify our hearts and hands, He gives us right relationship with Him. He doesn't want me to perform for Him. He just wants my devotion."

I smiled down at her sitting at my feet while the other girls were pondering what she had said. Tirzah had come so far in such a short time. Sometimes her faith seemed even bigger than my own. She was so hungry for more of Him every day. She wanted to taste Him and see Him and feel Him. She was beginning to want to know how to please Him as well. It was as if she had finally learned to let herself be loved by God, and what she wanted most was to love Him back.

But I felt at a loss on how to teach her that. It was my own daily struggle to know what He desired of me. *So how can He expect me to show her? Or anyone else?*

\* \* \*

The next morning, a messenger rapped on my door before the sun rose. I stumbled out of my stupor in my bedclothes and opened the door to see his eyes glimmering in the reflection of his torch.

"What is it?" I mumbled through the stickiness of my tongue.

"From Libnah, my queen. The king's search party found your sister and brought her back. Your mother awaits your arrival."

I gasped in awe, awaking fully at the thought of Hannah safe again.

"Thank you. Ready my carriage. We leave immediately—as soon as I can get dressed and packed."

\* \* \*

Tirzah insisted on coming with me to Libnah, as did the boys, who hadn't appreciated being left behind the last time. I prepared all of my personal items and ordered for our travel cakes and water to be packed into the carriage. As I was limping around the corner to gather the boys, I careened into Josiah in the corridor.

"Oh! Are you alright?" he asked. He held my elbows and my gaze to steady me.

I pulled away after a moment. "Yes, I'm fine."

"Where are you going in such a rush?"

"We're leaving for Libnah. It seems your search party found my sister last night."

"Good."

"Yes. Thank you."

"When do you plan to return?"

*Do I plan to return?* "I don't know."

He nodded, looking into my eyes again. "I hope you are able to bring some improvement to Hannah's situation."

"Me, too." I turned to walk around him. His eyes and his hands made my thoughts swim in confused swirls of anguish and anger.

"Hamutal ..." he called after me.

I turned again to face him and took a deep breath to brace myself.

"I'm so sorry."

I swallowed and nodded. It was all I could do.

# 27. JOSIAH

The day Hamutal left for Libnah, I gathered my men to finish the destruction of the idols we had brought from Samaria. The fire calmed me somewhat, but only slightly.

"Orders, my lord?" Asaiah asked once the gold was safely collected and the embers began to cool.

"All of the gold goes to the temple treasury. The other metals you can put in the palace treasury. I need to get a report from the national council today. Gather them to convene after midday."

"As you wish." He turned quickly to leave.

"Asaiah," I called after him.

"Yes?"

"Thank you." Our gazes met for a moment and I told him with my eyes the gratitude that words could not explain. He understood, evidenced by a smirk and a single nod.

I dismissed the rest of the men and palace servants so I could walk alone in the lush valley behind my home. The green of the meadow took my breath away, and the hearty scent of sheep basking in the hot sun was the welcome I needed. I greeted the shepherd, who turned to me, jumped back, and then knelt awkwardly.

"Good morning, my King. I didn't expect you!"

"Rise, brother," I said, scanning the hillside. The hearty smell of fleece filled my nostrils, and a refreshing breeze blew at my hair. "The flock has grown since I've been away. You must be doing something right."

"It honors me that you are pleased, sire."

"I want to warn you … We'll be sacrificing many of them in celebration of the LORD's faithfulness," I said.

"Of course. I expected as much." He followed my gaze and patted one of the ewes at his side. "It's one of the main reasons we raise them, isn't it?"

"Good man. And for today, do you have a nice yearling male for me?" I wanted my first sacrifice in the Temple since my return to be perfect.

"Of course. I know just the one." He loped off into the midst of the animals and returned promptly with a beautiful and clean ram. After setting him down in front of me, he reached into a pouch and pulled out a rope. I handed him a generous payment, but he didn't take it. "You would pay me for your own sheep, sire?"

"I pay you for your loyalty and service, and so that my offering today is truly a sacrifice. Jehovah deserves as much … and more."

The Temple felt empty when I entered, bereft of its previous shrines and extraneous altars, and vacant of any other worshippers. Hilkiah's apprentice was the one to take my lamb and spill its blood quietly on the altar. As the redness poured quickly, I dropped to my knees in confession and pleaded for the atonement to be enough for what I had done. I stayed there, crying muted tears and pleading for God's forgiveness, even as the flames roasted the meat. The nightmare of that night haunted me over and over as I pictured her body snapping over the wall of the hearth. I then recalled her frightened face when I reached for her. The two images danced back and forth in my mind, and I tortured myself with the grief they brought.

*Please, LORD; please grant me Your mercy. I repent, Father, I do. You know I never wanted to hurt her. Forgive me, God, for injuring Your precious daughter, my beautiful Angel. And please, if You have any forgiveness left over, plant a seed in her heart also. Oh, God, I need her to come back to me. I don't know how to go on without her.*

I bowed low to humble myself before Him, my head on the cold stone beneath. I don't know how long I prayed in that position, but it must have been a couple of hours, because I was startled out of my prayer by Jared's voice behind me.

"Excuse me, my King," he whispered.

"What is it, Jared?" I asked, pushing myself up.

"The council has been waiting. They were about to leave when you didn't show at the palace. Asaiah suggested I look for you here before we dismissed them."

"What hour is it?"

"The sixth," he answered.

I heaved a reluctant sigh and picked myself up, throwing my robes out of the way.

"Tell them I'm coming—don't let them go. I'll be down in a minute."

\* \* \*

Jared, Asaiah, Acbor, Hilkiah, and the others hushed their conversations as I entered. They bowed slightly as one and began to stand around the table-platform that held maps of the kingdom and scrolls of our records. I heaved a sigh to brace myself for the weight of decisions, large and small.

"Who wants to begin?"

Jerimoth, my foreign trade emissary, took a breath and spoke up tentatively. "I would like to discuss your plans for the wealth you have recently confiscated from the people."

"I'm sure you would," I replied.

"Your Highness, that gold puts us in a unique trade advantage which we haven't experienced since your grandfather Manasseh," he said.

"I don't follow. What would you have us do with it?"

"Well, my first proposal is to reinforce our caravans and security. They need improved conditions, which would greatly increase our ability to transport goods of all kinds to and from Joppa, as well as Tyre. There is also the matter of crossing the Jordan, Your Highness. If we just had a stronger fleet, we could trade with Assyria ..."

"Now, hold it right there, Jerimoth!" Asaiah said. "Who said anything about trading with the enemy?"

"Assyria has been quiet for two years," I said. "Perhaps it is Egypt we should worry about."

"Pharaoh sent a convoy just yesterday, my lord," Jerimoth said.

"And you entertained them?" I asked, bristling.

Something about Egypt concerned me. Perhaps it was because my own father was named after their god; perhaps it was what I knew of our forefathers' enslavement there; or perhaps it was something more. It could have been fear of their ominous power and legendary forces, but whatever it was, I had no desire for a new investment in their goods or treaties with their emissaries. Other nations, possibly—but never despicable Egypt.

"Only briefly, and simply to receive their message and send them on to Samaria with supplies of food and water."

"Hmmph," I grunted. *Harmless, maybe.* "The next time you conduct trade with Egypt, make sure they haven't doubled their pockets with our money. I don't trust them. Never have."

"The warning is noted, Highness."

Secretary Shaphan spoke up next: "There is also the matter of a new and quickly-rising nation. My latest correspondence with our emirates brings report of a powerful army under a man named Nabopolassar in the northeast."

"Who is that?" I asked.

"The king of Babylon, and he's as brutal and greedy as they come. A hundred thousand slaves he chains to build his city. A hundred thousand more to harvest the expanding land and territories he conquers in colonies near and far. They say Babylon is a city so big you cannot even see it all. Every merchant longs to travel there to sell wares; every slave trader calls it a paradise."

I shuddered at the thought of children, women, and men bound in chains. I prayed a silent plea, asking God to show me if this Nabopolassar was to be heeded as a threat.

Jerimoth repeated his request to fund trade increases, and I gave an amount to the treasurer to allot over the course of the following three seasons. After a few more discussions, matters of state could not hold my attention any longer, and my thoughts returned to Hamutal. *Was she alright? Was she still afraid and angry with me? Had she told her mother and siblings? What could I do to convince her it had been an accident? Could she ever forgive me? What of Jeremiah? Why had I been so cruel?*

"... Sire?" Asaiah said.

"I'm sorry—what did you say?"

"The Temple restoration, Your Majesty. How would you like to proceed?"

"Oh—er ... begin immediately. All repairs and materials are to be funded. Do whatever you must. I'll need a report, estimate, and date we can be finished—tomorrow."

Hilkiah spoke up to protest, as always. "Sire, you realize we have measurements to make, do you not? I highly doubt one day is enough time to—"

"Fine, High Priest. How long should I be prepared to wait until we know when, what, and how much it will take to repair God's House?"

"At least a week," he answered defensively.

"Make it so. Tell me what you need next week and when you think it will be done. I've waited long enough. My whole life, actually. And what could be more important to Judah?"

\* \* \*

That afternoon, I sent a messenger to find Jeremiah, who had set out the day before without telling me where. Though my words had been knives of accusation, I realized he had only been trying to help console Hamutal and rebuke my temper—trying to be the friend we both needed.

When I still had not received word from him or Hamutal a fortnight later, it was all I could do to pray and not rage. I spent nights and days in the Temple pleading with God to give me back my wife and my friend. He was silent, but I would not let the fire on the altar go out.

# 28. HAMUTAL

One morning at my mother's tent in Libnah, I awoke, startled at a strange dream. The details of it eluded me, but the subject matter was still as clear as it has been just moments before.

Josiah was calling my name.

I shook my thoughts free of his voice and tried for the first of what I already knew would be a hundred attempts to rid myself of my need of him that day. And, as I knew it would, the need remained. It seemed that the harder I tried to stay angry with him for what he had done, the more arduous it became to live without him. All I wanted to do was run back to him and find myself in his arms. Yet day after day, I stayed away.

Hannah lifted the flap of the tent, interrupting my thoughts, and dumped the swaddled baby into my lap. "I can't do this anymore," she said. "I've tried for long enough, and it's useless."

"What's useless?" I asked, rubbing the sleep from my eyes with one hand and scooping up the baby in my other.

"I'm not meant to mother this child. Or the other one, for that matter."

"What do you mean?" I asked. "You are his mother. If you are not meant to mother him, then who is?"

I soothed Jonah's hungry cries with my knuckle in his mouth and hushed him as I rocked. His sweet scent filled my lungs, and I wondered what would win her heart if not this charm and tenderness.

"I don't know. And I don't really care."

"Hannah!"

She stared blankly out the tent and hugged her arms around her shoulders as if to keep warm, though the sweltering heat already hung in the morning air.

"I want Matthias back. I'm going to find him, no matter what it takes."

"Hannah, he's gone. Dead. It doesn't matter where you go—you won't find him," I said.

"I'll try again …"

Suddenly, I realized my sister had departed me. As much as I could fight, scold, or lecture her, she would not come back—not even for her precious sons. She would go back to the medium who had enticed her with lies of bringing back Matthias's spirit with smoke and animal hearts. The king's search party had found her there—drunken, entranced, and painted in blood. Mother had washed her, nourished her, and tried to coax her out of the stupor of grief.

Only, she was long lost. Her eyes were as empty as a camel's, slain in exhaustion. That beautiful smile and clear singing voice were nothing but childhood memories. The woman who stood before me was not my sister. She had rejected my God and was chasing after a different one. One who existed only in the deep recesses of her mind. One who held none of the answers she sought and who shared her empty eyes and empty heart.

In that moment, I resolved to give her one last chance before relinquishing hope.

"Hannah, Jehovah can heal your pain if only you will call on His Name. He can give you a new husband and help you to raise your children. Will you come back to Jerusalem with me today? You will find Him waiting for you in the Temple. Let's go again—for Sabbath—like we did when we were girls."

She turned to look into my eyes for the first time in weeks. Her voice was flat and quiet like a cold stone in the morning: "No."

"Hannah, please don't do this—"

"Jehovah is nothing but a shadow—a myth. I don't want your Sabbath or your ritual … I don't want those lies ever again." She took a step closer to me and clutched my arm, anger filling the void. "What did your God ever do for me? I'll tell you what—He took my life, He threw my hopes on the ground, and trampled them," she spat. "Well, hear this, Sister—your precious Jehovah can stay away from me. I'll seek the power of Baal—my god and my husband's god—and I'll find out how to get to him."

Tears stung my eyes but the real pain was in my chest, behind my ribs. I shook my head. The words that came from my lips were not my words. I had no idea from where they came, but come they did: "Then you might as well be dead. Today you choose death forever."

"Good. Forget me. Run back to your palace and your beautiful king and your perfect children," she sneered. "Forget you ever knew me."

How cruelly she raged, taking every blame and piling it high and heavy on my shoulders. Forget her? How could I ever possibly? Erase from my memory the tender and soft arms that held me at night from the time she was but two years old? Throw out every song we ever wove together as if they were old and dirty rags? She knew I couldn't. She knew even as she hurled those stone-cold phrases at me that I wouldn't.

"Please don't do this," I sobbed again.

But she had stormed off, leaving the flap of the tent blowing in the wind. Little Jonah let out a fresh wail, and we cried together until my mother found us there on the bed mat, fuming and afraid.

It was not until that very moment that I understood what had angered Josiah. I had blamed him for killing Matthias, when Matthias had killed himself by his own rebellion. And now Hannah had united herself with him. Her choice was no more mine than it had been Josiah's to slay Matthias. The dismal truth sat like a rock in my stomach. They were dead the day they walked away from Him. The One who had offered life so freely had been left holding it while they turned their backs on His generosity.

And I had the audacity to fault the one man who had pleaded with them to receive it. Fresh tears stung my eyes and nose again, and my mother's sobs joined in with ours.

\* \* \*

The next day when we arrived in Jerusalem, I headed immediately for the palace baths behind the garden to wash the dust from my hair. I stopped short and ducked back behind the corner when I saw that he was already there, bathing alone.

I leaned hard against the wall and pressed back my longing for him with every bit of strength I possessed. Sucking in my breath sharply, I clenched my fists against my chest. As much as I tried, I could not help peeking back in at him. His back was to me. I stared, glued to the rivulets of water dripping down his wide shoulders into the tight angle that formed the small of his back. His hands reached up and found his wavy hair, and I noted how his arms swelled with new strength as they flexed.

Had it really been over a year since those arms held me, since those hands stroked my chin and neck, since his thirsty lips drank of mine? Carelessly, I let out a cry of regret. To my horror, he turned and I ducked back against the corridor just before his eyes met mine.

I knelt there, breathless as my thoughts raced, trying to contemplate an option that would save my pride and somehow also let me look into his eyes for just another moment. If I ran, I might avoid the awkward embarrassment of him finding me here. My frozen legs refused to move. I held my head in my hands and fought to think. Seconds later, I heard his quick, bare footfalls on the stone behind me.

"Hamutal?" His voice rang like a familiar song in my ears.

I stood and forced myself to face him. He had donned a wrap over his waist, but his broad chest was still uncovered and dripping. I swallowed hard and threw my gaze back at the stone floor.

"Oh, m—my lord," I said, trying to think of an excuse for being there. "I … I was coming to bathe and saw you here first. I wanted to let you finish."

"When did you get back?"

His smile was that of one delighted to see me. I looked up and took an extra moment to drown myself in the joy in his eyes. They bore none of the fiery anger I had seen that night. Only light and compassion remained to capture my heart again.

"Uh … just now … we arrived just now," I said, working hard to control the cracking in my voice.

"And how is Hannah? The baby?" His concern sounded so genuine. It broke my anger and my pride; it shattered my resistance into a thousand pieces. My tears came hot and fast, along with flooding remorse and repentance.

"She left again—gone back to the sorcerer in some far-off land. Mother decided to keep the babies with her. I did offer to bring the little one back here and find a nurse for him, but she refused." I shook my head and swiped at my tears. "Hannah chose death, the same as her husband."

My words sank in for a moment, and he furrowed his brow.

He asked about my hip and my hand. I pulled up my sleeve to show him the scar, healed over and pink. With a gentle caress, he took my arm, inspected it, and shook his head. When he looked back up into my face, his eyes were the ones pooled with tears.

"I'll never forgive myself for hurting you, my Love," he said, pulling my hand to his chest.

I sighed and reveled in touching him, finally. "Well, that's ironic."

"Why?"

"Because I don't think I can forgive myself for what I've done in my insolence. I never should have questioned your actions." I gazed steadily into his face now and said what I had needed for weeks to say: "I'm so sorry, Josiah."

He shook his head in disgust. "Don't ever apologize for that night, Angel," he said, pulling me into his arms. "I'll never lose my temper like that again—I promise."

His embrace was crushing, and I loved even the pain of it. I rested my head on his chest, further wetting my tear-stained cheek, and inhaled him deeply.

"Josiah, may I ask you a question? I realized today that something has been bothering me for a while." I pulled away slightly to see his expression.

"Yes, anything, Love," he answered.

"Why didn't you come back? When my father died?" I looked into his eyes, longing for understanding. "I really needed you. I needed someone to comfort me. I waited for you to come back—even if only for a few days. Why didn't you come?"

He scanned my face, looking from my eyes to my lips and back up again as I talked. His face pained when he heard my question. "Because He didn't release me, and because I knew you would be alright. Jehovah promised me a long time ago that He would be your Comforter. I knew in my absence He would dry your tears and embrace you with His love. He promised me as much many years ago. I heard Him in the fire."

I began to weep. And of course, He had comforted me. When I had finally chosen to turn to Him, it was exactly what I needed and longed for: soothing and peace. My God had carried me through that grief.

Josiah changed the subject. "What about your hip?" he asked, and dropped his hand to the top of my thigh.

I gasped with surprised delight and sudden desire.

"Oh, you are still hurting there?" he asked, immediately pulling his hand away.

"No," I said, pulling his head to mine. "I have no pain at all." He smiled in understanding and bent to press his lips to mine, threatening to devour me. In all trust and safety, I allowed him. Tantalizing joy swirled from my toes to my head as once again I was lost in his arms and enveloped in his longing.

\* \* \*

That night we lay under our blankets and spent the entire evening staring into the fire. Josiah had removed the stone hearth wall and there was nothing but the pit of sand in the floor to hold it in. The flames poured up like streams of yellow-orange water flowing heavenward. Wood crackled and snapped without ceasing, and when it even so much as slowed, Josiah would add more, leaning the logs dangerously close to the coals and flames.

"You know, that isn't safe for the children." I remarked. "What happened to the hearth?"

"I couldn't keep it. All I thought of every time I touched it was the frightened look in your eyes."

"But you loved that hearth. So did I."

"No, Hamutal. I love the flames ..." *Yes,* I agreed silently. *You have always needed the fire to calm you.* Like the flames, his passion consumed everything he had ever done. I traced the worry on his brow, and his eyes closed, relaxing slightly.

"What plagues your thoughts, my King?"

"Hmm?" He paused for a moment. "The Temple."

"Why?"

"Jehovah deserves more. Better," he replied, opening his eyes and sitting up on his elbow to look at me.

"You mean repairs."

"Smart woman." He grinned and brushed a strand of hair out of my face. His gaze remained over my shoulder, his face pensive once again. For long moments, he stayed that way, and I gave him the silence.

"Do you realize that I've been waiting years for someone to come and restore dignity to Jehovah's house?" I asked after a few moments.

I allowed the vision of richness and splendor to take my thoughts as I closed my eyes. Cracked beams replaced with new cedar. Shining stones, gold-plated gates and doors, and clean curtains. Rubble removed and cleared from every crevice.

"It will take years, you know," he said.

"I wonder what we will find ..."

# BOOK THREE

# 29. JOSIAH

For six long years, they had toiled. In the heat and the wind and the storms, I had visited every day, but I let them work. It was a slow work, the progress sluggish and infuriating. Hamutal forbade my daily marches up the hill when I began to come home raging. The seventh-day worship and sacrifices for Sabbath brought a cooling relief—for I could see some weekly change that was not there daily.

The muted brown dust swirled endlessly in my kingdom, and I feared my eyes would see no other color. Sand filled my cloaks and robes and sandals until I thought of nothing save the baths for day after sweltering day.

I had appointed Maaseiah as Jerusalem's mayor just after Hamutal came back from Libnah without Hannah. He had been her driver and assistant, and she recommended him for higher leadership based on his fierce loyalty and devotion to God. Her reasoning was wise: "He's too strong and loyal a leader to be merely my driver, Josiah," she had said. His actions proved her words true.

One day he came to my throne room with the daily report of Temple repairs: "My lord, the collection ..." he said and waved in six men who lugged three large chests into the court and dropped them on the marble with labored thumps.

I was confused. "What's this?"

Maaseiah replied, "Why, the funds for the Temple repairs, as you requested."

"But I ordered those two years ago. What is the meaning of all of this?"

"We've been paying for the workers' wages from the Temple treasury while the Levitical officers traveled the nation on collection duty."

"Oh," I said, the order of the matter and timing now becoming clear. "Well, it must be given to Hilkiah and the foreman, of course." He picked it back up off the marble. I spoke again. "Will this bring faster progress, in your estimates?"

"Yes, Your Highness. These funds will greatly increase our purchasing power for materials—both stone and lumber. And the foreman will be notified, of course," he said.

"Maaseiah," I said.

"Yes, sire?"

"Let's give them a bonus—that will be motivating, don't you think?"

"Indeed. And I will again express your desire for timely completion."

"Very good. I like your persuasive tone."

These Levitical priests and my foremen—Jahath, Obadiah, Zechariah, and Meshullam—all God-fearing and loyal to my crown, had overseen the Temple repairs thus far, taking orders only from Hilkiah and myself. They were supervisors in every area, masters at every trade, or so it seemed. How their knowledge stretched from the Temple traditions to heavy construction while working as skilled musicians and composers, I couldn't fathom, but gratitude overshadowed understanding of their talent.

\* \* \*

Jeremiah continued to come and go throughout my kingdom and to distant cities, declaring the judgment of God in any way possible. He came home to his room in the palace, where I insisted he stay when in Jerusalem, though I knew sometimes he secretly slept in the streets, so exhausted from preaching that he'd lie down where he was. One night, during the third watch, he knocked on the door to our quarters to let me know he had returned from prophesying in Samaria.

"I don't think I can do this any longer, Josiah," he said.

"Do what? Teach or preach?" I asked.

"Any of it."

"What is the word of the LORD, brother? You know I for one will listen."

"You don't want to know, my King."

"Try me."

"*Your wickedness will bring its own punishment. Your turning from Me will shame you. You will see what an evil, bitter thing it is to abandon the LORD your God and not to fear Him. I, the LORD, the LORD of Heaven's Armies, have spoken.*"

"You were right. So it hasn't changed, then. Even with the Temple repairs."

"No, it hasn't."

I walked him down the corridor to his room where he disrobed and fell into his bed. He stared up at me in silence for a long moment, pleading for a release he knew I couldn't give. My eyes pleaded his for the same.

* * *

I allowed the Levites to carry on the work of the Temple, satisfied at least with the generous response from the nation. My boys were maturing more and more each day, and knowing me less and less. Their studies of Hebrew and battle formation and time spent sparring with swords and shields kept them out of trouble in the city, though I worried about Eliakim from time to time. He seemed infatuated with the stars and with trying to read their positions in the night sky.

One night, I took a walk outside of the palace gates and found him gazing into the dark sky with a telescope he had made with his tutor that week. When I asked him what he saw, he abruptly dropped the scope from his eye to his side and stammered for words.

"Uh ... oh ... Father, I ... I, er, I didn't know you were there."

"How long have you been out here, son? The stars are glorious tonight—what do you see with that thing?"

"Oh … well," he said, "it just makes them look closer and bigger. I don't really see anything new."

"The heavens display the majesty of the LORD, don't they?"

"If you say so …" he replied, trailing off the last word in reflection.

"Eli, would you like to help me with the Temple plans this week? You can see the progress up close, you know. Would that interest you?"

"I don't know. I guess I could come for a day or two," he said.

"I think you'll enjoy the rebuilding. It is wise for a future king to know what it takes to restore an important monument. I've waited so long to see it purified, and now we have the finances to move forward with the building and repairs. Your mother and I are very excited."

"Have you seen Mother this evening?" he asked, changing the subject too obviously.

"Of course. She is in bed already, which is where you should be as well."

"Right. I'll be going, then." He looked up at the stars again, and I wondered again what he saw that pulled his heart so fiercely. I wondered, and I worried.

Once he had gone, I lost my gaze in the twinkling lights above. How clear and cloudless the night was—I marveled at the crisp, white light pouring from the moon. The throne room of the Almighty was a splendor I failed to praise Him for enough. I pictured Him seated among the stars and fell to my knees on the quiet sand.

"Jehovah, what majesty!" I whispered in wonder. *You reign over all this earth, LORD. Who am I that You would see me and help me? Oh, God that You would show my people who You are. That they would see You as I do now, that they would love You and forsake the idols of their hearts and their homes. Though I don't see the idols any longer in the streets, I still see them in my dreams. O God, take them from me—the nightmares. The burning gods cry out from the fire— LORD, do not let my mind ponder the horror of them!*

\* \* \*

The next morning, I read over the scrolls of King Solomon and traced a line that made me sit back in my seat with confusion. *God detests the prayers of a person who ignores the law.* My reasoning got the better of me, and I thought of my prayers the night before. Had God detested my requests and pleas? I did not know which law Solomon was referring to. I had scoured the palace library only to come away empty-handed. *What law, LORD—which one?*

And, as if on cue, Shaphan burst into my courtroom, breathless.

"My lord, we found a scroll!"

# 30. HAMUTAL

The day the Book of the Law was found was the beginning of the end.

That morning, the heat rose and fell in waves threatening to choke me. I gathered my hair that had fallen in wet pieces on my face and tucked it back into my shawl—the very same shawl I would have tossed had I not been in front of so many others. Had I been alone, it would have been a heap on the ground by now. But the ever-present stares of our subjects fixed the discomfort of heat on my head.

Dust flew with every step as I walked the distance from the Temple to the palace with my sons and tried not to drag my own feet in protest. Like the sun's penetrating rays, my dread pierced through the rhythm of our footfalls and blazed without relief.

Josiah had not come to the morning sacrifice for Sabbath. What could have happened that he would miss the worship? Only an emergency council meeting would keep him away. Fear rose in my chest and stole the little breath that the hot air had already robbed, and I put my hand to my throat to still my thoughts.

Was it an attack? Could it be Syria or Egypt or Moab? A battle to call my husband away? Rebellion in Samaria? Idolatry among the priests? My lungs longed for a breeze as my heart craved some kind of answers. Eli and Jeho covered their foreheads to shield their eyes from the dust and bright sun, and I ducked into the gate afraid.

Lord, *brace me. Prepare me for what I might find.*

Asaiah urgently summoned me to the courtroom, where I found Josiah wailing and tearing his clothes down to his under-linens. His

249

advisors and delegates stood around in confusion, shouting at him to stop and think rational thoughts. Just then Josiah stood, took the goblet from his table, and hurled it at the marble wall.

I demanded to know the source of his commotion, to which Secretary Shaphan took me by the shoulders and shouted into my face, "My lady, you *must* talk to him—he refuses to listen to me ..."

"What set him off?"

"All I did was read him the scroll Hilkiah found in the Temple this morning ... I read it for a short time, and then he burst out with this wailing. I don't know what it is. I don't know what to do. My Queen," he looked back at him again. "Hamutal, please ... do something!"

"Give me the scroll." I read it to myself quickly, following the lines with my finger, searching for the clue to the madness ... Moses ... wilderness ... fire and cloud ... Joshua ... King of Heshbon ... *I don't see anything here ...*

"Where were you reading when he started this?" I asked Shaphan.

Josiah ordered everyone out, shouting above their arguing. I pleaded with him and ran over to put my hands on his shoulders.

"Breathe, my King," I said over the commotion. "Tell me what it is, let me help you to—"

"There is no hope, no helping. We are all doomed!" he shouted and spun away to sob again, falling to his knees before the cold hearth.

Everyone had heeded his demand except Acbor and Jared, who looked to me for answers I didn't have.

"Build a fire in his hearth—quickly," I said. The room was already sweltering, but the flames would calm him. "Let me read the scroll some more. There's got to be something in there that upset him. I'll find it."

Shaphan rolled it out on the table and slid his finger next to the portion that had upset my husband so. "I think it started in here somewhere, and this is where he stopped me."

I read the portion carefully.

"'*So be careful not to break the covenant the* LORD *your God has made with you. Do not make idols of any shape or form, for the* LORD *your God has forbidden this. The* LORD *your God is a devouring fire; he is a jealous God. In the future, when you have children and grandchildren and have lived in the land a long time, do not corrupt yourselves by making idols of any kind. This is evil in the sight of the* LORD *your God and will arouse his anger. Today I call on heaven and earth as witnesses against you. If you break my covenant, you will quickly disappear from the land you are crossing the Jordan to occupy. You will live there only a short time; then you will be utterly destroyed.'"*

And I was frozen in grief too. "Utterly destroyed?"

Josiah was right—we were all doomed. The judgment of the LORD sank into my soul and forced my knees to hit the marble floor hard. I stared at him as he stared back at me, only tears and air separating our hearts. What were we to do? It was already over. His ruling already finished. We had absolutely no hope of ever going back and changing the past of our nation's evil. Though he himself had fought to rid this place of idols and bring true worshippers into the Temple, what good was it? The people were no closer to knowing God now than the day Josiah's arms had been burned rescuing the child from Molech's flames.

I picked up the scroll, wiped my tears, and read again, this time searching for a clause to God's wrath—an escape—though I knew none existed. A few lines later, I saw the beautiful promise we sang each Sabbath: *"If you obey all the decrees and commands I am giving you today, all will be well with you and your children. I am giving you these instructions so you will enjoy a long life in the land the* LORD *your God is giving you for all time."*

But I had never known what exactly those instructions were. The rules we followed for Sabbath? Temple traditions? Decrees of the Levites? I read on, searching for a clue. But what I found was not a clue. It was THE Law. All of it.

I cried out again, letting my wailing match the pitch Josiah had made when I first came in. I forced myself to read each law and decree aloud. Every one of them was like a knife to my flesh, a blade drawing the blood of my soul out in pain.

*"You must not have any other god but me.*

*"You must not make for yourself an idol of any kind, or an image of anything in the heavens or on the earth or in the sea. You must not bow down to them or worship them, for I, the* LORD *your God, am a jealous*

*God who will not tolerate your affection for any other gods. I lay the sins of the parents upon their children; the entire family is affected—even children in the third and fourth generations of those who reject me. But I lavish unfailing love for a thousand generations on those who love me and obey my commands.*"

Here, Josiah seemed to growl like an animal and then shouted, "No more!" I looked up from reading, but I could no more stop the commands from pouring from my mouth than I could stop the sun.

"*You must not misuse the name of the* LORD *your God. The* LORD *will not let you go unpunished if you misuse his name.*

"*Observe the Sabbath day by keeping it holy, as the* LORD *your God has commanded you. Remember that you were once slaves in Egypt, but the* LORD *your God brought you out with his strong hand and powerful arm. That is why the* LORD *your God has commanded you to rest on the Sabbath day.*

"*Honor your father and mother, as the* LORD *your God commanded you. Then you will live a long, full life in the land the* LORD *your God is giving you.*

"*You must not murder.*

"*You must not commit adultery.*

"*You must not steal.*

"*You must not testify falsely against your neighbor.*

"*You must not covet your neighbor's wife.*"

And they went on and on. Every law spelled out the heart of a loving God who had shielded our people since the beginning of time—a caring Father who wanted the best for His children and told us exactly how to live and succeed in this place He had given to us in generosity.

And we had desecrated every single one. Over and over, the book detailed the rules—promised blessing if we followed and guaranteed curses if we strayed. I kept reading into the afternoon, unable to halt my eyes or my voice until finally I was silenced by this: "*Just as the* LORD *has destroyed other nations in your path, you also will be destroyed if you refuse to obey the* LORD *your God.*"

Finally, I lifted my eyes to find him, but he was gone. The embers were dying out slowly. I rose to look about the room. I was alone with the Law. I held it to my breast and cherished the ancient smell of it for a long time. I was touching the same parchment our ancestors had written on so many years before. I pondered and wondered. *How long has it been hidden in the Temple? It must have been buried before anyone of our generation or our parents' generation, for my father surely would have told me about it had he known. How could we have strayed this far?* It was like every piece of this Scripture puzzle began to fit together in a horrible prediction of our future. I placed the scroll on the king's table and ran to find him.

\* \* \*

"Queen Hamutal, I've been searching the palace for you," Asaiah shouted across the courtyard, as I stepped out from the garden gate. Josiah was nowhere to be found. I had searched our chambers, the Temple, even the harem. Nothing.

"Have you seen the king?" I asked him.

He shook his head, desperation setting in. "What should we do? Matters of state are urgent, the Temple guard requests his presence for renovations, and he seemed more distraught than I've ever known him to be. What was it? Why did he grieve so?"

"It was the Law. The Book that has eluded him for years. It's everything we've done wrong for generations, all the ways we've disgraced God, and the guaranteed curse on his nation. Asaiah—this is our doom. God's words, promising His wrath. Josiah has been hoping to avoid it, but the Book says it will not be averted. We've fallen too far. We've all gone astray. Too far astray. Who knows how long we have. After all our nation has done, after the way our people have played the harlot with their idols—you must know that every hope the king had for his nation has been dashed with this curse of the Law."

"Can we do nothing for him?" He ventured to muster hope I didn't have.

"What is there to do?"

"Is there a prophet? A man of God? Perhaps we can know when this doom will be—if indeed it is eminent."

But Jeremiah was not here. God had called him away. And once again God had removed from my world what I most needed—in my most difficult hour. *Why won't You let me have them both when catastrophe hits? God, why? Why call Jeremiah to Samaria again? What next?*

"Let me think," I said. "I may know someone. I will pray. I'll be in the Temple. Please send Josiah or a messenger up if you find him. And I'll send for you if I find him as well. Understood?"

"Yes, my Queen."

I searched his eyes for assurance before he turned. They held none.

# 3I. JOSIAH

In the garden behind my palace, Hamutal had planted blooms, and the gardener lovingly tended them with time and toil. Each season brought a new color, fresh flowers, and a different scent. On hot days, I'd wait until the sun had nearly gone down and then set out into the stone paths where I could get away from the council and the Temple restoration crew. I would imagine my garden as Eden and lose myself in the fragrance of my would-be paradise.

The day Asaiah brought me the Book of the Law, I listened to Hamutal reading it until I could no longer stand to hear the reminders of disobedience and curses. I hurried to the garden for solace. In a small way, I suppose I found it, though not until several hours later when the sun began to set on the mountain like a ball of flames igniting the clouds.

Though I attempted many times to pray, all that would come were tears and groans. Failure screamed louder than the curses, and the burden of countless lives in my kingdom weighed heavier than I knew was possible. If I thought presiding over God's people was unmanageable before, that day in the garden I realized the true hopelessness of it all. And I had nothing to offer the LORD but anguish.

With rents in my robes and ashes in my hair, I staggered back to my quarters late that evening. The only comfort God offered me was that of my queen's embrace. Somehow, it was enough, and I slept.

\* \* \*

The next day, I stayed in bed, sick with fever and vomiting. Hamutal asked what was to be done, and I had no answer for her.

"What can anyone do now?" I rolled over to heave into my basin, and she wiped my head with the cool cloth again.

"I'm not sure, but the council needs some direction. What would you advise them to accomplish in this interim, while we wait to know what comes next?"

"Tell them to seek the LORD. Only He knows. I know nothing else to do. What is done is already finished. God's wrath is burning at us furiously now. We'll be consumed before we know it. Hamutal—think of all my grandfathers and fathers have done! Every ancient law—utterly disgraced! Who knows but that our captors will be advancing across the plains any day now."

"I know," she said with fresh tears again.

That afternoon, I sent the council to Huldah, the only prophet I trusted, and that was only because Jeremiah had shown her God's truth and how to wield it. Her powers were beyond my understanding, but the truth was based on Holy Scripture—on the Prophets and David's Songs and the Chronicles. Her words never came back wrong, and though she was a woman, she was true. That was all I cared about now. With Jeremiah off again in Samaria, her proximity brought hope of instruction even before sunset, while his reaching us could take days or weeks.

I pictured Asaiah, Shaphan, Hilkiah, Ahikam, and Acbor traveling down the streets to the Second Quarter and regretted this illness that held me fast to this bed. I wanted to be with them. And longed with all that was in me to hear her words from Jehovah for myself. Perhaps they would find a loophole. Could I hold onto hope for God's mercy? In the back of my mind, I knew it was for naught. God would not be made a liar. How could He say anything contrary to what He had said all along? How could He retract the curses when He had never once retracted a single promise? I had spent my entire life watching Him make His prophecies into manifested, visual truth. What made me think this one would be any different?

*Hope.* The answer to my question bounced back off of the corner of my thoughts and hung over my head in unspeakable peace.

And suddenly, I knew what I needed to do. I slung my feet over the bed and stood, reeling with dizziness and nausea. Immediately, I sat back down.

"What are you doing?" Hamutal rushed over from the table to steady me.

"Please, tell the council to convene. I've got to get rid of this illness today. I know what we must do. Everyone must be summoned now to—"

"What are you babbling about?" she asked, easing me back down. "They won't be back for a few hours. You need to rest now."

"Yes, yes—but when they come ... I must speak with Asaiah and Jared. Shaphan and Hilkiah, too."

"Alright, then. I'll tell them. Please—rest. If you're going to attend council you won't be able to bring your basin with you."

And for the first time in many days, I smiled. "No, Love. I suppose that wouldn't be effective leadership, now, would it?"

She smiled back and dabbed my forehead once again.

\* \* \*

When the council met that afternoon, I awaited their response from Huldah as eagerly as I anticipated revealing my plan. When the words from her prophecy came, however, dread set in once again.

"My lord, the words of Huldah, as you requested ..." Shaphan began and then trailed off, waiting for me to acknowledge my readiness, though I had already given it. *What is he waiting for?*

He shuffled his feet on the smooth marble and looked around to the others.

"Go on ..." I sat forward in my throne and removed the crown, placing it on the floor beside me, which my attendant quickly retrieved and placed on its table.

He cleared his throat again. "The words of Huldah the prophetess, wife of Shallum ..." Yet another hesitation.

"Shaphan, go on! Tell me all of it. Leave nothing out, not a single word!"

"Yes, Highness. She said: 'God's Word, the Word of the LORD—"All that was read to the king from the Book of the Law of Moses will indeed come to pass. Destruction and exile, the death and doom of nearly all of you! And why? Because you have defiled My Name with your idols and séances. No longer will I tolerate your belligerence. Prepare for the LORD's wrath. There is no satisfying this fire that rages against Israel."'"

I shook my head again at the curse. It was no different, but the confirmation hit with fresh relevance and urgency. God's message to us was the same. *Did I really expect it to change?* We might as well be dead already.

"There's more," Shaphan went on.

I nodded for him to continue. My stomach was rumbling again, and I suddenly wished for Hamutal's hand in mine to steady me. I reached beside me to grasp the scroll of the Law instead.

"She went on to say, 'Tell the king this: because he was repentant and tore his robes with tears at the reading of the Law—'"

"Wait!" I interrupted. "Did you tell her?"

"No, we didn't," said Jared, who stood behind Shaphan just slightly. "We only told her we found the Law and asked her what God would say to us and to you. She knew of your response on her own. Or, rather, from God—I presume."

Amazed once again that Jehovah saw me, even noticed my actions, I motioned for him to continue.

"'Because of his repentance, God has seen you. He says this to the king— "you will live and die in peace. This destruction will not come to you. I will hold My hand of judgment from you, and you will not live to see the destruction of your people. But make no mistake, My fire comes after your rule."'"

It gave new meaning to the phrase "Long live the king." Peace with me but curses and death once I died? What kind of prophecy was this? I was not sure whether to be relieved or afraid. I thought of my sons and of all of the hopes I had placed in them to rule Jerusalem well. I was enforcing hours of instruction as their tutors taught them matters of state and border policies. Doom promised to my children? I would rather have taken it on my own head.

I sat in stunned silence as they waited for me. *Peace? What would I do with promised peace only for my reign?* Only one option came to mind. If we had a few more decades, I would live to obey Him. And if I had anything to do with it, my subjects would respond likewise.

"Finish refurbishing the Temple by next Sabbath," I ordered. "The nation gathers in Jehovah's House on that day. And I mean *everyone.*"

# 32. HAMUTAL

No one could have known how the nation would respond with such devotion until they all came that day. So many subjects, more numerous than I had known existed in our lands, by decree from the king—all of them came, more than ready for what he asked of them. If Josiah had questioned his influence before that day, he would never do so again.

They came to Jerusalem from near and far. More than one hundred runners had been sent to the extents of our borders, and even beyond to any sons of Israel who would hear the king's decree: "Come! Come to Jerusalem—to the Temple of the Almighty, the God of our fathers, and gather to hear the Word. King Josiah summons you and your family." Not one person was left uninvited, so vast was the decree. Josiah asked for them all, and I had to believe they all had come.

Thousands of arms and legs were crowding into our small city, which had seemed so grand and spacious the day before. The smell of bodies crammed together in the heat was stifling, and I was thankful for my shawl, my custom, and my gender as I crossed the fabric over my nose and inhaled my mint oil from it. We watched from the palace towers—watched them streaming in without hesitation or fear. They came with smiles, and Josiah looked at me with apprehension. After gazing over the expanse of the city again, he shook his head in amazement.

"What, my King; didn't you think they'd come?" I said and patted his shoulder gently.

He chuckled at me a little and widened his eyes slightly. "I suppose I did have my doubts. There really are so many. How are we going to get them all within earshot of the Temple?"

It was my turn to shake my head in awe. I shrugged, unsure. "Callers in the streets to repeat it?"

"Hmm," he mused, rubbing his beard and twisting his lips. Calling a messenger over, he spoke my suggestion into being and had the instruction delivered to Asaiah.

Just then, Jeremiah strode across the courtyard with his scribe and attendant. We caught him in the corner of our eyes at the same time and turned simultaneously to greet him. His beard was darker and his hair lighter. He brushed the long locks back with his fingers as he rushed toward us with a broad smile.

"Jeremiah, where have you been all these weeks?" the king exclaimed.

"In the forsaken deserts of your land. You really must permit the beautification officers to plant more gardens and crops. The sand is endless in this kingdom of yours."

He embraced my husband and they laughed heartily. To have Jeremiah back for this was more than we could have asked. We had become used to the lack of him—accustomed to the desire to use his words as a crutch, with the powerlessness to do so because God had kept him inaccessible. Jehovah's plans often confused me. Though I loved the prophet dearly, and craved his presence and clear messages from God every bit as much as Josiah did, I wondered if the reason we were deprived of him was so that the king and I would seek the LORD for ourselves.

"In which barren place were you hiding all this time? Have you seen the decree?" I asked.

Jeremiah came to the ledge to scan the crowd as they pushed into the streets with polite impatience. They became more and more anxious as the minutes passed, curiosity rising like the stench from under their arms. Even with all of this in the atmosphere, when I looked at individual faces, nearly every one of them held a smile of tolerant courtesy.

"From the ends of Samaria, my Queen, and even there, I received the decree from the king to assemble today." He stared intently into my eyes for a moment, and I shrugged off his gaze with a chuckle.

"Well, stay awhile this time, Prophet. I do believe you'll want to examine the texts for yourself," Josiah said.

Jeremiah turned to my husband just as Asaiah rushed in and knelt before us.

"Ah, yes—what did you find?" Jeremiah asked.

Josiah put one finger up to the prophet and turned to his servant, nodding. "Yes?"

"Pardon the interruption, Your Highness, but Shaphan is ready. The masses are beginning to get restless. He believes it would be best to start immediately."

Josiah turned back to Jeremiah. "It seems you will get to hear it with the rest of my subjects, friend. For the record, I would have shown you first if we had more time. But fear not, we will have hours to pour over the words of Moses after I've read them to everyone."

Jeremiah was stunned. I had never seen him speechless, and yet, here he was, the great prophet without words, his jaw hanging agape. I worked to control my chiding within as Josiah took my hand and ushered us all down the palace steps to the courtyard below. He was headed to the Temple, to the king's pillar at the entrance. I prepared my heart to hear it again and bid him farewell with a kiss.

But his hand held my wrist unexpectedly.

We exchanged thoughts with our eyes—mine of confusion and his of insistence. "You think I'm doing this without you?" he asked.

I stammered for a moment. "I had thought ..." I looked to Asaiah and Jeremiah—highly qualified men to stand by the king.

"No, Love. You thought wrong. Shaphan will hold the scroll and be sure I read it all without missing a letter. But you ..." Here he paused and looked into my eyes with purpose. "You will stand beside me, just as you always have. Just as you always will."

I brushed a tear away and shook my head—not in argument, but in amazement. Such an honor was beyond my comprehension, and one I had not been prepared for—not in the slightest. But perhaps that's what God had planned, because just as I thought of an endless list of protests, we were whisked away by Jared and Asaiah to the top the Temple stairs where Shaphan was standing. Solomon's Porch never seemed so small, for standing before the entrance were all of Josiah's council and every priest, lined up with their shoulders arched in apprehension, their eyes all staring at my husband in the same way.

The king turned to whisper into my ear as we ascended the freshly swept stairs to the Temple, "By the way they glare, I'm either ignorant or insane."

"Both, my lord," I teased to cut the tension. "But they said the same of Moses and Samuel and David. It seems the insanity of this world is the intelligence of the LORD." I smiled reassuringly and squeezed his arm.

He stepped out from the portico and raised a hand to quiet the crowds. I stood at his side, holding onto him for dear life, even as he did the same to me. No one else felt him shaking. Only I was aware that under his great courage crouched fear—about to pounce at any moment. Scanning the crowds and the endless sea of faces in every direction, I struggled to steady myself so I could steady him. As the multitudes quieted gradually, we breathed together in unison, our chests pounding.

"I'm here," I whispered, tilting my mouth up to his ear.

He nodded, not taking his eyes from the streets below. The voices were still curious and jovial and showed no hint of riot that I could decipher. Jeremiah had come up behind us and now stood with his father and cousins who served in the Temple together. Jared and the guard waited for a sign from Josiah, but he gave none. The king felt unthreatened by his subjects. Though not unprepared for mutiny, he saw past their outward reaction to each heart, and we both stood firm, praying it would be more than ears that would hear the Law. We prayed it into their hearts and souls. As we had the night before, we whispered prayers of obedience.

When they had calmed a bit more, Josiah summoned Shaphan to bring the first scroll. He approached slowly and cautiously. Josiah looked up at the masses again.

"My brothers and sisters, sons and daughters of Jacob—you've come and I thank you. Your king acknowledges your obedient display."

They began to cheer and roar as one, but he raised a hand to silence them again.

"I've kept you in the dark as to the reason of my summons, but you need not be in suspense any longer. Last week as the Temple restoration came to a close, the priests found this ancient document here before me. Indeed, it is the very Law of Moses—hidden and buried these many years!"

He paused to gauge their response, but they remained silent. It seemed they all held their breath in unison. I glanced over at Jeremiah, who transferred his weight from one foot to the other, waiting to hear the Word of the LORD.

As Josiah began to read the history of Moses and the people on the mountain of Sinai, callers on rooftops repeated him every few sentences. The people gave rapt attention as he recounted and retold the stories in full, which they'd likely only heard previously only in pieces. It had never been told to them like this. Not in its entirety. Not as Moses had written. Looks of consternation fell over them as mothers hushed their babies so they could hear. I could imagine their thoughts racing, just as my own had when I was the one reading a week before: *Was this truly the writing of our father, Moses?*

Josiah kept reading, looking up every so often to check their countenance. Somehow, by something miraculous, they all kept listening. Every once in a while, we heard a slight communal sigh or gasp, but there was no interruption, no shout, not even a single protest. I held my husband's arm and nodded at him to continue whenever he seemed hesitant. Men echoed every word from the rooftops, as Moses's ancient words spread to every subject of our nation.

At last, he came to the warning before the commands, and he paused to brace himself with a breath. I knew that he would not interrupt the text with his own words once he had begun, but I felt his desire to preface the decrees with a warning or added admonition. He resisted and continued, as the sun rose in the sky and thickened the air with waves of heat.

"'This is the day I call on heaven and earth as witnesses. If you break these commands I give you today, you will not live in the land I have promised you. You will be destroyed and only a fragment of you will survive to be scattered among the nations where you will worship *statues and empty gods. But when you are there and you call on my Name I will rescue you.'"*

The priests began to look at one another in confusion, as did the people on the streets. They had begun to realize that this was more than a civics lesson from the king or the celebration of a holiday. The Law loomed before him, and the Spirit of God fell over all of us in an eerie hush as Josiah continued.

*"'Consider all of history and recall what has been done before you. Is there any other nation whose God has spoken to them as I have spoken to you? Is there any other people who have been delivered with signs, wonders, and miracles—as I have delivered my people Israel? So keep this in mind—I am giving you these commands today to keep in your mind and teach to your children. There is no other god in heaven or on earth. I am the LORD your God who loves you, and I give you this Law so that you may obey it and live for a long time in the blessed land I give you today.'"*

At this, the murmuring began. As if with one voice, I heard from the streets, "Law?" They looked at one another in confusion and then back to the king again. Their faces fell in fear as they considered the ramifications of the words in the scroll.

\* \* \*

Later that afternoon, my husband finished the last line on the last scroll and looked up to see the people still in the streets and courtyards below the Temple. They began to look at one another quizzically, wondering if he was finished. Josiah knew the last thing he had to do would be the hardest, but after murmuring a prayer for strength under his breath, he continued. I could only watch and hold his arm.

"Today, I vow as your king to uphold all of these laws and regulations, which you have heard in the presence of the LORD your God. You have heard the promises—the blessings if we obey and the curses if we do not. Brothers—we are children of the Most High God—Jehovah is His name. He has rescued us from Egypt, Cush, Moab, and Assyria—how can we *not* obey Him? How can we not serve Him with every breath we take?

"My countrymen, I plead with you to take this vow with me, lest we suffer the curse bearing down on us as we speak. Perhaps the LORD will have mercy on us if we will unite in obedience!"

# 33. JOSIAH

What I expected from my subjects was too much too soon, but zeal for the scrolls was all I could see. Like when the rain comes fast and out of nowhere, I was blind to all else. At night, I would burn candle after candle copying the Law onto my own parchment with Asaiah and Shaphan, though they would be asleep on the table long before I could bring myself to stop. Each day, I would study it with Hilkiah, and we'd debate over which points were enforceable and when. With the Temple finished and peace becoming more of a reality, I sought God in those texts like I never knew possible.

Hamutal began to worry. She claimed I was becoming obsessive, that the Law had consumed my time and attention. But I was pursuing Jehovah's righteousness—His ways—not only for me, but for everyone.

"I am the king. This is my duty. If not to make the people obey God, what else would I do?" I asked her. And she had no rebuttal.

That first year, I focused on two reforms—honoring the Passover Feast in Jerusalem and preventing intermarriage with foreigners. The first was a simple invitation and decree on the surface, but it required extensive time with Hilkiah and the other priests. By the time the festival drew near, the look on their faces had transformed from honor to dread when I approached. The second was a mere mandate to the priests and fathers of the land, and every marriage from that day forth would only be between a Hebrew man and a Hebrew woman. In practice it was simple enough, but we ran into trouble when it came to people who were already in unlawful marriages. I decided to permit them with the requirement that both spouses make weekly sacrifices on the Sabbath. The Passover was the greatest point of contention.

"But who are the singers of the line of Asaph?" I insisted one afternoon as we planned for Festival, looming only a month away.

"Unknown, sire," huffed Zechariah again.

"Listen—according to the book of David, the singers must be his descendants. Where are your genealogies?"

"I believe I saw them in the libraries, Your Highness. I might be able to find them."

"Wonderful," I said with not a little sarcasm. *As if it was so difficult.*

"Jeremiah—am I being unreasonably particular, or is this what God requires?" I knew he'd be in agreement like I knew the sun would set in a few hours. It was an easy vote, but in my mind, the only one I needed.

"No, Your Highness—you're right. The singers for the Passover should be—as for any feast—sons of Asaph. No doubt."

"But my choir has been rehearsing these songs for years," Hilkiah said. "This is ridiculous! Those fools haven't sung a note in their lives."

"Silence!" I shouted. "Just because you haven't kept this Temple as you should have been for these many years doesn't mean we give in now. The regulations of David say—appointed singers sing. Make it so."

Hilkiah's nostrils flared, and he shook his head only slightly. I raised my eyebrows in a challenge, to which he only shrugged.

"I thought so. Now, about the bread. How will we prepare the people? How can we enforce the No Leaven Law?" I looked around the circle, but no one met my eyes directly. "Jared—any ideas?"

He thought for a moment and then shrugged before he spoke: "I can only speak from personal experience. My wife makes delicious bread. One day she ran out of leaven, and tried to make it without. Sire—the loaf was terrible; we had to toss it out. We'll either need to teach the people how to prepare this bread as the LORD desires, or we'll have to provide it for them. Sort of like an exchange. 'Give us your leaven, and we'll give you our bread and instructions for making more'?"

"Hmm," I pondered. "I like it. Bread lessons. Make it so."

Jared balked and gestured toward himself in a silent, *"me?"* I nodded and smiled. He left the council room shaking his head, visibly irritated at how he had talked himself into the pit of women's work.

\* \* \*

That night as I was working on my copy of the Law, Hamutal came into our quarters and stood behind me, massaging my shoulders and neck. I groaned with relief as she kneaded, putting my head down on the table for a few moments. The scent of oils on her skin filled my nose and calmed me. For several minutes, she said nothing, working her healing on my tense muscles.

"I never knew you were a scribe, my lord," she said gently, gesturing over my shoulder to the parchment under my arms.

"I'm making my own copy, like it says."

"It says that? Where?" she asked.

"Here," I answered, rolling back the pages. "'*When he sits on the throne as king, he must copy for himself this body of instruction on a scroll in the presence of the Levitical priests.*'"

I turned to look into her face. She looked up and into the shadow beyond my desk to see Jeremiah and startled.

"You didn't even know I was here, did you, my Queen?" Jeremiah said.

She tossed her head back and laughed. "You frightened me, Jeremiah! Are you here to be sure he remembers his lessons properly?"

"Actually, I'm here to learn, but yes, I do fulfill the Levitical witness. He's quite the scribe—better than I ever was, truth be told. I prefer the reading to the writing or copying. I never saw anyone write so accurately with such speed. He hasn't made a single mistake yet, if you'll believe that."

"Really?" She examined my work, looking from the ancient scroll of the Law back to the fresh parchment. "What about that line there?" she chided.

"Where?" I jumped up, looking at the page where she pointed. Glancing back up at her grin, I chuckled and stood to pick her up in an embrace. "I'm such a fool for you, woman."

"Will you teach me?" She stood beside me with such curiosity and innocence that I could have taken a drink of it.

"To copy? What do you mean? Your father taught you to write. I've received many beautiful letters from you."

"Yes, but that's not like this, is it? Isn't this more complicated—more precise?"

"Yes, I suppose it is. I'll show you, but not tonight, Love. Your eyes are too sleepy, and it's late. For now, be thankful you're the queen instead of the king. Here, give me your hand."

She handed me her right hand, but I reached for the other. Her pale skin was so soft on mine and I couldn't help but kiss it before I took the stiff brush in my hand and dipped it in the ink.

"What are you doing?"

"This is all the copying you'd need, if it would stay. If His name was on your hand, you'd never forget to obey Him, would you?" She looked confused but didn't pull her hand away. I wrote steadily on her palm, even when she twitched with the tickling. When I had finished and blew on the ink to dry it, she gasped sharply.

"It's—it's His name!"

I had brushed on the letters we wrote but never spoke aloud. *Yahweh*—a mere breath of a name, and wasn't that what He'd always been? The breath of life to Adam, the wind and the whisper to Elijah—He was the invisible, yet all-powerful God. Hamutal stared for several minutes in adoration of the letters I'd written there on her palm—so close, so visible, and yet so far.

Her incredulous and innocent eyes searched mine quizzically. All at once, I realized our reversal, and for once, I was teaching her something she'd never learned of Jehovah.

"The prophet Isaiah wrote this: *'See, I have written your name on the palms of my hands. Always in my mind is a picture of Jerusalem's walls in ruins.'*"

Breathless, she closed her fingers around His Name and clutched that fist to her heart. "Thank you, Josiah. How amazing is our God! He never stops wooing me with His love."

I stood again to draw her into my arms and breathed in her loveliness. I couldn't help but agree with her—I too was so struck by this God of endless love. "How about you send the prophet to bed and take a break?" she suggested, burying her head in my chest.

"Alright. Let me finish this section. You lie down, and I'll be right there."

She sighed deeply and backed toward the bed in our adjoining chambers, nodding a farewell to Jeremiah before she turned. And I truly meant to follow her, but woke with a start in the middle of the night, my head snapping up sharply from my work.

* * *

Jeremiah and I continued to copy the Law by night and enforce it by day. I knew the days were dwindling and he would be sent off to some far land before I could protest, so each day with him I tried to stretch the hours. The Passover drew nearer, and I clung to the hope he would not leave before we could celebrate it together. Every letter of the Law was to be fulfilled in regard to the feast, and once again I performed several raids throughout Jerusalem to rid the homes and markets of idols and mediums. We drove out the latter and burned the former, and though I knew there were probably more, I put an end to the raids a week before the Feast began. The next morning, I met with Hilkiah, Zechariah, Jehiel, Conaniah, Hashabiah, Jeiel, and Jozabad—all of the priestly leaders who would be in charge of sacrifices.

"Are the preparations from Levi complete?" I asked.

"It is as you have commanded, Your Highness," Conaniah answered politely.

"Since the Temple has been thoroughly cleaned and consecrated, it will be acceptable to bring the Ark back into its resting place. No more carrying it back and forth to your homes, understood?"

"But I thought you had commanded—"

"Yes, I remember. But the Law clearly mandates the Ark to stay in the Holy of Holies. And now that we've driven out all unclean worshippers and images, it should be at rest, as it says. Let us keep the Presence where It was always determined to stay."

"As you have commanded," he said.

"Good. May the LORD bless your faithful service to His ceremony and His people," I blessed the priests collectively.

"And you, my lord," they answered in unison.

\* \* \*

On the eve of the Festival, I met with all of the priests at the Temple for consecration, prayer, and final preparations. We checked everything off of our list and tallied the people and lambs. Because the majority of people had traveled so far, and many more would come and go through-out the week, we overcompensated with extra livestock. My hands wouldn't stop sweating, and I couldn't rid my chest of a heaviness that had settled there since I'd found the Book of the Law. I unrolled my copy of it and took mental note of every detail about the Passover and the Festival that was to follow for seven days. The next day would be the Sabbath to begin it all—the initiation of atonement blood for the nation of Israel, and my nation of Judah. We had rid the city of leaven, selling and then eventually trading loaves to those who had no means. My troops and soldiers, as well as the Temple guards had been ordered to inspect every home within the radius of the city, but still I worried. *What if they've kept leaven in secret? How will we stave off the LORD's wrath then?*

"Are the priests and Levites trained and ready for all of the slaugh-ter?" I asked Hilkiah.

"Yes, of course."

"And they are in order of age, rank, and family?"

"Yes, Highness."

"What about the lambs? How many do we have?" It was the third time I'd asked in the last hour.

"Thirty-seven thousand lambs and goats, as well as sixty-five hundred bulls. Most of that from your personal donations. All of the priests have given from their flocks and herds as well," he repeated in rote.

"Will that be enough? We're redeeming the entire nation, I remind you."

"Sire," he assured me, "I cannot recall, nor can I find record of a larger offering since King Solomon dedicated this Temple upon its original foundation. If any amount of blood could redeem these people, this will be plenty."

I could only hope the high priest was correct. Only God could know the depth of our debt, the height of our sin, and the blood it would take to wash it away. For all of the idols I'd burned over the years, for all of the witchcraft still reported and the mediums still imprisoned in our land—our transgressions appeared insurmountable. Our only hope was the Law, and following every line of it. If I was to save my people, I needed to enforce it in every city, every home, every heart. Perhaps the LORD would spare my sons if we appeased His wrath with obedience.

I had to try.

# 34. HAMUTAL

In the years following the first Passover Josiah instated, he worked tirelessly to enforce every letter of the scroll he carried and kept by our bed. Though we knew God as One who wooed and rescued His people, to me He became something else. Angry—ever angry.

The Voice I'd heard as a girl calling me on the mountain, became a constant scolding and began to sound more and more like Josiah's voice in my recollection. For many years, I couldn't hear Him, though I could read the Book of the Law whenever I wanted to know His heart. The lines I first committed to memory were not the first ones the king remembered. In all reality, he remembered them all. With as much time as he spent reading them in the middle of the night, it was no wonder.

My treasures were the instructions for parents and children, and so I taught Eli and Jeho to say the beginning, and before long, they knew it as well as I did.

"'*Listen, O Israel! The* LORD *is our God, the* LORD *alone. And you must love the* LORD *your God with all your heart, all your soul, and all your strength. And you must commit yourselves wholeheartedly to these commands that I am giving you today.*'"

And then they were off to play and spar with one another again. I had tried everything I could think of to pass on my devotion, but it would always be rote for them. They only repeated it to be finished with me and run to the hills after lessons. Even the tutors could not find any desire in the boys to learn the Law. Josiah told me they would grow out of their restlessness, but I was not convinced. Morning by morning, I woke with a command on my lips to teach them, and day after day they rolled their eyes at me.

I began to wonder why the seeds I was planting in their hearts looked back at me like bare soil. None of their father's passion for worship manifested, and Eli especially grew to detest our hours with the scrolls. One day, he threw them across the room.

"Why do we have to do this again?" he shouted, picking up the others to hurl as well.

Mustering my sternest scowl, I rushed over to stay his hands. "No, son. You may *never* treat Jehovah's Law with contempt. Set them down and find your bow. Tempers are the worst companions to learning."

He shoved them into my hands and stormed out of the room. Though he never raged that way again, his quiet contempt grew, as did my worry. Those blue eyes of his held a brewing rebellion I could only pray would be snuffed in time.

An expanding cloud of failure settled over my heart. With Josiah's growing mandates, and arguments with the council members, I left the matters of state to his capable guidance, and resolved to keep my opinions to myself. What did I know anyway? Who cared that I thought some of the laws were too taxing for the average family? They were the Laws. From the LORD. By His command. What choice did we have?

\* \* \*

In that same year as the first Passover we celebrated, I became pregnant with my second son, Mattaniah. When he arrived in the gray chill of a very frigid winter, my heart warmed once again with a mother's joy. The wrinkled, soft skin of his arms and legs begged to be kissed, and for months I stayed in my chambers, drinking in his sweetness. Josiah spoke blessings over him, as he had the other boys, and began to read him the Law, too. At first, I chuckled at his silliness of proclaiming "thou shalt not's" to my nursing infant who had not once trespassed or even thought to, but Josiah's face hardened, silencing my laugh into a blush.

"It's never too early to begin. I was warming the throne at eight years old."

I nuzzled my nose into the baby's cheek, trying to picture him as a man, but I could not. That was always my weakness—I could only see this moment, while Josiah's view spanned years ahead. I know now it was the LORD's power within him, but at times I envied his visions. I longed to be the rock on the beach instead of the sand ever moving in the waves of circumstance.

As Mattaniah grew to a toddler, I was never far behind, and my world was consumed with monitoring his growth, counting new words, and showing him the kingdom. His nurse only took him from me for a few hours each day so that I could instruct the older boys. I'm not sure if I longed for those hours to pass quicker or if the boys did, but every time the nurse brought the baby back to me, I sighed with secret relief. I sent them off to Josiah to learn war strategies and politics, following which he sent them to Old Hilkiah for Temple lessons. As parents, we were doing all we could to show the LORD's ways to our sons. At least we were trying.

Though we never spoke of it, the worm of doubt chewed at Josiah's thoughts as much as they did mine. Huldah's words were like a daily echo we fought to reverse. Our sons were destined to bear the wrath of God. She said it was because of the idolatry of this generation and many before, and we fought with every weapon of righteousness we could summon to preserve hope for a new legacy. Our only measure was to teach them God's Law and pray they carried it on once we were gone.

Perhaps the LORD would restrain His anger from my boys if we did everything right.

\* \* \*

One warm day I heard Josiah in a rage. The target of his anger was none other than my own Jehoahaz. I walked into the dining hall to see what the commotion was, only to find my son cowering before his father on the floor while he ranted and paced.

"What were you thinking? What did you expect—that I wouldn't know? That the LORD would not see?"

"I'm sorry, Father," Jeho said. "I forgot."

"Forgot! You forgot?" He raised his open hand to our son and I sped between them before I could think.

"My lord, please!" I shouted, shielding the young man I loved from the husband I adored. Every emotion in me ripped to shreds. My presence and voice snapped the king back from rage, and he lowered his hand.

"What happened, Your Majesty?" I addressed him formally, gathering Jeho into my arms.

"Your son has eaten a raven. Shot his bow and proudly consumed the unclean flesh out in the field." He stopped short, thinking of something more: "Did you even bother to cook its blood out first?"

"Of course, Father. I don't eat blood," Jeho said.

I placed my hands over my eyes and sighed. It was not the first infraction that week, and Josiah's patience was already pressed thin. Not more than a day before, a subject was found with a statue of Baal in his home. Josiah confiscated and destroyed the figure and then imprisoned the man until his death sentence was to be executed. He had been beside himself with guilt and fury.

I turned to Jehoahaz. "Did you honestly forget, or did you disregard your father's instruction? You learned about clean and unclean meat just last week."

"I'm sorry. There are so many. I truly forgot, Mother. I'm not lying."

I looked at Josiah. "He's a boy. He is still learning. We all are."

"So be it. The bull comes from your herd, son. If I don't see you at morning sacrifice, you will pay. I can't watch over you every second. Or make up for your every mistake. This week, your study time with the Book of the Law will be doubled. I hope that will dispel the forgetfulness."

Jeho balked but didn't roll his eyes. The bull was nothing to him; though to a commoner, it would have been a year's wage. The extra memorization, on the other hand, would be more than painful.

\* \* \*

A few weeks later, it was more of the same. Josiah was consumed with the Law and sacrifices, and his council members were scrambling to keep up with his demands while simultaneously avoiding his wrath when those demands were not met. When they couldn't stand under his pressure, they tried coming to me.

"You must help us, my lady," Hilkiah said. He had come accompanied by Asaiah and Shaphan. "Every day is a new decree, and he threatens our livelihood if we are unable to make the people comply."

"And you think I have any say?" I echoed their cries for my own life in the palace as well.

"He adores you. He'll listen if you tell him. What he asks is impossible, and you know it."

I sighed, rubbing my temples. Clearly they did not know the weight of their request. Incur the king's rage on my own heart to spare their positions, families, and comfort? It was hardly a sacrifice I was willing to make.

"What does he want today?" I asked, turning the subject so as to suggest compromise.

"To destroy the entire town of Geba," Shaphan replied matter-of-factly.

"What!" I reeled. "But why?"

"Conspirators to idolatry. A group from the town has incited many of them to build a temple there and offer sacrifices."

"To Jehovah?" I asked.

"No. To an unknown Assyrian god. I don't remember the name."

"And the king has commanded what, exactly?"

Asaiah sighed deeply before answering. "He commands that we send troops to destroy the citizens with swords and burn all of the dwellings, taking no plunder, not even livestock."

My jaw fell wide open. I had read that decree in the Book of the Law and had immediately prayed we would never have to enforce it. I pictured women and children being put to the sword and shuddered. The husband I knew would never enforce such violence, I was sure. *He can't be serious. We'll never win their hearts by terror. What is he thinking? None of his soldiers will murder an infant.*

But there was no refuting the Law. If the accusations were proven true, the order would stand. Josiah had every right by God to demand it from his troops and his council.

I sat on my bench and put my head in my hands. My hair came over my face as I breathed in and out through my mouth, searching for any possible idea to get around this. But nothing came. I reached for the front of my dress to tear it, but stopped before shredding the fine, handspun linen.

"To the Temple; we have no choice—we must pray. God might show us another way."

"Yes, my lady," they replied.

\* \* \*

Though I didn't hear Jehovah's voice when we prayed, I did think to read the passage about destroying an idolatrous city. Josiah had allowed Hilkiah to keep the original scrolls in the Holy Place of the Temple, and he brought them out to me.

"*When you begin living in the towns the* LORD *your God is giving you, you may hear that scoundrels among you are leading their fellow citizens astray by saying, 'Let us go worship other gods'—gods you have not known before. In such cases, you must examine the facts carefully. If you find that the report is true and such a detestable act has been committed among you, you must attack that town and completely destroy all its inhabitants, as well as all the livestock. Then you must pile all the plunder in the middle of the open square and burn it. Burn the entire town as a burnt offering to the* LORD *your God. That town must remain a ruin forever; it may never be rebuilt. Keep none of the plunder that has been set apart for destruction. Then the* LORD *will turn from his fierce anger and be merciful to you. He will have compassion on you and make you a large nation, just as he swore to your ancestors.*"

The only thought I came up with after reading was to interrogate the entire town to find the perpetrators. Perhaps the LORD and Josiah would be appeased to punish only the men or women who had begun the conspiracy and spare the rest of the town. When I proposed it to the council, they thought it just might work.

\* \* \*

In the end Josiah agreed to have a committee of judges from his council and the Temple priests travel to Geba for the trial. What amazed me was the number of conspirators who admitted to the idolatry, knowing the death sentence they faced. Exactly twenty-six men and women swore allegiance to the Assyrian god, and exactly twenty-six were brought back in chains for punishment. Though Josiah had heard rumors of the entire town participating in blasphemous ceremonies, deserving holy destruction of the entire town, I knew he was relieved not to be obligated to carry out the penalty on everyone. The night after the executions, we lay in bed beside each other, sighing and crying.

It was Josiah who spoke first, breaking the silence like a shattered pot: "I know the Law becomes more burdensome every day. It's like a rope that hangs my kingdom, isn't it?"

"You know I love the Law. It is the breath of God, His voice and His instruction for our good. But ..." I couldn't finish. I didn't know how.

My husband did for me: "It doesn't feel possible to appease it."

"Yes. It's ... it's as if we break it without even knowing. The rules are so many, and even if we follow them, how can we be sure others do? How can we know?" I hadn't known the depths of his tension, or that it matched my own like a mirror.

"What do you think God wants from me?" He asked without really expecting an answer. It was the question he had always asked me.

"I—I don't know. But I can't imagine it's any more than you've already done. Look how far you've brought the people. Don't you remember when we were children and no one knew Him? He has to see our progress, doesn't He?"

His arm wrapped around my waist under the blanket and pulled my back into my stomach. "It feels like ..."

"A vice," I finished for him.

"Yes," he said with an undertone of shame. He sighed again, bowing his head into my back. "I've been thinking. I wish ... I just wish ..."

"What?"

"If only there was a way we could pay for everyone's sins once and for all, you know—I'd give anything for that. We sacrifice all of these animals for our sins and those of the people. What if ... what if there was one final lamb that would be pure enough to pay for every last one—for the rest of their lives? Do you think God would give us that?"

"Hmm … I never thought of that. How would we find or know about this special lamb?"

"I don't know. When we first found the Law, it was everything I'd ever searched for. The way to know what God wanted. How we were to please Him. I loved it so much. So how has it come to this now, that I can't get out from under the weight of it?"

"I hate this burden you carry. It's like you bear the weight of these multitudes of souls. It is far too much for any one man. Even a great and mighty man like yourself."

"I don't feel mighty at all."

His confession didn't surprise me, but it would have shocked any other person. The outward confidence was a mask for his growing insecurities. I struggled for the words to persuade him. But I knew there were none.

"Josiah?"

"Yes, Angel?"

"I love you." It was all I had.

He breathed deeply into my neck, thinking for long moments before he answered. "And it's your love that keeps me standing." I knew it was true. Like his backbone, I was his support, and for that I felt slightly content. "Hamutal?"

"Yes?"

"Let's pray for the Redeemer to come. You know, the one Isaiah spoke of … maybe he'll be able to lift the burden of the Law. Or show us how to follow it better."

"Yes. The Redeemer …"

# 35. JOSIAH

For many years we prayed for peace, and for many years the LORD granted it. At least we *saw* peace all around our borders. To the west, our ports were never attacked—only lucrative trading while our fleets of trade ships grew stronger. To the south, Egypt stayed distant, fighting every other nation and losing men and chariots by the hundreds. To the east, Babylon began to grow larger than Assyria, and my council began to worry about the size of King Assurbanipal's army as it invaded Sinsharishkun's land. Yet, no one attacked us, and we lived in harmony with Israel.

Civil war within the Assyrian borders did not help in the slightest, and rumors spread that Egypt would attempt to rescue them from the encroachment of Babylon. Those rumors left me unsettled. Our region's international powers began to crumble, and all we ever heard from the traders was how large Babylon's forces were, their cities towering over it all. Though I had never dared to travel or even send spies to Babylon, the picture of it continued to expand in my imagination, which only caused me to worry for my sons even more.

It was still the Assyrians I despised, however, with their Baals and child-sacrifices. When my trade emissaries returned one afternoon to report all about their travels, I grilled them for answers late into the afternoon.

"And what of the Egyptian traders and military presence along the coast?" I asked.

"No soldiers from Egypt, sire. Traders aplenty, bartering with us and others for goods—mostly they bring Pharaoh's gold and leave with spices or lumber. Occasionally, I see them leaving with bundles that look like weapons. Of course, sometimes plows are packed similarly. They could be tools."

"And the Assyrians?"

"None that I saw this trip, my lord. Though word among the cartels is they stay in their own provinces and train for battle. Babylon comes upon them at every town and village. Most Assyrians have fled to their walled cities, I hear. It shouldn't be long now before Ashur-uballit will be forced to surrender to Babylon the Great."

"He'll never do that without a bloody war," I said. "He'll send every living being into death by the sword before he allows them to become slaves. He is both arrogant and cowardly."

"Would you not do the same, my lord?" Asaiah interjected. Seated to my left as always, he laid his hands open on his lap and raised his eyebrows in honest curiosity.

"Hardly. Fight we must, but fall we will. And if the prophets have been right, even the crown will be led into slavery."

Murmuring began among the more than twenty council members and tradesmen around the room. Not more than a month previously, I had admitted this inevitable defeat to the LORD during morning sacrifice. I had told none of my attendants, commanders, or priests, however. This was the first they heard of a hint of the doom I'd succumbed to in faith. A faith no one would understand.

That morning in the Temple, I finally understood. *God, the kingdom grows too heavy for my arms. When will it be time for one of my sons to reign? I never want to stop serving You, LORD—and Your people—but I tire of the endless prosecutions. The Law pervades, and we obey, and then the people break it again. Is there any end to this punishment of the unclean and wayward?*

*"Yes, Josiah. I bring the end to them presently."*

*Wait—an end to the people? That's not what I meant. What do you mean?*

*"Why has Israel become a slave? Why has he been carried away as plunder?"*

I had read the passage once with Hamutal from Jeremiah's earliest written messages. We had both shuddered, immediately praying it wasn't us. We were pleading it would not be our sons, all the while knowing it was. I asked Hilkiah to bring the copy he kept in the Holy Place to my seat next to the altar. He came back with it a few moments later, as the worshippers filed out of the Temple and voices emerged from Solomon's Porch. Instead of following them, I unrolled my friend's prophetic words to our nation, written by his scribe not more than a decade before, and pleaded I wouldn't find them again like I had before. It could not be. I hoped I had been mistaken. But my heart sank as I realized my memory had served me correctly. They began with the line Jehovah had just reverberated into my heart.

*"Why has Israel become as a slave? Why has he been carried away as plunder? Strong lions have roared against him, and the land has been destroyed. The towns are now in ruins, and no one lives in them anymore. Egyptians, marching from their cities of Memphis and Tahpanhes, have destroyed Israel's glory and power. And you have brought this upon yourselves by rebelling against the LORD your God, even though He was leading you on the way! What have you gained by your alliances with Egypt and your covenants with Assyria? What good to you are the streams of the Nile or the waters of the Euphrates River? Your wickedness will bring its own punishment. Your turning from Me will shame you. You will see what an evil, bitter thing it is to abandon the LORD your God and not to fear him. I, the LORD, the LORD of Heaven's Armies, have spoken! Long ago I broke the yoke that oppressed you and tore away the chains of your slavery, but still you said, 'I will not serve you.' On every hill and under every green tree, you have prostituted yourselves by bowing down to idols. But I was the one who planted you, choosing a vine of the purest stock—the very best. How did you grow into this corrupt wild vine? No amount of soap or lye can make you clean. I still see the stain of your guilt. I, the Sovereign LORD, have spoken!"*

I dropped the scroll and fell to my knees. *Oh, LORD, do You mean to tell me we will be led to slavery? My family? My wife? My sons? What about Huldah's prophecy? Didn't she promise me peace?* I could not contain my grief. The only comfort came from old Hilkiah's chanting and the praises of the Temple singers behind me. I stopped caring who saw me weeping at the altar. They had grown accustomed to it over the years. Through my anguished choking, Jehovah spoke once more into the depths of my heart from the altar fire.

*"Peace for You, my Fire. Only for you. My anger comes for Judah. She will be captive before she will be Mine. It is not for you to see."*

\* \* \*

And that is why I knew it wasn't for me to form alliances with Neco against Babylon, even when my council suggested it. I would not stand for alliances with Egypt nor covenants with Assyria.

"My lord, he warns—this is not for you to involve yourself, if you are not on his side." Acbor inserted. "He goes to stand in battle with Assyria against Babylon. He said if you are not going to help, then stay out of it. Wouldn't it be for our benefit if we united with the nations that surround us?" Acbor was a man of logic. My problem was not for lack of logic, however. My problem was that God's Word defied most logic, and I was sold out to following it.

"No. Jeremiah's words from the LORD said not to ally with Egypt or Assyria."

"But, Highness—if Great Babylon takes Assyria, won't we … won't we be next?"

"The LORD only knows, Commander. We will not ever side with Egypt or Assyria, though. Not ever."

"Yes, Your Majesty."

"In fact," I said, "let us go out to meet him—Neco is weak. Perhaps we need to demonstrate Judah's power against Assyria once and for all."

"But," Jared said, "the messenger from Pharaoh said—"

"It doesn't matter what that pagan said! We can never side with any nation who claims another god! It's time they realized the power of Jehovah once and for all!"

They knew I'd never concede. With much reluctance they agreed, and we planned the attack for the following day. I was convinced we would return triumphant after teaching feeble Neco a lesson in Israel's power. My troops hadn't been defeated on a battlefront since I'd taken reign, and Jehovah had made it clear we were not to join forces with them. Once again, I would prove my loyalty to Him. I would obey at any cost. I knew God was on my side, as He always promised He would be.

# EPILOGUE

The bed shook beneath me in the early morning before Josiah rode to Megiddo. Earthquakes were not unheard of in our land, but neither were they commonplace. I awoke with a start as my favorite yellow flower pitcher shattered on the marble below. Through the shaking and tumbling, I managed to make it to Josiah in the next room. He clutched me, and we fought to hold one another upright. When all was settled, we were shocked to see so little damage to the palace.

"What does it mean?" I asked him.

"It means the Lord is Almighty," he declared. "Don't worry, my Love. This mission is simply a military training lesson for your princes. How will they ever know how to fight if they don't face any resistance? Come, come—it will be good for them!"

"Let's go away somewhere, then. When you come back," I said.

"Perfect! To the coast? The beach is warm this time of year."

"Yes—just us. We'll watch the sails of the ships and bask in the salty breezes." After he fastened his armor and sword, he kissed me lightly before he bounded up into the chariot with Jared. "Come back soon, my King," I called.

"Tomorrow night, Angel," he said. "Neco's soldiers are nothing more than palace princesses. We'll be back before you know it."

\* \* \*

But the next time I saw my king—my brave and strong husband—he was bloodied beyond life. When Eli brought news that Jared was driving him back in the chariot, wounded by Pharaoh's arrows, I didn't believe him at first. Not until my oldest son beat his chest and fell at my feet in tears did I realize he was serious. I ran up to the palace tower and looked north for the king's chariot.

The sight of dust rising in the wake of his horses ripped into my heart like a dagger. I ran out to meet them, cursing my skirts and garments as they slowed me. *No, God—No! No, no! Oh please,* LORD*; please don't take him from me.* The world blurred and spilled hot down my cheeks, but I kept running as fast as I could.

The stallions pulled up short of me, and Jared eased him onto the ground and into my arms. Two arrows rose up sharply from his chest, and blood covered the front of his tunic like too much red water. A scream pierced my ears before I realized it was my own. Stifling it into his shoulder, I eased one arm under him and waved the other for Jared to continue into the city gates to fetch the physician.

"My King, my King," I sobbed, "please don't leave me!"

"I'm so sorry, Love," he whispered and choked. I could barely read his lips to decipher his words. They were bloody as I kissed them, and he tried to speak again. Realization hit me hard and won over my denial. Josiah was going to leave me.

"I needed ... wanted—to see you again. Tell you ... I'm—I'm sorry," he sputtered. I tried to hush him. "I didn't know."

"Oh God!" I cried toward the Temple Mount above me on the hill. "Not this, not your king ..."

I felt utterly forsaken by Him. I had no idea why Josiah would have to die. He was the greatest man I'd ever known, and he loved the LORD more than anyone ever had.

I bent to kiss his face again, and he reached up to run his hand through my hair. Before he took his last breath, he had one final request of me. Through dust muddied by his blood, he whispered the words I would wake to every day for the rest of my life. They were the words that held me together, even through exile, slavery, and the betrayal of my own sons.

"You must love the LORD your God, Hamutal. Follow *His* voice to *His* heart. And serve Him—" he choked, "without me."

\* \* \*

My husband loved three things in this life—Jehovah, me, and fire. He often told me I was his cooling dew, the balance to his flames. While that may have been so, what I longed to be was his fuel—his branches and beams. Even when he had been gone for many years, I longed for him to consume me.

On one lonely night after Nebuchadnezzar led us all in chains to the Great Babylon, slaughtered my grandbabies in front of us, and then gouged out Mattaniah's eyes, I dreamed of becoming a tree. A lumberman cut me down by my trunk and fashioned my branches into three items: fuel for a fire on the Temple's holy altar, a manger for straw in a stable, and the beams of an executioner. The sound of Josiah's voice asking Jehovah for the Redeemer echoed through my dream, and God answered by placing a lamb on top of my altar wood, a baby boy into my manger, and a criminal upon my crossbeams. Though I never understood my dream, I always remembered it, and I thought of those three items any time I touched something made of wood.

I know now that none of my sons will be the Redeemer, but I have not lost hope that one will come. Although God has allowed me to suffer deep pain, He has never broken a promise. And I have not broken mine—the one I made to Josiah as he died in my lap. Though the burning pain of grief consumes my nights and my days, I still love Him … and I still serve Him. I know one day He will come for me, and for all of His people—because that is what He does, and that is who He is. Like an unfailing fire that always consumes, my merciful God is One who always redeems.

# A NOTE FROM THE AUTHOR

While King Josiah's is a story of tragedy, it is also one of his great passion, and even more so, God's. For generations, Jehovah had spared His kings and their subjects from doom, wanting to give them one more chance to repent and worship Him alone as Divine. But by the time Josiah was born, exile was already waiting in the wings, and despite his thorough reforms, God's plan to discipline His people was inevitable. The only way they would look for a Redeemer was if they needed One, so He gave the gift of need in the form of slavery in Babylon. Though I hated to leave the story on such a sad note, I have always been determined to tell it as it *might* have happened, adding the flesh of the story without changing or removing any of the bones.

Yet Hamutal's story is one of great hope, for she was of the Remnant whom God spared so they would look for the Messiah. Her recurring dream that you read in the epilogue is all of our Hope, all of our dreams come true. He is Christ the Lord, the sacrificial Lamb that would take away all of our sins, once and for all. He is the Babe in the manger, come down from on high to live among us and reveal His merciful love. He is the Son of Man who hung on the Cross, dying to set us free from idolizing ourselves, and from slavery to the Law.

When I was writing Consuming Fire, I wanted nothing more than to know it would encourage someone, even you, to believe with greater faith than you had yesterday, hope with greater confidence than you had before, and reciprocate God's love in faithfulness with greater passion than you knew possible. He is worthy. And we don't need any other reason.

If you enjoyed this book, would you consider passing it on or recommending it to someone who might enjoy it too? It's the greatest honor I can think of.

# ACKNOWLEDGMENTS

Thanks is given first to **Yahweh,** who downloaded this story to my brain over the course of a few weeks about 10 years ago, and has been so graciously patient with me between then and now to put it to words and finally to print for the people to read. He gives us beautiful gifts, and far be it from me to fail to thank Him for them. Thank you also to my husband, **Kris,** for believing in me and supporting my dreams. I couldn't have gotten a better Guy if I'd sent God specs. And to my children, **Korilynn** and **Josiah** (yes, I named my son after him, years before I had the idea for this book) for your support, patience, and understanding about all of the time I spend staring at my computer. You are more than gracious, and I hope that by holding this book in your hands, you will be inspired to follow your dreams—but only the ones God puts in your hearts. Thanks also goes to my proofreader/editor and sister-in-law, **Kelley Tuck,** for your careful and critical eye, especially for commas and repetitive words. I truly believe this work is much improved because of your dedication, affirmation, and love! Thank you also to my content editor, **John David Kudrick,** who did a fantastic and encouraging job with my messy first draft. Thank you to my parents and family and friends, who each played an integral role by simply giving me words of affirmation and not letting me give up. Thank you, Mom (**Terrilynn Zaharias**) for being my biggest fan. You know I'm yours too, so keep painting. Thank you to **Sarah Tolson** who took precious time out of a busy day and week to take and edit my headshot photos; you are so great at what you do. Finally, thank you, **Dear Reader,** for spending a few hours with me and King Josiah and Hamutal and Jehovah. I hope the next time you open your Bible to 2 Kings or 2 Chronicles and read his account that you will see it with fresh perspective, and that you will read the entirety of Scripture in light of God's unending love.

# ABOUT THE AUTHOR

photo credit: Sarah Tolson Photography

Robyn Langdon has loved writing since her childhood. Her stories and articles have been published in Chicken Soup for the Mother's Soul and Enrichment Magazine. *Consuming Fire* is her first novel and she hopes it will motivate her readers to examine the original accounts of King Josiah in the Bible. She is a wife, minister, mother, sister, author, and business owner, but, first and foremost, she is a daughter of the King of Kings. When she's not writing, Robyn enjoys hiking, playing games with her family, and helping people use essential oils.

CPSIA information can be obtained
at www.ICGtesting.com
Printed in the USA
LVHW090757031120
670551LV00004B/288